The Amish Voice

Book Three in The Amish Singer *Series*

by Bob Nailor

For I know the plans I have for you
declares the Lord,
Plans to prosper you, and not to harm you,
Plans to give you hope and a future.
~ Jeremiah 29:11

This page left blank

The Amish Voice

Discover other titles by Bob Nailor at
www.bobnailor.com

Cover collage by Bob Nailor

iii

This page left blank

iv

Table of Contents

PRELUDE

Music played. Daniel watched Martha walk the aisle of the church. Her white gown glistened with a myriad of sequins and beads. A veil hid her face as she walked with her father toward him. Her father's scowl caused Daniel to frown.

"He doesn't look happy." The voice was a whisper from beside him. "Are you sure you want to get married?"

Daniel gazed down. He didn't have on his boots; instead, they were shiny, black leather shoes. He stared at the pants. They weren't his regular blue pants, nor was this *his* shirt. He stared at the tuxedo and the blue ruffled shirt. Daniel felt the constriction of the bow tie around his neck. He couldn't breathe.

"Do you take this woman?"

Daniel stared at the *Englische* minister.

He couldn't breathe, the tie constricted tighter and tighter.

"I AM AMISH," he yelled and sat up in bed.

Realizing his surroundings, Daniel sat on the edge of his bed.

"I am Amish," Daniel whispered into the darkness of his bedroom.

CHAPTER ONE: The School

Sunday, July 21, 1963, 11 a.m.

Daniel gazed into her green eyes. "You know I love you, Martha." He reached up and tucked a few stray hairs with a light blue tint back within the confines of her bonnet.

"Remember, my name is Martha. Martha Noble." She giggled, knowing how difficult it would be to change after so many months of living as another person.

"You know I love you, Martha, Martha Noble."

She blushed. "And I love you, too, Daniel Yoder."

"Will you be staying close?" Daniel asked.

"I am sure if I ask my Aunt Mary, I may stay with them." She giggled. "Imagine, your Uncle Mark married my mother's sister."

"I am sure Uncle Mark will be happy to do that. Do I need to have another ask your father's permission to court?"

"My father is *Englische*. He doesn't care who I court, but you may want to have another ask Uncle Mark or my Uncle Paul..." She winked. "You know, just to be safe."

"I will ask my father to find a *Schteckleimann*."

"I better be about with my aunt and uncle. This is not New York City. A single Amish girl and Amish man shouldn't be alone." She leaned in and gave him a peck on the check then raced back toward the house where the other women congregated.

Daniel stood at the corner of the barn, leaning against it, watching Martha as she lifted her skirts to run toward the house. He smiled, knowing beneath that white bonnet was a crop of blue hair. He touched the side of his head above his ears and rubbed the stubble there. He would need to let his hair

2

grow out. His smile widened and he cupped his chin. *Maybe I will look good with a beard,* he thought and then sighed.

"Ah, there you are, Daniel." Noah Yoder, his father, came around the corner with a side glance at the escaping Martha in the distance. He cocked an eye at Daniel. "She has caught your eye?" He frowned. "Is she not your Aunt Mary's niece? The *Englische* girl?"

Daniel was unsure of how much to reveal about Martha. He nodded.

"She is a nice girl, Papa."

Once more Noah cast a glance at the receding Martha. "Yes, she does appear so, my son. But, enough of that. The Bishop would like to talk with you. Join us for a conversation."

Daniel hesitated. *Join us? Who is us?*

"Yes, Papa." He fell into step beside his father as they walked toward a group of men.

Daniel identified the men: Bishop Schmucker, Ezekiel Troyer, Paul Mueller, Reuben Metz, and Jeremiah Wyse. He attempted to guess the subject at hand, but was at a loss. The Bishop, four ministers, counting his father, Jeremiah and him. It was the last two who caused the conflict. How did he and Jeremiah work into the equation?

"What are we discussing, Papa?" Daniel asked as they came closer.

Noah slapped Daniel on the back. "Why, our new school, Daniel. What else could it be?"

Again, Daniel stared at the group. Still, Jeremiah seemed out of place. *I will be the teacher. How is Jeremiah involved?*

"Welcome, Daniel," Bishop Schmucker said. He glanced about the area. "The children have started a game of ball and the women are about getting the meal prepared." He gazed toward the pond. "Let us move to the seats by the pond so we may talk in privacy."

Noah noticed Hannah, Daniel's younger sister, running toward them to retrieve the ball.

"Hannah, go to your mother and fetch us a pitcher of lemonade and pie." He pointed at the pond. "We'll be down there discussing..." He paused. "Future details. Now, hurry about yourself."

Hannah tossed the ball toward the group and then raced to the house as requested.

The group of men ambled to the collection of roughly hewn log benches.

Bishop Schmucker held up his hand. "Before we sit, let me say a few words of prayer."

The group bowed their heads.

Dear Father. We come together in your name in search of the answer to these troubling times. Guide our feet as we proceed in our endeavors to continue our way of life for us and our little ones. We ask your attendance today and be with Daniel as we move forward. Amen.

Daniel drew in a deep breath. It was very unusual for the bishop to draw attention to one person.

"Ah, here comes Hannah with some refreshments."

"Momma said you could have some lemonade, but she wasn't about to allow you to ruin your meal with some pie." She giggled. "She sent each of you a glass of lemonade and a small cookie." Hannah straightened taller with pride. "I made them."

Noah took the tray with the lemonades and cookies to hand to Daniel. He then shooed her away with his hands. "Go play ball until we come for the meal." Noah turned to the group. "Enjoy." Daniel held the tray as each of the ministers and Jeremiah took a lemonade and cookie. Daniel placed the tray on the ground without spilling his drink or dropping any of the cookies. He grabbed his glass of lemonade and a cookie. He wasn't sure he wanted to eat the cookie his sister had made, but she'd been helping their mother with meals and most of them tasted fine. He bit the cookie. It was good.

Paul Mueller held up the remains of a cookie. "Your daughter will make a fine wife," he said. "I should have my grandson meet her."

Daniel winced at the thought of Isaac Mueller with his little sister. He knew Hannah would never agree to it.

"Perhaps in the future, Paul," Noah said, noticing his son's dour look. "Hannah is still young, a mere fourteen."

"First," Bishop Schmucker started. "We need to discuss

the land." He gazed at Jeremiah. "We have offered a fair price for the land you own, Brother Jeremiah. Do you agree to the sale?"

"I do, Bishop." He gazed at the group. "I discussed with Elizabeth the possibility of helping at the school. With our youngest almost four, she feels he will be disruptive to the class." He cast a sheepish look at Daniel. "Would it be possible for her to assist next year when Leroy will be closer to five?"

Daniel shrugged. "That would be fine with me. Is there another who could help? How many students are we discussing?"

Bishop Schmucker cast a glance at the group. "There should be thirty-four students."

Daniel tried not to look surprised. He tried to envision helping his siblings then enlarge it to encompass the actual number. *Have I made an error in judgment?*

"But..." Bishop Schmucker lifted a hand of assurance. "There are eleven who will be in the seventh and eighth grades. That is almost a third of the students. They will be able to help care and teach the younger ones." His eyes shifted to Daniel. "Is that not correct?"

Daniel nodded. "They could help with the younger ones." His voice was hesitant, but he smiled, more to confirm his thought. "Yes, that would work."

"Still," Paul interrupted. "It is my belief an older, mature person should be there to assist our new teacher." He smiled. "In case one of the older students decide to give Daniel a little guff."

The group of men chuckled.

"Do you have a person in mind, Paul?"

"I do," he replied. "My sister, Ruby has yet to settle on a man. She helps my wife, but I am sure she would agree to assist at the school." Paul gazed at Daniel. "Do you agree?"

Spinster Mueller? he thought, flabbergasted. *She has a quick and bitter tongue, plus she has no sense of humor.* "She would be an excellent choice," Daniel replied, realizing he had limited options.

"Then you agree to be the teacher? With the aide of Ruby Mueller?" Bishop Schmucker asked.

"Yes, Bishop," Daniel replied.

Bishop Schmucker turned to the other men. "We are in agreement?"

The men nodded their heads.

"Then we are committed." Bishop Schmucker stood. "A moment of silent prayer for the new school."

The men all stood, their heads bowed.

"Let us go and eat," Bishop Schmucker said after a few moments of silence.

# # #

Friday, July 26, 1963, 6:45 a.m.

Daniel watched Ben drive the car toward the house. *Last day to work this week*, he thought. *We will build the school tomorrow.* The car pulled into the driveway and Daniel squeezed into the back seat. As usual, Matthew Yoder and James Troyer, his cousins, were already in the backseat, waiting.

"Tomorrow will be a good day, Daniel," Matthew said. "They are calling for a warm day, no rain. It will be perfect to build the new school."

Daniel frowned. *How does he know tomorrow will be nice?*

"Don't fret, Daniel," Ben Hopkins said, watching him in the rearview mirror. "The weatherman announced the weather." He glanced at Daniel before putting the car in gear. "Do you allow the *Englische* to help on these events?" He grinned and gave Daniel a wink. "Asking for a friend."

"I see no reason you cannot help," Daniel said. "Be sure to bring a hammer, saw, and a tape measure."

"I was thinking of getting the generator from the mill and a couple of circular saws, drills, and... well, whatever else I'm able to convince Bob Sullivan to let me borrow."

"Mr. Sullivan has been generous in helping with the school." Daniel squirmed in his seat. "Do you think he will give even more?"

"There's Jack," James said.

6

"Stuffing his pipe into his shirt pocket." Matthew laughed. "One of these days he will set his shirt on fire, I am sure."

"Good morning, all," Jack said slipping into the front seat. "I know I have a busy day today with deliveries. I have two loads to take for the school." He leaned back and gave Daniel a scowl. "Are you worth all this effort? I don't normally go this far out of my way for teachers."

"I am sorry, Mr. Hall." Daniel hung his head.

"Don't fret, Daniel. You'll be a great teacher." He reached back with an apple in hand. "For the teacher. Guess I want to be the first to be the teacher's pet and give you an apple." He laughed, as did the others in the car. He turned to Ben. "Did you ask?"

Ben nodded.

"So, we'll be joining them?" Jack asked.

"Like I told Daniel. I'll see what I can borrow to make things a little easier." Ben turned into the parking lot of the mill. "But, Daniel told me to make sure I bring along a hammer, saw and tape measure. So, you'd better bring the same." He laughed.

"What time?" Jack asked.

"Daniel?" Ben queried. "What time is everyone getting together tomorrow morning?"

"We are to gather at eight," Matthew piped in. "We will be there, too."

"Of course you will," James said. "If there is food involved, you are there." He nudged his cousin in the ribs.

"I hope Aunt Sarah brings her macaroni." Matthew licked his lips. "It is the best in the world."

"I know my mother is bringing pies," James said. "She made apple, cherry, and gooseberry pies."

"Sounds like we'll be eating good tomorrow," Jack said.

Ben parked the car. "That is tomorrow. Today, we still need to work. So, everyone out of the car. All of you."

Daniel, Jack, Matthew and James headed toward the factory.

"Ben, do you..." Daniel noticed Ben wasn't with them. He turned to see Ben going into the office entrance.

Jack smiled. "Don't worry about Ben, Daniel. He is going to see if he can borrow the equipment." Jack winked. "If I know Ben, he will wrangle almost everything we need." He nodded. "Your new school will be up before the sun sets tomorrow night."

Matthew frowned. "Of course, it will. If we can build a barn in less than two days... I am sure we can build a small school in a day." He grinned. "Even if we do not get all those power tools." James and Matthew lifted their arms and flexed their muscles. "We are strong, young men." They posed.

Jack laughed. "No doubt. Now, get to work." He opened the factory door and let the three boys in.

# # #

Daniel noticed Jack looking around the factory. He frowned. *Jack should be on deliveries. Why is he here?*

"Ah, there you are. I got all the wood and supplies delivered." He nodded back toward the open door. "I heard the radio weatherman say it might rain tonight so I put a tarp over the stuff to keep it dry." He shrugged. "Of course, he also mentioned possible showers tomorrow." He frowned. "Did the elders have a backup if the weather was bad?"

Daniel thought for a moment. Matthew ambled toward them.

"If it rains, we Amish can build in the wet. This is a school, not a big barn." He smiled. "Unless, of course, the rain is pouring down hard."

"The weatherman said light showers possible," Jack added.

"Amish are not made of sugar," Matthew said. "We will not melt." He grinned at Jack. "Do *Englische* melt?"

Jack brought up a fisted hand. "I'll give you a melting Englische." He grinned and bandied his fists at Matthew.

Matthew fell back in mock fear.

"By the way, Mr. Sullivan told Ben he could borrow anything he needed. We must be sure to have it back by Monday morning for work."

"Mr. Sullivan is a very generous man," Daniel said.

"Actually, Daniel, Mr. Sullivan plans to be there, too." He leaned to whisper. "I also know Mr. Sullivan's wife has spoken to my wife and Ben's wife. She was going to check with the Bishop's wife to see if they could bring something to add to the meal."

Daniel frowned. He knew the Amish interacted with the *Englische* for work and shopping. He couldn't remember a time when the *Englische* united with the Amish community, especially to build a school.

#

Saturday, July 27, 1963, 6:30 a.m.

Daniel watched the buggy with his parents and younger siblings go to the building site of the new school. He glanced at the tools in the back of the wagon and held the mare still, stroking her forehead.

"Did I tell you I met your sister in Pennsylvania?" He straightened for the forelock of the mare. "Her name is Jezebel." Daniel smiled at the memory of visiting Jacob and Naomi Longenfelter. "Imagine if we named you something like that. Jacob said he chose that name because he was lured in by her beauty." Daniel snickered. "We decided to name you Beauty."

"Are you talking to the horse, Daniel?" Luke slapped Daniel on the back.

Startled, Daniel turned, his cheeks red. "Just biding time until you showed. Ready?"

Luke jumped onto the buckboard. "Waiting for you." He grabbed the reins. "Papa is probably already there." He gazed at the tools in the back. "I believe we've got everything." He scowled at Daniel. "I am going to count to three and then leave. Get in, Daniel." He paused. "Three."

Daniel jumped onto the buckboard. The leather reins snapped. Beauty trotted a path to the road.

"Do you think we can catch Papa?" Daniel asked.

"We will take our time and enjoy the ride," Luke replied. "It will be a busy day ahead."

Daniel sat back and watched the scenery. At the intersection, he noticed two other buggies. They turned in front of them and headed in the same direction.

Luke nodded at the buggies. "There goes the bishop with his wife. The first buggy was Isaac Graber and family."

"Do you think Miriam will be there?" Daniel's voice was subtle.

Luke jerked to stare at his younger brother. "I am sure she will come with her parents and I know her brother will be here to help." He smiled. "Trust me, little brother, I will be too busy helping to get your school built. I will not have time to court Miriam today." He grinned. "But, I am sure she will be with me at the sing tonight."

"If Martha is here today, I will ask her to join us if she can."

As they passed the tree row, buggies and cars littered the open field where the school would stand. People dotted the open area, creating work stations and preparing food.

"Look at all the people. I did not think this many *Englische* would show to help us." Luke pointed. "There is Ben. He is talking to Mr. Sullivan."

Daniel jumped from the buckboard and ran toward the two men. "Good morning," Daniel offered between deep breaths.

Bob Sullivan gazed at Daniel. "Who is the guy in charge? I am sure we will need to work out some logistics to get all this equipment to the right people."

"My Papa has the building plans. Jeremiah Wyse owns the land." Daniel scrunched up his nose in thought. "Of course, Bishop Schmucker could be the person in charge."

Ben placed a hand on Daniel's shoulder. "Tell you what, Daniel. We'll go discuss with your father since he has the plans, and from there, we'll figure out who needs what."

Daniel watched the two men leave in search of his father. Daniel's cousin, Matthew Yoder approached from the side.

"Daniel!" Matthew called. "Come see what we found in our barn for you."

Daniel ambled over to Matthew and then followed him to a wagon.

"This will keep the school warm in the winter," Matthew gushed. "I heard them talking about trying to get a stove for the school. I was out in the barn and found this sitting in a corner. I asked my father and he agreed it would be more useful in the school than sitting in the barn."

"It is very nice," Daniel said, noting the pot-belly stove with the flat top section. He noticed there was plenty of chimney piping to vent the stove, too.

The noise of the generator starting up caught their attention.

"That is very loud," Matthew said, gawking in the direction of the commotion.

"Ben said it is necessary to run the equipment which will make the jobs easier." Daniel shrugged. "Imagine how fast it will be to cut lumber with an electric saw rather than by hand."

Matthew nodded in agreement.

Bishop Schmucker called all the men to him.

"I need eight... no, ten men to start working the foundation. I need four teams of six each to start assembling the wall sections. Can I get eight men to start assembling the floor?" The bishop's voice continued to list assignments as the men broke into groups.

Daniel stood beside Luke, unsure of what to do.

"We will help with the wall," Luke said and pushed Daniel toward a group of four men. "That will make it six." He grinned at the three Amish men. A lone *Englische* man busied with hooking up the extension cord to the generator so he could use the saw.

Daniel gazed back at the group of women who hustled about with platters and bowls of food. He noticed Hannah who had finished her eighth-grade year of schooling. She was busy talking to her *Englische* friend, Susan. Daniel frowned. *Why would an Englische girl be here today?* He gazed at the gathered men. *One of the Englische must be her father*, Daniel thought. He spotted Susan's older brother, Jonathan, helping his father with the foundation. Daniel smiled. *It is good to see the Amish and Englische working together.*

"May I help with the wall?"

Daniel's thoughts shattered. He turned to see John Heffel

11

standing there, hammer in hand, and wanting to help. "It seems I may be one too many." John turned to gaze at the various groups of men working.

"Join us," Daniel said. "There is always room for one more." Daniel reached down and grabbed a stud. "We'll nail this one together."

Daniel and John placed the wall stud into place and nailed it. They worked furiously, pushing more studs into place and nailing them. Daniel stood, and noticed the group of men had the foundation almost finished. He glanced at the sun, it was almost to noon already. His stomach growled. John stood.

"Will Hannah be at the sing tonight?" John asked.

Daniel gazed at John dumbfounded. "I do not know," he replied with a shrug. "I can ask." He smiled, realizing why John was asking.

John stared at the ground by his boot. "She has a pretty voice."

Daniel leaned in. "I will find out and let you know."

John's eyes widened. "Do not tell her I asked."

"Of course not," Daniel replied. "I can ask Martha to ask her so Hannah will not know it is me asking."

John nodded approval. "*danke*."

CHAPTER TWO: An Amish Date

Saturday, July 27, 1963, about 4 p.m.

Daniel stood by the buckboard staring at the new school building. He absently stroked Beauty's mane.

"My school," he whispered. "I will be teaching here in September." He sighed. "Thank you, dear Lord, for this opportunity. My life is blessed."

"An idle mind is the devil's playground."

Daniel turned to face Martha.

"Not an idle mind," Daniel said. "I was thanking God for all the blessings I have been given." He glanced back at the school, grabbing her hands in his. "I will be a teacher." He smiled at Martha. "I always wondered why there was an urge within me to learn." He paused and squeezed Martha's hands. "They allowed me to attend school beyond the eighth grade. The Lord had a reason, one I was unsure of, but He has opened my eyes to His path for me."

"Yes, Daniel, the Lord is generous." She wrinkled her nose at Daniel. "He has brought us together."

Daniel smiled. "Another blessing." He squeezed her hands.

He wanted to kiss her, but he held back. They were not alone, and they wouldn't be left alone. There would be the chaperon. Hannah.

"Did you check with Hannah? Will she be joining us tonight at the sing?"

Martha nodded her head. "Our chaperon will ride with us to the sing."

"Stay here," Daniel said. "I must talk with a person. I will be right back."

Daniel let go of her hands and dashed away in search of John. He found the young man sitting under a tree eating a slice of apple pie. With him was Jonathan, Susan, and Hannah.

This is a problem, Daniel thought, but then had an idea.

"Hannah, I do not know if you have talked with Martha, but we wish to go to the sing tonight and..." He hesitated. "Will you be our chaperon?"

Hannah snickered. "I have already spoken with Martha." She nodded. "I will go with you."

Daniel looked at John who smiled and nodded his head. Daniel gazed at Jonathan and Susan.

"*Englische* are allowed to join us, if you wish," Hannah said.

Susan nodded approvingly. "That could be fun. It has been a fun day today."

Jonathan grimaced. "Saturday night? Here? Singing?"

Susan pretended to slap his arm. "It will be fun. Don't be such a Gloomy Gus."

"But it's Saturday night. I was going to..."

Susan glared at him.

"Fine. We will join you." Jonathan nodded. "What time?"

Daniel shrugged. "We usually get together about six. Tonight we are meeting at the bridge by the Dodson farm where the..."

"I know the place," Jonathan said. "Most Saturday mornings I love to race my corvette down the hill and around the curve at the bridge." He grinned. "Today? I had a blast building, of all things, a school I won't be attending." He laughed.

Martha eased behind Daniel and placed her hands over his eyes.

"Guess who," she whispered.

Daniel smiled, grabbing her hands in his. He turned to her. "Hannah will be joining us for the sing this evening."

"I know," she said, all the time smiling at the group sitting under the tree. "Hannah is like a younger sister to me." She gazed at Daniel. "I only had an older sister and..." She gazed off into the distance. "She is now somewhere in Canada with her..." She paused. "Definitely her boyfriend, could be

14

husband." Martha heaved a sigh. "I miss her."

Hannah stood to join Martha and hug her. "I will be your little sister, Martha. I will always be here for you."

Martha wiped a tear from her eye. "*danke*, Hannah." She hugged Hannah.

###

Daniel pulled the buggy next to his cousin's buggy by the end of the parked buggies on the north end of the bridge. If Abe Yoder was here, the possibility of Martha already being here was possible.

"I see Jonathan has made it here." He nodded toward the shiny blue corvette parked near where the road split. The main road coming north across the bridge while the other curved to go back up the hill to the east. He continued his search.

Hannah perked up and gazed at the gathered group on the bridge, looking for Susan and Jonathan.

John stood and waved. Sitting beside him on the stone bridge were Susan and Jonathan. Susan stood to wave.

Hannah stood, waved, and jumped from the buggy.

Daniel spotted Martha. She sat at the south end of the stone bridge, talking to Eli Troyer. Daniel frowned and a twinge of jealousy enveloped him. *Why is she talking to him? Why is he talking to her? He knows I am courting Martha.* He scowled.

Jumping from the buggy, Daniel tethered Beauty and sauntered to the south end of the bridge.

Eli lifted Martha from the bridge's stone wall. She raised her skirt a few inches and hustled toward Daniel.

"I have been waiting for you to arrive," she gushed breathlessly and grabbed his hand. "Follow me. Eli Troyer has been telling me about..."

Daniel balked, holding his ground, not moving.

Martha turned to stare at Daniel. "Is there a problem?" She released his hand.

"Why were you talking to Eli?"

Martha cocked an eye and watched Daniel. She grinned as the realization of the situation became clear. "Why Daniel

15

Yoder, you are jealous."

"What if I am?" He felt the flush of embarrassment come into his cheeks. *I am jealous*, he thought. He analyzed his thoughts. *I never felt this way about Molly.*

Martha inched back to him. "If you must know..." She wrinkled her nose at him. "Eli was telling me of a property that may become available soon – next summer, for sure." Once more she grabbed both his hands and pulled him in a circle as she moved around him. "If we are to marry, we will need a place of our own." She leaned in close to his ear. "Is that not true, my love?" She stepped back and, again, pulled him toward the end of the bridge where Eli stood waiting.

Daniel smiled. "When are we to marry?" He gave her a questioning look.

Martha shrugged. "I was thinking a spring wedding would be nice." She giggled. "The daffodils and tulips will be in blossom."

"What if I decide not to ask?" Daniel kept the smile from his face and stared at her.

She let go of his hands, dropping them with force. "Daniel Yoder! You dare to play this game?"

A curl of a smile turned the right side of his lips. "Only to see your temper." He leaned in.

Martha turned and stormed a path toward Eli.

Daniel raced to catch her and grab her hand.

"You know I love you, Martha... my Martha. I will not have another. Let us listen to Eli and discover the secret of this possible home."

Martha released his hand and placed her arm within his and leaned her head against his shoulder. "Like I would look at another, Daniel Yoder. Remember, I left New York City and came home for you."

Eli shook hands with Daniel.

"Tell me about this place, Eli," Daniel said.

In the distance, Daniel heard the group start to sing as Eli explained the details of a future home for the two of them.

I'm getting married, Daniel thought.

###

Saturday, July 27, 1963, about 9 p.m.

Daniel watched as Hannah ambled toward the buggy. She was with Jonathan. Daniel frowned. He thought Hannah would be with John.

"You best hurry," Daniel called to her. "It is getting late and I must have Martha back to Uncle Mark's place soon."

The sing ended twenty minutes earlier than usual, but Daniel saw no need to rush home. He felt comfortable dawdling to spend more time with Martha. Hannah was with Susan so Daniel saw no need for concern of his little sister. He searched the area.

He reconsidered his rash decision seeing Hannah and Jonathan together. *Where is Susan?* Daniel thought. *Hannah should not be alone with a young man, especially an Englische man.*

"Come along, Hannah. We must leave." Daniel motioned for her to get into the buggy.

Jonathan gazed up into the buggy at Daniel.

"If you want, I can get Susan and we could drive Hannah home." He winked at Daniel. "You could be alone with Martha."

"Nay. She must ride with us. She is our chaperon. It would not be right."

Jonathan gave a questioning look and shrugged. "As you wish." He turned to Hannah. "Good night."

Susan ran up to join them.

"I'm sorry, Hannah. I needed to..." She blushed. "I didn't mean to leave you, but I'm sure you understand."

"It is fine, Susan," Hannah replied with a grin. "Nature calls to every creature and when one must go, well..."

"Let's get you home, Susan. Mom will be wondering where we are." He again gazed at Daniel. "This was fun. I hope we can do this again soon."

"We do this each Saturday evening," Hannah said. "Next Saturday we will gather at Eli Troyer's farm."

"We need to leave," Daniel said and snapped the reins on Beauty.

17

"See you next Saturday?" Susan asked as the buggy left.

"I hope so," Hannah replied and watched the two disappear as they went crested the hill on the way to Uncle Mark's house.

"Did you and John have a good time tonight?" Daniel asked.

"John stayed with us for a little while before finally wandering off to join some of the other boys." Hannah straightened her dress. "I spent the whole evening with Susan and Jonathan. They didn't know some of the songs, but they enjoyed singing with us for those songs they did know."

Martha leaned against Daniel. "It was a good night, Daniel," she said. "Of course, any time I spend with you is good."

"Uncle Mark will be furious with me if I get you home too late."

"Uh, Daniel?" Martha's voice was a mere whisper.

"Yes?"

"You agree we should get married in the spring?"

"Married?" Hannah leaned forward from the back of the buggy. "You are getting married, Daniel?"

"We are discussing the matter, Miss Nosey Pants," Daniel said. "Now sit back and be silent. This does not concern you. You are our chaperon, not our moderator."

"If Daniel does not get cold feet," Martha said. "I was thinking of a wedding in the spring when the daffodils are in bloom." She hesitated. "What do you think?"

"It would be beautiful," Hannah gushed.

"Now, hush, Hannah," Daniel said. "Not a word of this to anyone. Do you understand? You are our chaperon and thus sworn to secrecy of what we discuss."

Hannah frowned. "I have never heard that before. You are making that up."

"Oh, no," Martha said. "All chaperons must keep all discussions heard in utmost secrecy." Martha attempted to keep a straight face. "In the *Englische* world, there is a confidence between a lawyer and client, a doctor and a patient, or even a minister with a sinner. Whatever is revealed between them, until death, it must never be told."

"Well, that does not make any sense. Next spring somebody is going to notice the two of you getting married."

Martha giggled. "True. But, at that time, you can tell others you knew about it."

"Fine," Hannah said. "I still do not believe you, but I will not tell anyone until you reveal your plans."

Daniel turned Beauty into Uncle Mark's lane.

"Uh-oh." Daniel nodded to the front porch of Uncle Mark's house. "He is sitting in his rocker, waiting for us. This could be bad."

Uncle Mark stood as they pulled closer to the house.

"It is about time you arrived home, Martha. We have been waiting for you."

We? Martha thought and then noticed the car around the corner of the house in the back. *My father or mother is here.*

"Your mother is waiting for you inside. Hustle yourself to see her." Uncle Mark held the handle of the front screen porch door, waiting for Martha to enter.

Daniel walked with Martha up the porch stairs and was to follow her in the door.

"We will wait out here, Daniel," Uncle Mark said, putting a hand on Daniel's shoulder. He turned to Hannah. "If you wish some lemonade, Aunt Mary is in the kitchen and will pour you some." He turned to Daniel. "Come. We will talk over there." He pointed to the rockers at the end of the porch.

Daniel frowned, unsure, but he moved to the rockers.

"Sit, Daniel." Uncle Mark eased into a rocker. Daniel took the other. Mark offered Daniel a glass of lemonade. "It is time for us to discuss matters."

"Discuss what, Uncle Mark?"

"Exactly what are your intentions with my niece?"

Daniel sipped his lemonade.

"I am courting Martha." He sipped more lemonade. "We are thinking of getting married. Perhaps this coming spring."

"Uh-huh," Mark grunted. "You understand she is *Englische,* not Amish." He paused. "Yes, I know – she dresses Amish and acts Amish, but she is still *Englische*. What are your plans?"

Daniel stared at the porch floor. He hadn't considered

19

those consequences. He was Amish. She was *Englische.*

"I am Amish, Uncle Mark. I will remain Amish."

"I understand that, Daniel. But, will you live as Amish? Or will you live as *Englische?* You can't be both. If you leave the Amish to be with an *Englische* person, having been recently baptized, you will be shunned. *Meidung.* Do you understand? Your mother. Your father. Your brothers and sisters. None of us may speak or see you. Do you fully understand the consequences?"

Daniel's throat dried. He sipped, then gulped the lemonade. His throat still dry.

"I will talk with Martha."

"My sister-in-law, Emma, Martha's mother, is discussing this with her now. We have discussed this and decided, at the current time, Martha should move back home until a decision is made."

Mark scrutinized Daniel.

"If you decide to become *Englische,* we will need to find a new teacher."

"I am Amish!" Daniel stood. "I will get my sister and leave now. Good night, Uncle Mark."

Daniel called through the screen into the house for Hannah. "I am leaving, Hannah."

The back screen door banged as Hannah came running. She climbed into the buggy beside Daniel who snapped the reins.

"Daniel!" Martha called from the front porch screen.

The buggy turned from the lane onto the dirt road and gained speed. Beauty trotted faster and faster toward home.

# # #

Daniel scowled in the darkness, thinking, brooding, and watching Beauty. The horse slowed and trotted on her way home, now that they were away from Uncle Mark's place.

"You are silent, Daniel," Hannah whispered, afraid to interrupt his thoughts.

"Why does everyone insist I want to be *Englische?*"

"I do not know," Hannah replied. She continued to look

20

forward. "Could your desire for learning make them think you will go *Englische*?"

Daniel heaved a sigh.

"I have given up that dream, Hannah. I no longer wish to attend school. I am the new schoolmaster." He paused. "I will teach others."

"Could it be due to Martha?" Hannah questioned.

Daniel rolled a shoulder and nodded in the shadowed darkness of the buggy. "Perhaps."

Hannah was silent. Other than the sounds of Beauty's trotting, the buggy's wheels on the road, and the songs of the crickets and frogs, silence encased the scene.

"I heard Martha's mother talking to her." Hannah's voice a mere whisper. "I should not have listened, but I did." She waited. "I only heard her talking when she raised her voice to Martha."

"She did?" Daniel queried.

"Martha's mother was upset. Martha wants to become Amish. She knows she must so the two of you can marry. Her mother does not think Martha understands what becoming Amish means or how her father will react."

Daniel gazed out the side of the buggy to the ditch.

"We should be silent and not discuss this, Hannah. The words spoken between Martha and her mother should remain between them." Daniel sighed. "Am I understood?"

"Yes, Daniel." Hannah straightened her dress. "So many secrets tonight."

"They will remain secret. Yes?"

"Yes, Daniel."

Daniel smiled. "*danke*, Hannah." He pointed to the house in the distance. "We are almost home. It appears everyone has gone to bed. We must be quiet so as not to wake them."

"I will be very quiet."

"And I will bed down Beauty for the night then come in."

Daniel turned the buggy into the lane of the farm and headed for the barn.

"Daniel?"

"Yes, Hannah."

"Are you still going to marry Martha?"

21

Daniel snickered. "If she will have me, yes." He cleared his throat. "Now, no more discussion of this subject – am I understood?"

"As you wish, brother." Hannah hopped from the buggy and ran for the back door of the house.

Daniel headed for the barn, jumped down and led Beauty to her stall.

"I love you, Martha Noble, and I *will* marry you." Daniel's voice whispered to the listening rafters of the barn. "Yes, I will marry you."

He opened the stall door and led the trotter in.

"I am Amish." He stroked Beauty's forelock, patting her on the forehead to finally reach the muzzle. He offered her a handful of grain. "Do you hear me, Beauty? I... am... Amish."

CHAPTER THREE: School Days

Saturday, August 3, 1963, 9 a.m.

Daniel opened the door of the schoolhouse and entered. The room still smelled of paint. He opened windows to allow the fresh air in. The late summer warm air flowed through the window.

In the one corner were the desks; piled and shoved together until he decided where and how he wanted them.

Daniel analyzed the room. It was obvious to him the choice had been made. The main blackboard was on the wall opposite the door he'd come in. There were two smaller blackboards on each sidewall. Daniel nodded and pointed at the far wall. *That will be the front of the classroom*, he thought.

He pulled out the sheet of paper with the list of his students.

Thirty-six.

Daniel inhaled deeply and gazed at the numbers for each class as he moved toward the front of the building.

First grade: 6.
Second grade: 3.
Third grade: 5.
Fourth grade: 4.
Fifth grade: 4.
Sixth grade: 3.
Seventh grade: 4.
Eighth grade: 7.

Reality hit. He leaned against the teacher's desk and stared at the room.

I will be a teacher, he thought. *I will have students.* He shoved off from the desk. *I am a teacher.*

The teacher's desk was near the pot-belly wood stove.

Daniel cocked his head in thought. *For now, it will be okay. This winter I will move my desk so it is not so close.* He moved the chair back and sat at the desk to survey the room from the new angle. He shook his head. *This will not work*, he thought. *My desk needs to be in the center.* Daniel stood and shoved the desk to the new position. He moved to the front of the desk and leaned against it to once more survey the room.

An aisle to the left. An aisle to the right. And a center aisle. Daniel nodded in agreement with his idea and walked to the blackboard. He drew.

Three seats in a row with six rows. That would be eighteen chairs in each section. No! Wait. He erased his sketch and started new. *I will make three sections of two chairs each. That way I can walk beside each student to help them, or..."* He sighed, allowing a shiver to curl up his back. *Or, make it easier for Miss Mueller to assist.*

He drew a diagram of the three sections with the four aisles. With only a few corrections, he had the final breakdown of the different grades. It started with the youngest at the front, the older ones to the rear.

There were forty desks. Daniel started to move the desks into position. He placed the remaining four desks off to the left of his desk.

Daniel smiled. *If a student gives me a problem, they can sit up here for all to see.* He nodded approval at his foresight of the possibility and possible punishment.

"I thought I would find you here, Daniel Yoder."

Daniel turned at the voice to see Martha standing at the entrance.

"It has been a week. I wondered if I would see you," Daniel said as he approached her. He glanced behind her to assure she was alone. "No chaperon?"

She shook her head. "Nay. I am alone, but only for a little while."

It was then Daniel noticed she was wearing *Englische* clothing.

"Yes, Daniel. I am dressed *Englische*." She hung her head. "My mother is a bit concerned I want to become Amish. She made me wear these clothes to see you so... so you would understand where I come from. My father is furious I am even thinking of becoming Amish – to marry you, an Amish man."

"Is being Amish so bad?" Daniel asked. The words echoed in his head, remembering Molly Pearce asking him if being *Englische* was a bad thing.

"My father didn't want me to come here today." Martha looked around the schoolroom. "He forbid it. He doesn't know I'm here."

"You disobeyed your father?"

"I needed to see you, Daniel. I love you. I can't..." She broke down and cried. "I'm sorry, Daniel. I've spent too many years in the *Englische* world. Can I be Amish?" She leaned in and placed her head on his shoulder. "It was so much easier in New York. Here? It's all different here."

"I love you, too, Martha. I want to marry you. You want to marry me. What is the problem? We want to get married." He stepped back and grabbed her hands in his. "I am Amish. You are..."

"Yes, Daniel. I am *Englische*. I know the Amish world, but I've always been *Englische*. I could play Amish with my cousins and then go back to my *Englische* world when I tired of it. Can I be Amish? Can I give up the *Englische* world? I mean – can I give it up completely? I don't..."

She pulled away from his hands. "I need time to think. I need to be alone. I need..." She turned and ran from the room, down the steps and to the car outside.

Daniel stood at the doorway watching her open the door of the car to get in.

"I love you, Daniel Yoder," Martha said and closed the door of the car. It pulled away, turning around in the small driveway. The window rolled down. "I will talk to you soon," she yelled as the car drove by Daniel.

Daniel watched the car pull onto the dirt road, the dust billowing up into the air as it raced away.

He heaved a sigh. The impetus and excitement of the new schoolroom drained from him. He sloughed his way back into the room and stared at the boxes of books and supplies he needed to deal with. He rolled a shoulder in a weak shrug and tromped to the desk, sat and stared at the room with the empty

25

desks.

Martha's words echoed in his mind. *It was so much easier in New York.*

#

Tuesday, September 3, 1963, 5:30 a.m.

Daniel walked with his father and brothers to the barn. Today was the first day of school and chores waited, starting with milking the cows. Daniel smiled, watching Jacob race ahead to the barn. It reminded him of when he would do that with Luke. On impulse, Daniel broke from his father and older brother and raced behind Jacob.

"I can beat you to the door," Daniel yelled as he sprinted up behind Jacob.

"If you think so," Jacob replied and went full out in a race. "But, you need to beat me." He laughed.

Daniel eased back to allow his younger brother to gain some distance and win the race.

Jacob opened the door. "I will go up and throw down the hay." He turned to his father. "Yes, Papa?"

"As you wish, Jacob," Noah Yoder replied. He turned to Luke and Daniel. "I will start at the far end. You two start here."

Daniel nodded agreement and grabbed a bucket and stool.

#

Tuesday, September 3, 1963, 7:30 a.m.

"Hannah," Rebecca Yoder called. "You make sure the twins have what they need for their first day of school." She grinned. "I heard the teacher is quite strict."

The twins, Joshua and Jonah, stared at their mother.

"But, Mama, the teacher is our brother. We know him," Joshua said.

"Daniel is fun to be with," Jonah added.

"Yes, but now he is your teacher. You will call him Mr.

Yoder while at school." She shook a chastising finger at the twins. "Remember that." She wiped her hands in a towel. "You are no different than any other student at the new school."

"Yes, Mama," the twins replied in unison.

Rebecca returned to the kitchen sink and finished washing the dishes. Hannah rushed about, helping Mary, Jacob, Anna, Joshua, and Jonah get ready for school. They would ride with Daniel to the new school.

"I want to go to school," little Ester whined. "There will be nobody to play with."

Rebecca turned from the sink to smile at her youngest child. "You can help Hannah and me in the garden and then we will come into the kitchen and play with the vegetables."

Ester clapped her hands.

Daniel came down and stood at the bottom of the stairs appraising the mayhem.

"Who is ready to go to school?" he asked. "Go get in the buggy."

Five children rushed out the kitchen door. Daniel grabbed the basket containing their lunch.

"Well, I for one am glad I am not going to school." Hannah stuck out her tongue at her brother. "Imagine, my brother trying to teach me." She offered a curtsy, turned and walked across the room. "Goodbye, Daniel," she said as she left the kitchen.

Rebecca grabbed Daniel by the shoulders and stood looking into his eyes.

"This is a momentous event for you, our family, and our community. A new school." She patted his shoulders. "A new teacher." Her lower lip quivered. She turned him toward the door. "Do not be late for school. Now hustle." She pushed him toward the door and immediately turned back to the sink, her head bent down.

"See you tonight, Mama," Daniel said and slipped out the kitchen door.

He got into the buggy. He jerked the reins and Beauty trotted out the lane onto the dusty dirt road.

First day of school, Daniel thought. He heaved a heavy sigh and closed his eyes.

Dear Lord, grant me the strength and knowledge to teach these children. Guide my feet and my words so they may learn. Amen.

"We are here!" Joshua exclaimed. "Hurry, Daniel – I mean, Mr. Yoder. I see James Troyer is already here. We can play."

Daniel and Jacob unharnessed Beauty so she could amble about and drink at the trough. Jacob quickly found his friends. Daniel stared at the yard around the school.

It will need to be mowed, he thought and smiled. *Another job for the schoolmaster*. He considered his options. *It should be fine until Saturday*, he thought. *Weather permitting*.

Daniel entered the school.

Tuesday, September 3, 1963, 8:00 a.m.

Miss Mueller stood by the front desk, hand on hip, surveying the room.

Daniel stared at the array of desks arranged in clusters. He glanced at each cluster which consisted of a different number of desks. Finally, he looked at Miss Mueller.

"It is a good thing I arrived early," she said. "These desks were in complete disarray. I rearranged them to accommodate the students by grade." She pinched her lips in disdain. "You gave no thought to the arrangement." She stepped down the one step from the platform and approached. "This is not an *Englische* classroom."

Daniel placed the basket with their lunches on the table to the left of the door.

"Miss Mueller," Daniel started. "I arranged the desks in three sections so we could assist the students with their needs."

Ignoring Daniel, she pointed at the different clusters of desks. "This is the first grade... this the second grade... this is the third grade..."

"Miss Mueller!" Daniel straightened to his full height. "I gave much thought to the layout of the desks and arranged

28

them as I wanted." He bit his tongue so he wouldn't add 'as the schoolmaster' and show disrespect to her.

"Fine, Mr. Yoder," Miss Mueller replied. "I was only attempting to be helpful." She straightened her dress. "Being older, I was offering my knowledge."

"I thank you for your thoughtfulness, Miss Mueller," Daniel said. "But, I believe, in the future, we will need to communicate our intentions before acting on them."

"As you wish, Mr. Yoder." The voice was icy as she moved toward the doors. "Should I call the children in, now?"

"First we will put the desks back in the arrangement I had."

The room transformed as the grade clusters disappeared, replaced by desks in straight rows and aisles.

"There is a bell on the table, Miss Mueller if you would like to call the students to class. Please tell them when they come into the school to please stand along the outside walls. I will assign them desks.

The students sauntered into the classroom, lining themselves against the walls. Their eyes were wide with excitement.

Daniel glanced at the diagram, remembering how he had assigned the desks for each grade.

"Let me have all the first graders to the front. There should six of you." He smiled and nodded at the twins who stood nearby. "That means you two."

Four young boys and two girls shuffled forward, unsure.

"Okay, there are two seats in a row." He grinned at the girls. "I believe you two will want to sit by each other. Yes?"

They nodded agreement.

"Fine, you both can take these first two desks. Now, I want Joshua in the next row with Leroy. Jonah and James will be in the back row."

"But I wanted to sit beside James," Joshua whined. "Why can't Jonah sit in that row?"

"Do you want to sit there, Jonah?" Daniel looked at his youngest brother.

Jonah shrugged. "Fine. I can sit there."

"Problem resolved," Daniel said and turned to glare at

29

Joshua. "But, if there is a problem with horseplay, I will move you to the front row. Is that understood, Joshua?"

"Yes, Daniel... I mean, Mr. Yoder."

Daniel arranged the remaining students into their designated desk groups. All this under the disapproving glare of Miss Mueller.

"Everyone has a desk." He nodded approval. "Now, the eighth graders will assist Miss Mueller to distribute the books and workbooks." The older students moved to help.

"When you get your workbooks, please write your name on the cover. You will find a pencil in your desk." Daniel smiled. "If you lose your workbook, and somebody finds it, we will know who it belongs to."

Daniel watched as the students received their books and workbooks. He noticed the frown on James Troyer's face.

"Is there a problem?"

"I do not know how to write my name," James said.

"Who else needs help?" Daniel asked.

Three other hands went up – Joshua and Jonah had already printed their names.

Daniel helped the four first-graders print their names by writing each of their names on a sheet of paper. They attempted to mimic the letters. He repressed a grin watching them struggle, but each student completed the task.

"Now, students, we will start the first day of school with prayer." The students bowed their heads.

> Heavenly Father. Today, as we begin our first day of school we ask Your blessing not only on our new school, but also our day as we study. We thank You for the beautiful day and I am sure the students look forward to recess. Guide our feet and minds as we learn. In Jesus' name, Amen.

"Now, first graders, take out your crayons..." Daniel handed out a plain piece of construction paper to each of the young students. "I want you to draw and color a picture of what you did this summer."

Daniel moved to the second graders. "I want you to do the same thing." He handed the three students each a construction sheet to use.

"Third graders. Open your readers and silently read the first story. Fourth, fifth, and sixth graders, you will open your math books and do the problems after reading the first chapter. You will find the problems at the end of the chapter." He smiled and gazed at the seventh and eighth graders. "You will write a small essay on what you did this summer." He turned to head back to the front, hesitated, and gazed back to the students. "I want a full page. No more than two pages. Any questions?"

"Mr. Yoder?" Sarah Troyer, James' older sister called. "I worked at the diner all summer." She gazed at Daniel expectedly. "That is one sentence."

"Sarah," Daniel started. "I am sure you can expand on what you did at the diner. Perhaps the people you met? Any accidents? Did I not see you at the bridge singing one Saturday?"

Sarah blushed.

"Our lives are not as exciting as your trip to New York City, Mr. Yoder," Samuel Heffel blurted. "We..."

"Mr. Yoder's trip to New York is not for discussion," Miss Mueller snipped. "Now be about your assignments.

"Yes, Miss Mueller," Samuel responded.

She pursed her lips. In silence, she began marching up and down the aisles, checking to make sure each student was working.

# # #

Monday, September 9, 1963, 9:30 a.m.

Daniel stood near the first graders as they worked on the letters of the alphabet. He enjoyed watching them gain confidence in printing their names. He leaned in to assist James to reverse the 's' of his name so it wasn't backward.

A knock at the door drew everyone's attention to the back. A darkened shadow of a young man stood in the bright doorway.

"Excuse me," the young man mumbled. "Da... Mr.

Yoder?"

"Yes," Daniel replied and walked toward the door.

The young man stepped into the schoolhouse.

Daniel stepped back, surprised.

A sheepish grin crossed the stranger's face. "Good morning... Do I call you Mr. Yoder or Daniel?"

"My name is Daniel Yoder." He grinned. "You, of all people, should know that, Jason Muirs." Daniel turned to Miss Mueller. "If you will watch over the students in my absence. I will attend to this gentleman's needs outside." He gave a cursory glance at the students. "I will be right outside. Continue your work. Miss Mueller is in charge and will handle any problems."

Miss Mueller cocked a questioning eye in his direction but finally nodded agreement.

"Come," Daniel said and placed an arm over Jason's shoulders to escort him outside. As they stepped away from the school and into the shade of a nearby tree, Daniel couldn't believe the visitor.

"What brings you to my school?"

"I heard you were the teacher. When did you get back from New York City? How did you get this job? I wanted to help build the school, but my family went on vacation and we were at Cedar Point on the other side of Toledo."

"I hoped you would stop by the house to visit."

Jason shrugged. "I had no idea what was going on." He scuffed his shoe on the ground. "Like, man, you vanished. You went to New York City." He grinned. "I heard that from Molly." He whistled. "Boy, was she ever mad at you. I'd see her at the pool and ask about you. She'd tell me you were in the big city being too big for your britches, hoping to be a movie star or something."

Daniel cocked his head and stared at Jason. "She said that?" He gazed anxiously at the school doors, waiting for them to open with a frantic Miss Mueller needing him. "Are you playing hooky from school?"

"Nah," Jason drawled. "Today is fair day so we didn't have school. I was going to ask if you wanted to go with me to the fair." Jason glanced at the school. "But, you have school."

He grinned and gave a short snicker. "Could the teacher let school out early for the day?"

Daniel gazed at Jason.

"Remember, Jason. I am Amish. I am a teacher, now." He shook his head. "I cannot allow such frivolities. I am a member of the church."

Jason's eyes widened. "You got baptized?"

Daniel nodded. "Come by the house tonight if you can. We can talk. I will tell you about New York City." Daniel smiled. "And I will tell you about Martha."

"An *Englische* girl?"

Daniel smiled and placed a finger to his lips. "That is a secret. Now, I need to get back to my students, Jason." Daniel headed back toward the school. "Of course, you could sit in the back and we can talk during lunch if you would like that."

"Is my car okay there?" Jason pointed to the dark blue 1958 Chevy Impala.

Daniel nodded approval. "Come on in and I will introduce you."

# # #

Daniel shared his lunch with Jason.

"I can't believe you were a suspect." Jason's eyes were wide. "Your roommate murdered?"

"So, tell me, Jason. How is high school this year?"

"It's neato," Jason replied. "So cool. Being a junior gives me a lot of benefits." He winked. "You should see the hotty freshmen girls this year."

"Hotty? What of Patty Zimmer? Did you take chorus?"

"Patty and I broke up. She thinks I'm immature. She's dating some senior. Chorus? Sure did. A new teacher and well, she is nice and all, but she isn't anything like Miss Bronson was. I miss her."

Daniel nodded in agreement. "I met Miss Bronson... I mean, Mrs. Jones while I was in New York City."

"No way! How cool. Now, tell me about this Martha. With a name like that, she has to be *Englische*. Is she from New York?"

Daniel grinned and gazed off toward the gathered students as they prepared to play ball.

"Martha's real name is Martha. I met her in New York City and she helped me adjust to the *Englische* world with new clothes and a haircut. We dated, sort of. She took me to visit some Amish people in Pennsylvania and then she left. When I got baptized, I was introduced to Martha Noble. It was Martha. Her mother was raised Amish, met an *Englische* man, and married him. She lives in Shipshewana." Daniel frowned. "We were going to get married, but..."

"Married?" Jason reared back in his chair to stare at Daniel.

"Yes," Daniel whispered. "We were. Now we are not. Her father, who is most definitely *Englische*, has forbidden it. He does not want Martha to become Amish." He shrugged.

Jason took a deep breath, a serious mood sitting in.

"There is a reason I came today," Jason said.

Daniel frowned and glanced at Jason. "Oh?"

Jason pointed at the school. "This." Jason inhaled deeply. "I've heard some grumbling at school." He shrugged. "Mostly students, but I've also heard a couple of the teachers making comments." He paused. "But, you know if the parents are talking, the kids are listening and repeating it."

"What are they saying?"

"Okay, yesterday, at church..." Jason paused momentarily, watching the young boys and girls playing a form of tag. "Remember, TJ? His father, Tom Hollis made a snide remark about how the Amish community helped vote to pass the consolidation. He says the Amish are snubbing the consolidation by building their school and taking needed students away."

Daniel considered Jason's words.

"I'm not going to say who, but the person he was talking with suggested the school be burned to the ground."

"Why would they want to burn your school?" Daniel asked.

Jason gazed in surprise. "Daniel. It isn't my school they want to burn. It is your school." Jason pointed at the school behind them. "This Amish school, Daniel. They were talking about burning this building."

Daniel's eyes widened in shock. "I need to think about this, Jason."

Jason nodded. "No doubt, buddy. I know how you want to learn and teach others. This would kill you."

"The students," Daniel started. "They could be in danger. I must tell the Bishop."

Jason raised a cautious hand. "Now, hold on a minute, buddy. I only heard them talking and you know how old man Hollis gets his dander up. I think it is all a bunch of steam."

Daniel gave Jason a quizzical look. "Steam?"

"Don't get your panties in a bunch. At least, not just yet, Daniel."

"Mr. Yoder?" Miss Mueller called from nearby. "Is it not time to begin class?"

"Yes, yes," Daniel replied absently. "Call the students in."

"Okay, dude," Jason said, gripping Daniel by the shoulders. "Keep calm. Understood?"

"I will keep calm," Daniel replied, once more taking command of the situation.

Miss Mueller rang the bell.

"Students!" Daniel hollered. "Time for class." He turned to Jason. "Thank you for visiting. If you would like to come over tonight, please do so."

Jason winked. "Tell you what, buddy. I'll see you this weekend. Okay?"

Daniel nodded.

CHAPTER FOUR: Going Home

September 10, 1963, 2:30 p.m.

"And just where do you think you are going?"

Martha hesitated at the front screen door.

"I asked where?" her mother repeated.

"I'm going to Mark Yoder's house to get the things I left there."

"I packed everything." Emma stood from her easy chair to join Martha at the door. "There is no reason for you to go." She pursed her lips. "That is your father's decision."

"Fine. I will go to Uncle Paul's house and get my things there."

"I don't believe that will be necessary," Dan Noble said coming from the kitchen. "You have nothing there you will need here."

Martha turned to face her father.

"I see we need to discuss this matter more," Dan said. "The three of us will go sit in the living room and hash this out once and for all."

Emma turned and headed to her chair in the living room.

"I don't see what you want to discuss. There won't be a discussion. You are going to demand me to do this or that." Martha put a hand to her hip. "So, it isn't a discussion."

"Watch the sass, young lady." Dan motioned for her to go to the living room. "Let's go argue."

Martha grimaced. "If you wish." She stomped to the couch in the living room knowing her father would sit in the BarcaLounger.

"So, where did you actually plan to go?" Dan asked.

"Being honest. I was going to see Daniel. I wanted to see how he is doing as a teacher for the new Amish school."

36

"Uh-huh. Then what?"

"I don't know, Daddy." Martha slumped on the couch, twisting a lock of hair about her index finger. "Maybe go to supper with him at this family's house?"

Dan cocked an eyebrow. "I told you. It is very simple. You are not to see him." He stood up from his BarcaLounger. "No daughter of mine is going to be marrying into a cult."

"Amish is not a cult," Emma said. "Remember, I was Amish."

"Yes, my darling wife. I married you and... well, I saved you from a life of drudgery." He strolled to Emma and reached out, caressing her face with his hand. "You wanted me to become Amish. I couldn't see you working so hard for so little. Plus, I had no urge to spend my time herding animals and working fields all day."

Emma cocked an eye at Dan. "So little? My Amish life was filled with love, laughter, and the Lord. It was not a life of misery as you think."

Dan waved his hand aside. "It doesn't matter. No daughter of mine is going to work her fingers to the bone from dawn to dusk." He glanced at Martha. "She deserves so much more... a car, pretty clothes, makeup, a home with modern conveniences." He paused. "And a husband who will provide all that for her."

Martha scowled at her father. "Daniel is a teacher. And he works at the mill during the summer."

"Need I say more? The answer is plain and simple." He turned to face Martha. "You are not allowed to see this Daniel Yoder. AND..." He hesitated. "You will not... I repeat... NOT marry him."

"I will do as I want," Martha yelled. "I survived in New York City." A tear welled in her eye. "Why did I come back?" she whispered and glared at her father. "You married Amish; why can't I? What's the difference?"

"The difference?" Dan's face reddened in anger. "The difference is simple. Your mother was almost eighteen. I had finished high school and was about to enter the Army. I went to boot camp and when I got back, I drove to her parent's house, proposed, and we married. She was about to get baptized."

"Well, I'm seventeen and Daniel is almost eighteen. I'll soon be eighteen." Martha sat up on the couch, hoping her father wouldn't do the math on her age. "No, Daniel isn't going off to the military, but we love..."

"Because you're the smart one," Dan blurted, cutting her words. "Alexander, your brother is at college studying some esoteric crap. He's joined some "Harry Christian" group and now runs around in a sheet. Your sister ran off with the first man who winked at her. And where is she now? Someplace up in God-forsaken Canada." Dan made a face. "Oh, yes, he's a jewel of a find. That so-called man she married wanted to avoid the draft. Yeah, there's a real man. I trudged through Europe fighting the Germans in World War II, living in foxholes."

"Smart one?" Martha echoed.

"That's right," Dan snapped. "You're going back to school. I'm tired of this nonsense about being Amish and no need to continue schooling."

Martha wiped the tears away.

Dan glared at her. "Do you understand me?"

"Yes, Daddy," she replied.

Emma stood and joined Martha on the couch.

"Tell you what, Martha." She ignored her husband. "How about you take a little breather. Time to get your wits about you. Go visit your friend, Hazel and talk about school." She winked at Martha. "If you want, I can call her mother and see if you could stay for the evening meal."

"You will be back home by no later than eight," Dan demanded. "Do you hear me?"

"Yes, Daddy," Martha whimpered. "Be home by eight o'clock." She gazed into her mother's eyes. "You don't need to call Hazel's mother. I'm sure it will be okay for me to stay for the meal tonight."

"I'll see you to the door," Emma said and stood to help Martha get up.

They walked silently together toward the door. Emma glanced back to assure herself Dan was sitting in the BarcaLounger and reading the newspaper. She leaned in close to Martha.

"Tell Uncle Paul I will try to get over to visit in the next couple of days." She smiled, grabbed Martha's hands and squeezed them. "This is our little secret." Emma gave Martha a small peck kiss. "Talk to Uncle Paul. Be sure this is what you want."

# # #

"Uncle Paul?"

"Yes, Martha."

She took a deep breath. "My father says being Amish is a cult and he has forbid me joining the church and community." She paused and took another deep breath. "I love Daniel Yoder. Is there any way we can marry and exist?"

"Come and sit with me, daughter of my sister." He smiled at her while leading her into the main sitting room. "This is not a simple yes or no answer." Paul nodded at his wife who sat in the rocker by his chair. Paul turned to Martha. "Are you thirsty? Hungry?"

Martha laughed. "I am fine, Uncle Paul." She hesitated. "But, may I join the family for the evening meal?"

"A blessing," Mary said. "I will place another plate on the table." She stood and left the room.

"Now, tell me, Martha. What is this about marriage?"

"My father is adamant. I am not to marry Daniel Yoder."

"Your father cannot decide who you love." Paul stroked his beard.

"He insists being Amish is like a cult. He says I will work all day and never have anything."

"Worldly goods." Paul nodded knowingly. "The *Englische* surround themselves with all the worldly things they can. All the modern conveniences."

Martha nodded her head.

"Amish is not a cult. It is a way of life. Many think it is a faith. We are Christians and a simple people. We see no reason to complicate our life with all the modern gadgets. Each Ordnung decides what is allowed and how it is allowed."

"I know all that, Uncle Paul. Is there a way for me to be *Englische* and Daniel to be Amish? And for us to be married?"

"Nay, Martha. The simplest answer is what you do not want to hear. Either you become Amish, or Daniel becomes *Englische*. Daniel has been baptized into the church. If he leaves the Amish, he will be shunned. *Meidung*. His family will not be able to speak to him." Paul searched Martha's eyes. "Is this what you wish for Daniel?"

Tears welled in Martha's eyes. "But, Uncle Paul, can I become Amish?"

"You know our life, Martha." Paul offered her a handkerchief. "You have lived as Amish over several summers with my family."

Martha nodded. "But, Uncle Paul, I always returned to my *Englische* home. I could do it at any time I wished." She gazed at her uncle. "It was fun playing Amish."

"Ah," Paul said and eased back into his chair. "Is that what you considered living with us, a type of playing?"

"I... uh... I meant that while I was here... I... uh..."

"Look in your heart, Martha. Did you play Amish, or did you embrace the Amish lifestyle when you stayed with us?"

Martha stared at the floor in thought.

"I think I tried to live as Amish when I was here." She once more gazed at Paul. "But, I knew I could leave any time I wanted." She paused. "I didn't want to, but I could." She reached out and put a hand on her Uncle's hands. "You are Amish. You have never lived in the *Englische* world."

Paul laughed, a gruff chuckle from deep inside his chest.

"Daughter of my sister. You do not know the young me. You only know the Amish me." Paul gazed off into the shadows of a corner of the room. "When I was young, I questioned everything. Grandfather Matthew was sure I would skip the first chance I got." He nodded, a small curl of a smile to his lips "I went on *Rumschpringe*. Do you think your little escapade to New York City was wild? I almost joined the Army, but instead, I joined a traveling circus, going from town to town."

Martha's eyes widened.

"Shocked, are you? I smoked. I drank. I... well, let us say I lived a life nothing to match what I had lived before. Each town we visited had plenty of pretty, young girls. They would ogle my muscles and physique as I worked putting up the tents. I considered the *Englische* lifestyle."

"But, you came home," Martha said.

"Yes, I came home." Paul smiled. "The *Englische* life was exhilarating, but I was missing something. I was missing family. I was missing my faith. I got very drunk one night." Paul placed a hand to the side of his head and mimicked a hangover. "The circus left town without me. When I awoke, I was alone with nowhere to go." Paul winked. "A young lady I had met suggested I come live with her." He shrugged. "I headed home. I was in Missouri." He laughed. "It was a long hike home, but I came home. Grandfather Matthew welcomed me. I joined the church and was baptized. Never once have I regretted my decision."

Martha shook her head. "I thought the murder in New York was exciting."

Paul put a finger to his lips. "This is a secret. Only Mary knows of my past. I shared this with you so you would consider my words."

Martha pretended to place a key to her lips and lock them. "Your secret is safe."

"So, once again, Martha, I say to you: search your heart and soul. Only you can decide about your life. Your father can forbid and bless, but he can't live your life, only you can do that." He stood. "It is now time for me to milk the cows."

"If you want, I will help you." Martha stood.

"I am sure the boys would love that." He winked. "Instead, help your aunt with the evening meal. There is only Fannie left to assist in the kitchen." He smiled. "You know the Amish and you are a girl." He cocked his head. "Do you understand?"

Martha laughed. "Right. Amish women cook. I will help Aunt Mary and Fannie fix supper."

"If you wish to discuss this more at a later time, see me."

"Thank you, Uncle Paul. Oh, by the way, mother says she will come to visit in a couple of days."

"It will be good to see my sister." Paul strode through the kitchen and out the door.

"Can I help with the vegetables?" Martha asked and

joined Aunt Mary at the sink.

###

Martha closed the front door of the house.

"Is that you, Martha?" Her father's voice was strong. "Come to the living room."

Martha stepped around the corner. "Who else were you expecting?" She noticed her mother sitting in her rocker, knitting. "Since Alexander moved out, and Bethany is now in Canada... who else did you expect?"

"Sit down, young lady. No more sass." Dan pointed at the chair opposite him. He took a deep breath. "Do you know what time it is?"

"About a quarter to eight," Martha replied. "I made the curfew you established. You said to be home by eight. I am here."

"It is ten of eight and you were cutting it close." He glared at her.

"Hazel and I lost track of time after supper." She kept her eyes staring at the floor, knowing full well if she looked at him, he would know she was lying.

"Oh, did you now?" The sarcasm in her father's voice was obvious.

Martha glanced up at her father.

"How is it when I called Hazel's father to let you know you could stay later..." He paused and offered a questioning look. "He had no idea where you were. They were just sitting down to the evening meal." Dan folded his arms before him and glared.

"Checking up on me?" she asked.

Dan brought a cautionary wagging finger before him. "No, but I do expect an answer. Where were you this evening?"

Martha stood and glared at her father. "To be honest, I visited Uncle Paul and had supper with them."

Dan lowered his head and sighed in disgust. "The Amish, again."

"Dan Noble!" Emma yelled. "That is MY brother."

Dan glanced at his wife before once more turning his

42

attention to Martha. Standing before his chair, he attempted to remain calm. "How many times must I tell you, Martha, I don't want you associating with the Amish. You're not Amish."

"Yes, father," Martha sneered. "That's right. I'm *Englische*. That is so much better than being a simple Amish person. How lucky I am. Why do you hate the Amish? Is being Amish such a bad thing?"

"No daughter of mine will marry an Amish boy." Dan waggled an admonishing index finger at his daughter as she stood glaring at him.

"But, you can marry an Amish woman?" Martha stabbed a finger in her mother's direction. "Remember, mother was Amish. More than half of my relatives are Amish."

Dan Noble inhaled, his chest expanding in the action. Trying to calm his temper, he exhaled slowly.

"Fine," Dan mumbled. "Why did you go to Uncle Paul's house?" He was tempted to add '*against my decision*' but decided against it.

"I needed to talk to somebody." She cocked her head to give her father a small glance. "It had to be somebody who would be impartial."

"An Amish man would be impartial?"

Emma stood and stepped between Martha and Dan.

"We all need to sit down and discuss this like rational adults." Emma turned to Martha and motioned for her daughter to sit in the chair. She turned to Dan. "You need to sit back in your recliner... and quit ranting at your daughter about the Amish." She placed a hand on her husband's shoulder and pushed, urging him to sit. "Whether you like it or not, here are some facts. I was born Amish, raised Amish, and even though I married an *Englische*, I am still Amish deep down inside. Now, whether Paul would be impartial? I believe he would be the best person to answer Martha's questions. Yes, Dan, he is Amish, but he would want what is best for Martha. He knows she is *Englische*, born *Englische*, and raised *Englische*. Knowing my brother when I was a little girl, he would probably tell her to stay *Englische* rather than attempt the... what you seemingly think to be the harsh lifestyle of the Amish."

Dan acquiesced to his wife's soft pressure. He sat in the BarcaLounger, watching his daughter sit in the chair opposite him.

"Will you at least go back to school?" Dan asked.

"I will," Martha replied.

Dan sighed, relieved.

"Can I convince you to not consider any marriage proposals until after you graduate high school?"

Martha closed her eyes in thought, considering her father's words and those Uncle Paul offered. She opened her eyes and stared at her father, taking a few minutes to straighten her dress.

"If I agree, and Daniel is willing to wait until then... can I then marry him?" Martha hesitated. "Although an Amish woman with a high school degree is a waste of time."

Martha watched her father's muscles tense. His fingers curled, tightening over the edges of the BarcaLounger. Finally, they relaxed.

"Until you graduate, I agree," he whispered. "I can only hope in the time span given you will find another to steal your heart and that person not be Amish."

Martha smiled and then snickered. "Maybe your wish will come true, but, please, Daddy, don't hold your breath. I love Daniel."

Dan shrugged. "One can hope." He stood, strode over to Martha and kissed her on the forehead. "I'm counting on proms, school dances, and other activities to work for me."

"Can I visit Daniel?" Martha asked.

Again, Dan tensed, his eyes squinting.

"Let me put it this way, Daddy. On a limited number of weekends and perhaps a few weeks during the summer break. May I also be allowed to stay with his Uncle Mark?"

"Not every weekend," Dan replied. "I want you to enjoy your days in high school. There will be many activities for you to participate in." He smiled. "Daniel is Amish. He won't dance or go to a home game."

Martha nodded in agreement. "Understood. But, do you agree to let me see him?"

"Yes."

"Thank you. I love Daniel so much."

Martha stood and kissed her father on the cheek, and then moved to her mother and kissed her on the cheek.

"Good night," she said and rushed up the stairs to her room.

CHAPTER FIVE: Citizen Unrest

Saturday, September 14, 1963, about 1 p.m.

Daniel got in the back seat of Ben Hopkins' station wagon. Luke slipped into the back seat from the other side of Ben's car. Their father got into the front passenger seat.

"Which store do you wish to visit in DeMotte, Mr. Yoder." Ben smiled at each of them, offering Noah Yoder a hand to shake.

"If you would take us to the courthouse and wait, that would be fine." Noah Yoder eased back into the seat, but still held a secure grip on the assist handle of the door.

Ben noted the death grip and smiled, looked into the rear mirror at Daniel, winked, and put the car into gear.

"How are things at the new school, Daniel?" He paused. "I miss you on the bus."

"Teaching is very interesting, Ben. I am enjoying it very much."

"Going to DeMotte for school supplies?"

Ben smiled. "Yes. I want to get some colored chalk and I need to replace a bottle of finger paint that was spilled." He paused. "Oh, and a couple of erasers for the younger ones to correct their spelling."

Daniel watched as Centertown came into view. He stretched to look at the new consolidated high school just beyond where Ben would turn to go to DeMotte.

Ben noticed Daniel's actions.

"Would you like me to drive by the new high school?" Ben kept one eye on the road and watched Daniel in the rearview mirror. "I can take another county road into DeMotte. It isn't a bother."

"There is no need," Noah said. "We must take care of our

business and be back to the farm to finish some of the fields yet today."

Daniel glanced at his father then leaned back into the seat. "No," he mumbled.

Ben sped toward DeMotte, cruising around the big "S" curve outside Hayton.

#

"I'll park the car here, Mr. Yoder," Ben said, pulling into a spot. He pointed at a bench under a shade tree near the courthouse. "And, I'll sit over there until you come back."

"We will not take long," Noah replied. "I need to pick up a few things for Rebecca at the Five and Dime. Luke will be at the hardware store." Noah glanced at Daniel. "He will be at the office store." He smiled. "Daniel should be back first."

Daniel heaved a sigh. He understood what his father's words meant. He shouldn't spend too much time at the store gawking about at everything. *Get what I need and come back,* he thought.

Daniel headed toward the office store on the west side of the courthouse square.

A ding-dong sounded as the door opened when Daniel entered. The perfumed scents of incense and potpourri included with each item in the gift section of the store assaulted him. Daniel hustled to the back of the store where office supplies were kept.

"May I help you?" The salt-and-pepper haired woman wearing too much perfume looked up from the counter. She smiled at him, but he could see the minute flicker of "*Oh, an Amish*" when she saw him.

"I need some colored chalk and a bottle of orange finger paint, please," Daniel replied.

"This way," she snipped and stepped from behind the counter. "Will you need poster paper, too?" She turned to face him. "I am guessing this is a craft project of some sort?"

"No, ma'am," Daniel said. "I am a teacher. I want the colored chalk to show the students my corrections." He smiled. "The paint is to replace the bottle dropped by accident."

"Oh." The voice was cold. "This is for the Amish school. I see."

Daniel noticed her name tag: Dorothy Pearce.

"Uh, Mrs. Pearce. Do you know a Molly Pearce by any chance?"

She handed Daniel a box of colored chalk. "She is my niece. Why do you..." She scrutinized Daniel before pursing her lips and glaring at him. "You're him. The Amish boy who Molly knows."

Daniel smiled. "Yes, Molly and I attended school together."

She shoved the orange finger paint at Daniel.

"There. Follow me, I'll ring it up and you can be on your way."

She turned and charged toward the front counter and cash register. Daniel placed the items on the counter. Mrs. Pearce rang the items into the cash register.

"That will be one dollar and seventy-two cents." She grabbed the two items and put them into a paper bag.

Daniel handed her two dollars.

"Your change," she said and placed the twenty-eight cents on the counter. "Thank you." She turned and walked away from him.

"The Amish shouldn't have built that school," she mumbled.

"What did you say?" Daniel asked.

"Nothing." She pursed her lips. "Good day."

Daniel left the store and headed back to Ben who sat on the bench he had designated.

#

A stranger spoke animatedly with Ben as Daniel approached. The stranger glanced up to see him.

"Here comes one of them, now. I'll talk to you later." The stranger shoved his hands into his pockets and stomped away.

Daniel joined Ben on the bench and gazed at the Five and Dime. He didn't see his father. He glanced at the hardware store to his left. He didn't see Luke.

48

"I guess my father was correct. I am the first one back." He smiled at Ben.

Ben laughed. "Something told me, listening to your father's voice, you had best be the first one back or you'd be in trouble."

Daniel shrugged. "It was strange. The woman who waited on me was Molly Pearce's aunt." He paused. "She was not friendly. She said the Amish should not have built the school."

"Funny you should mention that," Ben said. "Leon Milster - the guy I was talking to - told me the same thing." Ben frowned. "I'm not exactly sure what he meant. Just before you arrived, he said something that has me upset. He said 'the Amish will learn' and well, then he left because he saw you coming."

Daniel stared at the grass, watching the moving shadows of the tree flicker across the lawn. The wind gently blew the branches.

"Jason Muirs stopped by the school on Monday since it was fair day and did not have to go to school." Daniel sat back, folded his hands and placed them in his lap. "He said there was some grumbling about the Amish building a school. He even mentioned someone has considered burning my school down."

Daniel gazed up at Ben's shocked face.

"People can be mean, Daniel," Ben said. "They can also say things they don't intend to do." He paused and gave a deep sigh. "I've heard others complaining. Leon isn't the first." He looked up. "Here comes Luke. Your father should be coming soon."

"Please do not say anything to my father," Daniel whispered. "I do not wish to upset him."

Ben stood, placing a strong grip on Daniel's shoulder. "Mums the word." Ben stretched as Luke approached.

"Daniel!" Luke said. "We must talk," Luke spoke Amish. "There is talk about the new school."

"Please, Luke." Daniel glanced at Ben. "We will speak *Englische* in front of Ben. He knows."

Luke gave Ben a questioning look.

"What did you hear, Luke?" Ben gazed at the Five and Dime. "Your father isn't coming, yet."

49

"I was bent down, checking out items near the floor and they did not see me. They were talking about the Amish school and how it should not exist and something should be done."

Daniel nodded his head. "The woman at the office store said we should not have built the school."

Luke gazed at the Five and Dime. "The two men said if vandals destroyed the school perhaps the Amish would return to the *Englische* schools." Luke shook his head. "They do not understand we do not wish to have our children so far away." He glanced at the Five and Dime again. "Here comes father. We will not discuss this."

Daniel nodded.

"Take us home, Mr. Hopkins." There was an urgency and an unusual formality in Noah's voice. "I need to speak with the bishop immediately."

Ben nodded, knowing Noah had heard and realized the issues.

#

Tuesday, September 17, 1963, 7 p.m.

John Teegarden snapped the gavel on the table.

"This meeting of the Consolidated Northwest Schools is now called to order."

"Cut the crap, John." Tom Hollis slumped in his chair, tapping the rubber eraser of the pencil on the tabletop. "We all know why we're here." He paused. "It's the Amish."

John took a deep breath. "There are other issues to discuss, Tom."

Tom slapped his hand on the table. "Not so fast. Right now the main issue is the Amish and their new school." He nodded as he glanced about the table at the group assembled. "We need to address **that** issue before we amble down any other road tonight."

There was a small rumble of agreement from the assembled men.

"Since you seem to be spear-heading this..." John lifted an open-palmed hand to Tom. "Why not move forward with the discussion." He noted the other assembled eight men. "All nine of us are here tonight, so it is a full board meeting." He offered a weak smile. "We can vote and get it over with."

Tom stood, rolling his knuckles under, making fists on the table as he stood to full stature.

"We are well aware the Amish helped to railroad this consolidation of our schools during the vote. They were in full agreement with the project." He paused, lingering on the moment to take a deep breath. "Then, this summer, they went and built a new school." Tom leaned over the table, scrutinizing each man, making eye contact with them. "If they didn't want the consolidation, why did they vote for it?"

Jack Holland timidly raised a hand.

"What, Jack?" Tom snapped. *That Amish lover makes me sick,* he thought.

"The Amish have but one issue with the consolidation. I work with some of them at the mill. Their complaint was the fact their children would be bussed away from Centertown." He shrugged. "If the Centertown school had not become the new consolidated high school, the Amish might not have built the school." He offered a weak smile. "The Amish all live south and west of Centertown."

"He's partly right," Bob Hopkins added. "I was talking with the bishop the other day. They were concerned about the schooling... something about some law in New York state and taking God and prayer out of the schools."

"God doesn't need to be in the school," Tom said, taking charge of the discussion. "I've always thought prayer in school was a waste of time." He paused. "I believe in religion, but, we need to teach them the basic three R's: reading, 'riting, and 'rithmetic. If they want to learn about God, that's for them to go to church."

"But, for some students, this is their only introduction to God." Bob nervously fidgeted his fingers in a clasped hand grip.

"Again, not our problem, Bob." Tom stood tall. "If parents want their kids to learn about manners and playing nice – have the kids watch Captain Kangaroo. If they want them to learn about God, let the kids watch Davey and Goliath." He paused, narrowing his eyesight. "It is not, I repeat, NOT the duty of a school to teach children religion."

"Well, the Amish feel it is," Jack replied. "That's why they left, built a school, and now teach their kids."

John snapped the gavel on the table. "Gentlemen, we seemed to have veered from the discussion at hand."

Tom glared at John. "Tell you what. We burn down the Amish school and they will have to come back to us."

"Tom Hollis!!" Peter Udall jumped to his feet and glared at him. "If my sister heard you..."

"Your sister is dead. God rest her soul. Are you now her voice?" Tom glared at Peter. *Elizabeth Tremussen was always a thorn on almost every subject*, he thought. *Plus, she wasn't even on the board, but always got her two cents in.*

Peter stood. "Most of the time, Tom, I protect your back. I was there with you about Julie Bronson, but, this time? No. I can't sit here and listen to you advocate burning a school." He glared at the other men in the room. "I don't care whose school it is. You don't burn them down."

"Gentlemen. Gentlemen." John's voice lifted above them. "Sit and let's discuss this as logical, reasonable men." He turned to Tom. "Other than burning down the Amish school, do you have any suggestion of how to address the situation – as you call it?"

Tom sat in his chair, glowering at the others.

"Perhaps," Jack Holland whispered. "We should have the bishop... or even the new teacher, attend our next meeting so that person could explain the Amish reasoning."

"In other words," Tom sneered. "We table this topic until next month... or later?"

Jack smiled weakly. "Yes," he whispered.

Tom shrugged.

"Fine." John grabbed his gavel. "Unless someone disagrees, the Amish school discussion is tabled until an Amish representative can attend." He paused. "All in agreement say aye."

Seven men said aye.

"The ayes have it, with two nays" John rapped the gavel. "So passed." He fiddled with a pile of papers. "Next is the discussion about school menus. It has been suggested that all the schools serve the same meals. Discussion?"

Roy Bauers patted his rotund stomach. "I think that would be a wise decision."

The meeting continued for another forty minutes before ending.

CHAPTER SIX: Missing Martha

Tuesday, October 1, 1963, a little after 4 p.m.

Martha opened the front door. She was hesitant, having noticed her father's car in the driveway. He should have been at work. He was home early. She closed the door, the click of the door mechanism sounded like a jail door closing. She cringed. Taking one step, the floor creaked.

"Is that you, Martha?" Her father's voice called from the living room.

"Yes, father," Martha replied. "I'm on my way up to my room to do my homework." She quickened her steps across the foyer to the stairs.

"Come in here, please."

A shiver played its way down her spine. It was more a command than a request, even if he did say please.

"I've really got a lot of homework, daddy." She attempted to put him off and use an endearing term to aide her.

"It can wait. We need to talk."

Martha inhaled, pulling the air deep into her lungs. She realized she wasn't going to be able to put him off, and obviously, something was wrong. Martha clicked off the possibilities. There was only one she could think of.

"Now, young lady."

Martha sauntered into the living room and took the chair opposite his BarcaLounger. She noticed the television was off.

"Did you have a fun weekend?" He paused. "I mean, you did a sleepover with some school friend on Friday and Saturday."

"Yes, I enjoyed my weekend." Martha waited. She knew what was coming next. He was trapping her in a lie.

"Can you explain how it was my co-worker saw you at

the Mercantile parading around in Amish clothing with two other women."

"Oh, that," Martha replied. "Uh, Mary got sick on Friday and canceled. So, I decided to go to Uncle Paul's instead." She paused. "Was that a problem?"

Dan cocked his head, analyzing his daughter's words.

"That would depend on what happened. Did you see Daniel?"

Martha blinked and stared innocently at her father. "No. I had no way to contact him." She smiled. "Remember, Daddy, the Amish don't have telephones."

"Don't get sassy with me, Martha." Dan eased the BarcaLounger back. "Did you drive to Centertown to visit him?"

"No." Martha paused. "Even if I did, you said I could see him."

"Why, yes. Yes, I did." Dan sneered. "But, I also stipulated it was to be limited visits. You saw him last weekend. Am I correct?"

Martha nodded agreement. "But, only on Sunday. We went to church and I came home by supper time."

"Can I ask a question?" Dan asked.

"What?"

"Why do you want to be Amish?"

"I love Daniel. He loves me. He is Amish and if he was to become *Englische*, he would be shunned by his family. I don't want him to leave his family just so we can be together. I want my children to know their grandparents. If I become Amish, I can visit you and mom. Even Daniel can. If I remain *Englische*, we can't be married."

"So, how is schooling coming along?"

Martha was surprised by the discussion change, but accepted it, knowing if it continued on the Amish course, it would become an argument.

"Fine," she said. "I still don't see why I had to take algebra. I won't ever use it when I marry Daniel." She shook her head. "I really don't see any of the classes I'm taking to be of any help to me when I become Amish."

Like a tiger springing from its lair, Dan slammed the

BarcaLounger into an upright position.

"You don't get it." He stood. "Try to understand this. You're not going to waste your life. I won't let you become Amish."

"You promised," Martha screamed, stood, and ran from the room.

#

"You said I could see Daniel," Martha mumbled into her pillow. Her eyes narrowed to slits of anger. "You were lying." Her father's last words echoed in her mind – *I won't let you become Amish.*

Martha sat on the edge of her bed, staring at her bedroom and all the decorations.

So many distractions, Martha thought and shook her head. She smiled. *I like waking up at Uncle Paul's house. Simplicity.* She slipped the metallic charm bracelet from her wrist and glanced at the reflected image in the mirror. *I don't need the makeup.* She reached over and put a dab of hand cream on a tissue. She rubbed the tissue on her face, removing the light makeup – light pink lipstick, eyeliner, face powder, and pastel blue eye shadow.

"There," she whispered, looking at the plain girl reflected.

Martha pulled her hair back and put it up in a bun. Again, the words jumped forth in her thoughts – *I won't let you become Amish.*

"Watch me," she mumbled and fell to her knees on the floor. "There it is." She pulled the small suitcase from under the bed and tossed it on top of the pink chenille bedspread. The suitcase snaps clicked open under her fingers.

Martha gazed at the contents: three white bonnets, a black dress, a blue dress, and the third one in a shade of dark lavender. A set of respectable shoes nestled to the right.

"I am... do you hear me, Daddy? I am Amish."

She grabbed her Bible from the nightstand and placed it on top of the dresses. Martha closed the suitcase and slipped it back under the bed.

"Tonight," she whispered.

#

Wednesday, October 2, 1963, 1:45 a.m.

Martha awoke and looked at her alarm clock.

She listened. The house was quiet. Assured her parents were in bed, she moved out of bed. Already dressed in a blouse and Capri pants, Martha leaned down and grabbed the handle of the suitcase. She pulled it from under the bed.

It was a clear night. The almost full moon cast blue light into the room so Martha could see what she was doing without turning on a light. She absently reached for the Bible, her hands sliding over empty space.

"Oh," she whispered. "I've already packed that."

She reached for the car keys and immediately pulled back her hand.

"No, I can't take the car." Martha grimaced. "It will be a long walk, but it is the only way." She smiled. "I am Amish."

Martha slipped down the stairs and went to the kitchen. She grabbed a paper bag, placing a loaf of bread, the jar of peanut butter and its companion, a jar of strawberry jam. She grabbed a butter knife from the drawer and slipped it into the bag. She carefully folded the top down on the bag. She moved across the foyer, making sure to avoid the squeaky area near the front door. She opened the door, resetting the knob's lock so the door would be locked when she closed it from the outside. She gazed at her car sitting in the driveway.

"It would be so much easier," she whispered, then immediately shook her head. "No! I am Amish and do not need such things. I will walk."

She took two steps.

"But..." Martha turned toward the garage. "I have my old bike. Amish are allowed to ride bikes."

She put her suitcase and bag of food down. Martha opened the side door to the garage. It was dark, but she knew where her old bike hung from the rafters, waiting for her to use it at some point in the future. The moonlight glistened in through the windows showing her the path to the bicycle.

57

"And, the future is now." She lifted the bike from the hook, carefully guiding it out of the garage and into the moonlight. She grabbed the small suitcase and paper bag, placing them in the basket.

I hope the bread doesn't get smashed too badly, she thought.

Martha gazed up to the window in her parent's bedroom. "I love you," she whispered.

Pressing a foot down on the pedal, the bike moved down the driveway and Martha was on her way. The cool morning breeze chilled her.

Probably should have considered a sweater, she thought, shrugged, and continued on her bike.

Martha awoke to the sounds of men's voices. She peeked out of the small peephole she'd made in the hay.

Uncle Paul and two of his sons were in the barn preparing to milk the cows.

She watched as young Levi's head popped up by the ladder. He grabbed the pitchfork and headed toward her.

"Nay, Levi," Paul yelled. "From the other side first. It is older."

Martha sighed relief. She gazed at the pile on the other end of the loft. There was enough there for at least... she calculated. *I would say maybe eight to ten days*, she thought. *My hiding place is safe for at least a week.*

She pulled the hay back to hide her peephole. Her foot hit the chain on her bike. It made a small sound.

Levi turned, frowning and staring at the hay on the opposite side from him. He shrugged.

That was close, Martha thought. She curled into her hideaway and waited. The sounds of the men feeding and milking the cattle soothed. She fell asleep.

Wednesday, October 2, 1963, about 8 a.m.

58

"Paul Hershberger!"

The voice awoke Martha. It was her father.

"Be calm, husband of my sister," Paul said. "I am here with a late birth." He stood from a pen where a cow lay in labor.

"Where is Martha?" He charged through the barn doors. "I know you've got her."

"Martha?" Paul shook his head negatively. "Nay. I have not seen her today."

"She ran away from home last night." Dan glared at Paul. "She wants to be Amish and marry that boy over in Centertown." He took a deep breath while drawing himself to full height. "I forbid it."

Paul reached out to place a hand on Dan's shoulder.

"Don't bother touching me or try using your Amish magic on me." He pushed Paul's hand away.

"Amish magic?" Paul cocked his head with a frown. "I do not understand what you mean."

Dan folded his arms defiantly over his chest. "You know exactly what I mean. All the mumbo-jumbo about the simple life and how great it is. You know exactly what I mean."

"Perhaps we should go to the house and see if Mary has seen Martha." Once more Paul attempted to place a comforting hand on Dan's shoulder.

Once more Dan pushed it away.

Paul fell in step with Dan as they walked the open area between the barn and house.

"Tell me, Dan. Why do you hate the Amish? You married my sister."

"I married Emma because..." Paul stammered. "I.. I was enamored with her innocence. Everything I did with her was new and exciting to her. She made me feel important."

"Now that she is *Englische*... what?"

Martha strained to listen, but the men were walking away. Their voices faded. She pushed the hay away and dusted herself off, smoothing her Amish clothing. She slipped down the ladder and hid behind the big barn door to watch the two men enter the house.

I have to know what they are saying, Martha thought. She scanned the open area between the barn and the house. *Not too much cover, but I should be able to hide behind the lilac bush.*

Martha inhaled deeply and dashed to the buckboard, eased around it and raced for the cover of the lilac bush. She held her breath. The kitchen door didn't open, nor did anyone stand at a window. She hadn't been spotted.

This is not right. I shouldn't spy, but I need to know... Martha leaned in close to the open window of the living room. She watched the reflection of the two men on the pane of glass.

"I probably shouldn't have said that," Dan said. "I didn't realize she was that upset."

"I have not seen Martha, but I do know she is very happy and content when she is here."

Martha smiled at Uncle Paul's words. *He is right*, she thought. *I enjoy my life when I visit.*

"She left like a thief in the middle of the night. Neither Emma nor I heard her. She didn't take her car so she couldn't have gone too far." There was a pause as realization filled Dan's face. "I figure she came here and wanted a ride to Centertown." Another pause. "Who is a driver for the Amish?"

Paul smiled. "You mean beyond my sister, Emma? There is Steve Harnet and Lowell Bailey." Another pause. "Centertown is quite some drive."

Martha saw her father jump up.

"Why didn't I think of it?" he exclaimed. "Martha has a couple of school friends. They could have driven her to Centertown, or maybe to a bus station in Goshen or Ligonier."

"Martha is a smart, young lady," Paul said. "Are you sure she is not in school?"

"She wasn't in her bedroom this morning. There was no mess in the kitchen or bathroom. I don't think she went to school."

She watched her father's image start for the kitchen.

"I will check there." He turned to face Paul. "You **are** telling me the truth – Martha is not here."

Paul nodded. "I would not lie to you, Dan. You are family. Martha is not here."

"Fine," Dan replied. "If you hear from her, let me know."

Martha hugged the lilac bush so her father or Uncle Paul wouldn't see her. She waited.

Dan drove away. Uncle Paul waved and stood, watching.

Martha gazed at the chicken coop and the wooden gate to the field between the implement garage and barn. *It's a long path, but I can hide better on my way back to the barn*, she thought.

She ran toward the coop, lifting her skirts, hoping none in the house would see her.

If I make the barn, I can hide and be safe, Martha thought as she peeked around the corner of the chicken coop. She watched her uncle walk back into the house. Her father's car was already on the dirt road, raising dust into the air.

CHAPTER SEVEN: Daniel Accosted

Wednesday, October 2, 1963, 9:30 a.m.

"I'm sorry, Mr. Noble," Hazel said. "I have no idea where Martha is. She hasn't talked to me for two days." The young girl stared at the floor. "She thinks I snitched on her about Daniel."

Dan grimaced and nodded. He turned to the other young girl.

"Do you know anything? Martha seems to have run away." He leaned closer. "You do realize she could have been kidnapped?"

The other young girl with a beehive hairstyle stared wide-eyed at Dan. "No, sir." She sat shaking her head. "I waited for her at the entrance this morning. She never showed up. I was almost late to class because I kept waiting."

Thomas James, the principal, clapped his hands together. "There you have it, Mr. Noble. Neither of the girls saw your daughter today." He turned to the girls. "You may go back to your classes now."

The girls stood and scurried out of the office.

Dan slumped in the chair.

"I don't understand. Why would Martha run away? Who helped her?"

"Perhaps this Daniel person?" Thomas James offered.

Dan stared at the principal. "It's a possibility. Although, I think if they had tried to escape in a horse and buggy..." He smiled. "First, it's over an hour's drive by car. Plus, I'm sure there would have been some tale-tell signs. I didn't see anything to indicate a horse in the area." Dan paused. "At least, not in my neighborhood. Still... it might be worth checking."

Dan stood, shook hands with the principal, and exited the

office. A quick jaunt past three classrooms, down three steps, and he was out of the building, headed to his car. Centertown was a little over ninety minutes away.

I wonder how long it would take a horse and buggy? The thought boggled Dan.

Dan appraised the local grocery. *Beat up, run-down,* he thought. *I wouldn't shop here.* He entered the premises.

Aaron Shaw looked up from stocking items on the lower shelf. He stood. "May I help you?" he offered a hand to shake. "The name is Aaron Shaw."

"I'm trying to locate Mark Yoder's farm." Dan ignored Aaron's hand. "My wife always comes here to pick up our daughter when she visits. She knows where he lives. This is my first time to..." He awkwardly shrugged then waved his hand in the air. "Uh, Centertown. What is the quickest way to this Amish man's place?"

"Are you Martha Noble's father?"

"What of it?" Dan snapped. "Where's this Mark Yoder live?"

"Mark Yoder... Mark..." Aaron evaluated the man before him. Martha had mentioned her father didn't care for the Amish. "He lives about six miles from here." He paused and smiled. "Well, six miles as the crow flies. The best way to get to his farm would be... Hmm. Let me show you." Aaron placed his hand on Dan's shoulder and eased him toward the door. "This way." He opened the front door and escorted Dan out. "See that blinker light? Go through it and about three miles beyond you will turn right. That's Livingston Road. Go another two miles, turn left, go another two miles, turn left again, go..." Aaron frowned in thought. "Yes, that's right. Go another mile, make a right, go a mile, turn left and his farm is the first one on the right." Aaron smiled. "It's a big white house, probably fresh laundry on the line, more likely three kids playing in the yard and there's a large greenhouse on the south side of the house. You can't miss it."

Dan stared down the road in the direction Aaron pointed.

"Let's see if I got it right. Three and a right. Two and a left, another two and another left, then one and a right, one and left. First house on the right." Dan nodded his head. "Yeah, got it."

Dan hustled to his car, got in and sped away, making a cursory stop at the blinker light.

Aaron shook his head and smiled. "Or, you could just go six miles, make a right and it is the last house on the left in the first mile," he whispered and then cocked his head to look skyward. "Lord, forgive me."

Dan beat on the front door, yelling. "Mark Yoder, you answer the door right now. We need to talk."

Mary answered the door, the three young children sheepishly peeking around her skirt.

"I am Mary Yoder. How may I help you? Are you lost?" Her voice was soft and calm.

"No, I'm not lost. My name is Dan Noble. I want to talk to Mark Yoder." He stretched, angling to see around Mary hoping to see inside. He grabbed the screen door and yanked it open. He tried to step inside. "Where is my daughter? Are you hiding her?" Again, he stretched, attempting to see inside the house.

Mary held her position and glared at Dan. "This is my house, Mr. Noble. Emma is my sister, and you are my brother-in-law, but I have not asked you to enter. And, no I have not seen your daughter in over a week." She crossed her arms in front of her. "It is nice of you to finally visit. My husband is out in the barn if you wish to talk with him. Good day, Mr. Noble."

Mary pulled the screen door from Dan's hand, startling him. She hooked it into the eyelet then closed the front door.

Dan stepped back and stomped across the front porch and down the steps. He raced around the house to the barn.

"Mark Yoder!" Dan yelled.

"Aye, you called?" Mark stepped from the barn, shovel in hand.

"Is my daughter, Martha, here?"

64

"Martha Nobel? Nay. I am guessing you to be my brother-in-law. I have not seen you since you married Emma, Mr. Noble. As to Martha, she has not been here in over a week. She is a good girl. You should be proud."

"Right now I'm upset. She has run away. She wants to be with that Daniel boy."

"Mr. Noble," Mark started. "That Daniel boy is my nephew and is a member of good standing in our community. He is the teacher for our children."

Dan glared the Amish man before him. "This Daniel wants to marry my daughter." He paused. "I want my daughter to finish school, and go to college." Dan drew in a deep breath, allowing it to exhale slowly. "I want my daughter to remain *Englische* - as you Amish call it." He shook his head negatively. "I don't want her to ruin her life and become Amish."

Mark watched the man before him. It was obvious Dan was upset and any attempt to reason with him would be futile.

"Mr. Noble. Trust me. If your daughter, Martha, shows at my home, I will personally make sure she returns immediately to you."

Dan grimaced and offered Mark a disgusted look. "Really? Are you going to hogtie and throw her into the back of a buggy then trot all the way to Shipshewana to return her?"

Mark snickered. "Nay, Mr. Noble. I will have my *Englische* friend, Ben Hopkins, drive her back to you. I will also come along to assure she is returned to you," He offered a hand to shake.

"My daughter is not here?" Dan asked while scrutinizing the buildings.

"Nay." Again, Mark offered his hand to shake.

"Fine. If you Amish want to hide her, I'll find her myself." He mumbled something incoherent. "I'll find her no matter where you hide her."

Dan turned and ambled back to his car. He turned it around and raced away.

I should have asked where the school was located, Dan thought. *One of these houses should know.*

Dan strode up the two steps of the small schoolhouse, turned the knob and stood in the doorway.

All the students turned to see who had entered.

"Daniel Yoder?" Dan stood defiantly in the open doorway casting a dark shadow. The bright sun outside hid most of his features giving him an even more ominous appearance.

Daniel stood from his desk. "I am Daniel Yoder."

"Step outside, young man. We need to talk." Dan turned and stomped down the steps and into the bright sunlit schoolyard.

"Keep working on your studies," Daniel said as he strode toward the door. "Miss Mueller will answer any questions you have until I return." He turned to Miss Mueller and shrugged before stepping around the desk and walking the center aisle of students.

With legs spread slightly apart, arms folded before him, Dan watched through partially closed eyes as Daniel come down the two steps.

"Where is my daughter?" Dan glared at young Daniel.

"What is your daughter's name?" Daniel asked while moving toward the stranger with his hand extended to shake.

"You know very well who my daughter is. Martha Noble. Now, where are you hiding her?"

Daniel's hand dropped, he stepped back, surprised.

"Mr. Noble. I do not know where Martha is. I have not seen her in over a week when we went to church and had lunch together." Daniel stepped closer, again offering his hand to shake. "It is a pleasure to meet you."

"Well, Mr. Yoder, for your information." Dan glared at Daniel, again ignoring Daniel's offered hand. "My daughter, my precious little Martha, has run away, again. She told me she was going to marry you." Dan shrugged. "Obviously, to do that, she would have to be with you."

"Honest, Mr. Noble. I do not know where Martha is."

Dan stepped back and leaned against his car to study Daniel.

66

"She has to be here... somewhere," Dan said.

"Are you sure she has run away?" Daniel asked.

Dan nodded his head. "Just like the last time when she went to New York with her sister and cousin." He glared at Daniel. "Her Amish cousin who talked her into that *Rumschpringe* shenanigan of running off." Once more, Dan was the aggressor. "Martha said she was marrying you and didn't care what I wanted."

"Mr. Noble," Daniel started. "When I first asked Martha to marry me, I asked if I should get someone to ask you for permission. She said you didn't care who she married."

"Of course I care," Dan snapped. "She is my baby. I care."

Daniel watched Dan's lower lip quiver.

"Her sister ran off, got married, and now lives in Canada with some... some... I don't know what he is." Dan stared at the ground in thought. "Okay, most definitely a draft dodger, otherwise..."

"We, Martha and I, are not running off, sir," Daniel offered. "We planned to get married next spring." Daniel shrugged. "Now? I am not sure."

"Of course you're not sure. You're too young to know what you want." Dan once more took command of the situation, appraising Daniel. "Both of you both are just kids." He shrugged. "This is probably nothing more than simple puppy-love."

Daniel straightened his hat. "Sir, I assure you this is not puppy-love. I love your daughter. When we were in New York City, I considered becoming *Englische* just to be with her." Daniel stared Dan in the eyes. "If I am willing to question my being Amish for her, it is true love." He paused. "She ran away from me and I had no idea where. I came home, was baptized and am now Amish." Daniel cocked his head so the sunlight shone on his face. "If she asked me to become Englische..." Daniel left the sentence unfinished. "She said she wouldn't allow me to do that."

Dan flared in anger. "I won't allow my baby to become Amish. She'll not ruin her life that way. I want her to finish high school. I want her to go to college and make something of

67

herself."

Daniel nodded. "Should you not ask Martha what she wants, not what you want?"

Dan's hand fisted. "I'll not have some kid tell me how to—"

"Mr. Noble," Daniel said, cutting him off. "I am not a child. I have a school to run with students who need me as their teacher. If you want to discuss this more, may I suggest you visit the home of my parents tonight and we will discuss this in greater detail. Good day, Mr. Noble."

Daniel turned and walked toward the schoolhouse. He moved with deliberate steps, waiting for Dan Noble to take action. He heard the car door slam shut and the car's motor race. Dirt and grass flew in the air near Daniel as Dan's car sped from the grounds.

# # #

Thursday, October 3, 1963, 8 a.m.

Daniel opened the door of the school with a glance back at the children playing in the yard. He nodded approval. *I will call them shortly. Let them have fun*, he thought. He stepped inside expecting to see Miss Mueller hustling about making sure all the workbooks were prepared.

Immediately he noticed the paint splattered across the front wall chalkboard. Desks were no longer in neat rows but tossed about the room in disarray. Books were scattered everywhere. There was no Miss Mueller.

He shook his head in disgust as he continued to view the mess.

More splattered paint covered the sidewalls, the excess having run down the walls and windows.

The only item to have been untouched: his desk.

Daniel turned back to the schoolyard. He saw Miss Mueller getting out of her buggy.

"Elizabeth," he called and motioned to the student with his index finger.

She came running. "Yes, Mr. Yoder?"

Daniel pulled the door closed as he stepped outside. "I want you to keep the children playing out here until I come back out." He took a deep breath. "It may be a long time. Do you understand?"

Her eyebrows furrowed in question. "Yes, Mr. Yoder." Elizabeth nodded her head.

"Thank you," Daniel smiled. "Now, get about." He watched her run back out into the yard to oversee the activity.

Daniel motion for Miss Mueller to join him. He heaved a sigh, opened the door, stepped aside allowing Miss Mueller to enter. He closed the door behind them.

"What is this?" Miss Mueller's hand came to her lips to cover her gaping mouth. Her eyes widened as she scanned the mess.

"Lord, give me the strength."

Daniel stepped carefully around the desks to his desk. "This is what I opened the door to see this morning." He approached his desk.

He noticed a large hunting knife plunged into the middle of his desktop. It held a note.

Daniel read the scribbled words.

You have been warned.
Close this school.

Daniel worked the knife from the desk releasing the sheet of paper. Miss Mueller was busy picking up workbooks. He folded the note and stuck it inside his hat. Daniel stood by his desk and scanned the room, evaluating the devastation.

The walls can be painted. The windows can be cleaned. He scrutinized the chalkboard. *Maybe the paint can come off. The desks can be easily rearranged.* He gazed at books strewn around the room. He sighed., shaking his head. *Fortunately, most of the class have written their names in the book, so it should not be too difficult to put them to the proper desk.*

A tear well in his eye. Daniel leaned against the teacher's desk, seeing Miss Mueller begin to straighten desks.

"I need for the bishop to see this, Miss Mueller. Don't clean up too much."

"No school today," he whispered and shoved off the desk, once more stepping carefully through the mess. "I am canceling school. We will send the children home. I will speak with the bishop..." He heaved a long sigh. "Then I will come back this afternoon and clean this mess as best I can." He headed for the door.

"I will also come back," Miss Mueller offered. "I will bring others with me to assist."

Daniel opened the door.

"Time for school," Elizabeth yelled, noticing Daniel at the doorway. "Time for school." She clapped her hands to get the other students' attention.

Daniel held up his hand to stop the students at the bottom of the steps leading up to the school.

"There will be no school today," Daniel said then paused to consider his next words. "It seems we had visitors last night and they vandalized the room." He gazed at the students. "Do you understand what I am saying?"

"What do you mean? What is van... van... That word you said?" James Troyer's face wrinkled in a questioning gaze.

"Vandalized? It means somebody came in and ruined things. Desks have been moved and the books have been thrown about the room." He paused and drew in a long, deep breath. "Also, paint has been tossed on the walls and chalkboard."

"Can we see?" James Troyer asked.

"One at a time. Just come up to the door and look in."

Miss Mueller stepped aside.

Daniel opened the door as the children made a neat line. James Troyer was first in line.

Each child quietly stepped to the door and peeked into the schoolhouse. When the last person looked in, Daniel appraised the situation. Some students needed to get home.

"Okay, now, who has a buggy here? Each family with a buggy, go to it."

Daniel watched as most of the children rushed to a family buggy. Only two students remained, they were the Graber siblings in the second and fourth grades.

Miss Mueller leaned in. "I can take the Graber children

home with me. I go past their house on my way."

Daniel nodded and the Graber children ran over to Miss Mueller's buggy.

"Will there be school tomorrow?" Elizabeth asked.

"Nay," Daniel replied. "We will reopen school Monday."

He closed the door of the school and went to the buggy where his siblings waited to go home. Daniel got in and watched the other buggies leave the yard. He waited and was the last to depart.

Daniel pulled into the driveway of the house and let his younger brothers and sisters out.

"Mary, tell Momma about what has happened. I will tell Papa and then I am going to see the bishop."

Daniel snapped the reins and Beauty moved forward.

# # #

"That is what I opened the door and saw this morning." He reached into his hat to retrieve the note. "Plus, there was this." Daniel handed the note to the bishop.

Bishop Schmucker leaned back into the chair, stroking his beard while reading the note. He handed it to Noah Yoder, shaking his head disgustedly.

"Who do you think would do such a thing?" the bishop asked.

Noah glanced at the note. "It is obvious," Noah said. "The *Englische*. When I was to DeMotte and Centertown, I am certain the *Englische* are unhappy with our school."

"They would destroy our school?" the bishop asked.

"They are difficult to understand." Noah shook his head. "Many do not want us around, and yet they destroy our school, wanting our children to attend their school."

"Today is Thursday," Daniel said. "I will go and clean the chalkboard and paint the walls. I will attempt to get the paint removed from the glass." He paused. "Miss Mueller said she would return to help and hopes to bring others to assist."

"Nay. Nay." Bishop Schmucker raised a hand for silence. "We will assemble the community and all will help." He turned to Daniel. "You will gather the books and oversee their repair if needed." He hesitated. "Today you will go and get that which we need to fix the school. Tape for repairing the books. Paint for the walls." Bishop Schmucker nodded in approval at his plan. "Get whatever you feel is needed to clean the schoolroom." He smiled. "We are Amish, we can fix the desks." He leaned conspiratorially toward Noah. "I am sure you can convince your good wife to make my favorite pie for tomorrow?"

"Aye, that I can." Noah laughed. "Also, I will see what needs to be fixed and getting the wood necessary." Noah stood. "I am sure we can get a good price from Bob Sullivan at the mill." He winked at Daniel.

CHAPTER EIGHT: Martha Unhidden

Saturday, October 5, 1963, about noon.

Martha listened to the sounds beyond her hiding place. Uncle Paul left the barn for the house when Mary called him to a meal. She watched through the open barn door to see her cousins hustle into the house. Grabbing the jar of peanut butter, Martha scraped the bottom and edges to gather the last of her meager food. She spread the remaining peanut butter on the bread. The crust already had some mold growing on it; she'd thrown that away. The pigs enjoyed it. The jelly was gone.

Martha's stomach growled. She was hungry and a lone slice of bread with peanut butter was not going to suffice.

"I am sure Uncle Paul will understand," she mumbled, gazing at the meager slice of bread. "I will give it to the pigs." She sighed. "I hope Aunt Mary has made extra. I am starving."

Martha crawled down the ladder from the loft and tossed the bread into the pigs' pen. The old sow wallowed toward the offering. Her offspring raced to join her. The bread disappeared in seconds before any of the piglets could eat.

Dusting and straightening her skirt, Martha hustled across the open area between the barn and house. She tapped lightly on the screen door before going in.

"*hallo*," Martha said, speaking Amish to the couple sitting at the table with their four children. "May I enter?"

"Martha!" Paul stood from the table. "Come. My goodness, sit, my child. We have just finished most of our meal and are about to eat dessert." He helped her to the table. "Where have you been? How did you get here?" He stretched to gaze out the window. "I did not hear a car."

Martha bowed her head in shame. "I have been hiding in the barn. I listened to my father and you argue." A tear coursed

73

down her cheek. "He wishes me not to be Amish." Martha lifted a finger to her nose and sniffed. "I love Daniel. I want to marry him. I want to be Amish."

Mary placed a plate of hot food before Martha. "Eat, Martha. You must gain your strength. You appear so pale." Mary caressed Martha's cheek with the palm of her one hand while testing for a fever with her other hand.

"*danke*, Aunt Mary." Martha bowed her head and said a quick prayer of thanks to the Lord.

"Does your father know you are here?" Paul asked.

Martha shoved a full fork of potatoes into her mouth. The burst of flavor overwhelmed her after the days of peanut butter and jelly. Martha shook her head negatively.

"We must let him know."

The three sons and one daughter sat quietly, watching, listening.

"No!" Martha said between bites. "I need to think. He has forbidden me to see Daniel." She shrugged. "If I return to him now, I do not think he will allow me to visit the Amish ever again." Martha paused and munched on the warm buttered carrots. "He... he..." She shrugged again. "I will talk with him tomorrow."

"How did you get here?" Mary asked.

"I rode my bicycle." Martha snickered. "It is still hidden in the hayloft where I was hiding these last few days. Peanut butter and jelly sandwiches get boring after two days." She gave her uncle a sheepish look. "I beg your forgiveness, Uncle Paul. I took milk from the cows to drink." She quickly added. "Only a cup a day and from a different cow each time. Most of the time I drank water."

"You must be starving." Mary cut a large slice of cherry pie and placed it on her plate. "Eat."

"*danke*," Martha mumbled.

Paul leaned back in his chair. "This will need some discussion. Your father is furious. He accused me–"

"I know, Uncle Paul," Martha said, cutting him off between bites. "May we discuss this after the meal?"

"Eat, Martha," Paul said with a smile. "We will discuss this later." He picked up his fork and held it upright on the table. "Let us eat in silence and allow the Lord to clear our thoughts."

Martha nodded and shoved another mouthful of food into her mouth while eyeing the cherry pie.

"You boys finish feeding the stock." He offered a stern look at his older sons before turning to Martha. "Come," Paul said and motioned for her to follow.

"I should help Aunt Mary and Elizabeth with the cleanup," Martha offered.

"Both of you." He nodded at his wife. "We will discuss the matter and then you may clean the meal away." Paul gazed at his daughter. "Elizabeth knows how to clear the table." He walked into the main room and sat in his chair.

Paul sat silently, watching, analyzing his niece. She sat on the bench, dressed in Amish attire. He knew the ends of the hair hidden beneath the bonnet had tints of faded blue. Paul nodded. *She is Englische. She is Amish*, he thought, grimaced and shrugged. *She is a young girl caught between two worlds.*

"I am very sorry, Uncle Paul," Martha said. "I did not think my father would accuse you of lying and be so mean." A tear welled in her eye.

"Your father's anger directed to me was only his love for his youngest daughter who he fears he will lose." Paul paused. "He has lost one daughter – your sister in Canada."

Martha heaved a sigh and nodded. *Yes, Bethany is in Canada with... with...* Martha frowned in thought. *Who was Bethany with? What is his name?*

"I think I should take you back to your house. I am sure my sister, your mother, is frantic." Paul smiled. "That is, if your father's actions are any indication."

"My father's actions are such because he does not want me to be Amish." Martha straightened her skirt and gazed at her uncle. "He feels I am throwing my life away."

Paul nodded his head in thought.

"My father wants me to graduate from high school, go to college, get a degree, and, as he calls it, make something of myself." Martha paused. "In other words, marry an *Englische* boy."

"What do you want, Martha?" Paul asked.

"I want to marry Daniel. I love him." Martha smiled. "When we were in New York City, I thought maybe we could both be *Englische*, get married, and be happy there." Martha lowered her head. "But, Daniel is Amish. He was a lost little boy in the big city." She looked up at her uncle. "Do not get me wrong. Daniel is a strong and intelligent man who wants to learn, but he wants to learn only so he can deal with the *Englische*." Martha swelled with pride. "Daniel is Amish. He could barely wait to get back home. He would have left New York sooner if there hadn't been that murder."

Paul once again nodded his head, this time in agreement.

"Daniel is a good Amish man and will make some woman a good husband." He gazed at his niece. "Are you that woman?" He shrugged. "Only time will tell."

Martha glared at her uncle. "What do you mean? Do you think I am not good enough for him?"

"Martha, my sister's daughter, my darling niece. You are a wonderful young lady who is in love. I feel you and Daniel would make a good couple." Paul took a deep breath. "But, as I would expect from my children, they should heed the advice of their elders." He curled a shoulder. "Your father wishes you to continue your education. Should you not obey your elder? What does the Bible say?"

"Ephesians 6:1. Children, obey thy parents in the Lord: for this is right." Martha recited.

"And?" Paul added.

"Commandment five. Honor thy father and thy mother, that thy days may be long upon the land which the Lord, your God, is giving you." Martha quoted.

"Are you ready to go home, Martha?"

Mary reached over and hugged Martha. "Remember, Martha, 1 Corinthians 13:7, says Love bears all things, believes all things, hopes all things, endures all things. Love never ends." Mary caressed Martha's hands in a squeeze. "If you love Daniel and he loves you, the Lord will see to it your paths meet."

Martha inhaled deeply. "I will help Aunt Mary and Elizabeth with the kitchen and then you may take me home." She hung her head. "I have caused my parents enough heartache." She snickered. "Of course, I could ride my bicycle back home."

Paul cocked an eye in her direction. "I think not. I wish to see you home, safely."

#

Martha retrieved her small bag of clothes from the barn and walked her bicycle up to the side of the house. She ambled into the house.

"Uncle Paul," she called. "I have my bag of clothes and my bicycle."

Paul stood in the opening to the living room.

"I will have Levi harness the buggy and strap your bicycle to the back of it." Paul strode through the kitchen to the back door. He turned to Martha. "This is for the best."

Martha nodded as her uncle stepped out and disappeared.

"Aunt Mary." Martha turned to the older woman. "How can I get my father to understand I love Daniel, and I want to marry him? I want to be Amish."

"The Lord will guide you," Aunt Mary replied and turned to Elizabeth. "You may go outside." Elizabeth nodded. Mary turned and sat on the bench by the table and patted the area next to her. "Sit." She smiled at Martha. "It is every girl's wish to marry the man of her dreams." She gazed off into the distance. "I was sure I would marry Leroy Tr... his last name is unimportant" Again she gazed distantly into the air. "But, the Lord sent me your uncle." She shrugged. "I was not about to listen to my father who insisted I marry your uncle. In my heart I was sure my destiny would be with Leroy." Mary turned her gaze to the floor, then looked up to Martha and smiled. "But..." She took a deep breath. "The Lord showed me how much better Paul Hershberger was as a man than Leroy. I married Paul. He was been a wonderful husband and provides well for the family." Mary grimaced and shrugged. "Leroy? He married another woman and rumor has it he treated her mean. They left our Ordnung and moved to someplace in Iowa. He and she have never been heard from since."

Martha's eyes widened. "Are you saying I may not marry Daniel? The Lord has other plans?"

Mary's face glowed with love. "No, dear. I am saying the Lord will find you the proper mate." Her eyes twinkled. "I think Daniel is the right man, but, well, that may be just me."

The kitchen door opened, Paul walked in and joined them at the table.

"The buggy will be ready shortly. Is there anything you will need to go home?"

"No, Uncle Paul. I have what I need in the bag outside the door."

A car screeched it brakes in the driveway.

Martha ran to the window to see her father's car in a billowing cloud of dust.

"It's my father," she said. "And, he looks mad."

Paul stood and walked to the kitchen door.

"Paul Hershberger," Dan Noble yelled. He stood leaning against his car, legs and arms crossed in defiance. "You lied to me."

Paul pushed the screen door aside. "I have not lied to you, Dan." The Amish man's voice remained calm. "What has happened to make you think I am lying?"

"I just returned from Centertown. I spoke with Mark and this Daniel Yoder. I could tell they were telling me the truth. They've not seen Martha."

"No, father," Martha said from the other side of the door. She moved around her uncle to confront her father. "They've not seen me. I told you I had not been to see Daniel. In fact, until an hour ago, Uncle Paul had not seen me, either." She glared at her father. "I've been hiding." She glanced at the barn. "There. In the barn. Cousin Levi was about to stab me with the pitchfork when Uncle Paul told him to use the hay from the other side."

Martha stood defiantly on the back stoop of the house with her uncle.

"Uncle Paul was about to bring me home." She pointed at the buggy Levi had hooked up. "Ten more minutes and we wouldn't have been here, but in the buggy headed into town and home."

"I don't believe one word of that," Dan shouted. "Right now, you're going to get in the car. I'm taking you home." He gazed at Martha. "And I'm burning all your Amish clothing. I'm tired of you playing Amish. It is time for you to grow up and face facts."

"What facts is that, Daddy?" Martha asked. "Your facts?"

"Don't you get smart with me, young lady." He snapped an arm downward with his index finger pointing to a place beside him. "You get down here." Dan glared at his daughter. "You're *Englische.*"

Martha spread her skirt. "To me, Daddy, it appears I am Amish. That is what I want to be. Amish."

Dan stepped forward.

"Dan!" Paul shouted. "Come with me. We shall walk and talk." Paul stepped off the stoop toward Dan.

"I don't need you talking to me about any of your silly Amish voodoo."

Paul grinned at the connotation. "I will not discuss any Amish... as you call it... voodoo. I wish only to discuss your daughter." Paul placed a hand on Dan's shoulder. "Man to man. Come."

He pulled Dan from the car and headed him toward the side of the barn which led by the wooded fence row and path to the next field.

Martha watched as the two men walked side by side, talking, not yelling; no shouting, but talking like old friends. She wanted to know what they were saying.

"Come, Martha," Mary whispered from the kitchen doorway. "Let us sit, talk, or perhaps read the Bible until their return." She smiled. Martha was reminded of Mona Lisa. "Your Uncle Paul knows what to do and say." She nodded. "Trust me. Trust the Lord."

Martha followed her aunt into the main room and sat beside her. Aunt Mary opened the Bible and shared reading the story of Ruth and Naomi.

"Aunt Mary?" Martha grabbed her aunt's hand and held it. "What do you think my father would do if I was baptized into the community?"

Aunt Mary search Martha's eyes. "I believe that to be something you should discuss with your father. Today? Now? I would not suggest it, he seems quire upset by the prospect of you becoming Amish."

Martha scrunched up her lower lip. "But, I want to become Amish." She sighed loudly. "Does not my desire mean something? Must I always obey what my father wants?"

Mary gently turned the pages of the Bible from where they had read. She moved to Exodus 20 and pointed at verse 12. You answer is here."

Martha read.

Honor thy father and thy mother.

"So, I need to listen to my father." She scrunched up her nose. "How long do I need to listen to him. At what age do I get to do what I want?"

Mary smiled. "Your father is your father until you die."

"You mean when he dies," Martha countered.

"Nay, Martha. Even when your father goes to his eternal reward, your memory of him will still be held in your heart, and you will tend to his ways." She patted Martha's hand. "Your father is your father until your dying day. Obey him."

"But I want to be Amish."

"In time, Martha. In time."

Martha heard the back door open and Uncle Paul strolled into the room.

"Your father is waiting for you by the car."

Martha frowned at her uncle.

"All is well, Martha. Go with him."

Martha kissed Aunt Mary and gave Uncle Paul a hug.

"Thank you," she whispered into his ear then hustled from the house.

CHAPTER NINE: Uncle Mark's House

Saturday, October 5, 1963, 3 p.m.

Martha sat in the front seat. She remained silent, waiting for her father to begin the conversation - any conversation.

The silence confused Dan. He stretched out to turn on the radio – anything to break the ugly sounds of silence. His fingers curled around the knob. He pulled back.

"Are you going to say anything?" he asked. It wasn't directed at anyone in particular. He only wanted to have the silence end.

"What do you want me to say, Daddy." Martha continued to stare forward. "I love Daniel. I want to be Amish." She paused. "You want me to finish high school. You want me to go to college and receive a degree in some great academic endeavor." She heaved a sigh.

"I only want what is best for my baby girl," Dan replied. "Is that too much to ask?"

Martha pursed her lips and thought on his last sentence.

Dan glanced at her, evaluating.

"Your uncle feels I am pushing you to a choice and you will rebel." He paused. "You and your sister ran off with your cousin to experiment with *Rumschpringe*. He knows you ran away a second time and hid in his barn. He thinks you will run away, again." Dan paused then turned to stare at her in the late evening light. "Is that true?"

Martha squirmed in her seat. She knew her father was right. She would run, again, and again, until she got to marry Daniel.

"If I complete high school and college, will you let me marry Daniel and be Amish?"

Dan blinked, squeezing a tear from the eye. He didn't like

what he was hearing. He considered his options.

"If you became Amish, would you do that?"

"Do what, Daddy?"

"Complete your education?"

Martha smiled and gazed at her father. "What will I do with a college degree in the Amish world?"

Dan sighed and nodded. *She is right,* he thought. *She has more education than most of the Amish.* He shook his head in disgust. *I think Daniel has more education than any of his siblings or cousins.* Dan cocked his head as he thought. *Together, their children will be more educated than most.* He smiled. *Maybe a grandchild will wish to become Englische and I can offer them a college education.*

"If I relent and allow you to marry..." He paused for emphasis. "If one of your children wish to be *Englische*, will you allow them to live with us?"

Martha didn't hesitate. "I will need to speak with Daniel, but I see no problem with that. If one of my children wish to be Englische, I think Daniel would be okay with the choice. He wanted to learn more."

Silence once more enveloped the car. Martha waited.

Dan felt the lump in his throat grow bigger. He knew what to say, but could he say it. Martha was his baby. All his dreams were about to end. Dan swallowed.

"Your mother was Amish. She agrees you should follow your heart. Uncle Paul also agrees I should let you follow your heart. If you become Amish and marry Daniel, and decide later you no longer wish to be Amish..." Dan let the sentence dangle. "There will be repercussions." The car slowed and Dan looked at his daughter in the late twilight. "Can you handle that? I am sure Daniel will not become *Englische*. Could you leave him?"

"I love Daniel," Martha said. "We've been through too much to throw it away in a simple argument." A smile curled the edges of her lips. "Are you saying..." She gazed at her father.

Dan nodded. "Yes, Martha. I give my blessing to you becoming Amish and, if you so desire, you can marry Daniel." He paused. "With one exception."

Martha cocked her head, giving him a questioning look.

Dan smiled. "I am sure it is one you will agree to with no hesitation. I want to walk my little girl down the aisle. I didn't get to walk Bethany down the aisle." He shrugged. "If Alexander gets married, I figure we'll be lucky to be invited."

Martha leaned over carefully and hugged her father and gave him a peck of a kiss on the cheek. "I'd be proud to have you at my side when I walk the aisle to marry Daniel. I agree to your terms," she whispered.

"We're home," Dan said and heaved a long sigh. "Go tell your mother. If you wish to go back to Uncle Paul's place tonight, I will drive you."

"I will stay with you and mother until Monday morning," Martha said. "I will then return to Uncle Paul's house and notify Daniel I am becoming Amish."

Dan nodded. He knew when he needed to step back. Paul was correct. Dan put the car in park without driving it into the garage. He sat quietly, staring at the big white garage door.

Maybe, he thought. *Just maybe if I'd heeded Paul's advice earlier, I'd still have both my daughters with me.* Dan sighed and opened the car door.

# # #

Monday, October 7, 1963, 9 a.m.

Martha drove her car into Uncle Paul's driveway.

What am I thinking? she thought. *I won't be driving this anymore. I'm becoming Amish.*

Martha grabbed the small valise of her Amish belongings. Aunt Mary came through the kitchen door and hustled down the steps to embrace her.

"Welcome, Martha," Aunt Mary said. "I told you the Lord would see you through the trial."

Martha leaned against the car and patted it. "I won't be needing this after today," she said. "First I will take my things into the house then I will drive to see Daniel and tell him the news." Martha started for the steps and stopped. "What if he doesn't want me?" An expression of concern on her face.

"If Daniel truly loves you, he has not stopped loving you

because of all these issues." Mary embraced Martha. "Come, Martha, your room awaits and then it is off to see Daniel."

Together the two of them walked into the house.

# # #

Monday, October 7, 1963, 11:30 a.m.

Martha drove into the small schoolyard and parked her car. She jumped out and rushed to the steps leading to the one-room class where Daniel taught. She opened the door and watched as the students turned in unison to see who was at the door.

"Daniel?" she called. "May I speak with you outside for a moment?"

Daniel nodded to Miss Mueller who strode to the front of the classroom to oversee during his absence.

"I did not know teachers had so many interruptions." Miss Mueller pursed her lips in disdain then motioned for Daniel to leave.

Daniel smiled as he strode toward Martha.

"Does your father know you are here?" Daniel whispered as he approached her.

Martha nodded. "Yes, he does." Her smile was broad. "He will allow me to become Amish and..." She hesitated.

"We may marry?" Daniel finished the sentence.

Again, Martha nodded.

"But, first I must become Amish. I will be staying at Uncle Paul's house and I will speak with the bishop."

"You could stay with my Uncle Mark and talk with Bishop Schmucker." Daniel grabbed Martha's hands in his. "I mean, that is an option."

"True," Martha said. "But, I will honor my uncle and stay at   his house. He is the person who convinced my father to accept the fact I want to be Amish and marry you. I will talk with Bishop Beiler and explain the circumstances."

Daniel nodded. "That is a wise choice, Martha." The school door closed with a click. The students couldn't see them. Daniel leaned in and kissed her. "It is too late to have a fall wedding. Do you wish to wait until spring? I mean, there is not enough time to prepare..."

Martha put a finger to his lips. "You forget, my father is *Englische*. If we wish to get married yet this fall or winter, he will pay the expenses. He can buy the produce necessary; we need not harvest from the garden." She giggled.

Daniel nodded agreement. "As you wish. We will be eating soon. Will you join me?"

She hugged him. "Of course."

#

"Why are you here?" Dan's voice was brusque. "Done with the Amish already?"

Martha smiled at her father. "No, Daddy. I just came home so mother and I could decide on a date to get things going. Daniel wants to get married."

"A date?" Dan gazed up from the newspaper and frowned. "What date?"

"My wedding date, Daddy." Martha giggled.

Dan smashed the paper into his lap. "You have over a year to start planning that. You still have to graduate, young lady."

Martha stepped back, unsure of what to do.

"The other night when you brought me home from Uncle Paul's, you said I could become Amish and could marry Daniel."

Dan flipped the BarcaLounger upright. "Yes, I said that. I'm not denying the fact. But, I thought it was understood, you'd still finish high school, and the wedding would be after you graduated."

Martha leaned against the arch of the living room wall for support. Her legs weakened.

"But, if I'm Amish, I don't need a high school diploma." Martha paused and stared at her father. "You expect me to live with Uncle Paul and still go to high school? In Amish clothing?"

Dan shrugged, spreading his arms open. "You're the one who wants to be Amish."

Martha glared at her father.

"Fine. You're playing games. I can play games, too." She stomped to the front door. "I'll be back later with my things."

"Where are you going, Martha?"

"Back to Uncle Paul's place to get my things. I'll go to school, but I'll go to school dressed as an Amish girl. I will live an Amish life right here in this house..." She opened the door. "Yes, where all your neighbors can see me."

Martha slammed the front door behind her and ran for the car.

"Martha Noble, you get back here!" Dan screamed as she backed out of the driveway and sped away.

And the first thing, little Miss I-want-to-be-Amish, will be for you to lose your car, Dan thought as he walked back into the house. Amish don't own cars. As you said, Martha, two can play this game.

#

Tuesday, October 15, 1963, not quite 8 a.m.

Daniel eased Beauty to the hitching post at the school. He watched as his siblings jumped from the buggy and raced to play before school. Daniel stood for a moment and inhaled the cool, fall morning air.

Soon I will need to arrive earlier to start a fire to warm the classroom, he thought.

Another buggy arrived. It was Miss Mueller.

"*gute mariye*," Daniel said.

Miss Mueller nodded, offered her hand, and Daniel assisted her from the buggy.

"The students will be arriving shortly," Daniel said as they walked to the schoolhouse doors. "I think they can play for a little while as I get things prepared inside." He paused. "I do not believe I need to start a fire, yet." He turned to Miss Mueller. "Do you agree?"

She nodded approval. "I shall wait here and watch over the children."

Daniel walked up the steps to the doors and opened them.

He gasped.

Once more the classroom was a disheveled scene of destruction. This time – worse.

"Miss Mueller," Daniel whispered. "Come here."

He turned to watch her hustle up the two steps to the entrance. Daniel held the door open for her to see in.

"Again? Who would do this?" she asked while leaning in to view the destruction.

"It seems they do not wish us to teach our children." He smiled. "We will have class." Daniel held a hand to his brow and gazed at the sky. "What do you think, Miss Mueller? Shall we have class outside today?"

Miss Mueller continued to stare through the open door at the destroyed classroom.

"Miss Mueller?" Daniel called in an attempt to get her attention.

"Yes. Yes. Outside will be fine. It is a beautiful day." She gazed at the playing children. "They can sit on the grass and share reading books." She smiled. "We can make a fun day of the situation."

Daniel nodded agreement. "We can even make up questions for math and make a game of where things are located and the students point like a compass."

"But what of the mess?" Miss Mueller gazed back at the open door of the school.

"Here comes the Troyers. I will have Elizabeth seek out Bishop Schmucker." Daniel hailed the young girl as she tied up the horse.

Elizabeth ran at the beckon. "You need me, Mr. Yoder?"

"Go and find Bishop Schmucker. Tell him we need him at the school immediately, and it is very important. If you happen to go past my house, ask my father to come, also."

"I would ask you to get my brother," Miss Mueller said. "But, he is working at the wood mill today so I will not ask to bother him."

Elizabeth frowned at the request and backed away toward her buggy and horse.

"I will be quick about it, Mr. Yoder."

"Please watch the children, Miss Mueller," Daniel said. "I

am going in to assess the damage."

Daniel turned and disappeared behind the school doors.

He walked carefully between the torn books, loose papers, broken desks, and chairs. Daniel shook his head as he proceeded to the front. Once more tossed paint covered the walls and chalkboards. But, this time, he noticed the blackboards had been hit. They were cracked; some with pieces missing. They would need to be replaced. Three of the windows were broken. Daniel counted the desks; ten were smashed beyond easy repair. Books were shredded, many of their pages laying in pools of splattered paint on the floor.

Daniel reached his desk. A can of paint was turned upside down in the middle of his desk. Red paint spread out over the desktop and down the edges. Once more, a note was attached to his desk with a knife. It had red paint oozing around the note. The note was simple.

You were warned. You didn't listen. This is your final warning.

Daniel gazed at the pot-belly stove he had considered lighting. It had been turned over, the stove pipe reaching to the ceiling had been partially knocked down, a section still dangled from the roof.

He shook his head, disgusted.

Why do they destroy my school? What have I... what have the Amish done to them?

"Mr. Yoder," Miss Mueller called from the door. "Are you ready to start class today?"

Daniel nodded. "Assemble the students."

The door closed.

Daniel made his way through the mayhem of the room, trying not to get too much paint on his shoes. He grabbed a few tablets from a storage shelf which didn't seem to have been noticed during the rampage of the classroom.

The students were assembled at the bottom of the steps, their smiling faces shining in the early morning.

Daniel heaved a sigh.

"The school has been vandalized... again," he said. "This

time I am not closing the school, but we will have our classes outside. We will do reading, math, and geography." Daniel smiled. "But, we will have more fun doing it."

Daniel walked down the steps and led the students to the grassy area where the early morning dew had been burned off.

"To start, each of us, starting with the third graders, will read from the Bible to the whole class." Daniel nodded at Elias Mueller. "You will begin reading. I will stop you and point at the next reader until everyone has had a chance to read. If you need help, like always, Miss Mueller or I will assist." Daniel paused. "The first and second graders will draw pictures of what is being read." He turned to Elias. "Start reading, Elias."

Elias opened the Bible and began to read from Genesis.

Daniel listened, but kept one eye on the road, watching for Elizabeth or Bishop Schmucker to appear.

Papa said he had business to attend to, Daniel thought. *Perhaps he is with Bishop Schmucker. Only time will tell.*

He turned to gaze at Miss Mueller. She was staring at the doors of the school. Her face was troubled.

CHAPTER TEN: The Amish School

Tuesday, October 22, 1963, 7 p.m.

Daniel approached John Teegarden.

"You must be Daniel Yoder," John said, stretching out a hand to shake. "John Teegarden. I'm glad you could make it to our meeting." He rolled a shoulder. "I'll warn you ahead of time. The topics may get a bit heated. Some of the board members are quite fervent in their beliefs."

"Yes, I understand, Mr. Teegarden," Daniel replied.

"Let's go inside the room," John said and offered Daniel to proceed through the door first. "I'll have you sit over here." He indicated a chair.

Daniel sat, noticing a few people gathered, sitting around the room. His gaze went to the table at the front of the room where eight men sat. One chair, in the middle, was empty, but John Teegarden was quickly approaching it. John stood at the chair.

John picked up and snapped the gavel on the table three times to gain attention.

"This meeting of the Consolidated Northwest Schools is called to order," he said, then took his seat. "This evening we are here to discuss the Amish school. We have the teacher for the school with us tonight." John nodded toward Daniel. "That is Daniel Yoder. Now, so everyone knows everyone's name, starting with far-right, the board members are Gerald Miller, Jack Holland, Bob Hopkins, Roy Bauers, I'm John Teegarden, and continuing to my left are Peter Udall, Tom Hollis, Tony Thompson, and at the far left end, Steve Singer."

Tom Hollis glared at Daniel, then stood.

"Tell us, Mr. Yoder. Why did the Amish build a school?" Tom Hollis wasted no time in the attack.

90

Daniel stood.

"We built the school so our children wouldn't be bussed so far away from our homes."

"Aren't you a little young to be a teacher?" Tom Hollis stood, placing his fisted hands on the table and leaned forward toward Daniel.

"I am seventeen, sir. Also, I attended school through the tenth grade." Daniel paused. "Since most Amish only go to school through eighth grade, I am more educated than most."

"But, you're just a mere child," Roy Bauers said. "My son is a sophomore this year." He shook his head, his rotund body quivering in the action. "I would never trust him to attempt to teach a class, let alone a whole school."

"Gentlemen, I do not believe Mr. Yoder's age is the issue." John rapped the gavel and glared at Tom. "If you will please sit, Tom." John turned his attention to Daniel. "Are you saying that if the school in Centertown had been made an elementary school, the Amish would have let their children attend here?"

"Perhaps," Daniel replied. "I also know there was a discussion of possible changes in the near future where morning prayer could be removed from the school."

"The public schools don't need to teach or promote religion." Tom Hollis took his seat. "We are required to teach the basic - reading, writing, and arithmetic."

"Mr. Hollis," Daniel started. "We, at the Amish school, teach the basics, plus we teach the children to speak English since most basically only speak Amish. We also promote our faith, we teach the Bible, we offer prayer, we–."

"Waste a lot of time in school with things that don't help the child learn to take their place in society." Tom stood. "If a child needs to learn religion, that is the job of their church leaders, not the teachers at school."

"Gentlemen." Daniel addressed the school board. "The Amish teach and live the Bible every day of their lives. We are a simple people who–"

"Yes," Tom Hollis yelled, again cutting Daniel's speech. "You are a simple people. Why is that? Because you have no education beyond the eighth grade."

"Tom Hollis," John said. "You keep a civil tongue about you. The next time you speak out of turn without the acknowledgment of the board president... that's me, you will be removed from the room. Now, sit. Am I understood?"

A small murmur and weak applause filled the air of those sitting in the audience.

Tom Hollis sat, fuming, glaring at Daniel. The fingers of his one hand strummed the table, the other hand flipped open a Zippo lighter which his thumb quickly snapped closed. Tom repeated the action.

"I am here for one reason," Daniel ignored the repeated snapping open and closing of the lighter in Tom Hollis' hand. "The school has been vandalized twice. The first time it was petty stuff. The last time there was major damage including the desks, windows, chalkboards, and school material." Daniel strode to the middle of the open area. "We Amish only wish to teach our children in our manner. We did not build the school to offend the *Englische*." Daniel looked directly at John Teegarden. "What do the Amish need to do to make amends? What do we need to do so my... our school is no longer the target of vandals?"

Gerald Miller raised his hand and coughed to get attention.

"Yes, Gerald?" John nodded at the man on the far end.

"Mr. Yoder, it seems to me that you are accusing us... uh, the *Englische*, of vandalizing your school. What makes you think it is us?"

Daniel frowned at the question. "It is a fair question, but..." Daniel paused to consider his next words to be heard and understood. "Why would an Amish person want to destroy their property?"

Gerald scowled at the reply. "You said 'their' property. Why would you say that?"

"The school is the property of the Amish community. It belongs to all of the Amish. It is not MY school. It is not my Amish neighbor's school. It is OUR school. Does that make sense?"

Gerald nodded. "Do you have any idea who of us would do it?"

Daniel shook his head. "I do not."

Bob Hopkins raised his hand. "Offhand, do you know how much money the state gives you in assistance for the school?"

"They give us nothing, sir," Daniel replied. "It is our school. We paid for it. We support it."

"Then, who covers the expenses of repairing what the vandals destroyed?" Tony Thompson asked.

"We do. The Amish community."

"You mean the Amish built the school with their own money?" Tony asked.

"Yes, sir. Some of the *Englische* came to help and some, like Bob Sullivan, donated items."

John rapped the gavel. "We again are off-topic. Does anyone have a topic-related question?"

Tom Hollis raised his head. John nodded.

"So it is my understanding the Amish students will not be coming back to our schools. All the government assistance we received for them is gone. Is that correct?"

Daniel frowned. "I do not know the exact answer, but I know at the current time, the Amish children will not be coming back to the *Englische* school."

Tom Hollis slammed back into his chair and threw his hands into the air. "I rest my case. We've lost funds, gentlemen. As I said before, the Amish school must be closed and they return to our school so we can be financially stable." He scowled at the assembled group in the audience. "Unless, of course, you want to increase taxation to cover this loss."

John Teegarden rapped the gavel loudly on the table repeatedly.

"We will survive without the Amish students." John glared at Tom. "The Amish school is not our problem." John turned to Daniel. "Thank you for coming tonight. I'm not sure all has been settled, but answers have been forthcoming. I'm not sure we would have made another of the schools the high school, but now we know why the Amish built their school. Also, we know what must be done for the future of our school district."

Tom Hollis narrowed his eyelids to slits. "Yes, we know

what must be done," he mumbled.

Wednesday, October 30, 1963, early morning

"We must hurry. I must start the stove at the school so it will be warm when the students arrive." Daniel hustled his siblings about the kitchen.

Jacob scowled at his older brother. "Could you not go now and Mary bring us in the buggy later?"

The twins, Joshua and Jonah, gazed expectedly at Daniel, hoping they could go later.

"If Daniel goes early, he will take one horse and buggy. Then you will take another horse and buggy." Rebecca Yoder offered a stern look at her offspring. "How will I go into town today?" She smiled. "Do you want your mother to walk all the way into Centertown for groceries?" Rebecca paused. "And then carry the bags home?"

"Oh, no, momma," Jonah said. "I will stay home and go with you and carry the bags."

Rebecca laughed. "Thank you, but you all will go together to the school. Now be about yourselves and get a hustle on. Daniel must light the fire."

She placed the basket with the lunches for all the children on a stool near the door.

"Go bridle Beauty, Daniel." She pushed him toward the door. "I will make sure the children are ready to go when you return to leave."

Daniel stepped out of the house into the crisp late autumn air. Frost covered spots here and there in the yard. He ambled to the barn, watching his father and Luke leave the barn, leading the plow horses on their way to the fields. Daniel hummed, then burst into song, singing "Aborigine Stomp."

Beauty stood patiently as the bridle, harness, and buggy were attached.

Daniel continued to sing songs he'd learned in New York City, but stopped when he got into the buggy and snapped the reins for Beauty to move. He rode to the back door of the house.

The twins were the first ones out the door, followed by Anna and Jacob. Mary carried the basket of food as she carefully came down the steps. Daniel jumped down to grab the basket from her. He kissed his mother goodbye and hustled to the buggy.

"I guess Jonah and me can play..." Joshua started.

"It is Jonah and I," Daniel corrected.

"We are not in school, Daniel," Joshua countered. "We will play until James comes."

Daniel smiled. "You could study."

The only sound heard was that of Beauty's hooves on the dirt road and the creaks of the wheels.

#

"Jacob," Daniel said. "Could you help me bring in some wood for the burner?"

Jacob rushed to the long woodpile of split wood and grabbed several logs. He carried them into the school and placed them neatly near the wall.

"Thank you, Jacob," Daniel said. "Are you going back outside?"

Jacob nodded and quickly disappeared.

Daniel placed the paper and tinder into the big pot-bellied stove. He lit a match. The paper took immediately. Daniel placed a couple of larger pieces of wood on the small fire and closed the door. He adjusted the damper and stood by the stove, warming his hands before going to his desk and sitting. He sat and moved the stack of workbooks before him. He turned the pages and reviewed each student's work progress.

"I am glad to see you have a fire started," Miss Mueller said as she stepped into the schoolroom. "I came a little earlier, just in case you did not get here or thought a fire unnecessary."

Daniel smiled. "There is a nice fire. I can feel the stove's heat at the desk. It should warm the schoolroom very soon."

Miss Mueller nodded. "I could feel the difference when I walked through the door." She approached the desk. "Checking the workbooks?"

Daniel nodded.

Miss Mueller stood, fidgeting, waiting. She pursed her lips. "I will be quite honest, Mr. Yoder." She stood to full stature, hands clasped before her. "I did not think you would be a good teacher. I felt you were too young, too inexperienced."

Daniel gazed at her, searching her eyes.

"What I am saying..." She grimaced and grasped her hands together by the fingers. "You are an excellent teacher." She heaved a sigh. "The students respect you, Mr. Yoder."

"Thank you, Miss Mueller."

Miss Mueller bowed her head, lifted it quickly and smiled.

"If you wish, you may call me Ruby. That is my name. I do not feel we need to be so formal between us." She hesitated. "When the children are present, I think we should remain formal, but at moments like this, I do believe the formality could be friendlier."

"I agree, Miss Mu... Ruby. You may call me Daniel." He smiled. "It is Daniel – not Dan, Danny, or..." Daniel made a face. "Danny-boy." He sighed. "It is Daniel."

Ruby smiled. Daniel thought it was the first time he'd seen her smile; a true smile, not forced. Suddenly, she frowned.

"Tomorrow," she whispered.

Daniel cocked his head in question. "Tomorrow, yes?"

Ruby pursed her lips. "Tomorrow is Halloween." She paused, then drew in a deep breath. "I fear the *Englische* may attempt a prank on the school." Ruby rolled a shoulder. "Just a feeling."

Daniel nodded. "I agree." He gazed about the room. "Do you think a new coating of paint... perhaps a light blue or green might be interesting?" He grinned.

Ruby pensively sucked in her lower lip. "If that is the only damage."

Daniel heaved a deep breath. "True. We will wait and see what comes tomorrow night." He put down his pencil. "Right now, we need to start class. Do you want to come them in?"

She nodded, turned and took two steps before stopping. She turned back to Daniel.

"I have enjoyed our conversation this morning, Daniel. I

96

will have the students in their seats shortly, Mr. Yoder."

Daniel smiled.

# # #

Wednesday, October 30, 1963, late night

Daniel awoke to the sound of somebody pounding on the kitchen door. His siblings stirred in their beds, also awake, rubbing their eyes.

"Wake up, Yoders! The school is on fire!"

Daniel's eyes widened with the realization of the words. *The school is on fire.* He dashed to put on his shirt and trousers.

"Hurry, Daniel," his father's voice yelled from the hallway.

Daniel slipped on his boots and raced down the stairs. He saw his father's back as the man raced out the kitchen door. Daniel ran to join him as his father jumped on the wagon of men being pulled by Jeremiah Wyse's horses.

"I tried to put it out when I saw it, but the flames were too much," Jeremiah said. "My wife got two of the neighbors to assist and I went in search of others to gather more men to help."

The horses galloped the road and in the distance, Daniel saw the red glow of the school on fire. He knew it was useless, but still, he prayed.

Heavenly Father, please guide our hands to save the school. Amen.

Jeremiah pulled the horses as close as possible and the men jumped from the wagon. They rushed to help pump water into buckets to douse the flames. Now, two brigades of able-bodied men sloshed buckets of water in an attempt to save the structure.

Window glass shattered from the heat. Flickering flames danced within the billowing smoke clouds escaping the window frames.

Noah passed a bucket to Daniel. "Did you make sure the

97

fire was out when you left the school?"

Daniel nodded. "Yes, Papa. It was dead. I tested it with my hand. There was no heat. The children wanted me to keep the fire going longer, but I insisted it must be out before we left."

Bishop Schmucker threw the bucket of water on the flaming inferno. He gazed at the flames.

"This is useless," Bishop Schmucker said. "The school is lost." He stumbled across the open area to rest on a log near a tree. "Perhaps we were rash in our decision of one so young to be a teacher."

"Daniel said he made sure the fire was out in the stove before leaving." Noah strode to the bishop.

"He is right," Ruby said, an apparition stepping from the line of trees. "I was there. The fire was out. There was no possible way the stove caused this fire." She strode to the gathered men. "Daniel is very conscientious about his teaching." She stretched to full height. "I, too, was leery of one so young being in charge. Daniel has done nothing but been an inspiration to the children of the school. He frets and worries constantly that he might be failing the community as a teacher." She gazed at Daniel. "I, for one, am glad he is the teacher." She pointed to the school, now a mere skeleton of flaming, falling debris. "This is not his fault. We discussed the possibility of an *Englische* prank tomorrow night. Obviously, they did it tonight."

The Centertown community volunteer fire department howled into existence, arriving at the school with lights flashing.

"We cannot be assured this was done by the *Englische*." Bishop Schmucker stood to go to the firemen as they began to unload their equipment.

"There is no need, gentlemen. The school is lost. We thank you for your concern." He raised his hand. "Go home to your families. We will watch the fire until it burns out."

"Captain Zimmer, at your service. I apologize for our delay. It seems somebody muffled our fire alarm and it took longer to respond." He sheepishly glanced down at the ground. "It took me too long to figure out why the alarm wouldn't ring.

I kept pressing the button, but nothing happened."

"Just a Halloween prank, I fear," Bishop Schmucker said. "None were injured. All is well."

"No, not all is well," Captain Zimmer yelled, his eyebrows wrinkling in concern. "Somebody caused all this. Somebody is accountable. This goes beyond a prank. Stealing a watermelon, or turning over an outhouse, that is a prank. Hanging toilet paper on trees in a yard, that is a prank. Burning a school?" Captain Zimmer shook his head vehemently. "No, that's not a prank. That's arson." He turned to Bishop Schmucker. "Also, muffling the fire alarm so it wouldn't ring, that is not a prank, either." Captain Zimmer stared into Bishop Schmucker's eyes. "Somebody will be held accountable for all this mayhem tonight. This is no prank to be dismissed."

Ben Hopkins strode to Daniel and placed a comforting arm over the young man's shoulder.

"We will rebuild the school, Daniel," Ben whispered. "You will have your dream, again."

Daniel shrugged off the older man's arm.

"I am sorry, Ben, but the *Englische* are making it clear. The Amish should not have a school."

"You can't give up now, Daniel." Ben grabbed Daniel by the shoulders and held him at arm's length. "You fought for what you have." He grinned. "Do you wish to throw it away?"

"No," Daniel whispered.

"That's the Daniel I know," Ben said. "Let the fire of the school burn inside you. Let it glow and shine. You will have another school."

CHAPTER ELEVEN: Martha Visits

Thursday, October 31, 1963, 9 a.m.

"Where are you going, Daniel?" Hannah asked.

"To the school," he replied.

Hannah giggled. "But, you cannot expect the students to come today? Who will you teach? Where will you teach?"

"Hush, Hannah." Rebecca snapped a towel in Hannah's direction. "You be about your chores. If Daniel wishes to visit the ashes of the school, that is his decision, not yours."

"Thank you, Mama," Daniel said.

"Do you want me to make you a lunch to take?"

"No, Mama." Daniel pushed the kitchen door open. "I will walk to the school and should be back by lunchtime." He hesitated. "Maybe a little later." He shrugged and left the house, sauntering down the steps of the porch.

The sun shone brightly and there was a mild breeze. Daniel gazed off into the field across the road where he watched the *Englische* neighbor, Richard Jones, harvest the late soybeans. The harvest dust blew away from their house. Daniel smiled as he heard his mother's words: *When the Englische harvest with their big machines, my laundry needs to be washed as soon as it is dry.*

Not today, Mama, Daniel thought.

Daniel turned onto the dirt road and began the hike to the burned school. A song came unbidden to him and he sang softly.

Where're you walk, cool gales shall fan the glade.

Daniel stopped. He tried to remember the last time he had sung those words. He nodded his head, knowing the day. It was in New York City.

Daniel sighed. *New York City*, he thought. It seemed like so long ago, yet it was only this past summer. So much had happened. Suddenly, the smiling face of Adam Brown filled his memories. The sound of the didgeridoo and the tribal beat of 'Aborigine Stomp' urged Daniel to scuff his feet in tempo against the dry dirt of Fall.

Daniel stopped, wide-eyed, staring at the open fields around him.

"I... AM... AMISH!" he yelled. "I do not want to be *Englische*."

He fell to his knees, head bowed.

Forgive me, Father. I am weak. I pushed to learn, and now... Give me the strength to fight the *Englische* within me. I am Amish. I... am... Amish. In Jesus' name, Amen.

Daniel stood, inhaled deeply, and trudged forward. The school was only two more miles. To clear his head and assure his thoughts were proper, Daniel sang songs from the *Ausbund*.

As he turned to trudge the last mile, Daniel watched the distant school come closer with each step. Seeing the pile of ashes filled him with sorrow.

What will the children do? Thoughts raced through Daniel's mind. *How can I teach without books? Who started this fire? And, why?*

Daniel stood at the edge of the large pile of ash. The chalkboards lay among the burned wood, cracked and broken. He shook his head.

Near the front of the schoolroom, he saw the pot-bellied stove. The door stood open.

How strange? Daniel thought. *I know I closed and latched the door when I checked the fire to make sure it was out.*

Daniel strode across the open area toward the stove. Ash and dust swirled around his boots. He stooped to check the stove's door. His eye caught a glint. Something metallic lay hidden in the ash where he'd stepped. Daniel reached out to dust it off.

It was an open Zippo lighter, slightly damaged by the

heat of the fire.

Daniel picked it up to examine. He dusted more of the ash off. There was a Marine insignia on the side. Daniel moistened a finger and cleaned the opposite side. Initials were engraved on the lighter: TH.

Daniel stared at the lighter. He knew it was not one an Amish man would have, even covertly due to the military insignia. He stuck it in his pocket as a car pulled into the schoolyard.

"I figured you'd be here already," Captain Zimmer said. "Bill Meyers and I have come to see if we can figure out who the arson is, or..." He paused. "If the fire was caused due to somebody's negligence or not caring."

"I can assure you, Captain Zimmer," Daniel started. "I am very sure the fire was out when I left. I even closed and latched the stove's door." Daniel pointed to the pot-bellied stove. "Which is now open."

Bill Meyers rolled a shoulder. "That could have popped open in the heat. Doesn't prove anything."

Daniel reached into his pocket and fingered the lighter. He was about to show it when Bill Meyers yanked on the stove door.

"Yup, just as I thought," Bill said, flipping the handle of the stove. "Looks like the heat built up in the stove, the door wasn't closed properly, and the door popped open. Some embers probably fell out and well..." He glanced up at the space above them. "The rest is history. No sabotage or arson here. Just a simple case of negligence and immaturity." He cast a condescending eye at Daniel.

"Well, I don't see anything to say it was arson." Captain Zimmer tread through the ashes.

"Guess the Amish kids will be starting school in..." He grinned. "Oh, not my decision. I'll let the school board decide that tonight in an emergency meeting and they can notify the parents."

Daniel's fingers tightened around the lighter. The smugness on Bill Meyers' face irked Daniel, but he was not about to let it show.

"I will notify Bishop Schmucker," Daniel said.

"Okay, Bill, let's get out of here and get home."

"Nice try, kid," Bill whispered with a smirk at Daniel.

Daniel watched the two of them get in the car and leave. He sat on the school steps, thinking.

#

Daniel sat staring out at the openness of the schoolyard. To the side, swings moved ever so slightly in the breeze. Leaves scurried and rustled across the yard, sometimes in a whirlwind vortex, other times in a race against each other.

Another car appeared and pulled into the schoolyard.

Martha jumped from it wearing her Amish clothes.

"Daniel," she shouted. "I just heard on the news about the school." She stopped to stare at the destruction. "This is terrible." She raced to sit beside him on the stone steps.

Daniel stared at the car, then nodded toward it. "I thought you were becoming Amish."

Martha wrapped her arm within his. "I wanted to get here as fast as possible." She grinned. "I'm not baptized, so you could say I'm still officially on *Rumschpringe*."

Daniel shrugged.

"How did this happen?" she asked.

"They are claiming I was negligent. The one with the fire captain said it was an obvious case of me not making sure the door on the stove was closed and the fire out."

She leaned back and stared at Daniel. "That can't be true," she said. "You are the most conscientious person I know. You worry and fret about the smallest thing."

Daniel shook his head. "When they talk with the bishop, there will be consequences." He sighed. "They are already talking about the Amish children going to the *Englische* school."

Martha stood and stomped down the steps to the ground.

"Are you saying the Amish will not rebuild a new school? Why?"

"If the fire was my fault, it will be my responsibility to get a new school built." Daniel stood. "I do not have the funds for a new school and books."

Martha placed her hands on her hips. "They can't think you did this."

Daniel stepped down to join her.

"Martha, my love, you do not realize the full implication of this event."

She frowned, one eyebrow curled up in a questioning look.

"I will be shunned."

"Shunned?" She stepped closer and flung her arms around Daniel. "They would shun you?"

"Until I repent my transgressions, admitting my shame, and agreeing to restitution..." Daniel rolled a shoulder. "Yes, I will be shunned."

Martha pursed her lips and gave Daniel a determined look.

"I know you don't want to hear this, my love, but perhaps we should consider a life away from the Amish. A life with the *Englische*."

Daniel's eyes flared wide.

"No, I am Amish. If I were to leave the Amish now, I would be shunned, never able to talk to any of my family - my parents, my siblings, my aunts, uncles or cousins." He took a deep breath. "To them, I would be dead." He shook his head. "No, I must remain Amish." Daniel gazed at her. "Is this what you wish for us? I should leave the Amish? We become *Englische*?"

Martha once more embraced Daniel. "No, my love. I only wish to be with you. I only suggested an *Englische* lifestyle as a possibility. I will become Amish. We will be together."

Daniel smiled, grabbed her hand and squeezed it. He gazed at the car before looking her in the eye. "Are you sure you want to be Amish?"

Martha gave Daniel a peck on the cheek.

"I must get back home before my father discovers I have taken the car." She wrinkled her nose at Daniel. "He is agreeing to me becoming Amish."

"That is good," Daniel replied.

"But, I don't want to push him too much." She laughed. "I will talk with you later."

She got in the car and pulled from the schoolyard to disappear down the dirt road.

Daniel leaned against a hitching post, surveying the scene. He slipped his hand into the pocket with the lighter, gripped it, then flipped it over a couple of times in his hand, feeling the raised metal Marine insignia scrape against his palm.

"I may be shunned, but I will find out who did this." He cocked an eye to the sky. "With the Lord's guidance and assistance."

CHAPTER TWELVE: Sunday Church

Sunday, November 3, 1963, early morning

Daniel walked silently beside his father as they moved toward the barn to milk the cows and feed the animals. Jacob and twins ran eagerly to the barn door. Daniel smiled, remembering when he used to do such childish things.

"Daniel." His father's voice cut through the early morning brisk darkness.

"Yes, Papa."

"Bishop Schmucker spoke with me yesterday." Noah Yoder stopped and watched the younger boys dash through the barn door. "Feed them well," he yelled to the boys before turning back to Daniel. "He was visited by Captain Zimmer and Mr. Meyers." Noah paused. "They are claiming the fire was due to negligence on your behalf." Again, he paused. "Do you understand the meaning?"

"Yes, Papa," Daniel whispered. "It was my responsibility and so the fire was my fault."

Noah nodded, placing a hand on Daniel's shoulder. "Still, there is..."

"I understand, Papa. I will be shunned."

Noah sighed and dropped his hand. "Today, at church, it will be announced. Since you are my son, I was not allowed to participate in the decision."

"Papa, as God is my witness, I tell you the truth. The fire was out. I did not err." Daniel hesitated, searching for his words. "Even Miss Mueller stated the fire was out. Did you not hear her?"

"I am sure her words will be judged, Daniel." Noah placed an arm over Daniel's shoulder and urged him toward the barn. "Let us milk the cows, feed the animals, eat the breakfast your mother has prepared, and go to church. Your destiny is in God's hands."

Daniel ate his breakfast in silence, watching his siblings and parents. When his mother looked at him, he could see the redness in her eyes. Tears welled but did not run. Daniel wanted to go over and embrace her and tell her all would be well. Instead, he lowered his head and continued to eat.

Daniel rode with Luke in the second buggy. Another horse was tethered to the back of their buggy.

Daniel nodded, knowing the reason for the extra horse. He watched as Anna, the twins, Joshua and Jonah, and little Ester bounced around in the back of their parent's buggy. Hannah, Mary, and Jacob rode behind Daniel and Luke in the second buggy. They were on their way to the Graber house for church.

Daniel sighed. *I will be riding Bronk home when I am shunned.*

Luke smiled. "This morning, Bishop Schmucker will make an announcement."

Daniel rolled his shoulder with disinterest. "Yes, I know."

Luke nudged Daniel. "Do not be so glum, little brother. It was bound to happen and will not be that much of a change."

Daniel frowned, unsure of Luke's words. Daniel played the words over and over in his mind, trying to understand how Luke seemed unconcerned about the possible shunning.

"Everyone out," Luke yelled.

Daniel frowned. *There is only me,* he thought. "I will help with the horses," Daniel said, jumping from the buggy.

"Nay, little brother." Luke snapped the reins. "I will do it." He grinned. "See you later."

Daniel shuffled toward the Graber house. He saw the covert glances and obvious stares as he entered the house.

"We need to make several announcements." Bishop Schmucker raised his hand to get attention.

Daniel held his breath. *This is it.*

"First, I wish to announce the marriage of Emma Troyer. She has chosen Leroy Stoltzenberg to be her husband."

Daniel watched as many nodded approval of the announcement.

Elroy Troyer, Emma's father stood. "The date of the wedding will be the Thursday after next on November the fourteenth. All are invited."

Bishop Schmucker continued. "Also, I wish to announce the marriage of Miriam Lantz. She has chosen Luke Yoder to be her husband."

Samuel Lantz stood and nodded to those in attendance. "The date will be four Tuesdays hence on November twenty-sixth." Samuel smiled. "Everyone is invited."

Daniel's eyes widened, surprised. He searched for Luke, finally realizing his older brother was nowhere to be seen in the group of men.

I have been so preoccupied with teaching and the fire at the school, I did not know Luke had asked Miriam.

"Another announcement," Bishop Schmucker said, his voice more serious. "Tomorrow, our children will begin attending the *Englische* school. The bus will stop to pick them up and take them to Centertown." He shook his head. "Some will then go on to Hayton, the others will go to Myersville, depending upon their grade. Fifth grade and below will go to Hayton. Sixth grade and above will go to Myersville." Bishop Schmucker turned and glared at Daniel. "This is because our school burned last week." He sighed. "And now, the final announcement. Due to the negligence of Daniel Yoder, the school burned. Until further notice, Daniel Yoder is shunned. *Meidung.*"

Shunned?

Daniel stared at the assembled members of the community. John Heffel who sat next to him immediately turned so his back was to Daniel. Many others moved to distance themselves and not look at him.

Unsure what to do, but knowing he must leave, Daniel stood and left the room. Those sitting closest to him eased away to open the path for him to leave. He gazed at his father. Noah immediately dropped his gaze to the floor, as did Daniel's mother. Only little Ester grinned at him. All those in attendance ignored him, even Ruth Graber who had shown an interest in him before he left for New York. Today she shunned him.

Daniel stood outside the Graber house. He knew being shunned would mean none would talk to him, not even his parents and siblings. He attempted a smile.

The twins and little Ester might talk to him until they were reprimanded and learned better. Daniel sighed at the thought. *They weren't members of the church, yet. I am shunned.*

Daniel gazed about the Graber yard.

Best start my walk home. I will be allowed in the house, but I will not be allowed to join the family at the table. I must sit at a separate table.

Daniel looked up from his idle saunter toward the road. He gazed at the rows of buggies.

I think Luke brought Bronk for me to... Wait! Luke was not at church.

He saw the buggy, but saw no sign of the spare horse. Daniel grinned.

Luke took Bronk to go to the Lantz home. Miriam and Luke are having their first meal alone together. She is cooking for him. I should...

His thought trailed off realizing being shunned, he was not allowed to participate in any community activity.

Daniel continued his sauntering along the country dirt road, enjoying the newfound silence. Even nature seemed to realize he was being shunned. The wind blew, but the rustling leaves and dried grasses moved silently. Birds flitted about, resting on the wire fences. Again, silent. Daniel felt they were watching him, judging.

His stomach growled with hunger as the family home came into view.

At least my stomach will talk to me, Daniel thought and

109

smiled at the concept.

Daniel stepped into the kitchen and wondered what he could find to eat. The family would enjoy a part of the afternoon at the Graber home, then later at the Lantz home to help celebrate Luke's betrothal before coming home. On the counter, wrapped in a basket, he found two fried pieces of chicken and three biscuits. *Curious,* he thought.

Saying a quick grace, he enjoyed the meal.

As he slathered fresh homemade grape jelly over the last butter-laden biscuit, he suddenly realized, his father knew he would be shunned and his mother had food prepared for him in the event it did happen.

"Thank you, Papa," Daniel whispered. "And Mama, too. Luke, I am sorry I am missing your betrothal."

# # #

Monday, November 4, 1963, 7 a.m.

"You must hurry," Rebecca reprimanded. "The bus will be here shortly."

"Why must we go to the *Englische* school? We can build another." Jacob whined. "I will wait and help build it."

"Yes," the twins chimed in. "We want Daniel to be our teacher."

Rebecca scowled at the twins, then glared at Jacob. "Daniel is not the teacher."

"But..."

"Hush, Jacob." She put an index finger to her lips. "No more."

Daniel heaved a sigh as he sat in the corner of the kitchen watching his siblings prepare for school. He dared not assist. He kept silent, watching out the window for the big yellow bus to appear.

"Here are your lunches. The bus is coming. Now, hurry." Rebecca handed each child a brown bag.

Daniel was about to offer to get the books when he realized the error of his way. One, they had no *Englische* books as yet, and two, he was not allowed to assist now being

110

shunned.

He placed his dirty dishes in the sink.

"*danke*, Mama," he said. She couldn't respond, but he could still talk to her.

He opened the kitchen door and headed out to watch his siblings get on the bus. His younger siblings were not baptized members of the community and could, if they wished, talk to him. He waved and the twins waved back as they climbed the steps of the bus. Daniel smiled.

I can busy myself doing jobs around the farm, Daniel thought. He stuck a hand in his pocket and his fingers wrapped around the lighter. *Or, I could go to the school and learn when the board will meet next.*

He walked inside the house. His mother and Hannah were cleaning up the kitchen, finishing the dishes.

"I think I shall walk into Centertown," Daniel said to nobody in particular and grabbed his jacket. He turned and left, taking a leisurely stride, he headed toward town.

"Good morning, Mrs. Miller," Daniel said as he entered the school office.

"Good morning, to you. How may I help you?" Mrs. Miller stood from the desk and moved toward the counter. "Daniel Yoder?"

"Yes, ma'am," he replied.

"I heard about the school. That was truly tragic. Now, why are you here?" She smiled.

"I wanted to know when the school board would meet again," Daniel asked.

"Let me check the calendar." She reached behind to her desk and grabbed a datebook. "Let me see. They usually meet on the... oh, my, that is near Thanksgiving. Hm?" She flipped pages. "Ah, here it is. They moved it up much earlier. They will meet here at 7 p.m. on Tuesday, November 12th." She frowned. "Why, that's next week."

"Is that a problem?" Daniel asked.

"No. No, not at all. It seems the month is passing so

111

quickly." She placed the datebook on her desk. "Is there anything else you need?"

"No, Mrs. Miller. That is all. Thank you."

Daniel left the office, noticing the chorus room to his left. He moved to the door and reached for the handle. He wondered if the room was empty. A young girl's voice performed a crescendo as she went up the scale. A piano sounded.

Daniel pulled back his hand. He recognized the voice. Brenda Howsly was singing. He remembered listening to her practice when Julie Bronson was the chorus teacher.

He stepped back and started down the flight of steps. As he neared the main floor, Leroy Harrison, the janitor stopped him.

"Are you lost there, young Yoder?" He grinned.

"No, sir. Just on my way home."

"Between you, me, and banging pipes of this school, that burning of your school was not an accident." He leaned in close to Daniel. "I hear they say you did it... some type of negligence. I ain't buying into that." Leroy glanced about to see if anyone was near. "I heard them talking, saying somebody should burn the Amish school. Next thing I know, the school is done burnt."

Leroy grabbed Daniel's arm. "Be careful, young Yoder. If the Amish rebuild the school, you might be next." He released Daniel's arm and grinned. "When I told Big Bob about you being a teacher, he said he figured you'd be one. He said you're too Amish to be *Englische*." Leroy cackled. "Now, young Yoder, you have a good day."

Daniel nodded and hustled from the school to make his way home, noticing the grocery.

Mama needed some cinnamon to make more applesauce, Daniel thought. *I can get it.*

Daniel walked into the grocery. A small bell rang.

"Good morning, Mr. Shaw," Daniel said. "I need some cinnamon."

"Right here," Aaron said and handed him a small tin of the spice.

Daniel reached into his pocket to pull out the change to pay.

"No need, Daniel. I'll put it on the tab." Aaron leaned in close. "Is it true? Are you being shunned?"

Daniel nodded.

"Sorry to hear about that. How are you doing?"

"It is fine, Mr. Shaw. The Amish community may not speak to me, but the *Englische* know me and still talk to me." He grinned. "At least Martha is not baptized, yet."

"Ah, young love. If you need anything, let me know," Aaron said. "Have a good day."

Daniel turned and headed out of the store.

Daniel strolled into the yard. His mother and sister, Hannah, worked in the garden, harvesting the last of the vegetables and pulling plants in preparation for turning the ground. He went into the kitchen and placed the cinnamon on the counter.

Mama will be happy, Daniel thought and heaved a sigh. *But, she will not say anything.*

He saw the sandwich on the plate. It was for him. He took the meal and sat on his chair in the corner of the kitchen. He noticed a small table had been placed by the chair.

His mother and Hannah entered and placed the vegetables on the counter. His mother noticed the tin of cinnamon and placed it on the shelf with the other spices.

Hannah turned and mouthed the words 'Thank you, Daniel' and hoped Mama didn't see her.

Daniel lifted the sandwich and whispered '*danke*' back.

The twins raced into the kitchen with fluttering papers in hand.

"For you, Mama," they said in unison while handing their latest artwork to her.

Jacob trudged into the kitchen. "The *Englische* teachers gave me a stack of homework to do ." He placed a pile of books on the table. "I do not want to go back to the *Englische* school."

"You will go back," Rebecca said. "Until you finish eighth grade."

"Can Daniel help me?" Jacob whined and turned to look at Daniel. "Will you? It is math and you know I do not understand it.,"

Rebecca ever-so-slightly nodded and walked from the room.

"I will prepare the evening meal," Hannah said as she watched their mother leave.

"*danke*, Hannah," Rebecca answered.

Hannah leaned in close to Daniel. "Mama left so you can help Jacob. If she does not see you helping, then the shunning is upheld. We are not baptized and therefore not members who must adhere to the rules of *Meidung*."

Daniel quickly sat at the kitchen table and motioned for Jacob to join him.

"Show me your assignment," Daniel said.

Jacob opened the book and turned it so Daniel could see.

"This is how it is done, Jacob." Daniel wrote quickly to show Jacob how to do the math assignment homework.

Anna and Mary sat across from Daniel. "Can you help us, too?"

Daniel moved quickly to assist them, unsure of when his mother would return.

"Hurry, Daniel," Hannah said as she stretched and looked out the kitchen window. "Papa and Luke are coming in from the field. They are taking the horses to the barn, but they should be here soon."

"Hannah?" Rachel's voice called from the front room. "Do you need help?"

"Soon, Mama," Hannah replied. "Papa and Luke will be here shortly."

"Then I best come help you, Hannah," Rebecca said. "Your father will want the meal ready soon."

"Are you finished, Daniel?" Hannah asked, her voice raising in fear. "Papa and Luke are headed to the house."

Daniel looked at his siblings. "Is everything understood?"

They nodded and Daniel quickly moved to his chair in

the corner. His mother walked into the room and nodded approval of what she saw. As she started to peel a potato, Luke and Noah walked in the kitchen door.

Noah immediately noticed Daniel sitting in the corner, but said nothing.

"Children," Noah said. "Your mama will have the evening meal ready shortly. Be about finishing your homework so Hannah may set the table for our meal." Noah continued through the kitchen to his chair in the front room. Luke followed behind, avoiding eye contact with Daniel.

Wednesday, November 6, 1963, 2 p.m.

A car entered the Yoder driveway and stopped, pulling into the grass behind the house.

Rebecca stood at the window, peeling the last of the apples she'd collected.

"I wonder why Martha Noble has come? Surely she has heard the news."

"Mama," Hannah whispered. "She is not baptized and is still basically *Englische*. If she wishes to visit with him, to her, he is not shunned."

Rebecca drew in a deep breath. "As God wishes," she mumbled.

Daniel sat in the living room. He was considering collecting eggs from the hen house when he heard his mother talk about Martha. Daniel strode quickly through the house to the kitchen door.

Martha knocked just as he was about to open the door.

"I just heard this morning, Daniel," she gushed. "I took off from school and came immediately. How could they shun you, Daniel? You did nothing wrong."

"Let us sit out here on the kitchen stoop." Daniel urged her down the first step so they could sit and talk." He glanced at the kitchen window where his mother watched from a respectable distance. She nodded approval. *I may be shunned, but the rules still apply. We need a chaperon, or, at least be*

115

visible for all to see, he thought.

Martha straightened her dark Amish dress. "How can they do this to you?"

Daniel rolled a shoulder. "The Fire Captain decided it was not arson. The other person with him found the door of the stove open and decided the fire had not been put out." Daniel hung his head. "The only choice was my negligence. Hence, it is my fault. I must make restitution and ask forgiveness for my transgression." Daniel grimaced.

"But, it wasn't your fault. I know that. You know that. Many know the truth." She took Daniel's hands into hers. "Did they not ask the students if the fire was out?"

Daniel smiled. "Ruby Mueller said the fire was out. I am sure many of the students told the truth. Still, it was my word against that of Captain Zimmer and Bill Meyers." He gazed into her eyes. "I am young. Perhaps too young to be a teacher."

"How long are you shunned?" she asked, standing to face him. "When will this be over and we can marry?"

"Marry?" Daniel stood. "I am shunned. There can be no marriage. I am banned from the church, the community, my family and friends. I must be atoned of my sin."

Martha crossed her arms before her with a defiant gaze. "Exactly when will this happen?"

Daniel shoved his hands in his pockets. The fingers clutched the lighter. A smile spread over his face. "Soon, Martha. Very soon." He squeezed the lighter. "Perhaps next week."

Martha frowned. "Next week?"

Daniel nodded. "My brother, Luke, will marry on the twenty-fourth of this month. I wish to attend and..." He paused. "If I am shunned, I will not be allowed to participate in the event." He looked into Martha's eyes. "Will you come with me to Luke's wedding?"

Once more Martha frowned. "Are you sure you will be finished with the shunning by then?"

Daniel let go of the lighter and grabbed her hands. "I am pretty sure *Meidung* for me will be over and I will be able to attend Luke's wedding."

"I will go with you, Daniel," Martha said and flung her

arms around his neck to kiss him.

A rap on the window caught Daniel's attention. He removed her arms from his neck, but he kissed her on the forehead. He was sure it was his mother's hand tapping on the window, but she couldn't see the discreet kiss he gave Martha. He smiled.

"This shall be settled very soon." Daniel nodded to reassure himself. "A new school will be built and..." He grinned. "The *Englische* will help."

CHAPTER THIRTEEN: Confrontations

Tuesday, November 12, 1963, about 1 p.m.

Daniel finished the meal his mother had provided. She didn't serve him, she allowed him to take what he wished from the various bowls and plates. As usual, he sat at his little table and chair in the corner while his father, Luke, Hannah, Ester, and his mother sat at the table.

He stood, placed his dishes in the sink, turned and inhaled deeply.

"To anyone who might be interested." Daniel faced the table and spoke. "I am attending the school board meeting tonight at seven. I plan to confront them with the evidence it was not negligence, but deliberately set." Daniel stuck his hand in his pocket and clutched the lighter. "I have my proof."

Daniel turned and headed out the kitchen door. He did not expect a response, but waited, sitting on the kitchen stoop, hoping.

Noah stood at the kitchen entrance. "I must visit Bishop Schmucker," he said. "Since our children are attending the *Englische* schools again, we should attend the board meeting to see what they have planned."

"A wise decision, Papa," Luke replied. "I may attend, too."

"Perhaps a few others might find the meeting of interest," Noah added. "I will spread the word."

"I will take Bronk and see if any others would go, Papa," Luke said. "You go see the bishop."

Noah slipped out the door and walked around Daniel who still sat on the steps.

Luke waited at the screen door, watching his father head to the barn to harness Beauty and visit Bishop Schmucker.

118

When Noah was beyond hearing distance, Luke sauntered down the steps.

"I hope you have the proof, little brother," Luke whispered. He continued down the steps.

"I have," Daniel murmured while nodding. "I have."

He ambled to his father's buggy and waited before getting in. He was not allowed to assist.

# # #

Tuesday, November 12, 1963, a little before 7 p.m.

Daniel jumped from the buggy when it stopped for the light at the center of Centertown. It would not be good for his father if he were seen in the buggy. Daniel strolled the block to the high school and entered, taking the steps two at a time up to the classroom next to the office.

He opened the door and immediately noticed Bishop Schmucker, Ezekiel Troyer, and Rueben Metz sitting together. Daniel knew his father would join them. He noticed the superintendent, Jeremiah Harding, and beside him was the principal, James Franz. In the corner, standing, holding onto a broom was the janitor, Leroy Harrison who smiled and nodded at him. Daniel frowned when he noticed Captain Zimmer sitting directly behind the Amish group.

At the table, John Teegarden was in attendance. Also, sitting at the table and scowling at the group of Amish was Tom Hollis. Beside him was Peter Udall who appeared indifferent to the Amish in the audience.

Daniel nodded to the men at the table; most he recognized from his last interaction with them about the school. He wasn't sure about all the names, but was sure he'd remember when the time came.

Daniel took a chair across the room, distancing himself from the other Amish.

John Teegarden rapped the gavel to call the meeting to order.

"It appears we have more guests tonight than usual. We shall address the old issues from last month and then open the

119

floor to anything new."

"We don't have anything that is so important with the old business," Tom Hollis said. "I see no reason why we can't table it until next month." He thumped his pen on the table. "I make a motion we do such."

"I second it," Bob Hopkins said.

Tom Hollis stood, leaning forward over the table. "Now, let's see why the Amish have decided to grace us with their presence." He eased back in his chair with a smirk on his face.

John Teegarden rapped the gavel. "I open the floor to new issues."

He gazed at the Amish men gathered together, hoping one would say something. None spoke.

"I have a question for Tom Hollis," Daniel said. "If I may?"

John nodded agreement.

"Mr. Hollis, is it true you were in the Marines?"

"Semper fi!" Tom replied with a vigorous nod. "Although I don't see where this is of importance."

"I notice you are not playing with your lighter tonight." Daniel reached into his pocket and pulled the lighter out. "Is this your lighter, Mr. Hollis?"

Daniel walked forward to give Tom the lighter.

Tom grabbed and stared at it in his palm.

"Yes, this is my lighter. It even has my initials on it."

"Please note," Daniel started. "The lighter has a bluish rainbow burnish to it. I found it in the ashes beside the wood burner stove of the Amish school." Daniel paused. "After it had burned down."

Tom snapped the lighter open and flicked the wheel to ignite the wick. "Hrmph. Still works." He flicked the lid to close the lighter.

"Would you like to explain how I discovered that in the Amish school?" Daniel asked.

"I lost this lighter about three weeks ago," Tom said.

"Very convenient," John mumbled.

"I didn't set the fire to burn the Amish school," Tom yelled.

"And yet, by your admission, your lighter was in the

ashes," Bishop Schmucker said. "How is that?"

"I said, I lost it about three weeks ago." Tom slammed his hand on the table. "I didn't do it."

"Were you not the one who was saying we should burn the Amish school down?" John asked. "In fact, I'm quite sure I heard you say something of that persuasion to a few members of the church the Sunday before it was burnt."

"I didn't do it," Tom screamed, pushing his chair back from the table.

"Right now the evidence is pointing at you, Tom." Peter Udall stood. "As a member of this school board, your actions are a terrible example to the community." He put a hand on Tom's shoulder. "I've always backed you, but this time, you've gone too far. In fact, I think you should be removed from the school board."

"But, I didn't do it. I don't know how my lighter got inside an Amish school."

"Why didn't you show me this evidence?" Captain Zimmer asked.

"I was about to when Bill Meyers said it was obvious I had left the fire burning and was negligent." He gazed at Captain Zimmer. "Would you have believed me after that?"

Captain Zimmer nodded in understanding.

"It is easy to blame a young man," Daniel said. "But, why would I, the teacher, want to burn the school?"

"Until further investigation," John Teegarden rapped the gavel. "Tom Hollis, you are officially suspended pending an answer."

"You can't throw me off the school board," Tom screamed. "You can't."

"All those who agree, say aye."

A resounding 'aye' from the eight other members of the board filled the room.

"Tom," John said. "If you would, please excuse yourself from the meeting." John lifted the gavel to point at the door of the classroom.

Tom stood, glared at Daniel, and headed out of the room. At the door he turned. "This is not over, John. Not one iota. I will be vindicated. I did not burn the Amish school."

The glass of the door vibrated as Tom slammed the door behind him.

Daniel frowned, unsure exactly where this placed him.

"Mr. Yoder," John said to catch his attention. "I will have Captain Zimmer reopen the investigation." He scowled at Zimmer. "A thorough investigation." He gazed back at Daniel. "You have brought severe allegations against a member of the school board. Unfortunately, Tom's lighter in the ashes of your school does point a guilty finger. As you stated, the burnish of the lighter case easily indicated it had been in the fire."

John leaned to look at Captain Zimmer. "How long do you feel you will need to investigate this issue."

Captain Zimmer shrugged. "It will be difficult. The fire was almost two weeks ago, plus it has rained twice during the time." He grimaced. "Still, I will do what I can."

"Let me know immediately when you have finished." John rapped the gavel. "Is there any other new business?"

Daniel stepped back and sat in his chair, unsure of what to do next.

Noah Yoder stepped forward. "I do not know if this is the proper place or time, but I would like to assist in this fire investigation." He gazed at Daniel. "At the current time, the community holds my son accountable for the fire."

Bishop Schmucker stood. "In light of the evidence, I declare *Meidung* no longer. The church will await the verdict of the investigation."

"Thank you," Noah said and eased back to his chair.

Daniel smiled.

John frowned, his eyebrows knitting together. "You have shunned this young man?" He pointed to Daniel.

Bishop Schmucker held his place. "Captain Zimmer stated it was negligence on behalf of Daniel that the fire happened."

John glanced at Captain Zimmer. "You will make this investigation your number one priority."

"Yes, John," Captain Zimmer mumbled.

Once more John rapped the gavel. "Again, this matter is tabled until Captain Zimmer finishes his investigation. Does anyone else have a question?"

John waited. Nobody spoke.

"Fine." John banged the gavel. "Moving on. Let us begin with old matters." He turned to Tony Thompson. "Read the minutes of the last meeting." He watched as the six Amish men stood and moved toward the door.

"Thank you for joining us, gentlemen," John said as they approached the door.

Noah Yoder nodded and quietly closed the door behind him being the last to leave.

#

Tuesday, November 12, 1963, near 8:30 p.m.

"Daniel, go with Luke to unharness Beauty," Noah said as he climbed from the buggy. He smiled. "I will tell your mother about the good news."

Daniel watched his father move quickly to the kitchen steps and disappear inside the house.

"Papa is very happy," Luke said. "I knew you did not set the fire." He grinned. "You would set fire to our house before you even thought of doing so to a school." He nudged Daniel. "Mister I-want-to-learn." Luke shook his head. "Bishop Schmucker is getting old, but he acknowledges his errors." He laughed.

"It is good to hear your voice speaking to me," Daniel said. "I have so many questions. When did you decide to marry Miriam Lantz? I never heard Mama or Papa talk about it."

Luke laughed as he jumped from the buggy. "Help me unharness Beauty." He pulled the leads. "You were so busy with the school, Daniel, I do not believe you knew what was happening about you." He grinned. "Of course, Martha has kept you occupied, too."

Daniel felt the heat in his cheeks.

"Tell me, Daniel. What are your plans with Martha Noble? Do you wish to marry her?"

Daniel unhitched Beauty from the buggy.

"We have discussed it," Daniel mumbled. "Her father has some issues."

"Speak up, Daniel," Luke said. "I can barely hear you. What did you say?"

"I said her father wants Martha to finish high school and attend college. He hopes she will marry an *Englische*." Daniel sighed. "He does not want her to become Amish."

Luke placed an arm on Daniel's shoulder. "Perhaps you should seek one from the church who is already Amish."

"But, I love Martha," Daniel said as he brushed down Beauty. "She loves me."

"Come, little brother," Luke called. "Beauty is down for the night. Let us go see Mama."

They walked toward the house.

"You know, Luke," Daniel started. "I will be losing a brother in a short time." He grinned. "Of course, I will be gaining another sister." Daniel made a face in the darkness. "Just what I need, another sister."

Luke pushed him and hastened his steps to the kitchen door, before breaking into a run.

"Not fair," Daniel cried. "That's cheating." Daniel chased his older brother.

The two boys burst into the kitchen, startling their parents.

Rebecca moved to Daniel, her arms outstretched to embrace him.

Daniel enjoyed the touch of his mother's loving arms about him.

"My Daniel," Rebecca said. "Why did you not present the lighter when you found it?"

"I wanted to confront Tom Hollis face-to-face, Mama," Daniel replied. "He does not like the Amish. I was afraid if I released the lighter to an *Englische*, it would disappear, and Mr. Hollis would not be held accountable for the fire."

Rebecca stepped back. "You accepted *Meidung* to prove your point?"

Daniel grinned. "I hoped *Meidung* would not happen, but it did." He rolled a shoulder. "Now the *Englische* are aware of the lighter found in the school. Mr. Hollis even admitted it was his."

"A wise move," Noah said. "Best all us be to bed. The

morning comes quickly and it will be good to have three of us working in the field before winter comes."

Daniel nodded and headed up the stairs to the bedroom. Luke followed.

# # #

Tuesday, November 12, 1963, about 9 p.m.

Tom Hollis sat in his recliner, flipping the lighter open, spinning the igniter wheel, watching the flame flicker before snapping the lid down to snuff the flame. He repeated the action.

"How did this get in the Amish school?" he mumbled. "My lighter."

Tom Hollis Junior stood in the next room watching his dad.

"They threw me out of the school board meeting!" Tom's voice was a little louder. He glared at the flame before again snuffing it out. "My lighter – in the ashes of the Amish school. How?"

Tom Junior stepped into the living room.

"Dad?" he called. "Have you got a couple of minutes?"

"What do you need?" Tom flipped the lighter open and snapped a flame into existence.

"It was my fault," Tom Junior said and hung his head. "I'm sorry."

Tom Senior frowned and scrutinized his son. "What is your fault?"

"The fire, Dad." Tom Junior took a deep breath. "Me, Jimmy Hughes, and Terry Young. We started the fire at the Amish school."

"You did what?" Tom Senior bolted upright in the recliner. "You set the fire?"

Tom Junior hung his head. "Yes, Dad," he whispered. "We heard you talking at church about somebody should burn the Amish school..." He paused and rolled a shoulder "Well, we decided to do it."

"I may have said that," Tom Senior said. "But, I didn't

125

mean it. I'd never consider burning a school down. I was just blowing off steam."

"We thought you meant it." Tom Junior gazed at this father, tears welling. "We didn't think the fire would get that far out of hand."

"What possessed you to think that?"

"Uh, we figured somebody would see the flames and call the Centertown fire department and they'd put it out."

Tom Senior nodded. "Who was going to call? The Amish don't have telephones." He tapped his temple with his index finger. "You weren't thinking with this."

Tom Junior shrugged and shook his head.

"Now, how did my lighter come to be in the ashes?" Tom Senior held the lighter into the air.

Tom Junior glanced at his feet. "I took your lighter. I'm sorry. I figured it would be easier to start a fire with it than for us to use matches."

"Okay." Tom Senior nodded. "How'd the lighter get in the ashes?"

"I'm sorry, Dad. I snapped it open like you do and spun the igniter. The flame came on and I got a wad of paper to light. I went to push it into the stove and some of the papers fell out. I went to snap the lid shut like you do, but I burnt my fingers and I dropped the lighter. It caught some of the paper on fire that I'd dropped on the floor. I couldn't get the lighter. Jimmy and Terry had started fires in the corner and we had to leave."

"So, the three of you burnt the Amish school down, left my lighter there, and I get blamed for destroying it." He glared at his son. "Do you realize I've been banned from the school board until this is all investigated."

Tom Senior placed an arm over his son's shoulder. "I can't help you out of this one, Tommy. You're going to have to go to Captain Zimmer and explain all this." Tom paused. "Uh, make sure to have Jimmy and Terry with you, unless you want to be the only one to take the rap." He shook his head. "I don't know what the repercussions will be. Trust me, it will be more than Captain Zimmer saying, "Naughty boys" and a mild hand slapping."

Wednesday, November 13, 1963, 3:30 p.m.

"So, what do you three boys want to see me about?" Captain Zimmer looked up from his desk, a questioning look on his face. "Bill Meyers and I have been out to the Amish school trying to find any clues as to who may have set the fire." He heaved a heavy sigh and stared at Tom Hollis Junior. "Your dad's position on the school board depends a lot on what I discover."

The three boys sheepishly glanced at one another.

"So, you haven't figured out who did it?" Jimmy Hughes asked while sneaking a peek at Terry Young.

Captain Zimmer shook his head. "Bill thought it was a simple open and close incident, but when Daniel Yoder produced the lighter..." Captain Zimmer rolled a shoulder. "That implicated Tom Hollis." He glanced at young Tom. "It doesn't look good for your dad." He clapped his hands. "Enough about the fire. What brings you young men to me?"

Jimmy and Terry both ever-so-slightly shook their heads. Terry mouthed 'Don't do it' and nodded toward Captain Zimmer.

"This is about my father," young Tom said while glaring at his two buddies. He turned to Captain Zimmer. "We set the fire, Captain."

"No, you set the fire," Terry said. "We went along but you set the fire."

Tom glared at his friend. "I set the fire? Who started the fire in the corner? Me? No, I was by the stove where I dropped my dad's lighter."

"Well, I didn't set any fire," Terry said snidely. "You can't blame me."

"Of course not," Tom sneered. "You just threw a lot of loose papers onto the fire." He paused. "Plus, you stuffed the alarm bell. Remember?"

"Hold it," Captain Zimmer said. "Are you admitting to arson of the Amish school?"

"I... well... uh, we, uh..." Tom stammered. He shrugged. "We weren't thinking, plus we figured it wouldn't get to be that big of fire. We thought somebody would call it in and the fire department would respond and put it out." He wrung his hands nervously. "The only thing we forgot, the Amish don't have phones." He glanced at his companions. "By the time somebody with a phone could see the fire, the school was lost. We were hiding in the trees and ran away when the Amish arrived to put out the fire."

Captain Zimmer nodded. "Ah-ha," he said. "We found some tracks in the tree line but thought they might have belonged to one of the Amish students." He glanced down at the boys' shoes. "I wasn't thinking, either. Amish don't wear sneakers."

"What happens now?" Terry asked. "Do we go to jail?"

Captain Zimmer moved and sat at his desk. "At the current time, yes, I should have you arrested and placed in jail. But, I'm going to let you go on your recognizance until I have a chance to discuss this matter with others which will include your parents and the Amish."

"Yes, sir," the three boys responded together.

"If it means anything," young Tom said. "I'm really sorry. I know I can't go back and change it, but I will do whatever I can to make restitution."

"Me, too," Jimmy and Terry chimed in together.

Captain Zimmer clasped his hands together before him on the desk. "I'd like to say this was a simple case of a childish prank gone bad, but..." He grimaced. "Go home. I'll get back with you."

The three boys turned and walked out of Captain Zimmer's office.

"My parents are going to tan my hide when they find out," Terry said. "I'll be grounded until I turn thirty-five."

Jimmy shook his head. "My allowance is a thing of the past. Plus, I'll have to get a job after school to pay for this."

Tom shoved his hands into his pockets. "I don't get an allowance." He grimaced. "I got some money saved from mowing yards during the summer, but..." He shrugged. "Whatever."

Thursday, November 14, 1963, 9 a.m.

"That is what happened," Captain Zimmer said. "What do you want to do?"

Bishop Schmucker stroked his beard and stared out the window of the room.

"What do I want to do?" The bishop glanced about the room. "Three young *Englische* lads, no older than our school teacher, burned down the school." He sighed. "At the whim of one's father, is that not correct?"

Captain Zimmer nodded agreement.

"The Amish will rebuild the school. Young Daniel Yoder will be the teacher." He paused. "Now, about the three lads. I think they need to assist in the rebuilding." He eyed Captain Zimmer. "Perhaps they will have a better understanding of the Amish and our ways." He paused again. "If they would like to make some restitution, we will gladly accept that to buy new books and supplies."

Captain Zimmer narrowed his eyes, waiting for the other shoe to drop. "Do you wish to press charges? I mean, for arson?"

Bishop Schmucker eased back in his chair. "Nay. Nay. I would rather have had the boys push over the outhouse, but they were innocent of their doing." He frowned. "Not innocent, but naive in hoping to appease those older who should have known better."

Captain Zimmer stood and shook hands with Bishop Schmucker. "The parents will be relieved to know you aren't pressing charges."

"Ah, the parents. May I suggest they also help in the rebuilding of the school." Once more he stroked his beard. "I believe they need a better understanding of the Amish, too." He smiled. "We are not a vengeful people."

"As you wish, Bishop Schmucker," Captain Zimmer said. "Let me know when you plan to rebuild the school and I will personally make sure they are here to assist."

"We will rebuild this Saturday," Bishop Schmucker said. "I will notify Daniel and he will get the books ordered and create a lesson plan until their arrival." He shook hands with Zimmer. "We want to have our children back as soon as possible. They will start school this coming Monday."

Captain Zimmer nodded approval. "I understand. I will visit the Hollis family, the Hughes family, and the Young family and make sure they are agree to your request." He grimaced. "I'm sure they will – none of them will want to see their son arrested for arson." Captain Zimmer started for the door. "I will also notify John Teegarden of my findings and our decisions today."

CHAPTER FOURTEEN: New School

Saturday, November 16, 1963, 8 a.m.

Daniel rode with Luke in the buckboard. He was amazed to see so many cars.

"Look at all the cars," Daniel whispered. "There has to be about thirty or more." He placed an open hand over his eyebrows to view the scene. "I did not expect so many *Englische* to help."

Luke laughed. "The *Englische*, like the Amish, all show to help when needed." He pointed to the left. "Is that not Bob Sullivan's mill truck there?"

"Yes," Daniel replied. "They have already started working."

Luke pulled the buckboard next to the last buggy in the line, jumped off, and quickly tethered the horse. "We best be about. This is your school."

Noah pulled beside Luke's buckboard. "Tether Beauty," he said and turned to the twins. "You help your mama get this food about." He jumped down from the buggy, leaned into the buckboard and grabbed his tools. Noah glanced at his two older sons. "Do you want the *Englische* to do all the work? Now get about."

Tom Hollis Junior strode toward them, hand outstretched to shake.

"I am sorry, very sorry, Daniel," he said while vigorously shaking hands. "I didn't mean for your school to burn down." He hung his head. "I admit my shame and ask for your forgiveness." He looked up and gazed into Daniel's eyes. "I started the fire, but, I and my friends, we had nothing to do with the prior vandalisms." He let go of Daniel's hand. "If you need anything, call me..." He grinned. "Okay, let me know and

131

I will help in any way I can. I hope we can be friends."

"You are sincere in your words, Tom. I do not hold any grudge against you. We are friends." Daniel smiled. "Now, let us get with the other men and build this school."

Jonathan Bell strode toward the two.

"We need two more for a foursome," he said. "I have John Heffel to help." He nodded back at a group of men, "So, the four of us could help with a wall. Yes?"

Daniel smiled. *John Heffel*, he thought. *He likes Hannah and Hannah likes Jonathan.* Daniel shook his head. *I will never understand girls, especially my sister.*

"Is your sister with you?" Daniel asked.

"Yeah, she's helping Hannah with something in the kitchen area." He sniffed the air. "It smells like we will eat very well today." Jonathan grinned. "Of course, that means we have to build a school first. Let's go."

Jonathan headed back to the area where the men were gathered, directly to John Heffel.

"Hello, John," Daniel said. "It is good to see you again."

John nodded. "We have been assigned to a section of the north wall with one window."

Daniel noticed the pot-bellied stove. "I wonder if they can use that stove?"

"I don't think so," Jonathan said. "I heard Bob Sullivan say he is donating one to the school, along with a teacher's desk." He grinned at Daniel. "If it is the one I saw on the truck, it's a beauty and it might get hot. It definitely won't burn if the school catches fire again."

Tom Junior kicked the dirt with his shoe. "I don't plan to make that mistake, again."

"We had best get started on our section," Daniel said. He clapped his hands and smiled at the group. "We do not want to be the last wall to go up." He laughed.

# # #

Saturday, November 16, 1963, near sunset

Noah stepped beside Daniel and put an arm across

Daniel's shoulders.

"You have a new school," he said, standing back a ways from the new building, admiring it. "We corrected the mistakes made with the first one. He pointed. "A bigger overhang, actually, a porch so one can sit outside and watch the children at play." Noah nodded approvingly. "Better window placement for proper airflow." He grinned. "We were going to relocate the stove, but feel it was the best location to heat the room. But..." He held up a finger. "We added an attic for extra storage. That means a ceiling for the room rather than heating all that space above the rafters."

"The school looks very nice, Papa," Daniel said.

"Plus," John Teegarden said as he joined them. "You will fill this with students on Monday morning. I've notified the school of the changes."

"Thank you, Mr. Teegarden," Daniel said, and smiled. "I will be diligent about heating the new school. I don't want to see this one burn down."

Bishop Schmucker joined them. "I will make the announcement at church tomorrow." He grinned behind his beard. "Although I think most of the community knows already."

Daniel admired the building. Suddenly, his eyes widened.

"I must prepare lessons for Monday, Tuesday, and possible Wednesday," Daniel said. "The books will not arrive until Tuesday or Wednesday." He gave his father a frantic look. "May I leave for home, now?"

Noah patted Daniel on the back. "If you must," he said with a grin. "But, I would suggest you eat a meal before you leave." Noah cocked an eye. "Your mama will not be happy if you leave without eating something."

Bishop Schmucker laughed. "Let us gather together for grace."

Word spread among the gathered and Bishop Schmucker gave thanks, not only for the food, but also for those who joined to assist with the new school.

Daniel grabbed a chicken leg, some boiled potatoes, buttered corn, and a biscuit. He ambled to the new school and sat on the steps leading to the front door. He gazed down at his plate, letting the scents of the food assail him.

A woman joined him. Daniel gazed up to see Martha.

"When did you come?" Daniel asked. "Why did you not let me know you were here?"

Martha giggled. "You were too busy with your partners working to build the school. I saw no reason to bother you. I, like a proper Amish woman, assisted in the kitchen, helping to prepare the meals for the men to enjoy."

"Why did you not join me for lunch?" Daniel bit into the chicken leg.

"As I said, you were sitting with the men." Martha wrinkled her nose at Daniel. "I did not feel it proper for me to plop down beside you and the rest of the men." She shrugged. "I talked with your sisters Hannah, Mary, Anna, and Ester, plus your mother, and Hannah's *Englische* friend, Susan."

Daniel nodded as he munched his meal. Clearing his mouth, he turned to her.

"You know I must leave now so I can prepare lessons for Monday. With church tomorrow, I will not have a lot of time to work on lessons."

Martha looked hurt. "You have no time for me?" She pouted.

"I want to spend time with you, Martha." Daniel reached for her hand to hold. "I would love to take you to the sing..." Daniel heaved a deep breath. "But, I really need to get lessons ready for eight different grades. I do not have books yet for them to work on."

Martha pursed her lips. "Perhaps I should be on my way home to Shipshewana." She stood. "Obviously, I'm not needed here." She stepped down one stair to the ground. "Am I correct?"

Daniel put his plate to the side and stood. "I love you, Martha, but I have an obligation."

"I understand," Martha said. "I will go home and come back another time."

"Will you come back for Luke's wedding? Will you be my guest?"

"Do you want me to come back, Daniel?"

Daniel grabbed her hands in his. "Yes, Martha. I want

you beside me when my brother is married."

Martha leaned in and placed a peck of a kiss on his cheek. "I want to marry you, too, Daniel Yoder." She sighed. "I must learn to sit and be silent for the teacher." She grinned.

"And I want to marry you, Miss Martha Noble."

Daniel leaned in, about to offer her a kiss. An obvious cough caught their attention. Noah stood near.

"Are you heading home soon, Daniel?"

Daniel let go of Martha's hands. "Yes, Papa." He grabbed his plate, grabbed the chicken leg, biting off the last of the meat. "I will give my plate to Hannah and head home."

Noah nodded.

Daniel leaned in close to Martha. "I love you, Martha," he whispered then turned to his father. "I am leaving now, Papa."

"goodbye, Martha," Daniel said and headed to where the women still served food to give Hannah his dirty dish.

Daniel walked near Bishop Schmucker. "I am headed home to work on lessons for Monday." He headed for the buckboard.

Luke ran up to him. "Are you planning to leave me here?" he asked. "I need to go home so I can pick up Miriam. Papa said they would be home shortly. Hannah will be my chaperon. She said she wanted to go since Susan wanted to join the Amish tonight for the sing."

Daniel frowned. *If Susan comes, so will Jonathan*, Daniel thought. *I wonder if John Heffel asked Hannah this time?* Daniel shrugged. *Probably not since she wants to see Susan which means she really wants to be around Jonathan.*

CHAPTER FIFTEEN: The Wedding

Tuesday, November 26, 1963, early morning

Daniel walked with Jacob, Luke, and his father to the barn. He watched as Anna walked with the twins and little Ester toward the chicken coop. The cool morning embraced them, causing chills, but chores needed to be done whether it be a regular day or a special one, like a wedding day.

"Race you to the door, Daniel," Jacob yelled and dashed away in a run.

Daniel considered the race, but held back. He was maturing and gazed at his older brother, Luke.

Today is the last time Luke will join us to milk the cows or do chores at the farm, Daniel thought. Tonight he will be a married man.

Daniel absently gazed at the ground, deep in thought.

"Jacob is already to the barn," Noah said, nodding at the closing door. "He will go up into the loft to feed the cattle. So, Luke, you start milking on the left. Daniel, take the right. I will alternate back and forth from the other end until Jacob comes down from the hayloft."

"Yes, Papa," Daniel and Luke said in unison.

Noah stepped inside the barn. Luke followed. Daniel stared into the dark morning shadows to see his other siblings at the chicken coop. Daniel smiled. *Mama will need a lot of eggs today*, he thought.

Daniel ducked into the barn and prepared to milk the cows.

# # #

Daniel adjusted the bow tie then straightened the front of

136

his shirt. He hustled down the steps from the bedroom to join the rest of the family as they prepared to go to the Lantz farm for the wedding. Mama had plenty of baskets filled with baked goods, different foods, and all the eggs collected that morning. The bright blue autumn sky of the earlier morning now warned gray with ominous clouds.

I hope it does not rain, Daniel thought.

As if God were answering a prayer, a ray of sunshine broke through the gloom and shone in the direction they were headed. Daniel smiled. The clouds opened more revealing a beautiful cerulean-blue sky. He bowed his head.

Thank you, Heavenly Father, for a beautiful day. Amen.

Daniel jumped into the buggy beside Luke. Again, the thought struck him. *This is the last time we will do this.* He gazed at Luke, admiring the quiet strength and advice his older brother had given him over the years.

"Did you think to invite Martha?" Luke asked.

Daniel nodded, yet he was unsure if she would attend. He tried to remember the last time they'd talked. He sat silently mulling over his thoughts. They'd discussed the possibilities of being *Englische* or Amish. Sitting there, he rolled a shoulder at his thought. *She said she would be back.*

"Look at that," Luke whispered and pointed. "So many have arrived already."

Daniel looked up to see the Lantz farm. He was sure there had to be near one hundred buggies lined up in the field. He saw his father's buggy near the front. His mother and father had left early to help prepare for the event. He felt his heart swell. There was Uncle Mark's buggy and he watched as Uncle Mark and his sons headed for the house. Mary and the girls were missing.

Perhaps Martha came with Uncle Mark, Daniel thought and stretched to see if he could locate her. Daniel frowned. *She is not here*, he thought, not seeing her among the other young girls.

Luke leaned over. "Do not fret, little brother. We will have the horse and buggy tethered shortly." He grinned. "After all, it is *MY* wedding, remember? I do not wish to miss it." He slapped Daniel on the shoulder. "Then you can rush about to see if Martha has come." Luke winked. "Of course, she would be a fool not to attend a wedding."

Daniel frowned at his brother's words. "Why?"

Luke reared back in the buggy, surprised. "Daniel. You are an attractive, young Amish man. Any Amish, or even an *Englische* girl, would be lucky to have you as a husband." Luke nodded at the cluster of young girls eyeing them as Beauty trotted by pulling their buggy. "See? They are looking." Luke leaned in closer to Daniel to whisper conspiratorially. "Every single girl attending a wedding... she hopes to find the man to marry." Luke shrugged and heaved with laughter. "Of course, most single men think the same." He slapped Daniel on the back. "It is only the old married men who attend a wedding and discuss the crops, chores, and horses."

Daniel eyed Luke, a glint in his eye. "Is that your fate, Luke?"

Luke nodded. "It is one I look forward to, my dear brother. One I look forward to, indeed."

They stepped from the buggy and young Eli Lantz took the reins while stroking Beauty's forehead. "I will take good care of her, Luke," he said and led her away.

"Who is that I spy?" Luke nodded toward the steps leading to the kitchen.

Daniel gained speed as he walked toward Martha.

"I hoped you would be here today," Daniel said, taking her hands into his.

"We need to talk, Daniel."

He searched her eyes, hoping to find the reason for her concern.

"I need to help Aunt Mary with the meal." She gazed back toward the kitchen. "But, after the wedding, can we step away to discuss a matter?" Her eyes pleaded. "It is important."

"Of course," Daniel replied.

Martha squeezed his hands, turned, and hastened up the steps to the back kitchen door. "Later," she whispered from the door, and disappeared.

"Shall we go and get me married?" Luke asked, placing a

hand on Daniel's shoulder.

Daniel nodded and moved forward with the urging of Luke's grasp.

# # #

"I didn't realize an Amish wedding was an all-day event." Martha wrapped her arm within Daniel's. "I've never attended one before."

Daniel smiled. "Now you know what our wedding will be like," he whispered. He leaned in closer. "Where do you wish to get married? At my parent's house? Uncle Mark's? Or, perhaps you would prefer your Uncle Paul's house in Shipshewana?"

Martha frowned with a questioning look. "Why not my parent's house?"

Daniel leaned against the fence where the horses were tethered. Just beyond were rows and rows of buggies.

"Do you think they could accommodate this?" He swung his arm to encompass the horses and buggies. "Remember, an Amish wedding is a community event."

She wrinkled her nose at Daniel. "My parent's home with its small lot might not handle this well. Not to mention all the extra fertilizer I'm sure the neighbors would immediately notice."

Daniel placed his hand under Martha's chin. "What is it you wish to speak with me about?" He shrugged. "You seemed quite upset."

Martha straightened her apron and the folds of her skirt.

"My father has approved us getting married next year. He has decided not to fight me about becoming Amish."

Daniel cocked his head. "The issue?"

"He says he only has one demand and I must commit to it for his full approval." She shrugged and held up a hand to silence him. "I don't know what he is going to ask of me."

Daniel reached and locked her fingers within his grasp. "Whatever it is, I am sure we can make it work."

Martha gazed at Daniel then laid her head on his shoulder. She heaved a sigh.

He squeezed her hand. "It is only a matter of time, Martha. Next spring will be here very quickly."

She nodded agreement.

"We shall meet the problems together as a team." She gazed up into Daniel's face. "You and me. Together."

Daniel kissed her forehead.

"Little brother?" Luke approached. "You are missed at the table. Come. Join us."

Daniel sighed and pushed away from the fence he and Martha leaned on together.

"Go," Martha whispered. "It is your brother's wedding. We will talk later or tomorrow." She gently pushed him toward Luke. "Go!" She grinned at Luke. "He is on his way, Luke. You dare to leave your new bride alone?"

"Even Nature has its demands." Luke snickered as he headed to the outhouse.

CHAPTER SIXTEEN: Conflicts

Tuesday, December 3, 1963, 6 a.m.

"It snowed last night," Daniel said. "I must get to the school early to start a fire to heat the room and clear some of the snow, if only the steps and sidewalk."

Joshua glared at his older brother.

"We will leave in about half an hour so we must get our chores finished." He gazed at Joshua. "For those who have not completed their morning chores... as yet."

"Half an hour?" Joshua's eyes widened. "The school bus will not come by for another hour to pick up the *Englische* students. Why so early?"

"Get about, Joshua." Rebecca stood at the stove making more pancakes. "Eat and get about your last chores." She turned to face the children at the kitchen table. Like any mother, she crossed her arms before her to ward off any further whining. "Am I understood?"

"Yes, Mama," Joshua mumbled before stuffing another large forkful of syrup laden pancakes into his mouth.

Jonah snickered quietly once his mother had turned back to the stove.

"I heard that," Rebecca said. "That means you, too, Jonah. Get a hustle about you."

"But, Mama..."

"Hush," Rebecca stated. "Daniel is the schoolmaster and must be at the school before the other students arrive." Once more she turned to gaze at her young offspring at the table and smiled. "It is his job. Think how lucky you are to have the teacher here to help you."

Daniel stepped into the kitchen. "What about the teacher?"

"It is nothing, Daniel," Rebecca said. "Your students will be ready shortly. Once more she turned to the young ones. "Now, finish quickly and get your chores finished. Daniel is waiting to leave."

"Yes, I am," Daniel said. "I will go out and get Beauty ready for the day. I will take a blanket along to help keep her warm and..."

"I need to go to town today," Rebecca said, cutting Daniel off. "I will ride along and bring the buggy back for Hannah and I to shop." She smiled. "I will make sure Hannah has the buggy back at the school by the time you are finished with teaching."

#

"Jacob?" Daniel turned to his younger brother. "Will you shovel the snow from the steps and sidewalk?"

"Yes," Jacob replied.

"That will allow me to attend to heating the school." Daniel reined Beauty into the schoolyard. He laughed. "I was about to ask the twins to pasture Beauty." He turned to his mother who had ridden quietly in the back of the buggy. "Everyone out," Daniel said. "Now, Mama, you can take Beauty and return home." He frowned. "Still, I do not understand why you did not have Hannah come rather than you."

Rebecca watched the youngest ones run through the snow to the swings.

"I wanted to make sure Joshua did not complain on the way here about the cold and having to come early."

The Troyer buggy arrived and James immediately jumped out to join Joshua by the swings. Daniel grinned.

"Those two are inseparable. Still, as long as they continue to pay attention in class, do their homework, and do not cause problems in class–" Daniel rolled a shoulder. "I will allow them to sit together in class."

Rebecca nodded and moved to the front seat of the buggy. "The twins are always together at home. It is wise to separate them at school." She watched as another buggy

142

arrived. "I will see that Hannah has the buggy here this afternoon when you are ready to come home." She snapped the reins.

"Yes, Mama," Daniel said, waved, and headed into the school to start the fire.

He turned at the school door to watch his mother turn onto the road and head home. He noticed Miss Mueller's buggy coming down the road.

"I better get the fire going," Daniel said and stepped inside the school.,

# # #

Daniel watched as the tinder ignited, scorching the smaller wood and flickering fingers of flame tinging the three logs.

It is a good fire, Daniel thought. *The room will be warm in a short amount of time.*

He moved to the desk and began to straighten papers, all the while keeping an eye on the front door, waiting for Miss Mueller to arrive.

She should be here by now, Daniel thought. He stood and gazed out the window. Her buggy was not there. This puzzled him and he quickly stepped to the front door. Opening it, in the distance he could see Miss Mueller's buggy and his mother's buggy – side by side. They were visiting.

Daniel quickly closed the door and went back to his desk.

# # #

Miss Mueller entered, pulling her coat off and hanging it in the closet.

"I hoped you would arrive early to start a fire," she said as she approached the stove, rubbing her hands together before spreading them out to absorb heat.

Daniel looked up from the papers he was grading.

"Good morning, Ruby." He snickered. "I will tell you I did meet with a little resistance this morning. Joshua felt it was unfair he had to come to school so early just so I could start a

143

fire and get the snow removed."

"You shoveled the snow?" Ruby asked.

"Nay," Daniel replied. "I asked Jacob to do it. I think he did a proper job."

"He not only did the steps and sidewalk," Ruby started. "He also shoveled an area around where we tether the horses. Your brother did an excellent job."

Daniel held up a paper. "I just wish he would put as much effort into his school work."

"Give him time." Ruby took the sheet of paper. "This is not that bad. He seems to have good penmanship. His sentences are correct." She frowned. "What is the problem?"

"Perhaps I am too critical of my siblings." Daniel took the essay back. "I was going to give him a 'C' for this."

Ruby snatched the paper from Daniel's hand and waved it in front of his face.

"Daniel Yoder! This is most definitely a 'B' if not an 'A' essay." She pursed her lips and scowled at him. "I think you are being too critical. You said to write about what interested them. Maybe you do not like his subject? Could that be it?"

Daniel shrugged. "Growing greens and beets to sell. I was hoping for something more." He picked up another essay. "See this one? Samuel's? He wrote about the proper harnessing of a horse team to a plow."

She grabbed the essay and scanned the page. "It is well written for a twelve-year old, but then again, most Amish boys know how to harness horses by the time they can walk." She giggled. "Jacob is only ten. Right? What were you interested in at that age?"

Daniel grinned. "Fine. I will learn to be more considerate of my siblings. Shall we agree this is a 'B+' essay?"

Ruby winked. "I was hoping for an 'A' but you are the teacher."

Daniel snickered. "Fine, a 'B+' it is. I certainly do not want the other students thinking I am favoring my brothers and sisters."

Ruby nodded. "I will call the students in to start classes."

"*danke*."

Daniel carefully placed Jacob's essay on the desk and

with his red pencil placed a 'B+' on the sheet.

# # #

Saturday, December 7, 1963, 2 p.m.

"I wondered when you would return home." Dan Noble glared at his daughter as she closed the front door to their home. "I haven't seen you in an over a week."

"Sorry, Daddy," she muttered and headed for the stairs and her room.

"When you change out of those ridiculous clothes, come back down here so we can talk."

Martha made a face her father couldn't see and heaved a heavy sigh. *I wonder what he wants to discuss now*, she thought. At the top of the stairs, she opened her bedroom door and stared at all the pink and frills. *Definitely not Amish*, she thought as she changed from her Amish garments into the more modern *Englische* clothes of a teenager her father wished her to wear. She sat on the edge of the bed. *Best go listen to what he has to say*, she thought.

She sauntered down the stairs and into the living room where her father was stretched out in his BarcaLounger.

"You wanted to talk to me?"

Dan moved the lounger into an upright position. "That's right." He glared at her. "About this wedding..."

"You've already agreed that Daniel and I can marry next spring," Martha said defensively.

"That's correct." He smiled. "But, of course, I did have one stipulation you had to agree with." He motioned her to the chair opposite him. "Sit down so we can discuss this civilly."

She cocked a questioning eyebrow in his direction. *Civilly?* she thought. Immediately her defenses were up. She knew he was going to demand something to cause a problem.

"I'm putting my cards on the table," Dan said. "I'll be honest. You're my only hope. I received a letter earlier in the week from your sister in Canada. She is married, so she says, to Mark English who she met in New York City." Dan took a deep breath. "Until this Vietnam issue is resolved, they will remain in Canada." He shook his head. "So, we won't be seeing her for some time unless we go up there." Dan leaned forward in his BarcaLounger. "As to your brother, Alexander." Again, he shook his head. "I don't know where I went wrong with him. He called yesterday to inform me he is dropping out of college and is moving to California. He mentioned something about some peace group he plans to devote his life to. It's called Harry something."

"Hare Krishna?" Martha offered, remembering the group in New York City with their robes of yellow sheets, bald heads, and all the banging on tambourines and finger cymbals.

Dan nodded. "That might have been it. So, if Alex decides to get married, but I think he plans to be some sort of monk, we probably won't be told about it." Dan shrugged. "At least, that is his useless plan. Anyway, your older sister is now married." Dan folded his hand together. "The one thing every father dreams about when a daughter is born... the day he will walk her down the wedding aisle." He sniffed. "I want to make sure I get the chance. I want my due. I want my right. It was denied me with your older sister. I want to proudly walk you down the aisle and give you away to Daniel." He paused. "Is that too much to ask? Demand?"

Martha grimaced. "In an Amish wedding, there is no walking down the aisle. There is no giving away of the bride. It is totally different."

Dan stiffened.

"Please, Daddy. It is a beautiful wedding. It is an all-day event and the whole community attends." She hesitated. "But, it is different than a standard church wedding."

Dan placed a hand below his chin, stroking it in thought.

Time passed. Silence.

"I told you. I will allow you to marry in the spring on one condition. That is my condition. I want to walk my little girl down the aisle." Dan stood. "I don't care how it is done, but those are my demands. If I don't walk you down a wedding aisle, there will be no wedding with my blessing." He cocked his head. "Understood?"

"But, Daddy." She gazed up at her father.

"There is no 'but' – that is my final word." Dan strode

146

across the living room.

"Fine," Martha yelled while standing up. "We do it your way."

Dan stopped at the arch leading from the living room to the foyer and front door. He turned.

"Since Amish don't have the bride walk the aisle..." She rolled a nonchalant shoulder. "What do you suggest?"

Dan stared at his daughter, a curl of a smile at the edge of his lips. "I will tell you this, Martha. You have two choices."

"And they are?" she asked.

"A real wedding at our church." He hesitated. "Or, no wedding."

Martha's eyes flared wide. "An *Englische* wedding?" She shook her head. "There is no way Daniel could do that. He'd be shunned." She sat in the chair, almost in tears. "That is no way to start a life together."

Dan's face softened. He had won the battle.

"Next year you turn eighteen. Finish your schooling." Dan strode back into the room. "Forget this Amish foolishness. You're too young to marry."

Martha turned to glare at her father.

"Before you say anything. Next year, being eighteen, you can do as you please and I can't stop you. If you want to get married, you can without my permission. I would want to walk you down the aisle, but... but, if that isn't possible, then I will just have to deal with that."

Martha narrowed her eyelids, anger welled up inside her. *He is playing a game*, she thought. *I can play this game, too.* She smiled. *After all, I am my father's daughter.*

"I will discuss this with Daniel and see what he has to say." Martha stood. "I wasn't going back to Uncle Paul's until Monday." She grinned at her father. "But, I think I will return yet today so I can go see Daniel tomorrow."

Dan rolled a shoulder. "As you wish."

CHAPTER SEVENTEEN: The Fight

Saturday, December 7, 1963, 5 p.m.

"Hi, Aunt Mary," Martha said as she entered the kitchen. "Can I help you?"

"Is that your car I see out there, Martha?" Mary never turned to face Martha.

Martha sighed. "Yes, Aunt Mary." She paused. "Yes, I know I shouldn't be driving it, but there is an issue that must be addressed."

"We do not drive cars, Martha." The voice was cold.

"I need to visit Daniel tomorrow and I do not know how it will turn out."

Mary turned to face Martha, squinching her face in displeasure.

"We are Amish here, Martha. If you wish to be Amish, you must give up your *Englische* ways." Mary dried her hands on a towel. "I thought you understood that."

Martha pulled out the bench of the table and sat.

"My father gave me an ultimatum. He will allow me to marry... IF he is allowed to walk me down the aisle."

Mary frowned. "Amish weddings do not..."

"Yes, I know, Aunt Mary. I tried to explain that to him. He is bullying me to come home and return to the *Englische* lifestyle."

Mary glanced out the window. "Is that what you wish?" She nodded toward the car.

Martha smiled. "No, Aunt Mary. I want to be Amish. I want to marry Daniel."

"Then, my dear child, you need to completely give up your *Englische* ways." Once more she nodded at the car. "Go hide the car by the corn crib. Your uncle will be here shortly."

She paused. "He will not be pleased."

"Maybe I should just go to Centertown before he comes home. I need to speak with Daniel."

Mary nodded. "Perhaps that would be best." She turned back to the sink and continued to wash the potatoes.

"When I return, I will take the car back to my parent's home and ride my bicycle here."

"A wise choice, Martha. When can we expect you back?"

"I will go to Uncle Mark tonight. I will see Daniel tomorrow for church. If all goes well, I should be back here tomorrow night." She hesitated. "Is that okay?"

"That is fine, dear." She gazed out the window. "You'd best hurry. I believe that is your uncle coming in from the field."

Martha rushed over and hugged Aunt Mary. "Thank you." She hustled out the door, running to the car, and quickly drove away. All the while she hoped Uncle Paul hadn't seen her or the car.

Saturday, December 7, 1963, 7 p.m.

"So, that, Uncle Mark, is what my father wishes... or rather, demands."

"There is no way Daniel can do that," Mark said. "He would be immediately shunned by the community." He grimaced. "He has already been shunned once. For one so young, twice in one year..." Mark shook his head. "Not good for him."

"Is there no way the bishop could allow my father to walk me down the aisle?"

"It is not the Amish way," Mark said.

Mark's wife, Mary, shook her head. "My sister's husband is not making life for you very easy. I don't understand his dislike of the Amish."

Martha shook her head. "Oh, Aunt Mary. My father doesn't dislike the Amish. Remember, he married one. His problem is me becoming Amish. He says he had high hopes for

149

me. He wanted me to be a doctor, lawyer, teacher, or somebody who the community looked up to. He feels I am throwing my life away if I become Amish."

Mary rolled a shoulder. "Still sounds like he doesn't like us."

Martha grimaced. "I will discuss this with Daniel tomorrow after church."

Sunday, December 8, 1963, 1 p.m.

"We really need to talk, Daniel." Martha moved away from the people and toward where the horses were tethered.

A few wandered outside in the cold, but most were indoors, preparing to enjoy the meal. The snow crunched under their feet and she shivered in her coat. Daniel reached up and rubbed her shoulders and arms, hoping to warm her.

"What is so important we must be out here?"

Martha turned to him, tears welled in her eyes. "It is my father."

Daniel scowled. "Your father?"

She sighed. "He told me the condition to our being allowed to marry." She rolled a shoulder. "He wants to walk me down the aisle." Martha grabbed Daniel's hands into hers. "He wants to give me away." A tear traced a path down her cheek. "My sister ran off to Canada and got married. My father didn't get the chance to give her away."

"What is this 'giving away' you are talking about?" Daniel gripped her hands tightly in his.

"In an *Englische* wedding, it is customary for the father of the bride to walk her down the aisle and ceremoniously gift her hand to the groom. It is his way of blessing the marriage."

"Amish weddings do not have this custom," Daniel said. "Does he not understand this?"

Martha bowed her head. "I tried to explain."

They stood quietly, pondering.

"How does your father expect to give you away?" Daniel finally asked.

Martha inhaled deeply. "He said if the Amish wedding does not allow this..." She paused. "He said it would have to be an *Englische* wedding."

Daniel stepped back, letting go of her hands. "*Englische?*"

Martha shrugged, then stepped closer to him.

"Perhaps we could have a small *Englische* wedding to appease him and then have an Amish wedding?" Martha gazed into Daniel's eyes, hoping he could see the possibility.

"If I were to marry in an *Englische* ceremony, I would be shunned." Daniel stared at her in disbelief. "You know that."

"I realize that, Daniel." She grabbed his hands, again. "But, that would happen only if the Amish discover it. The *Englische* wedding could be a quiet, discreet affair." She shrugged. "Maybe the Amish would not even know or realize it."

"For us to marry, Martha, you must be Amish. If you are Amish and we have an *Englische* wedding..." He stared toward the house. "Not only I would be shunned, but you also." He watched as his father came out the kitchen door. "Do we wish to start our life together, shunned?"

"Daniel!" Noah Yoder yelled. "Come into the house."

Martha looked into his eyes. Tears filled her eyes.

Daniel shook his head. "This will not work. I am sorry. No *Englische* wedding. I cannot allow myself to be shunned again."

"Daniel!" Noah yelled again.

"We will discuss this more," Daniel said. "I must attend to my father's calling."

Martha nodded.

Daniel turned and ran to the house. Opening the kitchen door, he gave a quick look at Martha who had remained by the horses. Daniel heaved a heavy sigh, and stepped into the house.

# # #

"I will bring Martha home, Uncle Mark," Daniel said. "I will take my siblings home, then Hannah will ride with Martha and I to your place."

Mark Yoder considered the situation before he nodded approval.

"Thank you, Uncle Mark." Daniel helped Martha into the buggy. "We have much to discuss."

"Yes, I know," Uncle Mark said. "Think wisely on your choices." He smiled. "You are both still quite young. Do not be rash in your judgments."

Daniel frowned. *How much does Uncle Mark know?* he thought as he climbed into the buggy and grabbed the reins.

Martha intertwined her fingers with Daniel's free hand and leaned her head against his shoulder. They rode in silence listening to the younger children discuss the day's events.

"Everyone out," Daniel said when he pulled the reins to stop Beauty by the kitchen door. Hannah assisted getting them out of the buggy before getting back in.

Daniel snapped the reins and Beauty continued around the house and headed for Uncle Mark's place. They rode in silence.

"Are we going to talk, or not?" Martha asked.

"What?" Hannah asked.

Daniel turned to his younger sister. "You are the chaperon. What Martha and I are about to discuss, you need not concern yourself." In the dimming light of the evening, he smiled at Hannah. "Enjoy the ride."

Hannah sat back in the darkness of the buggy.

"What your father is asking..." Daniel heaved a sigh. "I cannot agree with. We do not have what he wishes in an Amish wedding." He paused. "As to the other option. No. I cannot."

Martha whimpered. "I fear we will not marry. My father is adamant."

"Perhaps I should discuss this matter with him," Daniel offered. "If I explain, maybe he will understand."

Martha shook her head. "He is bullheaded. My father has made his decision and he will not budge." Martha leaned back to gaze at him. "Do you not see? This is his way of controlling me. He is forcing me to decide between us and him." She turned away to watch the scenery pass as Beauty continued to trot on the way to Uncle Mark's place.

"I still do not understand this need to give you away by

him."

"Every *Englische* girl grows up dreaming about her wedding day. Every *Englische* father sees himself walking down the aisle with his daughter and offering her to the man she loves. To an *Englische* girl, her father has been the love of her life as she grows up. Then she meets a man she loves." Martha hesitated. "It is a ceremony to transfer the love of her father to the new husband. Do you understand?"

Daniel rolled a shoulder. "It is not how the Amish get married."

"But, Daniel..." She turned from him and stared at the road they traveled.

Silence.

"We are almost to Uncle Mark's place," Daniel said. "We have not solved the problem."

"Maybe if..." Hannah started.

"You are the chaperon. Be silent." Daniel's voice was curt.

"Let her speak, Daniel. Maybe she sees something we have missed."

"Fine." Daniel snapped the reins on Beauty, pulling the one to urge her to turn into the driveway at Uncle Mark's.

"Could you discuss this with Bishop Schmucker? Maybe the Amish wedding ceremony could be changed to include whatever it is Martha's father is wanting."

Martha snickered. "What does an Amish girl wear to her wedding?"

"Well, she wears–"

"Before you start," Martha said, cutting Hannah off. "My father wishes me to wear a fancy, white wedding dress, a veil, and holding a bouquet of roses and carnations. He wants to be in a tuxedo." Martha giggled. "Can you see that at an Amish wedding?"

Daniel shook his head at the image.

"I know the Amish do not want to stand out. At an *Englische* wedding, the bride is the center of attention. Plus, there is music..." Martha sighed. "Plus, Hannah, he wishes to have a big party after with over sixty *Englische* friends. He wants champagne." Martha shook her head. "*Englische*

153

weddings can be quite lavish and be the social event for the newspapers."

Hannah hung her head. "I am sorry," she whispered.

"Social event?" Daniel queried. "And the Amish will not know?" Daniel shook his head disgustedly. "A secret? I do not think so."

He pulled the reins on Beauty to stop her. The buggy was near the front porch. Aunt Mary stood in the window, watching.

Martha leaned close to Daniel. "I want to marry you, Daniel Yoder. What do we do?"

She turned and jumped from the buggy. Hannah moved to the front seat. Aunt Mary nodded approval and walked from the window. Uncle Mark met her at the front door and waved to Daniel.

"What are you and Martha going—" Hannah started to ask.

"We will not discuss this," Daniel snapped. "Am I understood?"

"Yes," Hannah whispered.

They rode home in silence.

Friday, December 13, 1963, 4 p.m.

Daniel was alone. He sat at his desk, grading papers. Miss Mueller had gone home, as well as all the children. Mary was going to take the buggy with the children, but Miss Mueller offered to take his siblings home.

He stared out the window, watching Beauty munch on hay given to her before the students left. There was a chill in the air. He glanced at the pot-bellied stove. Embers glowed. The fire was dying. He considered another log when he noticed Beauty rear up, startled.

Daniel frowned. The front door opened.

"I was told I'd find you here," Martha said, silhouetted against the bright, reflecting snow.

"I am glad to see you, Martha. Come in." Daniel moved toward her.

"No, I'll not be staying long." She closed the door, then defiantly folded her arms before her. "I attempted to reason with my father about his demand." She sniffed.

She is crying, he thought and once more moved toward her.

"I said stay there." She held up her hand to stop him. "I love you, Daniel Yoder. You know that. I know you love me. We wish to marry."

Daniel cocked his head in question. "That is true."

"I fought with my father." Once more she sniffed then reached up to wipe away a tear. "If you truly loved me..." She paused. "And, as my father said, you respected him..." She turned her head and gazed down. Her head snapped up. "If that were true, you would agree to his terms."

Daniel frowned.

"I love you, Martha Noble. I love you with all my heart. There is none other I wish to marry, but you." He sighed. "But, I am Amish. I cannot be married in an *Englische* ceremony. If–"

"If you loved me, you would, no matter the consequences. Shunned?" Martha threw her hands into the air, exasperated. "What is it with you Amish and shunning? Can you not make a mistake, ask forgiveness, and move on?"

"I do not believe you are ready to embrace the Amish, Martha." It was his turn to fold arms defiantly across the chest. "It is not a game. It is a life choice. We live by the Ordnung." He paused. "Consider this. In New York City, the light turns red and the cars stop. Is this not correct?"

Martha nodded.

"What happens when a car does not abide by that rule?" he raised an eyebrow.

"Worst case?" Martha rolled a shoulder. "There would be an accident."

"Worst case," Daniel repeated. "Somebody could die. Best case, a ticket is given. We live by the Ordnung; the whole community agrees to the rules. If I break the rule, marry you in an *Englische* ceremony..." He grinned. "I would not die, but I have broken the rule. I must learn my lesson; I am given a ticket. Hence, the shunning and my need to atone for my

155

mistake."

Martha grimaced. "I think some of your rules are silly."

Daniel moved forward and took her hands into his. "I think you need to learn the Amish way. Not play Amish, but embrace the Amish." He gazed beyond her, outside where her car was parked. He gazed at her clothes. Amish. "You drove here in your car. You want to be Amish, but still, you slide back to the convenience of your *Englische* lifestyle." He released her hands. "Until you are truly, fully Amish, I do not believe we can marry."

A tear welled in Martha's eye. "As you wish," she whispered. "I love you." She stood on tiptoe and kissed him on the cheek.

Turning, she ran from the school and down the few steps and to her car. She opened the door, gazed up at the school where Daniel stood in the doorway. She heaved a sigh. "I guess we..." She shook her head. "I won't be back, Daniel Yoder. Goodbye."

Martha got in the car and drove away. Daniel watched until he could no longer see the vehicle. Sighing, he turned, closed the school door and sloughed his way back to his desk. He glanced at the waning embers in the stove, shrugged, and continued to the desk.

He picked up the paper he had been grading and held it between his hands.

Martha is gone, he thought. *Gone. I am Amish. I. AM. AMISH.*

"I am Amish," he yelled in anger, his voice lifting to the ceiling of the school. His hands pulled the paper taunt, Elizabeth's math quiz tore in the process.

CHAPTER EIGHTEEN: Life Goes On

Friday, January 17, 1964, 4 p.m.

Daniel watched the snow float down, swirling every so often when the wind blew. He stood and walked to the window. Beauty waited, munching on her treat.

The snow is increasing, he thought. He could no longer see the footprints of the children when they left. Only a slight rut marked where the different buggies had headed out.

An ember snapped in the pot-bellied stove. Daniel turned, grabbed a small log and headed to the stove.

I will be here for a little longer, a little more heat would be nice, he thought and opened the door of the stove and tossed the log onto the remaining embers of the fire. He turned to the desk. *Best be about the grading*, he thought. He whistled and shuffled the papers on his desk.

He stopped whistling.

That was 'Wherever Ye Walk,' he thought. *I have not thought of it for quite some time.*

Memories of high school, Miss Bronson, and New York City flooded him.

Martha. The image flared in his memory.

He held the pencil in his hand, ready to circle a misspelling.

The door opened. A burst of snow-ridden wind blew into the room.

Daniel looked up, hoping to see her.

"Miss Mueller," Daniel gasped. "What brings you back here?"

"It is Ruby, Daniel." She closed the door and stomped her feet to remove the stuck snow. "The snow is getting deeper." She moved into the room toward him. "We need to talk."

157

"Is there a problem in class?" Daniel asked.

"Nay, Daniel." She moved a chair to the desk and sat. "The problem is you."

"Me?"

"I have not seen Martha of late. Is there a problem?"

Daniel shrugged. Ruby glared at him.

"Fine," she said. "If you do not want to discuss it, so be it." She sighed and grimaced. "But, if you continue like this, I will be forced to inform the elders." She placed her hands on the desk. "Daniel. You have not been yourself for almost a month." She pursed her lips. "I heard your sister, Mary, whisper to Rachel about you and Martha. She said you two were not going to marry."

Daniel raised his eyebrows. "My sister said this?"

"Aye, Daniel. I am not the only one to notice the change."

Daniel shrugged. "Martha and I do not agree on some things. I think she is trying to be Amish and *Englische* at the same time. It will not work. I told her she has to embrace the Amish, or return to the *Englische*."

"Daniel Yoder!" Ruby's loud voice echoed. "If this is your one true love..."

"I love Martha," Daniel said. "That is the problem."

Ruby reached out and grabbed Daniel's hands.

"May I give you some advice?" She blinked and inhaled. "I once had a friend. We were to marry. He was *Englische*."

Daniel turned to face her, surprise on his face.

"You are not the first person to date an *Englische*, Daniel. You will not be the last. Still, I loved him, but I could not give up my Amish ways. He tried to become Amish, but, in the end, he could not do it. He wanted to be an architect, not a farmer." A tear welled in Ruby's eye. "I thought he would come back. He never did." She let go of Daniel's hands and spread her arms out. "Now? Here I am, an old spinster. I loved Harold. There was no other." Again, she sighed. "Yes, there were others over the years. Mostly Amish." Ruby gazed out the window, seeing something Daniel couldn't. "I have only loved Harold." She turned back to Daniel. "I still do. I saw him a while back. We were at the grocery. He didn't recognize me, but I recognized him. He married and has a family. And, yes, he is an architect."

"Martha wants to be Amish," Daniel whispered. "She... she has issues with her father."

Ruby grabbed his hands. "If you love her, Daniel, do not let her escape."

Daniel reared back in his chair, pulling his hands from Ruby.

"I am Amish," he said. "I could not be *Englische*. I... I..."

"You must make that decision, Daniel. Talk with Martha. Leaving the Amish now that you have been baptized is a major step–"

"I said I am Amish," Daniel cut her off.

"And you love an *Englische* girl. Daniel, do what is needed."

"I will not leave the Amish," Daniel insisted. "There are other Amish girls who would be happy to marry the schoolmaster."

"But, Daniel. Will you be happy in your heart. Be honest with your decision." Ruby stood. "I have had my say. I will leave you to your thoughts." Ruby headed for the door, but turned when she reached the stove. "Do not tarry in your decision. I did and that was my mistake."

"I am Amish, Miss Mueller," Daniel stated.

"I am not telling you to become *Englische*, Daniel. I am telling you to step away from your Amish bullheadedness and create the life you want." Ruby stretched out her arms with palms up. "Or else you will be like me when you are old."

Again, Ruby turned to the door and disappeared.

Daniel sat at the desk, hands stretched out before him. Slowly the fingers interlocked and he started his prayer.

Heavenly Father. I beseech You in guidance. Do I leave the life I know to be with the one I love? Do I break the Ordnung to marry Martha? Guide my feet. Amen.

Daniel picked up the papers he'd been grading.

I will do this tonight and over the weekend, he thought. He gazed out at Beauty. *She should be in a nice barn, not standing in the snow.*

Just then Beauty shook her mane to dislodge the snow. Daniel smiled.

#

Daniel bedded Beauty down in the barn then headed for the house, school work under his arm. His mother and Hannah were working in the kitchen where the other siblings studied and finished their homework.

"Daniel," Rebecca said, wiping her hands on a dishcloth. "I did not expect you home so early."

"Daniel!" his father called from the main room.

Rebecca motioned for Daniel to attend to his father.

"Yes, Papa," Daniel said stepping into the main room.

"Sit," Noah said and pointed to the chair next to him. "We need to talk."

Daniel walked across the room and joined his father. *I wonder what he wishes to discuss,* Daniel thought.

Noah folded the newspaper and set it aside, motioning for Daniel to sit beside him.

"Daniel," he started. "Is it my imagination, or have I not seen Martha here of late? Is she ill?"

"No, Papa," Daniel said. "Martha is fine." He paused. "We had a... a... I guess you would call it a fight. She is not talking to me."

"Uh-huh. Whose fault?"

Daniel hesitated, considering the best answer.

"I would say it is her father," Daniel replied. "He has made certain demands of Martha for us to marry."

"Marry? My son is considering marriage? Why have I not heard of this?"

"We are only talking, Papa." Daniel squirmed in the chair. "We were considering a spring wedding, but her father has issues with–"

"You being Amish? I have met Mr. Noble." Noah nodded, staring at the wall opposite them. "He has always felt the Amish were unacceptable. Yes, he married an Amish girl, but he felt he was saving her from a life worse than death."

"He does not want Martha to become Amish."

Noah smiled, a small grunt of mirth escaping. "Of that, I am sure, Daniel." He slapped Daniel on the knee. "So, my son,

160

what are going to do? It is obvious you love Martha and she loves you. What is the problem?"

Daniel felt his mouth dry. *How much do I tell my father?* he thought. Be honest, came the answer.

"Mr. Noble wishes to walk down the aisle and give his daughter away." Daniel winced. "I think it is part of the *Englische* ceremony."

"It is," Noah replied. "I attended an *Englische* wedding."

Daniel turned to gaze at his father. This was the first time he had heard his father state he had attended an *Englische* wedding, although, as Daniel considered it, it seemed right.

"Marta wants to become Amish, but she continues to slip back to her *Englische* ways," Daniel added.

Noah nodded.

"Did Martha explain to her father that an Amish wedding is different than an *Englische* one and the father does not give away the bride?"

Again, Daniel squirmed in his chair.

"She said she did, but he is demanding he do this or there will be no wedding. Something about it being his right."

Noah reached over and grabbed the newspaper.

"So, my son, what are you going to do?"

Daniel stared at his father in disbelief. "Papa! I am Amish. I cannot allow myself to marry in an *Englische* ceremony. Martha and I want to be married as Amish."

Noah shrugged. "Perhaps I have missed something. She is *Englische*. You are Amish. To be married Amish, both must be Amish. To be married in an *Englische* ceremony, you can be *Englische* or Amish."

"If I marred *Englische*, I would be shunned," Daniel whispered.

"Yes." He paused. "But, do you love Martha?"

Noah snapped open the newspaper and read, ignoring the young man beside him.

Daniel stood, tightening his hands into fists. "I. AM. AMISH," he mumbled and left the room.

CHAPTER NINETEEN: Wedding Plans

Saturday, January 18, 1964, 10 a.m.

Daniel waited by the kitchen window, watching for Ben Hopkins to arrive. He smiled as the station wagon pulled into the driveway.

"I hope to be back by tomorrow night, Mama," he said as he put his coat and hat on. He rolled a shoulder. "Of course, I might be back yet today."

"Good luck, Daniel," Rebecca said and kissed him on the cheek. "Tell Martha hello for me."

"Yes, Mama," Daniel replied and rushed out the door to the waiting car.

"So, you want to go to Shipshewana. Is that correct?" Ben shook hands and smiled at Daniel.

"Yes, Ben. I thank you for the ride." He hesitated. "I must see Martha and discuss our marriage." Daniel winced. "Of course, that is if she still wants to marry me."

Ben slapped Daniel on the shoulder. "Why wouldn't she want to marry a good looking, young man like you?"

Daniel shrugged. "I am hoping she is at her Uncle Paul's house," Daniel said. "Do you know how to get to it?"

"Yes, Daniel. I know where he lives. It will take not quite two hours to get to Shipshewana. Do you wish to listen to the radio or would you prefer to talk?"

"This is your car, Ben. Do you wish to listen to the radio?"

"CKLW it is then," Ben said and turned the radio knob on. A little static and then music. 'Anyone Who Had A Heart' by Dionne Warwick flooded the car.

"She has a nice voice," Daniel said.

Ben nodded.

"And now, the number two song this week. 'Louie, Louie' by The Kingsmen."

Daniel frowned as the words came from the speakers.

"Not your cup of tea, Daniel? I could find a different station." Ben leaned over and turned the knob to off. "Or we could just talk."

Daniel nodded.

"How is Martha?" Ben asked.

"I do not know," Daniel replied and stared at his shoes. "I have not seen her since before Christmas."

Ben raised an eyebrow. "Oh?"

Daniel grimaced. "We had a fight."

"Really?"

"Martha's father wishes to walk her down the aisle at the wedding." Daniel gazed at Ben who nodded. "Amish do not do that." Again, Ben nodded. "Her father suggested we get married in an *Englische* church."

Ben turned to face Daniel while keeping one eye on the highway. "And?" he said.

"I am Amish, Ben. You know I have been baptized." Daniel sighed. "I cannot be married in an *Englische* ceremony. I have been shunned once, I do not wish to be shunned again." Daniel bit on the inner side of his lower lip. "I am the schoolmaster. I must set an example."

"You have strong shoulders, Daniel," Ben said. "But, you can't hold all the problems of the world on them alone."

Daniel shrugged.

"Do you love Martha?" Ben asked.

Daniel glared at Ben. "Of course I do. You, of all people, should know that."

Ben grinned and nodded. "Do you wish to marry her?"

Daniel nodded. "Yes," he mumbled.

"Then marry Martha," Ben stated. "Be a man. Take the bull by the horn. If need be, run off and get married."

"We are only seventeen," Daniel said. "We need our parents' approval." He paused. "At least, her parent's approval. We cannot be married by Bishop Schmucker since she is not Amish."

"There are courthouses, Daniel. A judge can marry you."

"It is something to consider, Ben." Daniel folded his hands together on his lap, and closed his eyes in silent prayer.

Guide my feet. Give me the wisdom to make the correct decision. Amen.

"We are coming to Shipshewana," Ben said. "If I remember correctly, to go to Uncle Paul's place, it is a right at the center of town, two miles, a left and north about a half-mile. The house should be on the right side." He glanced at Daniel. "Correct?"

Daniel nodded. "I hope Martha is there. Otherwise, we will need to go into town to her parent's home."

#

Ben pulled into the driveway. Daniel got out and approached the front door.

"Daniel Yoder," Mary Hershberger said as she stepped onto the front porch. "Is that truly you?"

"Yes," Daniel replied. "Is Martha here?"

"She is," Mary said. "She is in the barn with the younger ones. They are hunting stray eggs in the hayloft. Come in." She stretched to get Ben's attention. "Oh, go and get that man in the car. He shouldn't sit out here in the cold."

"*danke*," Daniel replied and hustled to get Ben from the car.

"Please come in and wait with me. I do not know if she will talk to me. If not, I will be ready to go back home."

"No problem, Daniel." Ben got out of the car and followed him into the house.

#

"Daniel!" Martha came running into the house. "What a surprise."

Daniel stood and grabbed her hands in his.

"It is good to see you, Martha," Daniel said. He gazed down at his shoes. "I came to... I..."

Martha hugged him. "It does not matter, Daniel. You are here."

"My last words to you were harsh," Daniel muttered. "Forgive me."

"You were right, Daniel." She flounced onto a bench, motioning Daniel to join her. "I was playing Amish. I gave my car back to my father, rode my bicycle out here, and have embraced the Amish lifestyle completely."

Mary entered the room with cups of coffee. "I brought warm beverages."

Ben stood. "Would it be okay if I had my coffee in the kitchen?" He nodded toward Daniel and Martha. "I believe they would like to talk and they don't need an old man like me listening."

"Certainly," Mary said and led Ben from the main room to the kitchen.

"Do you still love me, Martha?" Daniel asked.

"Yes, you silly goof," she replied. "I told you that when I left." She hesitated. "I had to do some very deep soul searching. It was then I realized you were right. I was playing Amish. Uncle Paul made me realize it and so did my father. But, it took you to point it out."

"I am sorry I was so harsh," Daniel said.

"Nay, my love. I left my father and all my *Englische* belongings at my parent's home. I have lived with Uncle Paul since I left you. I am thinking of discussing my conversion to Amish and being baptized."

"What of your father's wishes? An *Englische* wedding?"

"Amish do not walk down the aisle in a white dress," Martha said and giggled.

"But, your father will not allow you to marry unless–"

She placed her fingers to Daniel's lips. "Hush. We will cross that bridge when we arrive there."

"I will marry you in an *Englische* ceremony," Daniel blurted.

"You what?"

"If you wish, we can get married in an *Englische* church to appease your father."

"But, you will be shunned," she said, her eyes wide in

165

surprise.

"If you love someone, you will do what is necessary." He smiled. "Plus, you said it could be a small, discreet wedding. Perhaps my Ordnung will not learn of it."

Martha flung her arms around Daniel and kissed him.

Daniel quickly removed her arms. "We are not married, yet. We are still courting." He grinned. "This familiarity is not allowed."

"Shh," Martha whispered and grabbed his hands to kiss them. "I will tell my father. Nay, we will tell my father tomorrow." She gazed at him, her eyes alight. "You will stay the night?"

"If your Uncle Paul will allow it," Daniel replied. He stood and stepped to the kitchen. "May I stay the night so I can talk with Marth's father this afternoon?" He glanced at Ben. "I am sure you wish to go home."

"No bundling," Mary said with a grin. "You may sleep in Micah's bed and he will double with his brother, Aaron."

"*danke*," Daniel said then turned to Ben. "I will be staying. Can you pick me up tomorrow?"

"What time would you like me to be here, Daniel?" Ben asked.

"If you arrive a little before five, you may join us for an evening meal," Mary said. "That way, the two of you can travel back to Centertown with full stomachs."

"Thank you, Mrs. Hershberger," Ben said. "I will see you all tomorrow. Pick you up here, Daniel?"

Mary smiled, Daniel nodded, and Ben departed.

"We had better go talk to my parents," Martha said. "We can ride bicycles into town."

Daniel nodded.

"We will be back later tonight, Aunt Mary." She paused. "We will probably eat supper with my parents."

Aunt Mary nodded. "See you later, Martha." She grinned. "You, too, Daniel."

#

Saturday, December 14, 1964, 2:30 p.m.

166

Daniel and Martha rode their bicycles into the Noble residence yard. She motioned and Daniel followed.

"We can put them here," she said putting her bike by the garage wall. "C'mon. Let's go inside." She rushed to the side door.

Daniel followed, removing his hat as he entered the house. He checked the wall by the door. There was nowhere to hang his hat. He held it and followed her up the steps and into the kitchen.

"Daddy?" Martha hollered. "Are you home?"

"Is that you, Martha?" her mother answered. "It is so good to see you, again." Emma turned the corner into the kitchen and immediately spotted Daniel. She frowned and faltered in her footsteps. "Your father went to the store. He should be back any minute." She hugged Martha. "May I ask the reason of you coming?" She pursed her lips, all the while watching Daniel.

"We wish to get married." Martha wrapped her arm within Daniel's. "We agree to Daddy's wishes."

Emma smiled. "Well, have you set a date?"

"This spring," Martha replied.

"Oh, my," Emma exclaimed. "That doesn't give us much time." She paused. "It will be an *Englische* wedding? Correct?"

Daniel nodded. "A small one."

Emma nodded. "Yes, just a few family and friends."

"Family? You mean your brother and sister will be included?"

"Of course." Emma's eyes widened in surprise. "And, of course, your parents and siblings would be included."

"Who left bikes out by the garage?" Dan Noble stumbled into the house. "I nearly killed myself coming out the garage side door."

"I'm sorry, Daddy," Martha said. "I told Daniel to put his behind mine."

Dan stopped at the top of the steps to the kitchen and stared at the three standing before.

"Why are you here?" Dan demanded. "You stormed out of here last month and we've not heard from you. Your last

167

words were 'I becoming a proper Amish woman,' slammed the door, and left on your bike."

"We agree to your terms of the marriage, Daddy," Martha said. "You can walk me down the aisle and give my hand to Daniel."

Dan raised an eyebrow. "Oh, I can? And when will this happen?"

"This spring, dear," Emma interjected.

Dan leaned against the doorway for support. "This spring, eh?"

Martha walked over to him and put her arms around his neck. "Yes, Daddy. You said we could get married, but demanded you be allowed to walk me down the aisle. Daniel has agreed to an *Englische* wedding."

"Yes, dear," Emma said. "We were just discussing the guest list. They want a small wedding." She raised her eyebrows. "I wanted to invite family and friends. Seems there might be a snag on the family attendees."

Dan furrowed his eyebrows. "Snag?"

"Remember, dear, I was Amish." Emma walked over to Dan and put her arm around him. "Let's all go into the living room and discuss this."

Dan gave her a questioning frown as she escorted him through the kitchen. Emma winked at Daniel as they passed.

"Everyone have a seat," Emma said, taking command of the situation while gracefully adjusting into the plush chair. "As I said, having been raised Amish, I think I understand where Daniel has issues. He has been baptized into the community."

Daniel nodded agreement as Martha sat beside him.

"As such, for him to be married in an *Englische* ceremony..." She paused. "He is allowing himself to the possibility of being shunned by the community."

Again, Daniel nodded. Martha squeezed his hand.

"Well, I don't give a damn about him being shunned." He glared at Daniel. "I made my demands, knowing this. I figured he would back out and Martha would come to her senses." He stood from his BarcaLounger and paced the room. "I never considered he would agree to the terms."

"Daddy!" Martha glared at her father.

"I love your daughter, sir," Daniel said. "If it means I am shunned to marry her... then so be it. I realize while shunned, I will not be able to teach or be recognized by my family or those of the community." Daniel gazed at Martha. "This is how much I love your daughter."

"You love my daughter, but yet you wish to marry her in secret. Is that correct?" Dan towered before Daniel.

Daniel stood, forcing Dan to step back.

"My idea was to marry your daughter on a weekend in an *Englische* church." Daniel looked Dan in the eye. "On the following Thursday, Martha and I would be married in an Amish ceremony."

A curl twisted the edge of Dan's lips into an ugly smile. "I see. You planned to squeeze through and hoped none would know." Dan thumped Daniel on the chest with his index finger. "Is this correct?" He shook his head. "A marriage of deceit by my future son-in-law." Dan grunted. "A great way to start a life together... on lies."

"Dan," Emma said. "You agreed to them marrying on a condition. They are agreeing to your condition." She grunted. "I'd call it a demand. I say let them marry."

"If I am paying for a wedding, I want more than five people in the church," Dan said.

"Five?" Martha questioned.

"You two, your mother and me, and, of course, the minister." He made a face.

"Maybe we could invite Beth, her husband, and even Alex... if we can find him," Martha suggested. She rolled a shoulder. "You could invite your coworkers. Some neighbors?"

Dan shook his head. "There is no way Bethany is coming back from Canada any time soon, and especially that loser of a husband. Forget Alex. I got a letter from him last week. He is in California, living in a commune somewhere, and spends a lot of his time at the San Francisco airport selling stuff."

"Wait a minute," Emma said. "Daniel, you said the two of you would be married the following Thursday? How? Martha must be Amish to marry in an Amish wedding."

Martha got a sheepish look on her face. "I am working

with Bishop Beiler, learning the proper ways of the Amish so I can be baptized the Sunday before we get married." She smiled. "I will be *Englische* at the first wedding, baptized the next day, and be Amish for the Thursday wedding."

"Seems you have it all planned," Dan said. "So, who will be your best man, Daniel. And, the other groomsmen?" Dan looked at Martha. "How many bridesmaids do you expect to have? Oh, and your maid of honor?"

"The what?" Daniel asked.

"We will discuss that later, Daniel." Martha glared at her father. "You're being mean, Daddy."

"Just trying to make sure you have all the bases covered, darling." He offered a Cheshire smile to his daughter. "Remember, he is Amish."

"DANIEL WEBSTER NOBLE!" Emma yelled and scowled at him.

Daniel stiffened, but remained calm. It wasn't him.

# # #

Emma continued to glare at Dan. He rolled a shoulder then sat in his BarcaLounger.

"It is quite obvious the boy has no understanding of an *Englische* wedding," Dan mumbled.

"Then we will teach him," Emma snapped. She cocked her head while glaring at him. "No, I think YOU should teach him." She paused. "With Martha's help, of course." She smiled at her husband. "Remember, he will be your son-in-law."

Daniel watched. He didn't feel her smile was an honest one. Also, he was leery of Dan.

"Now, I think I'll go into the kitchen and figure out something to eat." She headed for the kitchen, stopping at the archway. "What do you like to eat, Daniel?"

"Whatever is set before me, Mrs. Noble," Daniel replied. "I do not wish to be a burden."

Dan grunted.

Emma cocked a raised eyebrow in Dan's direction. "Behave."

"I can help, Mother," Martha said and grinned at her

mother. "I have been learning a lot of cooking methods from Aunt Mary."

"On a cold, wintry day like today..." She furrowed her brow. "Ah, yes, I think vegetable soup would be an excellent choice." She grinned. "I'll make it with hamburger, some potatoes, carrots, peas, celery, and whatever else I find in the kitchen."

"I will peel the potatoes," Martha offered.

Emma gazed at her daughter. "I think it prudent you stay here and assist in teaching Daniel about an *Englische* wedding." She winked at Martha.

"Yes, Mother," Martha said, realizing it would be a wise choice. She sat beside Daniel on the couch.

"A best man–" Dan started.

"He is your best *Englische* friend who will stand beside you at the front of the church," Martha said, finishing her father's sentence. "You do have an *Englische* friend. Yes?"

Daniel nodded. "His name is Jason Muirs."

"Jason Muirs?" She frowned in thought. "Oh, I remember him. He would make an excellent best man."

"Well," Dan said. "Seems we have the awkward part taken care of. Now, about your dress. The reception. The food." He glared at Daniel. "And, of course, the invitees." He grinned. "No, I haven't forgotten that. So, who do we invite?"

Martha grabbed Daniel's hand and squeezed it. "We will send an invitation to Alexander and Bethany. Whether they come or not will be their decision."

"I can open it to the people in the office," Dan added, and again stared at Daniel. "Since it seems there won't be that many attending from the groom's side." He paused. "Or the bride's mother's side."

Martha scowled at her father. "Again, you're being mean, Daddy. We have your side of the family to invite. That would be Uncle Bob and Aunt Susan, Uncle Jeff and Aunt Barb." She frowned. "If I remember correctly two of Uncle Bob's children are married and three of Uncle Jeff's are married." She smiled. "And they have children."

Dan rolled a shoulder. "You've upped the attendance list by less than twenty. With maybe another dozen from the office." He shook his head. "Yeah, a whopping maybe three dozen people."

"I'm not looking for a large wedding, Daddy." She smiled at Daniel, her eyes beaming with joy. "I just want to marry the man I love."

Emma ambled into the room and sat in her favorite chair. "The soup is cooking. It should be ready within the hour." She gazed at the group. "So, what are we talking about?"

Dan grimaced and nodded to his daughter. "Ask Martha."

"The attendees." Martha shrugged. "Daddy is upset that none of Daniel's family, or even your side of the family, won't be at the wedding."

Emma leaned forward in the chair, placing her hands on her knees. "Dan, you have to understand exactly how important it is to Daniel that the Ordnung does not find out about this Englische wedding."

Dan raised his eyebrows and shrugged. "Not my problem."

"If they find out, it most definitely will be your problem," Emma said in a stern voice. "Do you have any idea what that will do to our daughter? If Daniel is shunned–"

"Then maybe she shouldn't marry Daniel." Dan stood up from his BarcaLounger. "I'm not all that hungry." He strode across the living room. "I think I need to take a little walk around the neighborhood." He waved his hand in the air. "You know – to clear my head."

"DANIEL WEBSTER NOBEL!" Emma jumped to her feet.

Martha shook her head. This was the second time her mother had used her father's full name. She was mad.

"You will do no such thing." Emma waggled a warning index finger at her husband. "It is cold out there, plus, we need to discuss this wedding before they leave." She turned to Martha. "Or, you could stay here tonight." She glanced up at the ceiling. "In your old room." Emma turned to Daniel. "And you could stay in Alexander's old room."

"I'm sorry, Mother, but I told Aunt Mary we would be home shortly after the evening meal."

"Well, we can phone..." She paused, then giggled. "I

guess I won't be doing that."

Emma stared at Dan. "Since he doesn't seem to want to be involved..." She pursed her lips. "How about we go to the kitchen table to discuss this more. Daniel, you come with us, if for no other reason than for your protection." She turned Dan. "If you want, and can be civil, you can join us, too." She strutted from the room.

Martha stood, still holding Daniel's hand. "Come. We will go to the kitchen." She pulled him along the way.

Dan sighed and shuffled behind.

"It's too cold and dark for you two to ride bikes back to Uncle Paul's," Dan said. "You really should stay the night." He opened the kitchen door to the garage. "Look. It's even snowing."

Martha stared out the door. "But, I told Aunt Mary we would be back tonight."

Dan sighed. "Fine. I'll stick the bikes into the back of the car." He frowned. "Somehow. And I'll drive you back to Paul's house."

"Thank you, Mr. Noble," Daniel said. "Church starts early tomorrow morning."

Dan cast a wary gaze in Daniel's direction. "Right, the church," he mumbled. "I'll need to discuss things with Elder Hawkins at the United Methodist Church." He held the door open. "Guess we'd best get a move on. You two said you'd like a May wedding. Is that correct?"

"Yes, Daddy," Martha said and she swept past him to the garage to retrieve her bike.

Daniel followed.

"Fine," Dan said, opening the car's trunk. "A spring wedding in May it is."

CHAPTER TWENTY: Life Goes On

Sunday, January 19, 1964, about 6 p.m.

"Ben, can I ask you for a favor?" Daniel stared at the countryside as they drove back to Centertown.

"Sure, Daniel. Anything."

"You still drive the bus. Right?"

"Yup," Ben said.

"Do you see my friend, Jason Muirs? I do not believe you still drive my route."

"Actually, I still drive the old route." He smiled at Daniel. "I go by your house every day. Sort of strange not to stop, but to answer your question. Yes, I see Jason. Why?"

"Could you ask him to visit me? I have a question to ask him." Daniel squirmed in the seat, unsure how much to tell Ben.

"I'll let him know when he gets on the bus tomorrow morning. That soon enough?"

"Thank you, Ben," Daniel replied and once more was silent.

They rode in silence. As they drove through LaGrange, Ben kept an eye on his silent rider.

"Is there something bothering you, Daniel? Ben finally asked. "What I mean, is everything good between you and Martha? Is there a problem you'd like to discuss?" He paused. "I'm not trying to pry, but your silence is unusual, and I could see there was a strained air at the table as if you were afraid a secret would be discovered."

"There is a secret, Ben." Daniel turned slightly to face his driver. "I will be needing to come to Shipshewana to see Martha more." He hesitated. "There are other things, but..."

"But what, Daniel?" Ben reached over and placed a hand

on Daniel's shoulder. "You, of all people, know I would never divulge a secret."

"Martha and I are getting married," Daniel blurted.

Ben snickered. "Yes, I know that."

"No, Ben, what you don't know is it will be an *Englische* wedding."

Ben took his foot off the gas pedal and the car coasted. "What?"

"I have agreed to an *Englische* wedding to appease Martha's father. Then Martha will be baptized and we will have an Amish wedding."

Ben pulled into an open area at a small gas station along the highway.

"Won't you be shunned when the Amish discover what you have done?" He turned to face Daniel. "I remember you were shunned not too long ago. You're the teacher. What would the students do?"

"We hope the Amish do not learn of it," Daniel whispered. "We hope to marry on a Saturday in May, have Martha baptized by the next week, and our wedding the following Thursday after her baptism." Daniel heaved a sigh. "We hope the Amish would not have enough time to learn of the *Englische* wedding, if at all."

"That is pretty thin ice you're skating on, Daniel." Ben turned to face Daniel as he spoke. "I'm not Amish, but I know news travels fast and..." He shrugged. "That news would travel even faster. How do you plan to keep it a secret?"

"Well, none of Martha's Amish relatives, nor any of mine, will be invited to the *Englische* wedding. I will have Jason be my best man." Daniel smiled. "Plus, you'd be there since I hope you will drive me over on the wedding day. It would be her parents, her siblings – Beth and Alex, if they come home, some of her father's relations, and some of his coworkers."

Ben nodded his head. "Just the *Englische*?"

Daniel nodded. "Yes," he mumbled.

"What will you do, I mean, once Martha is baptized and the Amish discover you were married in an *Englische* ceremony?"

Daniel stared down at his shoes. "I am not sure. I hope we

can beg forgiveness and not be shunned."

"I will not say a word, Daniel. My lips are sealed." He smiled at the young boy. "May I bring my wife to the wedding?"

"Of course." Daniel's eyes lit up. "It would be nice. I figure Jason might bring a girlfriend, if he has one then."

Ben slapped Daniel on the knee. "Okie-dokie, then. Let's get you home." He pulled from the gas station onto U.S. 20. "Angola and Centertown, here we come."

# # #

Thursday, January 23, 1964. About 4 p.m.

"Excuse me?"

The deep, husky voice startled Daniel as he sat the desk grading papers.

"I'm looking for the young schoolmaster. A Daniel Yoder?"

Daniel looked up to see a dark figure standing at the door to the schoolroom.

"I am the schoolmaster," Daniel said, laying his grading pencil aside. "Come in and close the door."

"Well, aren't you the hoity-toity one?" Jason closed the door and strode out of the shadows into the classroom. "Nice digs, buddy."

"Jason!" Daniel jumped to his feet and rushed toward the newcomer.

"I was told you wanted to speak with me?" He offered his hand to shake. "Ben said it was very important."

Daniel grabbed the proffered hand and pumped it excitedly.

"I am getting married," Daniel gushed while stretching an arm about Jason's shoulders and moving him toward the front desk.

"So I've heard." He gave a small shrug. "Molly was whispering about it to Patty. Of course, Molly thinks the idea of you getting married is ridiculous. She said you're too young."

Daniel grinned. "I am Amish, Jason. Some get married when they are only sixteen."

"But, you're only seventeen, Daniel."

"I will be eighteen this year," Daniel rebutted. "I have been baptized and am a member of the community. Martha and I want to get married as soon as possible."

"This is the girl you met in New York City, right?"

Daniel nodded.

"So, why is that so important you would have Ben tell me to come see you?"

Daniel sat behind his desk, folded his hands together and waited until Jason took the chair opposite the desk.

"I want you to be my best man, Jason."

"You what?" Jason frowned at the prospect. "How? I'm not Amish."

"We will be having..." Daniel stopped. "This is a secret, Jason. You cannot tell anyone. Understood?"

Jason nodded slowly. "Promise," he said.

"Martha and I will get married in an *Englische* ceremony in Shipshewana. Her parents are *Englische* and her father is demanding to walk her down the aisle."

Jason frowned. "Uh..."

"Yes, if the Amish find out, I will be shunned. Martha and I believe we have it figured out. She is becoming Amish. We will get married as her father wishes, then she will be baptized, and, if all goes well, we will have an Amish wedding the following Thursday after her baptism." Daniel grimaced and rolled a shoulder. "In all, about a week and a half between the two weddings. One *Englische*. One Amish." He sighed. "It will be a busy May."

"Daniel, you do realize all weddings hit the newspapers. Right?"

Daniel frowned.

"Of course," Jason continued. "This will be in Shipshewana. At least your family won't know about it."

Daniel shook his head. "Martha's mother was Amish. All her siblings are still Amish." He grimaced in thought. "I know her Uncle Paul reads The Budget. I do not know if there is a local newspaper in Shipshewana." He rolled a shoulder. "But, there probably is one."

Jason cocked an eye in Daniel's direction.

"Yes, I know. News travels very fast by word of mouth." Daniel sighed. "I can only hope this works."

"So, buddy, about the best man thing. Do I need to rent a tux?"

Daniel's eyes widened. "I do not know. I will ask."

Jason stood and stretched out his hand to Daniel. "Okay, buddy. I'm your best man and got your back. Let's get you married." He paused. "Do I get invited to the Amish wedding?"

"It is a Thursday, Jason. Do you not have school that day?"

Jason's shoulders slumped. "Yeah." He grinned. "But, I'll skip that day." Jason snickered. "They shouldn't flunk me for that."

"I am going to Shipshewana this weekend. Do you wish to go along? You can help with the wedding plans."

"Sure. I can drive." Jason stood. "Uh, you do know how to get there?"

Daniel nodded. "Yes. Can you stay overnight?"

"Sure," Jason said. "This will be a total gas." He turned to head out of the classroom. "What time? About 9 a.m.?"

"That will be good, Jason. Thank you."

"See you Saturday, buddy." He walked through the classroom, glancing at the different desks. He stopped and turned to Daniel. "Do you enjoy being a teacher?"

Daniel smiled. "Yes."

"How many students?"

"I have thirty-six, but I have Miss Mueller to assist me. I do not do this all alone." He grinned and heaved a sigh. "Of course, getting here early during the winter to light the stove so it is warm..." He paused. "Let me say my siblings do not enjoy that." He grinned.

"I can't wait to tell Molly Pearson that I'll be in your wedding," Jason said as he grabbed the doorknob to open the door.

"You cannot tell her, Jason. This is a secret. You must not tell anyone." Daniel's eyes pleaded. "Please?"

Jason placed his hand to his lips and twisted it like he was locking a door. "Mums the word." He left.

# # #

Saturday, January 25, 1964, 11:45 a.m.

"It is good to meet you, Jason." Martha smiled at the young man standing beside Daniel.

"Anything to help a buddy out," Jason said. "I've never been–"

"To Shipshewana," Daniel added to cut Jason off. He watched as Aunt Mary maneuvered down the kitchen steps, being careful of the ice and snow.

Jason fumbled a few minutes. "Yes, to Shipshewana."

"This is my Aunt Mary," Martha said. "Her husband, my Uncle Paul, is my mother's older brother." She glanced about the farm. "He is out there somewhere – probably the barn."

"It is cold out here. Come inside," Aunt Mary said and turned to walk back up the steps.

"Since we hope to marry in May, Aunt Mary, I think we will go visit my parents." She smiled at the older woman. "In fact, I think it best so Jason doesn't get too scared of the Amish ways. We will stay overnight with my parents."

"Before you leave, will you come in and get warm? I have a nice lunch ready." Aunt Mary turned to Daniel. "Would you go fetch Uncle Paul?"

Daniel nodded. "Do you wish to come along, Jason?"

"Sure." Jason rubbed his hands together before lifting them to his mouth and blowing on them. "It really is cold today."

"Come," Daniel said and headed for the barn.

Jason followed.

"Sorry, man. I almost blew it." Jason whispered to Daniel as the hustled to the protection of the barn.

"It is fine," Daniel replied.

"What is fine?" Uncle Paul asked as he stepped from the barn. "Who is this?" He surveyed the *Englische* boy before him.

"This is my best friend... well, *Englische* friend. This is

179

Jason Muirs. We went to school together."

Jason stretched out a hand to shake.

Paul grabbed the hand in a hearty shake. "Glad to meet you, Jason Muirs." He turned to Daniel. "Now, what is fine?"

"We almost had an accident," Daniel said. He didn't want to lie and this was only stretching the truth a little. "Aunt Mary sent us to find you. Lunch is ready." He turned to head back to the house. "Let us hurry. It is cold out here."

The three hustled to the house where Daniel held the door open for Paul and Jason to enter.

"Close the door," Mary yelled. "The wind is gusting in and it will chill the food."

Daniel hustled in and closed the door.

Mary pointed to the far bench at the table. "You and Jason sit there."

Others were already at the table, waiting. They took the open spot near Paul.

"Let us give thanks," Paul said, closed his eyes and silence ensued.

Jason had visited Daniel many times and knew the way of a meal. Being Catholic, he made the sign of the cross and said his personal grace.

"Let us eat," Paul said and the food was passed around.

Everyone ate in silence.

Jason enjoyed the meal, cleaning his dish of the food he'd taken. "The meal was delicious." He looked directly at Mary. "Now, may I be excused?" He bowed his head. "Nature calls."

"To the left side of the barn, Jason," Paul said and shoved another large spoonful of potatoes into his mouth.

Jason left the table and made his way to the kitchen door and disappeared.

"I have dessert," Mary said. "Who wishes to have a slice of cherry pie?" She placed the pie on the table and soon only one slice remained.

Jason came back into the house.

"There is pie," Paul said. "If you like dessert."

"Thank you," Jason said and sat at the table.

He leaned to Daniel. "The water to wash my hands was almost ice cubes." He held them up for Daniel to see their

180

redness. "At least the pump worked."

Daniel grinned. "Eat and enjoy that slice of pie. It is yours," he whispered. "We will be leaving soon."

"Hi, Mother," Martha said. "Daniel and his best friend, Jason Muirs, came to see us and help plan more of the wedding."

"Oh, I'm so sorry, Martha," Emma said. "Your father really did try. He spoke with Elder Hawkins about a May wedding. There are no open dates in May. The best your father could do was April 4th."

"So soon?" Martha questioned. "I... I don't know if that will work. I won't be baptized until May."

"Your father booked the date since he didn't want to lose it." She glanced at Martha and Daniel. "We can get this all put together by then. I'm sure we can."

Martha sat beside her mother at the kitchen table. "I think you understand. We need to keep this Englische wedding a secret. If we get married in April, it will be over a month before we can get married after I get baptized. Do you see the problem?"

Emma grimaced. "We can only hope the secret is kept secret. I would love to have my side of the family at the wedding..." She gazed at Daniel. "But, I understand the situation. Shunning is no simple matter."

Martha grabbed both Daniel's hands. "Do we get married in April?" she asked.

"We must if we wish to marry in May," Daniel replied.

"About this *Englische* wedding," Jason started. "Do I need to rent a tux? Or can I just wear a dark suit?"

"You both will be in tuxes," Emma said. "If we're doing an *Englische* wedding, we're doing it up right." She grinned. "I don't believe your father has been in a tuxedo since our wedding day." She nodded while smiling. "This will prove interesting."

Martha gazed into Daniel's eyes. "It will be nice to see you in a tux." She giggled. "Do I need to take you tux shopping like I did in New York City?" She reached up and ruffled his hair which now appeared more bowl cut. "But, I won't force you to get a haircut."

Jason laughed. "Daniel cut his hair? He wore *Englische* clothes? I wished I'd seen that."

"It was my *Rumschpringe*, Jason." He frowned. "I did many *Englische* things while in New York City."

"But, you wouldn't perform nude for the musical you were to star in." Martha shook her head. "When they told me the costume you'd be wearing, I knew the Amish in you wouldn't allow it. I was amazed Peter even allowed you to wear jeans during rehearsal."

Daniel's face reddened. "Did you see the final costume? It was appalling. You left, but Preston had the costume changed. I still wouldn't wear it."

"That was one of the reasons I left, Daniel," Martha said. "That Mephistopheles costume was trash and an insult to good taste."

"A costume? You?" Jason grinned, his teeth glistening.

"That is the past," Emma said. "Daniel is now Amish. Shall we discuss the wedding? But, first, are you staying the night and what would you like for supper?"

"Whatever you want, Mother," Martha said. "We can stay the night – if that is okay with you and Daddy."

"Stay the night. No problem. You in your room." She turned to Jason and Daniel. "Are you two willing to share a full bed in Alexander's room?"

"We have shared a bed before at my house," Daniel said. "Is it okay with you, Jason?"

Jason nodded approval.

"Fine," Emma said. "How about pancakes and bacon for supper?"

"That sounds great to me," Jason said.

Daniel nodded in agreement.

"Pancakes and bacon it is," Martha said. "I will help make the pancakes."

"That's settled," Emma said. "Now, let's all sit at the kitchen table and discuss wedding plans.

\# \# \#

Sunday, January 26, 1964, 3 p.m.

Jason got in the car. Daniel stood with Martha on the other side of the car.

"Go ahead. Kiss her," Jason ribbed. "Then we can go." He laughed.

"I will see you soon," Daniel said and hugged her. Snuggling into her neck, he caressed the soft skin so none would see. The cold wind blew and she shivered. "I love you," Daniel whispered.

"I love you, too," Martha replied.

Daniel got in the car and waved as Jason drove out the driveway of Paul's house.

"What shall we discuss on the way home?" Jason asked.

"What would you like to?"

"Tell me more about your trip to New York City. How much do you remember about your roommate who got killed?"

Daniel frowned. It was a memory he tried to forget.

"Adam Brown," Daniel whispered. "Well, he was from Australia. He was tall, blond hair, blue eyes, and had an interesting accent. He spoke with funny words from time to time." Daniel smiled as he envisioned Adam.

"He was the one who had written an opera or play?" Jason questioned.

Daniel nodded. "Yes. It had a very good song I enjoyed. The name was 'Aborigine Stomp.'" Daniel paused as he thought. "Uh, I think this was the beat. He attempted to repeat the tempo he'd been taught. "No, it was more like..." He tried again, tapping out the beat on the dash over the glovebox. "Yes, this was it." He increased the sound.

"That is too cool," Jason said. "I mean, way out of sight."

Suddenly, Daniel envisioned the words. He sang.

My feet caress Mother Earth
I feel her essence seek me
I stomp. She is pleased.
The dust curls around my foot

We are one. She is me. I am her.

"Of course, it sounded much better with the didgeridoo." Daniel leaned back in the seat.

"A what?"

Daniel laughed. "It is a long tube they play in the outback of Australia."

"Outback?"

"From what I understood, it was mostly desert, some trees, and basically away from civilization. It was where the natives lived."

Jason shrugged. "If you say so. You seem to be the well-traveled man." He laughed. "Hey, remember when we sang 'Row, row, row your boat' our first year in high school?"

Daniel nodded.

Jason broke into song, singing the verse. Daniel waited, then started to sing so it was in rounds. They sang the song about six times.

"That was cool and fun," Jason said.

"I have not sung like that since I returned from New York City." Daniel paused to think.

"How about you belt out the song you sang for competition?"

Daniel shook his head, not wanting to sing.

"Hey, buddy. It is just you and me. I'm not going to tell."

Daniel grinned, hesitated, then began to sing 'Where'er Ye Walk' as he'd been taught to sing on stage. The car filled with his rich voice.

Jason nodded, enjoying the moment to listen to Daniel sing.

"Now, you sing the song you sang in competition," Daniel demanded.

"That was a quartet; not the same, buddy," Jason responded.

"Sing," Daniel demanded.

Jason inhaled deeply knowing full well he couldn't avoid the demand. He started with 'Sweet Adeline' followed by 'Baby Face' and finally 'Five Foot Two' to finish.

"Are you happy, now?" Jason asked. "Wow! We're

already to Angola. That was fast."

"We were so busy singing we didn't notice," Daniel said, smiling.

"Well, I sure wish I could hear Adam's music," Jason said. "It would be neat."

"I do not believe it will happen," Daniel said.

CHAPTER TWENTY-ONE: Singing In School

Monday, February 17, 1964, 9 a.m.

"Today I want to try something new," Daniel said and went to the chalkboard. He printed carefully for all to read.

Row, row, row your boat.
Gently down the stream.
Merrily, merrily, merrily, merrily
Life is but a dream.

"These are words to a song. Does anyone know them?"

He watched for a show of hands. Three hands went into the air. They were the older, eight graders.

"Elizabeth. Where did you learn them?" he asked.

"In the *Englische* school, Mr. Yoder."

Daniel turned to the youngest students.

"This is a song I learned when I attended the *Englische* high school. This is how it goes." He picked up a ruler. "As I sing, I will point at the word so the younger ones will learn."

Daniel sang. With each word, he pointed at it with a ruler.

"Now, let us all sing this together." Daniel led them and they sang. "Now, we will sing the song three times then stop."

Miss Mueller stood in the back of the class, arms folded defiantly before her; lips pursed, and a scowl on her face.

"Okay, this time we are going to do it three times, but..." He grinned at the group. "I want this group..." He pointed at the left-most rows of seats. "You will start singing. When they finish singing 'down the stream' I want this group..." He pointed at the middle row of seats. "I will point to you and you will start singing." He moved to the right of the room. "And, when that group finishes 'down the stream' I want this group..."

He, again, pointed to the row of seats on the right. "You will start." He moved toward the center of the room. "Remember, you sing it three times and then stop." He pointed to the first group. "Begin."

The students sang. Miss Mueller squirmed, glaring at Daniel the whole time. Yet, she said nothing. The song ended.

"That, students, is what you call a round." He nodded approval. "I think we will start to include some time to sing, if not each day, at least two or three times a week."

Watching the students smile at him, he knew they agreed.

#

"Mr. Yoder," Miss Mueller said when the students were outside for a short recess. "I feel you may have overstepped the bounds of teaching. The Amish do not need to learn to sing songs about rowing a boat." She pursed her lips and heaved a sigh. "They are here to learn. We are to teach them *Englische*, math, reading, and writing."

"They are here to learn and play, Ruby," Daniel said, sitting at the desk, checking his notes. "I do not feel a few moments of singing will damage them being Amish."

Miss Mueller stared at Daniel. "Did you not learn to sing in the *Englische* school?"

"Yes," Daniel replied. "Is that a problem?"

"Did you not go to New York City to discover how to sing better? The Amish do not need to sing better. They have learned the songs necessary for church." She paused and inhaled deeply. "If you wish to continue this nonsense, I will be forced to bring this to the bishop's attention."

"Miss Mueller." Daniel stood. "If you feel it necessary – please, notify the bishop of my flagrant *Englische* manner."

Ruby grimaced, huffed, and turned away. "I will go check on the children." She hustled toward the door, grabbing her coat on the way, and disappeared.

Daniel sat at his desk, his hand shaking from the encounter.

I am Amish, he thought. *Singing is not only for the Englische. I am Amish.*

The words of 'Where'er Ye Walk' flooded his mind. He inhaled slowly, letting the words fill him.

"I am Amish," he yelled, and pushed the papers away on his desk. He stood.

"Daniel! Come quick!" Ruby stood at the doorway calling him.

He ran to join her.

"Look!" She said and pointed at the children playing. "Listen."

The children were singing. They were singing 'Row, row, row" and they were doing it in rounds.

Daniel smiled.

"This is what I meant." She pursed her lips and folded her arms defiantly over her chest. "This must be reported to the bishop." She glared at Daniel. "At once."

Ruby stomped down the steps and hurried to her buggy. "I will return." She stepped into the buggy. "With Bishop Schmucker."

"Is there a problem?" Elizabeth asked as she approached. "Miss Mueller seemed quite upset."

"Nothing for you to worry about," Daniel replied and smiled. "Call the children in and we will begin classes again."

# # #

"Mr. Yoder," Bishop Schmucker called as he entered the schoolhouse, quickly noticing the students. "Good afternoon, students," he added and strode to the front of the class. He turned to face the children.

"Mr. Yoder. Is it true you taught the children to sing an *Englische* song?"

Daniel stood. "Yes, sir. It is one I learned while I attended the *Englische* school."

"Would it not be better to have the students sing..." He paused. "A song more in conjunction with the Amish life?"

Daniel nodded. "Perhaps."

Bishop Schmucker noted a chair to the edge of the raised platform and pulled it over to Daniel's desk. "Have the children sing this song Miss Mueller has spoken of – let me decide if it

188

is fitting."

"I taught them the song so they could learn about a term in music called 'rounds' which is easily exampled by the song."

Bishop Schmucker nodded. "Fine. Have them sing." He sat.

Daniel moved to the center of the platform. "As we did it this morning," he said. Once more he pointed to the left two rows. "You will start."

The students began to sing. The next group joined. Finally, the third group joined.

Bishop Schmucker listened, his eyes closed. A smile crossed his lips.

The students finished.

"You have beautiful voices," Bishop Schmucker said. "It is a pleasure to listen to you." He turned to Miss Mueller. "This, Ruby, is a song I learned early in my *Englische* school days." He paused. "You are correct, it is not an Amish song, but it is one easily learned by the young. I feel what Mr. Yoder has done today is within reason. I see no reason to nip this travesty, as you put it."

Daniel glanced at Ruby.

Her face was stoic. She stood silent, taking the chastisement. She quietly nodded to acknowledge the Bishop's words before speaking.

"Perhaps I was rash in my decision," she whispered. "I ask your pardon, Mr. Yoder."

"All is fine with me," Miss Mueller. "You only did what you felt necessary."

Miss Mueller bowed her head and stood silent.

"Now, Daniel," Bishop Schmucker said. "Teaching our children is a grave job and too much levity will encourage rebellion. I would suggest you keep singing to more traditional songs." He smiled. "After all, do you single people not gather for sings on a Saturday night?"

"Aye, we do, Bishop."

"Therefore, singing is not a sin nor against our Amish ways." He paused then lifted his hand with the cautionary index finger raised. "IF done in an appropriate manner. Am I understood?"

"Yes, Bishop."

Bishop Schmucker stood and gazed about the classroom, nodding in approval. "Perhaps I should visit more often."

"We would like that," Daniel said.

"Fine." Bishop Schmucker stepped down and proceeded down an aisle to the door. "Until next time."

"I will take the bishop home," Miss Mueller said. "I will return shortly." She gave Daniel a sheepish look. "I am truly sorry, Daniel."

"All is forgiven, Ruby. Hurry back."

Daniel watched her as she joined the bishop at the door and they left.

I am Amish, he thought. *I. AM. AMISH.*

Songs rushed through his mind as he tried to think which ones would be appropriate and useful to teach the students. He grinned.

"Now, we need to get back to our studies," Daniel said while clapping his hands twice. "Fifth, sixth, seventh and eighth graders, you do your next math assignment. Third and fourth graders – get out your *Englische* books and work on sentence structure." He turned to the first and second graders. "You all will join me up here, sitting on the floor. We will learn another song to learn numbers. Have you ever heard of the ant song? It is called 'The Ants Go Marching.' Does anyone know it?"

Daniel stared at their expectant faces. None knew the song.

"It is a simple song and it will teach how to count. It goes like this...

> The ants go marching one by one, hurrah, hurrah
> The ants go marching one by one, hurrah, hurrah
> The ants go marching one by one,
> The little one stops to suck her thumb
> And they all go marching down to the ground
> To get out of the rain, BOOM! BOOM! BOOM!

Then it will two by two, three by three, four by four, all the way up to ten. Want to try it? I will tell you the next number to sing. Okay?"

190

The children were excited.

Daniel wrote the numbers one through ten on the blackboard. Using a yardstick, he was able to point to the number so the children saw it as they sang.

He looked up and noticed a few of the older students watching. He motioned them back to their work. The young ones were at number ten when Miss Mueller returned. She scowled as she removed her coat and walked into the classroom. She shrugged and joined them on the platform, sitting in the chair Bishop Schmucker had sit in.

The children finished.

"Another song?" she asked.

"Yes, Miss Mueller," Daniel said. "One to help teach them numbers." He stood, erased the numbers and wrote the letters of the alphabet. "This will help them learn the *Englische* letters." He turned to her. "Yes, another song. It is called the 'Alphabet Song' and will make it fun to learn."

Ruby sniffed loudly to show her displeasure while rolling a shoulder. "As you wish."

Daniel sang the letters of the alphabet while pointing at each letter as he sang it. When he finished, he turned to the students.

"Now, you can all join me."

They sang, sometimes everyone, sometimes a few voices were lost of those who didn't recognize the letter.

"We will work on this again tomorrow." He smiled.

CHAPTER TWENTY-TWO: *Englische* Wedding

Saturday, April 4, 1964, 9:45 a.m.

"I'm totally psyched, Daniel," Jason said as he drove to Shipshewana. "Tonight you will be a married man. Totally unreal, man."

Daniel stared at the highway, the passing vehicles, and absolutely nothing in general. He fidgeted in his seat.

"You okay?" Jason asked, noticing Daniel's silence.

"Yes, Jason," Daniel said. "I am fine." His voice was dull, uninterested, absent.

"You sure? You don't seem like your regular self."

"Today I am getting married in an *Englische* church." He paused. "Against my better judgment. If the Amish Church finds out..." He left the sentence unfinished.

"Hey, buddy. You love Martha. She loves you. Who is anyone to judge you for marrying her?"

"They are not judging me," Daniel replied. "They are judging my decision." He gazed out the window to his right. "I am Amish," he whispered. "I am not *Englische*. I should not marry in an *Englische* church."

"You are doing this because you love Martha and her father is a demanding–"

"He is her father and she must obey," Daniel said, cutting Jason off. "If I wish to marry her, I must abide by his decisions."

"Then an *Englische* wedding it is," Jason said. "First we will stop by and get our tuxedos then go to Martha's house to change." He laughed. "I don't think stopping at Uncle Paul's would be a wise choice." He grinned at Daniel.

"Nay. A bad choice, indeed."

"You seem distant, Daniel."

"I was thinking," Daniel said. "Martha said she would be at the church all day to get ready." He shrugged. "Something about it being a bad thing to see the bride before the wedding. Anyway, that means we will be at the Noble house with Mr. Noble. Alone."

"Yeah, he is sort of a jerk," Jason said.

"We will not have Martha or her mother to..." He searched for the word.

"Buffer? Head off?"

Daniel nodded.

"Don't worry, buddy. I got your back. I'm *Englische*. He'll have to deal with me."

Daniel grinned.

Jason took the sheet of paper from his shirt pocket. "This is the address. Let's go in and get our penguin outfits."

Daniel frowned. "Penguin?"

"Just another term for a tuxedo. Don't sweat it." Jason slapped Daniel on the shoulder and guided him toward the front door.

#

Saturday, April 4, 1964, about 6:30 p.m.

Jason pulled the car into the parking lot of the United Methodist Church.

"We're here, buddy. This is your last chance to back out." Jason nodded toward the church. "Once in there, you will become a married man and Martha will be your wife for the rest of your life."

Daniel gazed down at his shiny shoes. He noticed the blue ruffled shirt. *The dream*, he thought. *I. AM. AMISH. This is Englische. I am doing this for Martha. I love her.* Daniel sighed deeply then nodded. "Let us go," he said.

"It's your death," Jason said and laughed. "This is so cool. Who knew Daniel Yoder would be the first guy of our high school class to get married?"

"I am not of your class, Jason." Daniel opened the door of the church. "I left. Remember?"

"You may have left, Daniel, but you'll always be a classmate to me." Jason wrapped an arm around Daniel's shoulder. "Best buds forever."

Daniel nodded, stopping to stare the strangeness of the church.

"Is there a problem, Daniel?"

"I have never been inside an *Englische* church before," Daniel whispered. "It is different."

Dan Noble appeared out of the shadows.

"Follow me, Mr. Yoder," he said. "I will show you where you need to be. Elder Hawkins will tell you when and what you need to do." He glanced at Jason. "I'm sure you know what to do – being *Englische*. This shouldn't seem strange and alien."

Jason held his breath and counted to ten. *I'm totally right. This guy is a jerk*, he thought. He nodded at Mr. Noble.

"C'mon, Daniel," Jason whispered and followed Dan Noble toward the front of the church to a room off to the side.

Elder Hawkins sat at a desk, and stood as they entered.

"Welcome, gentlemen," he said, offering his hand to shake. "My name is Elmer Hawkins. I'm an Elder here at United Methodist Church." He smiled as he shook hands, listening to the names. "This should be a very nice wedding, indeed." He turned to Daniel. "You, sir, are very lucky. I've known Martha for many years – watching her grow up. A good, Christian girl."

Dan Noble frowned then glared at Daniel.

"Now," Elder Hawkins continued, ignoring the hidden hostility. "I will walk out to the center." He looked at Daniel. "Once there, I will nod in your direction. At that time you will walk out, and you–" He turned to Jason. "You will follow the groom." He smiled at the two young men. "Shall we give a rehearsal?"

Daniel nodded.

Elder Hawkins strolled out and stood in front of the altar. He nodded to Daniel who ambled out with Jason following.

Elder Hawkins pointed to a location. "Stand there," he said, pointing at a location a few feet from him before moving closer and readjusting where Daniel should stand. He moved to Jason and had him stand a little behind Daniel. "There, that should do." Elder Hawkins moved back to his position. "We will stand here a few minutes and then the back doors will open and the bridesmaid will enter. Shortly thereafter, your bride will be escorted by her father down the center aisle. The bridesmaid will move to this side." He pointed to the opposite side.

Daniel nodded.

"The bride and father will join us, at which time you, Daniel, will move to stand beside Mr. Noble. Understood?"

Again, Daniel nodded.

"Are you sure? I've never married an Amish before."

Daniel bristled at the mention of being Amish. "Yes," Daniel said.

"If there's a problem," Jason said. "I'll tell Daniel what to do. Don't worry, sir."

"Oh, you're not Amish?" Elder Hawkins seemed surprised.

"No, I'm *Englische*, if you must know." Jason remained calm. "The Amish are not total idiots."

"I meant no offense," Elder Hawkins stammered. "I was under the impression that... never mind." He took a deep breath. "We should all get back to the room and wait. In fact, I think I will go and make sure everything is ready at the bride's end." He grinned. "After all, she is the show."

Daniel frowned, unsure what he meant.

# # #

"Getting nervous?" Jason quipped.

"About what?"

"Hey, buddy, you're getting hitched – married. You know, the old ball-and-chain. You don't have any jitters?" Jason paced in front of the window, staring through the colored glass to watch whatever he could see outside.

"I am getting married at an *Englische* church in an *Englische* ceremony. To me, it is not a wedding. Why should I be nervous?"

"Well, I'm nervous and I'm not getting married." Jason laughed.

Elder Hawkins stepped into the room. "We are almost ready. The organist will play two songs and then we will walk out."

Daniel nodded.

"How many are out there?" Jason asked.

Elder Hawkins squinted his face in thought. "I would say maybe about... hm... say fifty?"

Jason nodded.

"If you'd like to see," Elder Hawkins said. "Use the door I came in and you can see who all is out there." He paused. "I hoped there would be more Amish. I don't see any Amish in the pews. In fact, Daniel, there are only a few people on your side of the church."

"My side?" Daniel asked.

Jason laughed. "Attendees sit either on the left or right, depending if they're friends with the bride or groom." He stepped down to the door and opened it. "Okay, I see Ben Hopkins and his wife, and... I'm not sure, is that Bob Sullivan and his wife?"

"What?" Daniel rushed for the door.

In the front pew sat Ben and Bob with their respective wives. They waved.

"Did you tell?" Daniel glared at Jason.

"You invited Ben," Jason said defensively. "He probably told Bob Sullivan, your old boss."

"I hope nobody else shows," Daniel whispered. "The Amish cannot find out."

"I'm sure Ben was discreet, Daniel. He's a good friend."

The music stopped.

Daniel looked at Elder Hawkins.

"It's time." Elder Hawkins nodded and stepped out to the chancel.

Daniel and Jason moved to the other door and waited for the signal. Elder Hawkins nodded. Daniel stepped out with Jason a few feet behind him. He saw the people on the opposite side of the church. There were many.

So much for a secret, he thought. He turned and gazed at Ben and Bob.

They discreetly waved. Daniel nodded acknowledgment

and offered a weak smile. Daniel stood in his appointed place, and waited. Music started and a young girl stepped through the opening in the back. She moved toward the front of the church. Daniel frowned. This was not Martha. The girl moved up the steps of the chancel and stood to the opposite side. The music stopped momentarily before the notes of 'The Wedding March' filled the church. Daniel watched.

Martha appeared with her father at the door. They walked solemnly forward. She smiled.

Daniel's breath came in short gasps. She was beautiful. The white dress flowed around her and the veil fluttered in the movement. He was mesmerized. The sequins and beads glittered with each measured slow step Martha took.

So, this is an Englische wedding, he thought. A tear formed in the eye, but he held it. *She is like an angel and she is mine.*

Jason leaned forward. "You got a winner, Daniel. She is beautiful," he whispered.

Daniel nodded ever so lightly in agreement.

Dan Noble glared at Daniel, a smug smile on his face. Daniel moved to stand beside his future father-in-law.

"I'm willing to bet you're wishing you were *Englische* about now, eh?" Dan whispered.

Daniel stiffened at the words.

I am Amish, Daniel thought. *This is wrong.* He wanted to bolt, but the image of Martha filled his mind. He stood his ground.

Elder Hawkins started the ceremony. He droned on. Finally he asked, "Who gives this woman."

Dan Noble stepped back. "Her mother and I do." Dan took Martha's hand and placed it in Daniel's hand with another quick glare at the young man. Dan stepped back, turned, and joined Emma in the front pew.

Elder Hawkins continued with the ceremony.

"Do you, Daniel Yoder, take Martha Noble to be your lawful wife?"

Daniel stood silent.

Jason leaned forward. "Say I do."

"I do," Daniel repeated.

"Do you, Martha Elaine Noble, take Daniel Yoder to be your lawful husband?"

"I do," Martha said. She beamed at Daniel.

"You may now exchange rings."

Daniel froze. Jason leaned forward, pulling a simple ring from his pocket. "I knew you wouldn't know about this. Hope you don't mind." He offered the ring to Daniel to put on Martha's hand. It was a small birthstone ring.

Daniel placed the ring on Martha's finger. She offered her left hand with the ring finger sticking out. She then grabbed Daniel's hand and placed a simple band on his left hand.

He frowned, unsure of the jewelry.

"We can take them off after the party," she whispered.

"I now pronounce you husband and wife," Elder Hawkins said. "Daniel, you may kiss your bride."

Daniel felt awkward, to kiss in public. Martha leaned in and he kissed her.

"May I introduce Mr. and Mrs. Daniel Yoder." He turned the couple to face those who sat in the pews.

Martha pulled Daniel by the hand, they stepped down from the chancel and scurried along the main aisle.

"We will stand back here and welcome those who attended," she said.

Daniel nodded.

Jason strutted the aisle with the bridesmaid's arm entwined with his.

"Congratulation, Daniel. Martha," Jason said, shaking Daniel's hand vigorously then leaning in to kiss Martha's cheek.

The bridesmaid shook Daniel's hand. "It is good to finally meet you, Daniel." She jumped to Martha and embraced her. "I can't believe you're married."

"First. Hazel, meet Jason Muirs from Centertown." Martha turned to Jason. "Jason, this is my best friend, Hazel Langfield." She squealed and hugged Hazel. "I'm married."

Dan and Emma Noble were next. Daniel was unsure when Dan grabbed his hand and shook it.

"So, you are my son-in-law." He grimaced, leaned in to whisper in Daniel's ear. "Not who I would have chosen, Daniel.

I think my daughter deserves better, but..." He left the sentence unfinished.

Emma hugged Daniel. "Welcome to the family, son." She was crying. "I'm so happy."

Others soon joined them.

Ben Hopkins shook Daniel's hand. "Now, to see what the future will hold, Daniel." He pulled Bob Sullivan next to him. "I invited him and told him it was a secret. He assured me he would not tell."

"So, my favorite summer worker is now a married man." Bob shook Daniel's hand. "Congratulations. By the way, you will be coming to see me next month so we can discuss your summer employment. Right?" He winked. "I've got some big plans."

"Thank you, Mr. Sullivan," Daniel said.

The last of the guests filed by and Daniel sighed. Today had not been what he expected.

"Now for the fun," Jason said. "Out to the car so we can drive around town."

Daniel frowned. "Why?"

"Part of the tradition of an *Englische* wedding. The best man drives the couple around to let everyone know you were married."

"But I wish to keep this secret," Daniel said. His eyes widened in surprise.

"Nobody will know who it is," Jason said. "All they know is there's a happy newly wedded couple in the car. It will be quick and then we will go to the hall where the party is being held."

"Why?" Daniel asked.

"This gives the guests time to get to the hall to see the new bride and groom come in. Now, get moving."

# # #

Daniel and Martha walked into the community room, followed by Jason and Hazel who eased to the side and away from the limelight.

"Welcome the new couple, Mr. and Mrs. Daniel Yoder."

199

People stood and applauded.

Daniel was unsure, standing out like this was not part of his Amish upbringing. He wanted to shy away.

"C'mon, Daniel," Martha said and pulled him toward a table at the front of the group where Jason and Hazel already sat.

"What are we doing?" Daniel asked.

"This is all part of the *Englische* wedding," Martha said. "Soon we'll cut the wedding cake."

Daniel shook his head. "This is totally unlike an Amish wedding."

"I know, Daniel," Martha said. "I look forward to our Amish wedding. This bishop said I will be baptized on May 10th and we can be married on May 14th. My father has agreed to pay for all the expenses."

"There are no expenses. The community provides. Everyone donates. This is all strange."

"Nonetheless, my father said if there are costs, he will pay."

Daniel shrugged. "I am learning to not fight with your father. He wants his way."

Martha frowned. "He let me marry you," she said. "He was definitely against that."

"Yes, but it had to be an *Englische* wedding." Daniel stared at the gathered crowd. "I hope it remains a secret." He noticed Ben Hopkins lift a glass in their direction. "There are four from Centertown. They are *Englische*, but if one even mentions they were at a wedding – there will be questions and I fear the secret will be known."

"You worry too much, my love," Martha said and leaned her head on his shoulder. "Stop fretting and enjoy the evening."

The sound of clinking glass filled the room.

Daniel frowned. "What is that?"

"They want us to kiss," Martha said and leaned toward Daniel.

He kissed her and immediately gazed at the crowd as they hooped and hollered.

I hope this ends soon, Daniel thought.

Two people approached with plates in each hand. "Your

dinner." They placed the dishes in front of the four.

"Now we eat, Daniel," Martha said. "Then we will cut the cake." She grabbed a fork and began to eat. "Eat as fast as you can, Daniel. They will be clinking the glass soon. It is customary to keep the couple kissing so they can't eat."

Daniel took a bite.

Glasses clinked. Daniel leaned over and kissed Martha. They immediately went back to eating, trying to get as much food in before the next kiss.

Tonight, I am Englische, Daniel thought. Immediately he panicked. Molly Pearson's words flashed in his mind – Would it be so terrible to be *Englische*? Daniel closed his eyes. *I. AM. AMISH*. he thought.

Daniel took the last bite of food from the plate.

"I see the couple are finished. It is time to cut the cake."

Daniel surveyed the area, trying to locate the voice.

Martha grabbed Daniel's hand. "Let's go."

She led him to the table with a small three-tiered cake. A couple stood on the top tier with a lace heart behind them. Daniel frowned at the strangeness of the ceremony. Martha picked up the knife, put his hand with hers and they cut a small piece from the lower tier. Martha offered a small piece to Daniel.

"We feed each other the first pieces of cake." She opened her mouth to let Daniel feed her the piece. "My turn." She pushed the piece into Daniel's mouth, smearing the cake across his lips.

"What?" Daniel was surprised by the action, listening to the attendees laugh.

"Part of the tradition," Martha said. "I love you."

She leaned up and kissed him, smearing some of the cake on her face. Martha then took a napkin and cleaned his face of the cake before removing it from her face.

Daniel grimaced. "This *Englische* wedding is very strange with stranger customs."

Martha laughed.

"Now, my mother and her friend will cut the cake for everyone to have some," Martha said. "We can sit back down until the dance."

"Dance?" Daniel shook his head. "I do not dance. Amish do not dance. I do not know how to dance."

"It is very simple," Martha said. "We will go out on the floor, just you and me. You will hold me in your arms and I will lead you, moving about the dance floor. It is a slow dance. Nobody will be the wiser."

Daniel sighed and took his seat at the main table. Jason leaned over.

"You having fun?"

"No, Jason. When I agreed to this *Englische* wedding, I thought it was only so Dan Noble could walk his daughter down the aisle." He waved his hand at the group of people. "All of this? I do not understand this. Why?"

Jason grinned. "It is all part of the ceremony. What do the Amish do for a wedding that takes all day?"

Daniel thought. *We do not dance. We eat. We do not have a fancy ceremony or fancy clothes. It is a happy occasion, but it is held with reverence.*

He looked at the gathered crowd as they laughed, ate, and drank. *We do not party like this.*

"It is different," Daniel said, unsure of how to respond.

"Can I be nosey?" Jason asked. He didn't wait for an answer. "I will be staying in Alexander's room tonight. Correct? Uh... er... will you be sleeping with Martha?"

"I... I..." Daniel frowned. "Yes, we are married, but... It was not an Amish wedding."

"What wasn't an Amish wedding?" Martha asked.

"Jason asked if I would be sleeping with you tonight," Daniel said.

Martha blushed. "We are married."

Daniel shrugged. "It was an *Englische* wedding. I do not feel married. It was not an Amish wedding."

Martha pouted. "It was a real wedding for me."

Again, Daniel shrugged. "I guess we could do bundling until the Amish wedding."

Martha frowned with a grimace. "Not what I expected on my wedding night."

Daniel stared at her. "Do you actually think your father will allow us to sleep together?"

"Well, we definitely can't go to Uncle Paul's, either," she retorted.

"Perhaps it would be best if I slept in Alexander's room with Jason."

Jason shook his head and grunted. "Just what I want – to sleep with the groom on his wedding night."

"We will see how the evening ends," Martha said. "Now we celebrate our wedding."

# # #

Daniel saw Ben Hopkins and his wife to the door and waved them goodbye when they left. He did the same for Bob Sullivan and his wife.

"You be sure to see me next month, Daniel," Bob said as they shook hands. "You're a married man. You need to support your lovely wife."

"Yes, sir," Daniel said.

"And, you, Martha Yoder, make sure he does it." Bob leaned in and kissed her on the cheek. "Again, congratulations you two."

Mrs. Sullivan giggled and tittered, whispering to Martha before nodding to Daniel. They left.

Daniel stood at the door watching the taillights fade into the distance.

"I hope they keep the secret," he whispered to nobody in particular.

Dan Noble joined them at the door.

"I can't wait. The Polaroid picture was excellent. I dropped it off with a little notice about the marriage of my daughter. It should be in this week's paper."

"You what?" Daniel stood in shock.

"I put a notice in the paper about my daughter's marriage. It is customary for the parents of the bride to brag."

"Daddy!" Martha yelled. "We wanted to keep this marriage secret."

Dan huffed. "Don't worry. The Amish don't read the local paper."

Daniel bowed his head and shuffled back into the room to

203

Jason.

"A wedding picture will be in the paper," Daniel moaned. "Dan Noble thinks the Amish will not see it." He sighed heavily. "It will not be a secret for long."

"I'm sorry, buddy. We can only hope for the best." Jason patted the newly married man's back.

CHAPTER TWENTY-THREE: Discovery

Sunday, April 5, 1964, 3:45 p.m.

"Am I to understand this correctly?" Dan yelled. "My new son-in-law slept in Alex's bedroom with his buddy? Why?"

Martha sat in the living room chair, her hands fingering the handkerchief. "He doesn't consider us married."

"What did I pay for?" Dan paced the living room. "What does he think last night was? And the church?"

"It was an *Englische* marriage, Daddy," Martha answered. "Daniel only did what was requested. He is Amish, not *Englische*. The ceremony was just some ritualistic motions for him to perform. It meant nothing to him."

"Nothing?" Dan exploded. "I spent a lot of good money for... for... NOTHING? That young man is about to get an earful. I'm going to Centertown and let him know exactly what this is all about."

"You will do no such thing," Emma said.

"You were Amish," Dan said. "Did you think our *Englische* wedding was just malarkey? It didn't mean anything?"

"That's the difference, dear," Emma said, keeping her voice calm. "I left the Amish. I became *Englische* and THEN we got married. Yes, it was a short time of being *Englische*. But, that's the difference. I was *Englische*. Daniel is Amish." She shook her head. "He is Amish through and through."

Martha giggled. "That he is."

"So, he marries my daughter. Leaves her alone on their wedding night. And, now, the next day, runs back home to play Amish?"

"You seem to forget one little detail," Emma said. "You

205

demanded they get married in an *Englische* ceremony. Daniel agreed to your terms, knowing full well if word of it gets out, he will be shunned, maybe banished from the Amish community."

"That's not my problem," Daniel said with a shrug.

"Yes, it is your problem," Emma said. "Your son-in-law loves your daughter so much, he is willing to jeopardize his standing in the Amish community for her... and to appease you."

"He could have said no at any point," Dan said as he slumped into his BarcaLounger.

"Which is what you wanted, Daddy," Martha said. "You didn't want us to get married. You kept fighting it, even to the point of forcing Daniel into an *Englische* wedding."

"Fine," Dan said. "When the paper comes out this week – well, his secret won't be a secret. The whole world will see he married my little girl in an *Englische* ceremony. What's he going to do then?" One side of Dan's lips curled in a smile. "As I see it, I win. He will be cast out of the Amish and will be forced to become *Englische*. Being *Englische* with no formal education, he won't be able to support Martha and, if all goes as I see it, they will be forced into a divorce. That's the end of that marriage."

"DANIEL WEBSTER NOBLE!" Emma glared at her husband. "That was your plan all along. You've done some devilish deeds over the years, but this one..."

Martha jumped up and ran from the room, up the stairs, slamming her bedroom door before falling on her bed in tears.

"Well, at least I won't have to pay for an Amish wedding next month," Dan said snidely.

Emma shook her head and stomped from the room to attend to her daughter.

# # #

Thursday, April 9, 1964, 3:45 p.m.

Daniel pulled the buggy into their home's driveway to let his siblings out so they could start on their homework.

"If you have any questions, I will be in shortly. I will unharness Beauty first." Daniel snapped the reins and Beauty headed for the barn.

He finished the chore quickly, making sure Beauty had a few extra oats and new hay. He headed into the house. His mother glanced up from the sink, nodded, and returned to her work. His sister, Hannah, peeked around, eyes wide, she raised her eyebrows, glanced toward the living room, and nodded.

"Is that you, Daniel?"

Daniel recognized the voice. His father. He also recognized the tone. Somebody was in trouble. Daniel frowned. Hannah rolled a shoulder, turned her back to him and returned to her chore beside her mother.

"Yes, Papa," Daniel answered.

"Join me."

Daniel recognized that command. He was in trouble.

"Coming."

"Daniel, to do this math question, I need–"

"He will answer your question later, Jacob," Noah said from the living room. "I need to speak with him now."

Daniel nodded to Jacob and mouthed 'I will be back' before going into the living room.

"Sit." Noah pointed at the chair on the other side of the room from him.

Daniel moved to the chair and sat. He gazed at his father.

"I was in town today, Daniel. Jeremiah Wyse approached me."

Daniel nodded.

"Do you know why?" He paused. "He had a copy of the local newspaper from Shipshewana."

Daniel nodded.

"Do you know what he showed me?"

Daniel shook his head back and forth, all the while hoping it wasn't what he thought it might be.

Noah pulled a folded newspaper from the side of his rocker. He snapped the paper open and jabbed a finger at a picture. "Who is this?"

Daniel stood and crossed the room to look at the picture in the paper. His heart sank. There, in blazing black and white

207

was a picture of him and Martha. He was in a tuxedo; Martha in a white wedding gown.

"I can explain, Papa," Daniel offered.

"You need not explain it to me, Daniel. You need to explain this blasphemy to the community, especially Bishop Schmucker."

"But, Papa," Daniel pleaded. "Martha's father would not allow her to marry unless it was in an Englische ceremony. It meant nothing to me. It was only to appease Dan Noble. Now, Martha and I can be married after her baptism and becomes Amish. We will have an Amish wedding, which is what we wanted."

Noah stared at his son. "So this is true?" He repeatedly jabbed his index finger at the picture. "You married an *Englische* in an *Englische* ceremony." Noah inhaled deeply. "Do you know what that means?"

"Yes, Papa." Daniel stepped back to his chair and slumped into it.

"I have waited to hear the truth. Now, I must go speak with the bishop." Noah stood. "Hopefully, none have brought this to his attention, yet."

Noah strode from the room.

"I will be back," he said to Rebecca. "I am going to see the bishop."

Rebecca nodded and began to dry her hands.

The kitchen door slammed as Noah left. Daniel's sibling's attention snapped from their homework to gaze at the door.

"How could you, Daniel," his mother asked. "An *Englische* wedding?"

Daniel watched his younger siblings. They stared at him and listened to the conversation.

"Back to your homework," Rebecca said. "This be none of your business."

The young ones at the table once more turned their attention to their homework.

Hannah stood by the sink. She shook her head in disbelief.

"I did it to appease her father," Daniel said. "Martha and I plan to have an Amish wedding right after she is baptized into the church."

"Do you think she will be allowed to join the church, Daniel?"

"I... We... I do not know," Daniel whispered.

"Think, Daniel. What were you thinking?"

"I do not know," Daniel replied, standing with his hands folded in front of him as he was being chastised. "I do not know."

The kitchen door snapped open. Noah stood there.

"You had best come with me, Daniel. I am sure the Bishop will wish to discuss this... this... this abomination." Noah shook his head disgustedly. "The teacher, no less," he whispered.

Daniel grabbed his hat and followed his father to the buggy.

# # #

Daniel followed behind his father as they walked to Bishop Schmucker's door.

Noah turned to Daniel. "Allow me to speak. You will have your turn."

Daniel nodded agreement.

The door opened.

"Noah Yoder. Young Daniel Yoder." Bishop Schmucker held open the screen door. "What a pleasant surprise. Please, come in."

The bishop guided them to the main room. "Please. Sit. To what do I owe this visit?"

Noah settled into a chair and motioned for Daniel to sit beside him.

"Have you seen the latest newspaper from Shipshewana?" Noah asked.

"Nay."

Noah handed the paper to the bishop. It was folded so the picture of Daniel and Martha was easily visible. The bishop scanned the page before gazing from the paper to Daniel.

"Is this you, Daniel?" he asked.

Daniel nodded, not saying a word.

"You are a married man?" He paused then snapped his fingers at the picture. "An *Englische* wedding?"

Once more Daniel nodded.

"Speak up, Daniel," Noah said. "Now is your time to confess."

Daniel hung his head and heaved a heavy sigh.

"Martha and I planned to wed in an Amish wedding next month after she is baptized into the church." He rolled a shoulder. "Her father, Dan Noble demanded to be allowed to walk her down the aisle like in an *Englische* wedding. He claimed it was his right since Martha's older sister had moved to Canada and eloped." Daniel gazed at Bishop Schmucker. "This wedding meant nothing to us." Daniel bit back his lower lip. "Our *Englische* wedding night was spent apart. I slept in a separate room with my friend, Jason. Martha slept in her bedroom."

Noah huffed.

Bishop Schmucker glared at Daniel. "You expect your father and I to believe you did not perform your duty?"

Daniel's face burned in a blush. "We did not," he said. "Jason and I returned to Centertown the next day."

Bishop Schmucker nodded. "Uh-huh."

"If you wish, talk with Jason Muirs and he will tell you what happened that night."

"The fact remains, Daniel," the bishop said. "You are married... and in an *Englische* ceremony." He paused. "*Englische*."

Noah shook his head, all the while letting it droop to gaze at his feet.

"I have no other choice, Daniel," Bishop Schmucker said. "I must, again, have you shunned." He sighed. "For how long? Until you have committed yourself for sin repentance." He grimaced. "Do you understand? Tomorrow I will be at the school to explain this to the students and place Miss Mueller in charge."

Daniel snapped his head up to look into the bishop's eyes.

"I will not be allowed to teach?" he asked.

"You are shunned, Daniel. The community will be notified on Sunday, at least for those who do not know by then." He smiled. "There is one exception. You are the schoolmaster, therefore I will grant you the ability to attend and oversee the classes and assist Miss Mueller. Being shunned, she will not be allowed to talk to you." He sighed. "Now, since the students are not baptized, they may talk with you for any clarifications when Miss Mueller assigns the studies." The bishop inhaled deeply. "You can speak to the wind to express your needs. If Miss Mueller happens to hear, that is her choice."

"Thank you, Bishop Schmucker," Daniel said.

Noah glared at Daniel. "This is your second shunning." He shook his head. "You have too much *Englische* in you, Daniel." Noah squinted his eyes, searching for an answer in Daniel. "Did I err in allowing you to attend high school?"

Bishop Schmucker stood and placed a comforting hand on Noah. "Rashness, Noah. Daniel is a good lad but needs guidance." He gazed at Daniel. "I am sure he will find a way to offer sin repentance."

"What of Martha?" Daniel asked.

Bishop Schmucker and Noah turned and left the room.

Daniel was shunned.

# # #

Sunday, April 12, 1964, early

Daniel followed the family into the Jacob Metz home. His older sister, Rachel Metz glanced at him, averted her eyes and shook her head. Daniel approached.

"Why Daniel?" she whispered. "Shunned?"

Daniel nodded and continued to the entrance of the main room. He took a seat just outside the main room. Being shunned he wasn't allowed the fellowship of the church. He watched several pass him by, ignoring him, turning their heads to avoid eye contact.

Bishop Schmucker strolled past Daniel, ignoring him.

Daniel listened, participating quietly from his position in the kitchen.

Bishop Schmucker finally made the announcement

Daniel dreaded – he was being shunned. Now, Daniel knew the whole community was aware of his transgressions. He stood and sloughed his way out of the kitchen to the back door.

It was a beautiful, spring morning. He considered waiting for the family in the buggy, but decided it would be better for him to walk home since the family wouldn't be headed home until late in the day. He would get hungry. Daniel was sure his mother had left something out for him to eat when he got home. She might openly shun him, but she still mothered him when none watched. He smiled at the thought.

CHAPTER TWENTY-FOUR: Baptism

Sunday, April 19, 1964, early

Martha followed behind Uncle Paul and Aunt Mary. She grinned as her younger cousins bounced their way up the steps into Amos Troyer's home for church.

Mr. Troyer gave her an odd look and pulled Uncle Paul to the side. They whispered. Amos Troyer offered furtive glances at Martha.

"If you feel it necessary, then by means, bring it to Bishop Beiler's attention." Paul stepped away and moved toward the main room.

"Is there a problem?" asked his wife.

Paul hesitated, holding still. "Perhaps," he replied and glanced at Martha."

Martha enjoyed the service and sought out Bishop Beiler after the meal had been served. She spied him outside; he was speaking with Amos Troyer. She felt concern and waited until Amos stepped away.

"Bishop Beiler," she called. "May I speak with you?"

He nodded and she approached him, hoping no others would bother them.

"Bishop," she started. "I wish to become Amish. I want to join the church."

He gave her a somber look. "Come see me tomorrow," he said and stroked his beard. "After the noon meal, about one?" He smiled. "I am sure my wife will have some fresh meadow tea and perhaps cookies ready."

Martha nodded approval. "Very well, until one tomorrow," she said and walked back to see if she could help the women in the kitchen with the meal cleanup. She felt the sensation of happiness exude.

Soon, she thought. *Very soon, Daniel and I will be married.* She tittered. *Of course, we are already married... but not in Daniel's eyes.* She stopped and gazed toward Centertown. *Soon, my love*, she thought. *Soon I will be Amish and we can be married.*

Martha entered the house.

# # #

Monday, April 20, 1964, 1 p.m.

Bishop Beiler led Martha into the main room of his house.

"Now, what was this about you wishing to become Amish?" he asked as he sat in a chair.

"Bishop Beiler," she started. "I wish to be baptized and join the church."

"May I ask who you are? I do not recognize you, yet you seem familiar."

"My name is Martha Noble. I am the daughter of Dan and Emma Noble." She paused to allow the bishop time to think. "They are *Englische*. My mother is Paul Hershberger's sister." Again, she paused to allow her words to be considered. "She left the Amish during her *Rumschpringe*."

Bishop Beiler nodded in understanding.

"Why do you wish to become Amish?" He watched her, analyzing her actions and words. "Most *Englische* do not want the life of the Amish." He gazed at her Amish attire. "You are *Englische*, are you not?"

"Yes, I am *Englische*," Martha replied. "My mother allowed me to spend my summers with her brother, my Uncle Paul, to learn the Amish lifestyle and my heritage."

"Ah-ha." The old bishop held up a hand in comprehending the situation. "Now, I recognize you. The young girl who attended service from time to time." He tugged on his beard and once more scrutinized Martha. "Tell me. Why do you wish to be Amish?"

"I want to be baptized so I may marry an Amish man I love. He will not become *Englische*..." Martha snickered. "He

214

did *Rumshpringe* in New York City and did not enjoy the experience. He is a true Amish and I love him."

The old bishop shook his head. "I fear you wish to be Amish for the wrong reasons.'"

Martha narrowed her eyelids. "Is not love a valid reason? I wish to embrace the Amish life. Yes, I know it will be difficult. Yes, I will give up my *Englische* ways. Yes, I know I will be shunned if I decide differently after baptism. And, yes, the love of my life is Amish."

Bishop Beiler smiled. "We will welcome you into the community. I will prepare you for the baptism." He hesitated. "Who is this Amish man you love so much?"

"His name is Daniel Yoder. He lives in Centertown. He is the new Amish schoolteacher."

Bishop Beiler nodded. "Yes, I have heard of this young man. Did he not attend high school before going to New York City?"

Martha nodded in agreement. "It was in New York where I met Daniel." She shook her head back and forth in disgust. "His friend was killed, and he needed to stay there longer than he wished. He questioned his faith, his possible lifestyle as *Englische*. I took him to visit my uncle in Pennsylvania, an Amish family. He enjoyed working with his hands, wearing his Amish clothes. It was then both he and I knew he was truly Amish and wanted to return to his home in Ohio." She gave the bishop a sly grin and gazed at him. "He was only staying to be with me." She paused. "It was then I decided to come home to Shipshewana." She rolled a shoulder. "He had to make his own decision." She giggled. "I suggested my uncle visit his sister in Centertown. We went. It was then I discovered Daniel had returned home. The day of his baptism, I went to him. It was then I realized he loved me and I loved him."

The bishop placed a finger to his lower lip. "Ah, so he was on *Rumschpringe* then?"

Again, Martha nodded. "Daniel is now baptized and teaching the children at a new Amish school."

"Is that not the one which burned down? Was not the young man shunned?"

Martha nodded agreement. "It was not his fault as

215

originally thought. A new school was built."

Bishop Beiler nodded. "Yes. Yes. I remember." He sat in the chair, his woolly eyebrows knitting into almost one solid line. He paused, watching Martha. "I have one question, Miss Noble." He pulled out a newspaper sheet. "Is this not you?" He pointed at the wedding picture. "Are you not married?"

Martha's heart fell to the floor as she stared at the glaring image of her and Daniel. She sighed heavily and nodded.

"Yes, that is us," she whispered.

"I am not one to condemn without hearing both sides of the story." He eased back into the chair. "Do you wish to explain?"

Martha faltered then let the story flow from her lips about the demands of her father.

Bishop Beiler nodded. "Still, Martha, the truth stands – you are married. An *Englische* wedding." He paused and stared off into the distance beyond the walls of the room. "I am sure this Daniel Yoder you love is shunned, if not now, he will be when it is discovered."

Martha hung her head, shoulders slumped. "What must I do?" she whispered.

Bishop Beiler rolled a shoulder. "You are married. You are *Englische*." He pointed at her clothing. "You may dress Amish, but you are still *Englische*." He shook his head. "I cannot bring you into the fold of the church."

Martha stood.

"Let me walk you out to your bicycle."

Martha gazed up at Bishop Belier, tears welling in her eyes.

Martha rode her bike, ignoring most she passed. Tears flowed. Her mind raced.

I can't be baptized into the Amish church. They consider me an *Englische* married woman. Daniel and I can't be together. She shook her head. Daniel will never become *Englische*. He married me in an *Englische* church to appease my father, but he won't leave the Amish for me.

216

She stopped the bicycle and ran to sit under a large maple tree. With arms wrapped around her pulled up knees, she bent her head to rest on them and let the tears fall. She cried.

"Are you okay?" a young man asked.

Martha looked up to see the man watching her.

"I saw you get off your bicycle. I thought you might have hurt yourself. Did you?" He bent down close.

"No, I'm fine," Martha said. "I... I..." She gazed at the young man. "John Kurtz? Right?"

He nodded. "That's me. I'm home from college." He grinned. He squinted in thought. "You're Martha... Martha Noble." He reared back to study her clothes. "You're Amish now?" A frown covered his face. "Didn't you just get married?"

Martha wiped the tears from her eyes and smiled. "That's part of the problem." She pulled at her skirt. "I want to be Amish. My boyfriend is Amish." She shrugged and shook her head. "It's a long story."

John sat down beside her. "I can listen. Tell me."

"I can't," Martha said. "I need to see my mother." She sniffed. "I'm feeling a little better now, so I'll get along home." She smiled at John. "Thanks for the concern."

"Not a problem." He gazed back at the house and the barn beyond. "Guess I could help my father in the barn. I need to go back to college tomorrow." A silly grin crossed his face. "Plus, it will be good to see Adeline, again." He winked. "She's my girlfriend."

Martha picked up her bike, waved, and headed on into Shipshewana.

#

Martha rode the bicycle into her parent's yard and dropped it. Once more the words of Bishop Beiler rang in her ears and the tears flowed. She ran into the house.

"Who's there?" her mother's voice called from the kitchen.

"Just me," Martha said as she slumped into a chair in the living room. She let loose the tears and cried.

Her mother walked in.

217

"Whatever is the matter, Martha?"

"Bishop Beiler won't let me... that *Englische* wedding. I never should have talked Daniel into it." She wiped the tears from her eyes. "Bishop Beiler saw the picture in the paper. Who put it in?" She looked to her mother, hoping for an answer.

"Your father did," Emma said flatly. "After forcing Daniel to marry you in an *Englische* ceremony... and knowing it was to be kept secret; he took a picture and had it placed in the paper with a write up about the marriage." Her eyes narrowed. "He deliberately planned it."

Martha heaved a heavy sigh. "Daniel and I will never be allowed to marry in an Amish ceremony."

"What one plans, another can unplan," Emma said.

Martha frowned at her mother's words. "What do you mean? Bishop Beiler was adamant. Since we are married under *Englische* law, we can't be married as an Amish couple."

"What if you weren't married?" Emma asked.

"You mean divorce?" Martha's eyes widened in surprise. "Even divorced, as long as one spouse is alive, the other may not marry." She attempted a smile. "I remember Aunt Mary telling me about Liza Troyer who jumped the fence to become *Englische* after ten years of marriage to Leroy Troyer. He begged her to return and repent, but she was determined she wasn't staying Amish. He finally divorced her and she remarried *Englische*, but he couldn't remarry because she was still alive. There was that horrible accident on the interstate and she was killed. It was then Leroy was able to remarry."

"Honey," Emma said. "I know the story, too. I think I have the answer." She offered Martha a sly grin. "Your father gave me the idea when he stated you and Daniel would be divorced in a short time. Are you willing to take a car ride?"

"Daddy said we'd be divorced? A ride? Sure," Martha replied. "Where are we going?"

Emma smiled. "Hopefully to answer all your prayers and get this corrected." Emma stepped into the hallway and picked up her purse from the table, checking to make sure the keys to the car were in it. "Let's go." She opened the door for Martha.

Martha stared at the large window of the building. 'Troyer and Smith - Attorneys at Law' was printed in large print on the glass.

"Here?" Martha asked.

Emma nodded and held the door open.

"May I help you?" the woman at the desk asked.

"Is William Smith available?" Emma asked.

"Do you have an appointment?"

Emma shook her head. "No."

"I'll see if he is available. Your name? Reason for the visit?" the lady asked.

"Emma Noble is the name, Mrs. Dan Noble. We're curious about a marriage dissolution."

"I see," the woman said and stepped away from the desk to a doorway down the hallway.

Martha watched as the woman knocked on the door frame before leaning into the room. Moments later she leaned back out and motioned for them to come to the office.

"Mr. Smith will see you, Mrs. Noble." She motioned for them to enter the office and closed the door after Martha was in.

A tall gentleman wearing glasses, dressed in a three-piece suit and showing maturity with a few graying hairs stood.

"So glad to meet you, Mrs. Noble." He glanced at Martha. "And your name is?"

"I am Martha Noble... uh, I mean, Martha Yoder, Mrs. Daniel Yoder," Martha said.

"Please, sit ladies." He moved to the front of his desk, crossed his legs, and leaned against the desk. "Now, exactly what is the marriage issue? Divorce?"

"No, no," replied Emma. "My daughter was married on April 4th. My husband sort of forced the issue, demanding if they wished to get married, it would be an *Englische* wedding."

Smith frowned. "I'm confused." He glanced at Martha. "This is your daughter? She is Amish?"

Emma smiled. "Let me see if I can explain this quickly." She began the explanation.

Smith nodded, listening and making notes on a tablet to his side. He turned to Martha.

"So, Mrs. Yoder, you are only seventeen. Is that correct?"

Martha nodded. "Yes, sir," she said.

"And your husband, this Daniel Yoder is also only seventeen?"

Again, Martha nodded.

Smith grimaced and offered a huge sigh. "Both minors. Was there any parental consent?"

Emma suddenly had the look of a deer caught in bright car lights. "I guess my husband and I agreed, but I don't remember signing anything."

"What of this Amish Yoder boy?" Smith asked.

"Definitely not," Martha said. "His parents may not even know we're married."

"May I ask a delicate question?" Smith braced both his hands on the desk behind him. "An awkward one."

"I guess you can," Emma said when Martha didn't reply.

He looked directly at Martha.

"Martha, tell me. Was the marriage consummated?"

Martha felt the heat of blush fill her cheeks. "No," she whispered. "On our wedding night..." She took a deep breath. "He slept in my brother's room with his friend. I slept alone in my room."

Smith nodded. "So, now you don't love him and want out of this marriage? Is that it?"

"No, I love him with all my heart," Martha said. "I want to become Amish, but because we are married, I won't be allowed to join the church, and therefore can't marry Daniel in an Amish wedding. Daniel doesn't feel the *Englische* wedding was the real thing, hence why he slept in another room that night."

"Is there anyone to vouch for this sleeping arrangement?"

"Well, her father and I know they didn't sleep together," Emma said.

"Plus, the best man is Daniel's *Englische* friend who stayed with him in my brother's room."

Smith stood and moved to his chair behind the desk.

"Seems very simple. You were too young to marry

without proper consent from all parents concerned. The marriage was not consummated. And, as strange as it sounds, it appears the marriage could be considered forced. All of these facts point to an easy annulment of the marriage." He wrote on this notepad. "For a small fee, we can have this marriage annulled." He smiled at Martha. "For all practical purposes, the marriage didn't happen." He gazed at Emma. "Is this what you were hoping for?"

Emma looked at Martha. "I think if I talk with Bishop Beiler, you will be allowed to join the Amish church."

"What of daddy?" Martha asked.

"It is about time your father learned the Amish are not ignorant bumpkins. He has always thought himself better than my family. It is about time he was served some humble pie." She paused. "This was his ploy to keep you from becoming Amish." Emma leaned back in the chair, placing her arms over her chest defiantly. "Well, it just backfired." She turned to Smith. "Get the paperwork together. I'll write you a check."

Smith stood. "I will have the papers drawn and processed." He stepped to the door and opened it. "If you wish to have a cup of coffee and a slice of pie, I recommend the Country Kitchen restaurant at the corner of routes 5 and 20 on the south end of town. Give me about an hour and come back. Everything should be ready by then."

# # #

Tuesday, April 21, 1964, 9 a.m.

Martha sat in the main room of Bishop Beiler's house. Naomi Beiler, the bishop's wife sauntered into the room with a tray of meadow tea and freshly baked muffins.

"He should be home anytime, Martha," Naomi said, placing the tray on a small table near her. "He left early this morning for town to get more chicken feed." She frowned. "Unless, of course, he was detained by somebody."

The back kitchen door opened.

"That has to be him, now." Naomi smiled and hustled to the kitchen.

Martha took a muffin and pulled it apart, inhaling the scent. She nibbled, listening to the muffled voices in the kitchen before Bishop Beiler entered the room.

"So, you are back, Martha Yoder." He stood before the table near her. "Allow me a second to get a muffin..." He frowned and studied the tray. "Naomi? Where is the butter?"

Martha nibbled another section of her muffin.

"I just noticed it on the counter." She tittered as she hastened into the room. "My apologies. I forgot to put it on the tray." She handed the fat butter knife to her husband.

"The meadow tea is delicious, Mrs. Beiler," Martha said after sipping some from a glass. "Did you use fresh mint?"

Naomi smiled. "Why, yes, I did. Found a sprig or two this morning."

Martha took another sip and nodded. "Definitely fresh," she murmured.

Bishop Beiler smeared the butter on the muffin and grabbed a glass of meadow tea.

"Now, tell me, Martha, what is the purpose of this visit?"

"I wish to discuss, once more, about being baptized, joining the Amish church, and getting married." She popped the last of the muffin in her mouth and carefully brushed the crumbs into hand and placed them in the pocket of her apron.

"As I stated, quite clearly yesterday, you are married and *Englische*. There is no way–"

"But, there is," Martha said interrupting the bishop. "My *Englische* wedding is no more."

"Divorce is not the answer," the bishop reprimanded.

"Not divorce," Martha said. "My mother and I went to a lawyer. My *Englische* marriage has been annulled. There was no license. We were too young and didn't have Daniel's parent's approval." She grimaced, ending with a frown. "Also, my father forced this wedding by demanding he be allowed to walk me down the aisle. All three of those are grounds to end the marriage. In the eyes of the law, the marriage never happened."

"But, Martha Yoder, in the eyes of God you are married. You are man and wife. You have a union."

Martha blushed. "There was no union, bishop." She

bowed her head. "We never consummated the marriage vows." She held her head up high. "We did not sleep together on our wedding night."

Bishop Beiler's eyebrows knitted together into one dark, hairy line above his eyes. "Is this true?"

Martha nodded. "We slept in separate rooms."

He nodded his head, pulling on his beard as he thought.

"Allow me to mull these events overnight." He rolled a shoulder. "This is most unusual." He stood. "Until tomorrow, Mrs. Yo... Miss Noble."

"I will be staying with my uncle, Paul Hershberger."

Bishop Beiler nodded.

CHAPTER TWENTY-FIVE: Classes

Friday, April 24, 1964, 10 a.m.

Bishop Beiler knocked on the door of the Hershberger residence. Aunt Mary answered and welcomed him into the main room.

"Is Martha Noble here?" he asked.

Aunt Mary nodded and offered him a seat before going to the kitchen door to call her from the garden.

"I only have a few more potatoes to plant, Aunt Mary. Let me finish and I will be in."

"You have a visitor. Bishop Beiler is here."

Martha dropped the bag with the remaining potatoes, lifted her skirts and ran to the back door. She stopped at the hand pump to wash her hands of the dirt, and hopefully, the smell of old potatoes. She straightened her dress and apron, made sure her bonnet was proper on her head, then went into the house.

Aunt Mary nodded to the front room. "He waits for you there." She poured glasses of water and placed cookies on a tray. Aunt Mary lifted the tray and headed for the main room. Martha followed behind.

As Aunt Mary entered, Bishop Beiler stood. "You need not have bothered," he said, then noticed Martha behind her. "My apologies, Martha, for not getting back to you sooner. This took many prayers from me and several discussions with others of the Ordnung."

Martha watched as the bishop took a cookie and glass of water. She motioned for him to sit as she took a seat opposite him. She watched him with expectation, and yet, some trepidation.

"Your decision?" she asked, not waiting.

"After extensive questioning, and much praying, it was decided you are not married in the eyes of God." He smiled. "Therefore, you are not married in the eyes of our Ordnung. If you wish to become Amish, we can begin study. Only then may you be allowed a baptism." He paused and gazed into her eyes. "Understood?"

Martha nodded, suppressing a smile. "Yes," she whispered. "I understand."

"So, you wish to marry this young Amish boy from Centertown. Is that not correct?"

Martha's face beamed. "I most certainly do."

"When? A nice fall October day would be nice," he suggested. "Most of the harvests will be done. It will be cool weather and the colors of fall will be at their best." He winked. "A perfect day for a wedding."

"I would like a spring wedding," Martha said. "If possible, next month, if I can be baptized in time."

Bishop Beiler's expression changed to surprise. "So soon?" He immediately looked to her stomach. "Why?"

Noticing his gaze, Martha grabbed her stomach. "No. No. Never. I want to get married as soon as possible so my father does not have time to plot another way to stop us."

He nodded, knowingly. "It will be a strain on the community. All the food to prepare. Crops to plant." He rolled a shoulder. "You are asking much for a spring wedding. Are you sure you cannot wait until later in the fall?"

A glint showed in Martha's eye. "My father will pay for much of the food. He will get it catered." She grinned. "It is the *Englische* way. Plus, my mother, having been raised Amish, will make sure he pays." She shrugged. "If the community wants to contribute, so be it. I will appreciate the help, but I understand the need to get the fields ready." Martha straightened in her chair. "So, when do I start my studies and get ready for baptism?"

Bishop Beiler almost choked on the cookie he'd bitten, her forwardness catching him off-guard. "We may start tomorrow and study each day for one hour. Can you come to my house at ten each morning?"

Martha gazed into the kitchen where Aunt Mary stood

near the doorway, watching and trying not to be obvious she was listening. She nodded.

"I can," Martha said.

"We will start with basics which will be simple enough." He gazed at her clothes. "You seem to have a grasp of being Amish. We will spend more time on the rules."

"Do you think I can be baptized before the end of May? Daniel and I spoke of possibly getting married on Thursday, May 28th."

Bishop Beiler inhaled deeply. "I see no problem. The water may be cold for immersion."

Martha grinned. "If need be, I will break the ice myself if it is there and jump in."

He held up a hand with a large grin crossing his face. "We do not need to be quite that enthusiastic. We will wait and see what the Lord gives us for weather at that time."

"I will notify Daniel of this meeting," she said.

Bishop Beiler frowned. "There could be one problem. I have heard Daniel Yoder is currently shunned." He squirmed in his chair. "I do not feel it would be proper to talk with him." He paused. "Especially if you wish to become Amish."

"But–"

"Martha," Aunt Mary said. "Do you wish to be Amish, or not? Best heed the words of Bishop Beiler."

"Yes, Aunt Mary," Martha said and hung her head. "May I write him the news?"

Bishop Beiler lowered his gaze and shook his head. "Daniel is shunned. You may not communicate with him. Talk. Write. It is communicating." He rolled a shoulder. "The Amish must obey the laws of the Ordnung."

"Yes, Bishop Beiler," Martha said.

There has to be a way, Martha thought. *Perhaps...* Martha let the thought smolder in her mind.

# # #

Martha sat at the table watching her aunt, uncle, and their offspring enjoy lunch. She nibbled at the slice of ham, and rolled the peas around on her plate. She was thinking.

Uncle Paul placed his fork on the plate with a loud clang. The children stopped eating and gazed at their father.

"Is there a problem, Martha?" he asked, watching her.

"Nay," Martha replied. "I was thinking of visiting my mother this afternoon. Would that be okay?"

"Of course," Paul said. "We are not monsters." He grinned. "You may visit your mother anytime you wish. Will you be staying overnight?"

Her forehead wrinkled in thought.

"I do not think so..." She gazed off into the distance. "But, it could be late when I arrive back. Is that okay?"

"Step quietly if we are asleep," he said with a smile.

"Thank you. May I be excused?" Martha started to stand.

"Do you not wish a slice of fresh apple pie?" Aunt Mary asked.

Martha hesitated. "Your pies are delicious." She made a face. "May I take a slice with me?"

Aunt Mary nodded, stood and went to get the pie. Martha followed, taking the slice offered and then running out the door. She grabbed her bike and carefully maneuvered it so she didn't drop the pie. She started out the driveway, pedaling, using one hand on the handlebar, the other hand to feed herself the pie.

Aunt Mary stood at the kitchen door to watch, shaking her head, smiling, enjoying the view.

"Mother? Mother?" Martha ran into the house searching.

"I'm in the kitchen."

"Can you drive me to Centertown? I need to see Daniel. It is important."

"Why don't you drive yourself?" Emma asked.

Martha gave her mother an exasperated gaze. "I am Amish, mother. The Amish do not drive cars."

Emma stepped back from the stove, placed a hand on her hip, and cocked a raised eyebrow glance at her daughter. "You're still *Englische*, Martha. You want to be Amish, but you're still *Englische*. Remember?"

Martha heaved a large sigh. "Yes, I am *Englische*, but I want to be Amish and must now begin to live as an Amish person. I start classes tomorrow with Bishop Beiler so I can be baptized."

Emma turned back to the pot on the stove and stirred it. "So, tell me, my dear want-to-be-Amish daughter. Why do we need to go to Centertown. To see Daniel?"

"Yes," Martha said emphatically. "He is being shunned." Again, she sighed. "More likely because they learned he got married in an *Englische* wedding. I know Mr. Smith sent a copy of the annulment, but that could take over a week to get to him." She paused and gazed at her mother who appeared unconcerned. "Do you remember the Sears and Roebuck bill you got a few months back? It took 3 days for it to come from them to you. I remember you paying the bill the next day and because of mail service and other issues, it didn't get to them for almost two weeks. They posted a late fee. Remember?"

Emma slapped the spoon on the counter, then placed both hands on the counter before looking at Martha. She took a deep breath. "I remember."

"So, can we go and I will take my copy of the annulment so Daniel can use it to stop the shunning?" She pleaded with her eyes. "We can't be married if he is being shunned."

"Fine," her mother said. "I'll put this in the oven for your father's meal." She grinned at Martha. "I don't figure we'll be back in time, so I'll leave him a note."

Emma put a cover over the pot and placed it in the oven before setting the temperature. She looked at the clock.

"I'll set it on low and it will cook for the next three hours until he gets home." She paused. "You know he will want to know why we went to Centertown." She held her index finger to her lips. "He still doesn't know about the annulment."

"Mother!" Martha exclaimed. "You didn't tell him?"

Emma grinned. "How do you kids say it? No way, man."

They laughed. Emma grabbed her purse and the car keys. "Let's go."

# # #

228

Martha explained her plan to her mother on the trip to Centertown. She knew Daniel would be at home since he was shunned and she figured he wouldn't be allowed to teach.

"I can't go in," Martha said. "He is being shunned and Bishop Beiler was adamant I am not to talk with him." She grimaced. "The Amish seem to have a very strong and tight network and learn things faster than the *Englische* can even imagine." She laughed.

Emma pulled the car into the Yoder farm driveway. "I'll go in," she said.

"Thank you, mother."

Emma walked to the back kitchen door and knocked.

Hannah Yoder answered. Martha watched as the two talked. She noticed Hannah shake her head and point toward the school. Her mother nodded approval and came back to the car.

"He is at the school." Emma frowned. "You're right, he is being shunned, but he is allowed to assist the children, but not allowed to teach them. It seems a Miss Mueller is helping him." She gave Martha a questioning look. "Who is she?"

"Me in another twenty-five years if I don't get to marry Daniel." Martha laughed. "She is his assistant."

"Oh," Emma replied. "So, off to the school?"

Martha nodded. "Sure."

# # #

They drove by the school. The children were just leaving the building.

"We will need to wait until Miss Mueller leaves," Martha said. She pointed at an intersection about half a mile from the school.

"We can wait there and not be noticed," Martha said.

Emma nodded and drove the car to the corner, drove on, turned around and parked the car a little back from the intersection. They waited and watched as buggies filled with children passed them.

They continued their watch. Finally, Miss Mueller appeared at the door. She turned and carried on a conversation with another inside the school. A few moments later she got in her buggy and headed toward them.

"Hurry, mother," Martha said. "Pull through the intersection before she can see me. Keep going and we'll go around the mile square. If Daniel heads out, we'll see him since he will be going the opposite direction Miss Mueller is headed." She smiled. "Hopefully, he will stay in the school until we get back."

Emma roared the engine into life, pulled to the stop sign, checked for traffic – the only other person on the road was Miss Mueller. Emma pulled through the intersection and continued to the end of the mile to the next stop sign. She waited, turned left and went another mile and turned left again. Another mile and they were at the last stop sign. Daniel was nowhere to be seen on the road in either direction, She turned left and headed for the school. Daniel's lone horse stood, waiting, enjoying the new growth to chew on.

"I'll go in and give him the paper and explain everything," Emma said and opened the car door.

"No, I'll go in, too," Martha said. She surveyed the area. There was nobody to be seen.

She opened the door and rushed across the short open area, up the steps, and into the school. Emma strolled casually to join her seconds later.

"Daniel?" Martha called.

"Here," the reply came from the front of the school. He stood and ran to her. "Why are you here? I am being shunned. You should not have come." He held her. "I must repent of my transgressions." He shook his head. "The *Englische* wedding was not kept a secret." He gazed at his mother-in-law. "Somebody put our picture in the newspaper."

Emma nodded. "Your father-in-law is a jerk. He did it." She grimaced. "It was his feeble attempt to keep Martha from joining the Amish. He calculated you'd be shunned and the two of you wouldn't be able to marry."

Daniel gazed at Emma. "He was right."

Emma grinned. "Was. That is the correct term. Was."

Martha pulled a folded paper from her apron. "This is a marriage annulment. Our *Englische* wedding is no more. I spoke with Bishop Beiler about becoming Amish. Because of the wedding, he wouldn't allow it. But, we had the marriage annulled. I went back to Bishop Beiler and he said if the eyes of the law do not acknowledge it, the Amish will abide with it." Crimson filled her cheeks. "Plus, the fact we did not consummate the marriage that night, Bishop Beiler says in the eyes of God we are not married." She grabbed Daniel's hands. "We can get married in an Amish wedding – just as you wanted. I will be baptized soon and I told Bishop Beiler we hoped to marry before the end of May." She gazed into Daniel's eyes. "You do still want to marry me, yes?"

"Of course, I do," Daniel said, picking her up and twirling her in a circle. "Now, you'd best disappear before somebody sees you talking to me."

"Take this paper to your bishop," Emma said pointing to the paper Martha held. "Show him the marriage was annulled. It is not a divorce. You should be able to have the shunning removed." She grabbed Martha's hand. "Now, let's get out of here before there is even more trouble."

Emma pulled Martha down the aisle toward the front door.

It opened.

"Is there a problem?" Miss Mueller stepped in.

"No," Emma said. "I just needed to speak with Daniel."

Miss Mueller cocked an eyebrow, glancing at Martha. "Martha Noble... or should I say Martha Yoder?"

"It is Martha Noble, Miss Mueller," Martha said icily. "The wedding was annulled. Daniel and I are not married."

"Yet, you came here to talk with him?" She glanced at Daniel who stood a few feet behind them. "He is shunned." Miss Mueller turned her attention back to Martha. "You are dressed as Amish. You should know better. This will need to be reported to Bishop Schmucker."

Emma stepped forward to confront Miss Mueller, towering just an inch taller.

"My daughter did not speak to Daniel," she lied. "She came with me to show me where the school is located. I needed to make sure Mr. Yoder received the annulment papers." She pointed at the paper in Daniel's hand. "Besides, my daughter may dress as Amish, she is still *Englische* and as such, if she decided, she should be able to speak with Daniel whether he is shunned or not."

Miss Mueller smiled. "I have been corrected. I see no reason Bishop Schmucker should be involved." She sighed. "I wish I had the conviction these two have for each other. If I had, I would be married and not Miss Mueller, the spinster who will never marry." She turned to walk away.

"Miss Mueller?" Martha called.

"Yes?"

"When Daniel and I are married, would do us the honor of being a *newehocker*?"

"But I have–"

"Please?" Martha begged. "Unless you cannot make it to Shipshewana."

Miss Mueller grinned. "I will be there."

"*danke*," Martha said and watched Miss Mueller leave the school.

Emma turned to Martha. "We must go now before another comes." She turned to Daniel. "Do you have any questions?"

"No," Daniel replied, a small frown creasing his brow.

"What is it, Daniel?" Martha asked.

Daniel shrugged. "I just guessed we would be married here."

"If you wish, Daniel," Martha said. "First, get unshunned." She giggled. "I will see you soon when we can talk."

Emma and Martha left the school, rushing to the car and driving away. Emma glanced at her watch.

"We should be home shortly after your father arrives. Will you stay to eat? He can drive you home."

"I have my bike..."

"He can put it in the trunk," Emma said. "I think we need to tell him about the annulment."

# # #

Martha finished her meal. They'd eaten in silence and she

232

was reminded of the meals at Uncle Paul's home.

The lull before the storm, Martha thought. She took a deep breath. *It will hit the fan when he learns about the annulment.*

"How about we go into the living room and talk," Emma said. "I'll make some Kool-Aid to drink. Everyone like strawberry?"

Dan grunted and nodded approval. He stood and ambled into the living room to sit in his Barca-Lounger. "Turn on the television, Martha," he said as she walked into the room. "You buy the best available on the market and the stupid remote only works when it wants." He lifted the remote and repeatedly punched the button to no avail.

Martha pulled the knob and walked to the chair opposite him. Emma strolled in with a tray of plastic red glasses filled with strawberry Kook-Aid. Dan took one and sit it on the table next to him.

"Use a coaster, dear," Emma chastised.

Dan grunted and slid the coaster under the glass. "Done," he mumbled.

Martha took her glass and sipped. *This is not going to be a good thing*, she thought.

"So, where did you two go? Shopping?" Dan asked.

Emma sat on the couch with her drink. "We went to Centertown today," she said nonchalantly.

"Oh?" Dan raised an eyebrow with a questioning gaze. "Why?"

"We discovered Daniel was being shunned for marrying in an *Englische* church." Emma took a sip.

"Yeah, well, that's his problem. Not mine." Dan gazed back to the television, watching 'Mr. Ed.' He lifted the remote and punched a button. Out of exasperation, he slammed the remote on the table beside him. "Martha, would you turn up the volume?"

Martha moved to stand.

"We don't need it on right now," Emma said and motioned for her to stay seated. "We need to tell you something, Dan."

Dan stared at the television, straining to listen. "What?"

"I had Martha's wedding annulled earlier this week." Emma lifted the glass to her lips, waiting.

"You what?" Dan yelled, slamming the Barca-Lounger into an upright position. "You had no right to–"

"I had every right," Emma said quietly. "You forced this wedding so you could control our daughter. It was your plan to make Daniel either back away from marrying our daughter, or put him in the position they couldn't get married in an Amish ceremony."

Dan eased his Barca-Lounger back. "You can't prove it."

"I don't need to," Emma said. "The kids needed our approval to get married. Daniel's parents knew nothing of this *Englische* wedding. Plus, they never consummated the marriage." She grinned. "Remember, you were so thrilled your little girl was sleeping alone on her wedding night. The groom was sleeping in the next room."

"Daddy!" Martha raised her voice. "Is this true? You were happy I was alone?" She frowned. "Yet, you acted mad when you discovered I slept alone on my wedding night."

"Now, now, Martha. You're too young to understand, and–"

"And you forced all this, didn't you, Dan Noble," asked Emma.

He shrugged.

"Well, I took Martha to a lawyer when she was denied joining the Amish. Mr. Smith was quite helpful in getting the marriage annulled. By the way, did you get a license for them?"

Dan winced. "I got one the next day and forged all the signatures."

"You what?" Emma yelled. "Forged?"

"For an extra fifty bucks, I got the kid to let me do it." He shrugged. "So, sue me."

"No need," Emma said. "The annulment went through. We gave Daniel a copy so he can show his bishop. Martha has already shown Bishop Beiler the annulment. You'll be happy to know she starts her Amish training tomorrow. She'll be learning the ways of the Ordnung and will be baptized next month." Without too much hesitation for Dan to interrupt, she continued. "And, near the end of May, she will marry Daniel." She grinned. "In an Amish wedding. Yes, you will be paying for another wedding."

"I will do no such thing," Dan said, once more slamming his chair upright. He stood. "I'll have the annulment voided."

"You will do no such thing, Dan Noble. If you do, you will also be signing divorce papers." Emma stood. "I am tired of your damning my heritage. I was raised Amish. You fell in love with me, an Amish girl. I married you, giving up my heritage. If my youngest daughter wants to embrace my background, you will bite your tongue and agree to it." She stomped over to him. "Do you understand?" She glared at him as he remained silent. "I love you, Dan Noble. Martha loves Daniel. There is no difference. I am your wife and, as a wife, I am to be submissive to you as stated in the Bible, but I will not allow you to ordain our daughter's life."

Martha stood. "I love you both," she said and rushed over and embraced them in a group hug. "I don't want to see you getting a divorce over me." She hesitated. "But, I am going to marry Daniel Yoder, Daddy."

Dan leaned over and kissed the top of Martha's head. "I know, honey." He sighed. "I just need to learn to give up my little girl."

"Trust me, Daddy," Martha said. "Daniel will treat me well."

"I know," Dan said. "He is a good man. Can you forgive me?"

"Oh, Daddy," Martha said. She leaned up to kiss him on the cheek. "You'll always be my daddy." She smiled.

"Now," Emma said. "We'd best get her to Uncle Paul's before they all go to sleep." She grinned. "I remember, the Amish tend to awake very early in the morning to start work."

"I'll drive," Dan said. "Maybe we – all of us – will visit with Paul and Mary for a little while tonight... and again, this weekend."

Martha and Emma smiled at Dan.

CHAPTER TWENTY-SIX: Sin Repentance

Saturday, April 25, 1964, 12:45 p.m.

Daniel watched as Hannah and his mother cleaned the dishes and food from the table. Once the table had been washed, he placed the sheet of paper on the table.

"My marriage was annulled," he whispered. He walked from the kitchen to the main room. He sat in the chair opposite his father and waited, watching the activity in the kitchen.

Hannah leaned over and adjusted the paper so she could read it.

"Mama," she called. "You should read this." Hannah turned the paper so her mother could see it.

Daniel watched his mother read the document, point to a word and look to Hannah, who would shrug. Finally, Rebecca picked up the paper and walked into the main room to show Noah. He put down The Budget at her request and took the sheet of paper. They gazed at him.

Daniel took a deep breath.

"It is a document which says the marriage – the *Englische* wedding – between Martha and I has been voided. We are no longer married. I am a single man."

Noah nodded. Rebecca smiled and returned to the kitchen. No words were spoken by either. Noah stood and walked toward the kitchen. He carried the sheet of paper with him.

"I am going to visit the bishop," he stated at the doorway between the rooms. "I am taking the buckboard so more than one may ride."

Daniel realized he was being invited, stood and quietly followed his father through the kitchen, out the door, and to the barn. Without a spoken word, the two prepared Beauty for the

236

trip. Noah got in the buckboard and took the reins. Daniel hopped into the back and sat facing backward. He spoke aloud to no particular person, explaining how the annulment worked and what the Shipshewana bishop had said. Daniel felt he was getting the facts correct within his mind. Noah listened without comment.

It was a quick ride to Bishop Schmucker's home.

Noah knocked on the door. Daniel stood at the bottom of the steps, waiting.

Mrs. Schmucker answered the door, smiled at Noah, and frowned when she noticed Daniel at the bottom of the steps.

"Is the bishop in?" Noah asked.

She pursed her lips. "I will get him," she said and hurried away.

"Come in. Come in," Bishop Schmucker said. He noticed Daniel and held the door open as Noah walked in. He continued to hold the door open which allowed Daniel to enter.

"To what do I owe this visit, Noah Yoder?"

Noah pulled the folded paper from inside his hat and handed it to the bishop.

"This was brought to my attention," Noah said. "It is an annulment of Daniel's *Englische* marriage."

"Annulment? So he is divorced?"

"Nay, bishop. This piece of paper claims the marriage to never have happened." He shrugged. "I heard the bishop in Shipshewana has agreed that in the eyes of the law and God, they are not married; therefore the Ordnung has agreed to it and will be allowing Martha Noble to join the church after proper education and baptism – if she so desires."

Bishop Schmucker tugged on his beard and nodded. "What Shipshewana agrees to does not concern us. We will make our own decision."

He reached for his reading glasses and scrutinized the paper.

"I am confused." He shook his head. "It says the marriage was never consummated." He stared at Daniel. "Is this correct?"

Daniel nodded, a slight blush to cheeks.

Bishop Schmucker nodded. "Ah, so this is where the eyes

of God comes to play. Interesting." He sat and carefully read the document again.

"I will need to discuss this with others," he said. "When a decision is made..." He paused. "Daniel will still need to address Sin Repentance and ask forgiveness of this act."

Daniel nodded.

"I will make an announcement at church when the decision is made." He stood. "Is there anything else you wish to discuss?"

"Nay," Noah said. "My family will await your decision."

He turned and headed for the door. Daniel followed, unhappy an ending of the shunning did not happen. He would wait.

# # #

Sunday, May 3, 1964, 8 a.m.

Daniel stood outside the entrance to the main room. Church was being held and he was still shunned. But, Bishop Schmucker had informed Noah of Daniel's attendance being necessary. He didn't say if the shunning would be canceled, but wished for Daniel to be there. If *Meidung* was revoked, he could ask for Sin Repentance before the community.

Bishop Schmucker droned on. Daniel waited.

"It was brought to my attention Daniel Yoder married in an *Englische* wedding, outside the Amish Ordnung. He has been shunned for his sin. It was also brought to my attention that an annulment has been performed on this marriage and therefore, in the *Englische* eyes, never happened. In Amish eyes, it still happened." Bishop Schmucker bowed his head slightly, pausing to think. "However, it was also brought to my attention the reason for the annulment was threefold per the document. One point of the annulment cleared Daniel before the eyes of God. Therefore, the marriage never happened." He turned to gaze in Daniel's direction. "If Daniel would come forward and confess his sin."

All eyes turned toward the direction Bishop Schmucker gazed. Daniel stepped from the kitchen into the meeting room.

"I so desire," Daniel said, and walked between the two groups to join Bishop Schmucker.

He stood there, head bowed, hands together in front of him.

"In my youthful eagerness, I agreed to terms against my Amish training. I wanted to appease my future bride's father. It was a mistake to marry an *Englische* girl in an *Englische* wedding. I repent of this sin and ask forgiveness."

"Do you truly repent, Daniel Yoder?" Bishop Schmucker asked.

Daniel raised his head to look into the bishop's eyes. "Yes, I truly repent my sin."

Bishop Schmucker placed his hands on Daniel's shoulders. "Welcome back, my son," he said. "You are no longer shunned."

Daniel felt the weight lifted from inside him. He was once again one with the community. He would be able to teach, again.

# # #

Wednesday, May 6, 1964, 9:30 a.m.

Daniel was glad to be back to teaching. Even his students seemed more invigorated. Miss Mueller had taught well, but used a different method. She also had eliminated all singing as nonsense.

The first and second graders were having fun singing the 'alphabet' song. Daniel introduced 'One Little Indian' as a way to learn numbers. Many of the second graders had mastered the numbers one through ten in both directions. The first graders were still having problems, but they enjoyed the chance to learn.

A knock o the school door caught everyone's attention. Paul Mueller stood in the doorway. He pulled his hat off and shuffled forward.

"What is it, Paul," Ruby Mueller asked of her brother. "Why are you not at work?"

"May I speak with you two privately?" he asked.

239

"Continue your studies," Daniel said.

He followed Ruby down the aisle to the school door.

"Why so secretive?" whispered Ruby.

"I bring tidings," Paul said. "Bishop Schmucker has died and is now with God."

"Does my sister, Ruth, know?" Daniel asked.

"She bid me to come here," Paul said. "The home viewing will be later tonight."

Daniel nodded. "I must attend to classes."

He left Paul and Ruby to talk, if they so desired. As he strode back into the classroom, all eyes were on him. Daniel reached the front of the class and clapped his hands for attention.

"I was informed Bishop Schmucker has died and now rests with God." He paused. "I will allow an early out this afternoon so you may go home and if your parents so wish, they may attend the home service for our bishop."

The remainder of the day was somber, yet there was an air of joy knowing Bishop Schmucker had moved on to meet his Creator.

That evening, Daniel, with his parents and siblings, attended the home viewing of Bishop Schmucker. Daniel was reminded of when his grandfather died. It was sad, yet there was an air of joy. He wanted to cry. This man had seen him at his worst and best. Daniel couldn't express it, but he was glad Bishop Schmucker knew he was no longer shunned before passing. The bishop knew Daniel was teaching – just as the bishop had planned.

Friday, May 8, 1964, 10 a.m.

Daniel canceled school for the day so all could attend the funeral for Bishop Schmucker. The ministers, including his father, oversaw the funeral and attended the graveside viewing.

240

Daniel was amazed to see what he considered perfect attendance of the community. Bishop Schmucker had been an influence on the community.

# # #

Sunday, May 10, 1964, early morning

Noah fidgeted in the buggy. It was a beautiful day with the sun shining brightly and a mild, warm breeze.

Perhaps we can fly kites this afternoon, Daniel thought.

Again, Noah squirmed in his seat as the buggy trundled down the road. Daniel had never seen his father act in such a manner. It was then Noah pulled at his collar as if it restricted his breathing. His father's forehead beaded with perspiration.

Why is he acting so? Daniel wondered. *Is he not well?*

Noah urged Beauty into the Ezekiel Troyer driveway. Daniel noticed it seemed the whole community had come to church that day. In fact, most headed for the barn, not the house. Only a few women were headed into the house.

Daniel followed his father and siblings to the barn. His mother hustled with the basket of food toward the house.

Noah took a deep breath and entered the barn.

"*guder mariye*, Noah," Ezekiel Troyer said. "Today shall prove interesting."

Noah nodded.

Daniel saw his friend, John Heffel. He quickly left his father's side to join John and discuss things before church started.

Minister Troyer opened the service. The *Vorsänger* started *O Gott, Vader* and members joined in the sing, raising their voices to God. The service continued as always, except Bishop Schmucker wasn't there. It was different.

"Now," Minister Troyer said. "We pick a new bishop. We shall kneel in silent prayer."

The congregation knelt.

"I call on Deacon Jacob Metz to come forward."

Rueben's son came forward carrying five copies of the Ausbund. He placed them on the table and turned to face the

241

ministers. "I now call those in the lot to come forward." Jacob paused before saying the names. "Rueben Metz, Elmer Holtz, Joseph Langenstott, Noah Yoder, and Ezekiel Troyer."

Daniel watched as his father moved to join the other men. The hymn books had been tied with a string. One of the books contained a slip of paper on which the words of Acts 1:24 had been written:

> "And they prayed, and said, Thou, Lord, which knowest the hearts of all men, show whether of these thou has chosen."

Daniel glanced at his sister, Rachel. She tried not to smile as she watched her husband, Jacob, perform the duties of deacon.

In order of age, each man stepped forward to choose a hymn book then stepped back to sit on the bench, and wait.

Deacon Metz stepped before Rueben Metz, took the hymnal from his father, and untied the string. He searched the hymn book for the slip of paper. He found none.

Next, he moved to Elmer Holtz, repeating the procedure. Again, no slip was found.

Deacon Metz moved to Joseph Langenstott. He took the hymnal, untied the string, and searched the book.

Daniel glanced at his father who was next in line. He could see the look in his father's eyes. The stress of the lot was showing as he nervously watched for a slip to show itself in Joseph's hymnal.

Deacon Metz moved to Noah Yoder. Noah handed the hymnal to Rueben. Once more the deacon untied the string and opened the book. He flipped through the pages when the book slipped from his hands. Rueben snatched it from the air. A lone white slip of paper floated to the ground.

Noah bowed his head. The lot had fallen to him. He was now the new bishop for their Ordnung.

Daniel glanced at Ezekiel Troyer who was taking a deep breath of relief.

Deacon Metz extended his hand. "Rise, Noah Yoder, and receive your charge. I assure you, God will guide and strengthen you in your work."

Minister Troyer moved to greet Noah with a holy kiss and the assurance of support before leading him to the side where the congregation could pass and congratulate him.

Daniel quietly nodded. He now understood his father's edginess earlier. He may not have known he was chosen for the lot, but every man in the community when baptized agrees to be chosen. Daniel wondered if he would be as nervous as his father. It was then he realized, he could very well be chosen in the next lot for minister.

CHAPTER TWENTY-SEVEN: Martha's Baptism

Wednesday, May 13, 1964, 1 p.m.

Martha jumped from the car and rushed up the steps to the schoolhouse. Her mother, Emma, attempted to keep up. Martha knocked and opened the school door.

"Daniel?" she called out. "May I speak with you?"

He looked up from the student's work and saw her. He motioned for Ruby Mueller to assist young Aaron with his math, then quickly hustled to the door.

"What is the problem?" he asked, grabbing her hands into his. "Good afternoon, Mrs. Noble."

"I will be baptized this Sunday at church," she gushed. "Can you come?"

Daniel's eyes widened, both in surprise and concern.

"Oh, is there a problem?" she asked. "You do not wish to come?"

"Nay, Martha," Daniel said. "This Sunday is my father's first Sunday as the new bishop." He paused. "I hoped to attend."

Martha gazed down at the floor. "I understand." She sighed. "Bishop Beiler will be surprised by your absence. I will attempt to make him understand."

Daniel frowned. "Could you not be baptized here? By my father?"

"Daniel, I have been taught the ways of the Ordnung in Shipshewana. I do not wish to delay my baptism any longer. I want to marry you."

Daniel bit his lower lip. "If we marry, my job is here. We will live in Centertown – somewhere. In time we will find a home here."

Martha looked to her mother with questioning eyes. "I

244

will live here," she murmured. "I did not think about that."

"Let me discuss this with my father tonight." He gazed at her with hope. "Would you stay for supper?"

Martha again looked to her mother.

"I don't think it would hurt," Emma said. "I think we need to discuss this and the wedding." She smiled at Martha. "I don't think you two have given it much thought beyond the idea of getting married." She grabbed the keys from her purse. "I will drive into town and call home to let your father know we'll be home later tonight." Emma gazed at Daniel. "That is if she can stay here until I return."

"Yes," Daniel said. "I will finish teaching today and we will go to my parent's home."

"Daniel?" Ruby called.

He ambled to her. "What is it, Miss Mueller?"

"If you wish to leave when Mrs. Noble returns, I can finish teaching class today." She smiled. "I agree with her. You and Martha have much to talk about. You have many decisions to make."

"*danke*, Miss Mueller," Daniel said and hurried back to Martha and her mother.

"When you return from town, Mrs. Noble, we will go to my house." He nodded to Miss Mueller. "She will finish the classes for today."

Emma nodded and left.

Martha sat in a chair at the back of the schoolroom and watched Daniel teach.

#

Wednesday, May 13, 1964, near 5 p.m.

"Mrs. Noble," Rebecca said with a nod to Emma Noble. "How nice of you to visit." She smiled at Martha. "Welcome, Martha. Always a pleasure to see you."

"I asked them supper meal, Mama," Daniel said.

Rebecca smiled. "A blessing. There is always plenty." She looked at the guests. "Only two?"

Emma and Martha nodded.

"Hannah, set two more places at the table." Rebecca returned to her work at the counter, peeling the potatoes.

"Come," Daniel said and led the two into the main room. "Papa, I have brought Martha and Emma Noble to discuss a matter with you."

Noah stood from his rocker. "A pleasure," he said and motioned for them to sit. "What is this about?"

"Martha is to be baptized this weekend in Shipshewana," Daniel started. "We wish to marry later this month." He paused. "Martha will join our Ordnung."

Noah tugged on his beard, a slight frown creasing his forehead.

"Before she can join our Ordnung, she must learn our rules." Noah rolled a shoulder. "That is normally learned growing up in the community and at baptism when they join the church." Noah nodded. "I will talk with her after she is baptized, if she still wants to marry you, Daniel. Then we will see if she wants to be part of our community."

"Mr. Yoder," Martha started. "I wish to marry Daniel. I will do whatever is necessary. My mother was Amish. I've spent many summers with my Amish aunts, uncles and cousins. In fact, I now live with my Uncle Paul and Aunt Mary while I attend proper training in Shipshewana with Bishop Beiler."

Noah nodded.

"When I am baptized, if your brother, my Uncle Mark, is agreeable, I will move in with them." A small grin of happiness lighted her face. "I have lived with Uncle Mark before." She nodded acquiescence to Noah. "I know many of the rules of your Ordnung."

Once more Noah nodded. "That will make my job much easier. Come see me when you have moved in with my brother, Mark." He paused. "Then we will discuss what is necessary." Noah cocked an eyebrow. "Married?" He gazed at Daniel. "So young, my son?"

"We have known each other since last summer, Papa," Daniel replied. "We met in New York City."

Noah's faced darkened. "Ah, yes. *Rumschpringe.*" He turned his attention to Martha. "Tell me, Martha, do you truly

246

wish to give up your *Englische* ways?" He turned to Emma. "Are you happy with your daughter's decision?"

"I was raised Amish," Emma said. "My brother, Paul Hershberger and my sister, Mary Yoder, your sister-in-law, are still Amish. "

"I know your family," Noah replied. "I asked if you are happy with your daughter's decision to become Amish."

He watched Emma and she could feel his eyes searching.

"Yes," Emma said, pulling herself to full stature in the chair. "I am proud my daughter wishes to embrace my heritage. I left the church for love."

Noah cocked an eye of surprise. "Left?" he echoed.

Emma raised a hand to ward off where the conversation could be headed. "No, I went on *Rumschpringe*. I met Dan Noble and... well, we fell in love. It was a whirlwind affair and we married. I wanted Dan to become Amish." She snickered. "There is no way he would possibly consider it. He is most definitely very *Englische*."

Martha snickered. Noah glanced at her. She muffled the rest of her laughing.

"It was either I leave the Amish, or I give up my love of Dan. I was young. I became *Englische*." Emma sighed. "Before you ask, yes, there are times I regret doing so." Emma glanced at Martha. "Especially when I see these two so much in love and what my husband has done to sabotage it."

"Sabotage?" Noah repeated. "How?"

"It was Dan who demanded your son marry my daughter in an *Englische* ceremony." Emma nodded to Daniel.

Noah glanced at Daniel who sat with head bowed.

"It was Dan who put the picture in the newspaper. These two hoped to keep it secret. I thought it might work. Dan felt by doing what he did, possibly Martha would come to her senses and leave Daniel and come back to the *Englische* lifestyle. Dan felt he "saved me" from a life of drudgery and self-inflicted servitude when he married me." Emma sighed. "If I'd known that, I would have never married him. Dan can't see the good of the Amish lifestyle." Again, she snickered. "We went camping a few years back when the kids were much younger. As we sat by the campfire, the children in bed inside the tent, Dan and I enjoyed the simplicity and silence. He said, I quote - 'This is how life should be, simple; no hustle and bustle.' I don't think he grasped the irony of his words."

Noah nodded, understanding. "So, you have no issues with your daughter joining the church?"

Emma shook her head. "None what-so-ever."

"Fine," Noah said. "I see no problem, except for the possibility of your husband."

"Excuse me?" Emma asked.

"Your husband. I get the feeling he is not in agreement with Martha joining the Amish. Am I correct?"

Rebecca walked into the room. "The meal is ready..."

"Not now, Rebecca. We are in the middle of a very important discussion. We will be out shortly." He smiled at his wife. "This matter must be settled."

"Dan has come to realize that Martha loves Daniel, and Daniel loves Martha." She gazed lovingly at Daniel. "When I explained what Daniel had done in support of his love for Martha, my husband realized how much he had been wrong..." She paused. "For so many years." She paused again. "He actually fell to knees and begged my forgiveness for even thinking he had 'saved me' from the ravages of the Amish life."

Martha had been staring at the floor. She snapped her head up to gaze at her mother. "Father did what?" she asked.

"He begged forgiveness." Emma smiled at Martha. "I think if I'd asked him to become Amish at that moment, he would have." Emma stood and walked over to Martha, taking Martha's hands into hers, Emma knelt before her daughter. "You see, Martha? Your father truly loves you and only wanted the best for you – or, at least, what he thought was the best. He now realizes Daniel Yoder is a fine, upstanding young man and you could do no better in finding a husband than him." Again, Emma gazed at Daniel with a smile. "He said he would be proud to have you as a son-in-law." She grinned. "He hopes perhaps if Alex comes home, you could talk some simple sense into him."

Emma stood and faced Noah.

"You, Mr. Yoder, have a fine son in Daniel, one to be proud of. Yes, I know the Amish and pride. Just be assured, in the *Englische* world, Daniel is a model for others to live by." Once more Emma crossed the room to sit in the chair she'd been in.

"As you know, Mrs. Noble, we are a simple and humble people. Daniel is still young." He smiled. "He makes mistakes. He gets corrected, but, I still love him for what he is, an Amish lad on the brink of manhood."

Noah turned to Martha. "As I stated earlier, when you have settled in at Uncle Mark's, be sure to visit me and we will do what is necessary. Of course, time is of the essence. When did you two plan to marry?"

"Thursday, May 28th," Martha blurted. "This year."

"That is soon," Noah said while pulling on his beard. "Where will the ceremony be held? Shipshewana? Centertown? Whose home?"

Martha's eyes widened. "I don't know," she said. "I assumed in Shipshewana, but that would mean all of your family and friends would need to come there." She sighed. "Uncle Mark lives here. For family, there would be Uncle Paul, a few cousins, and my parents from Shipshewana." Martha turned to gaze at Daniel who had been silent. "Which do you prefer?"

"I do not care, Martha," Daniel said slowly. "It might be easier here in Centertown."

"Of course," Martha said. "If any of my friends from school want to come, they can drive here." She giggled. "That would be easier than many of your family trying to get rides to Shipshewana." She turned to Noah. "We will get married in Centertown. I will ask Uncle Mark if he will host my wedding." Martha stuck her index finger to her lips and chewed on the nail. "If not?" She gave Noah a hopeful look. "Perhaps here?"

"Definitely," Rebecca said, standing in the doorway to the kitchen.

"Fine. That little detail needed to be decided." Noah stood. "Now, my wife has prepared us a meal. Let us go and give thanks before we enjoy the food." He motioned to the kitchen.

As the group proceeded to the kitchen, Noah motioned

for Daniel to linger back.

"Arrange with Ben to go to Shipshewana on Saturday and to pick you up on Sunday afternoon." He smiled and placed a firm hand on Daniel's shoulder. "You must attend your future bride's baptism. I am the bishop. I am the bishop every day until I pass. Martha will only be baptized once. Go. Plus, I will announce the wedding this Sunday." He gently pushed Daniel into the kitchen.

"Yes, Papa," Daniel replied.

# # #

Sunday, May 24, 1964, about 11:30-ish

"Today we baptize Martha Noble into our church," Bishop Beiler announced then turned, walked to the water's edge, removed his shoes and waded into the pond behind the Hershberger barn.

"Join me, Martha Noble."

Martha approached the water. She removed her shoes at the edge and the ripples of cold pond water ran a shiver along her back. She inhaled deeply and braced herself as she waded into the barely warm spring pond water. It grew colder as it moved up to her waist. She fought the shudder. *I said I would break the ice if necessary*, she thought.

"As I told you yesterday, we will make this fast," Bishop Beiler whispered.

Deacon Kurtz moved beside her to assist the bishop.

Bishop Beiler's face was somber. He turned to Martha. She had her head bowed, right hand covering it as the prayed.

"Do you, Martha, renounce the devil, the world, and your own flesh and blood?"

"Yes," Martha answered.

"Do you, Martha, commit yourself to Christ and His church, and to abide by it and therein to live and to die?"

"Yes," Martha answered.

"Do you, Martha, in all order of the church, according to the word of the Lord, to be obedient and submissive to it and to help therein?"

"Yes," Martha answered.

Bishop Beiler leaned closer to Martha and nodded to Deacon Kurtz who moved closer to support Martha as she submerged into the water for baptism. "I baptize you."

Deacon Kurtz lowered her into the waters which flowed over her. She pinched her nose at the very last moment before the embrace of the cold waters chilled her to the bone. He pulled her back up, the water rushing away. Martha gasped, her breath taken away by the shock of the water's temperature.

"I welcome you into the fellowship of the church," Bishop Beiler said, then grinned, his back to those on the beach, watching. "At least, until Thursday when you marry that young man from Centertown."

Martha sloughed through the water to the beach and the waiting blanket to dry her.

"Welcome, Martha Noble," Naomi Beiler said, greeting her with a hug and kiss.

Martha shivered beneath the blanket.

I am Amish, she thought. Her eyes widened. *Daniel and I can marry, now.*

On queue, Bishop Beiler announced. "Martha Noble has chosen Daniel Yoder as a husband. This Thursday, May 28th, in Centertown, they will be wed."

Paul Hershberger stepped from the group and headed to Martha. "The wedding will be at the home of my sister, Mary Yoder. All are welcome. If you need a place to lay your head that night, let me know, I am sure we can find a room for you and your family." Reaching Martha, he stood beside her. "I am pleased to welcome my niece into the church." He motioned for Daniel to join them. "And for her chosen, Daniel Yoder." He placed an arm over Daniel's shoulder. "Allow Bishop Beiler to finish church, then we will all enjoy the festivities for today with a big meal."

Bishop Beiler resumed the remainder of the morning service.

Daniel sat with the other young men, watching, silently smiling at his future bride.

CHAPTER TWENTY-EIGHT: The Wedding Week

Monday, May 25, 1964, 8 a.m.

Daniel and Martha sat in the back of her father's car while her father drove and her mother rode silently beside him.

"It is very nice of you to drive us back to Centertown," Daniel said.

Dan Noble snapped his eyes to the rearview mirror to look at Daniel. "You're family, Daniel. It isn't a problem. If you need a ride, remember, call us any time and we will be there to help."

Emma giggled.

"What?" Dan asked.

"You seem to forget, dear. Daniel won't just be picking up the phone to call." She paused. "And, neither will Martha."

Dan smiled. "Yeah, I keep forgetting those little details." Once more he glanced in the rearview mirror to see Daniel. "Go to one of your *Englische* friends and have them call us collect. Okay?"

"Yes, sir," Daniel replied.

"You don't need to call me sir, lad. I am... I was... whatever. I will be your father-in-law in a few days. If you want, you can call me 'dad' or 'Dan' or whatever you feel comfortable with. Okay?"

"Yes, si... I mean, yes, uh... Dan?"

Dan nodded. "It will take some getting used to. I think we were married almost a year before I felt comfortable calling my father-in-law anything other than Matthew."

Emma lovingly slapped Dan's upper arm. "You had problems calling him 'dad' for almost five years."

Dan rolled a shoulder. "Maybe, I guess." Once more he

252

glanced in the rearview mirror. "Are you sure your uncle doesn't mind us coming to stay a whole week in preparation of the wedding?"

Once more Emma slapped Dan's upper arm. "I told you, I spoke with my sister about this. They insisted. After all, they are hosting the wedding at their house. It will make things much easier. We will drop Daniel at his house and then go visit Mark and Mary. Okay?"

"As you say," Dan replied.

# # #

"I will be over tomorrow morning," Rebecca said as she waved goodbye to the Noble family.

Daniel smiled, watching Martha stare out the back window of her parent's car as it pulled around the driveway and onto the road.

Rebecca placed an arm over Daniel's shoulder as they entered the house. "Do you realize in four days you will be a married man, Daniel?"

Daniel stumbled in his footsteps. *Married*, he thought. Suddenly, he felt giddy, light-headed, and, at the same time, overwhelmed.

"Yes, Mama," he replied.

I was married in an Englische wedding, but it did not feel like a marriage, he thought. *This? This is Amish. This is real, at least, to me.*

"I better get to school," Daniel said. "I do not want Miss Mueller to be overwhelmed too long." He grinned. "I am glad she offered to oversee the classes until I got there, allowing me another day in Shipshewana."

Rebecca grabbed the bag with his lunch. "Here. Now, get about," she said while shooing him out of the kitchen. "The schoolmaster is late."

# # #

Daniel rode the horse into the schoolyard, noticing the children outside playing. *Lunch time*, he thought. He tied up

253

the horse and raced inside to see how things were with Ruby.

"Ah, Daniel," Ruby said. "I wondered when you would arrive."

"My apologies, Ruby," Daniel said. "I did not think it would take all morning to come from Shipshewana. Are there any problems?"

Ruby smiled. "None." She frowned. "Well, there is one little itty-bitty problem." She broke into a large grin. "But, it is not school related."

Daniel scowled. "Oh?"

"I am to make a pie for Thursday. I know you like peach. I learned Martha likes strawberry." She frowned. "They asked me to make an apple pie."

"Ruby," Daniel said. "I know how tasty your peach pies are." He hesitated. "Okay, your apple pies are quite well-known." Daniel sat and leaned back in his chair at the desk. "Of course, your strawberry pies in the spring are some of the best."

Ruby cocked an eye at Daniel. "Your point is?"

"Well, the answer is quite simple," Daniel said. "You should make a pie of each." He grinned and winked at Ruby. "Of course, you could make two peach pies instead of one... for a total of four pies." He leaned forward and placed his hands on the desk. "With four pies, they wouldn't know how to respond." His grin widened. "Plus, I would have a whole peach pie to myself."

Ruby was silent for a few seconds. "Four pies, it is," she said. "Now, eat your lunch and I will go watch the students. A few extra minutes of play should not hurt before we begin classes."

Daniel opened his bag and placed his meal before him on the desk. He gazed at the extra large slice of meatloaf.

I hope Martha can cook, Daniel thought and his mouth watered at the memory of yesterday's special meal she had prepared. He smiled. *Yes, she knows how to cook.*

He put the large hunk of meatloaf between the two thick slices of bread and watched as Ruby headed toward the door.

"By the way, Daniel," Ruby said, as she approached the back of the classroom. She turned, a sly grin curling her lips.

"The children were very disappointed to learn there would be no school this coming Thursday."

Daniel laughed, almost choking on the bite of sandwich he'd taken. He nodded. "I am very sure," he coughed.

CHAPTER TWENTY-NINE: The Wedding Dress

Tuesday, May 26, 1964, 8 a.m.

Hannah tied Beauty up near Uncle Mark's barn while Rebecca grabbed the baskets from the buggy of items she'd brought in preparation for cooking some of the food for the big day. She handed a bag to her youngest child, Ester. The other children were at school.

"*guder mariye*," Martha yelled as she ran from the house to greet them.

"*guder mariye*," Rebecca replied. "Can you help me carry in some of this?"

Martha grabbed some bags to assist and smiled at Hannah who was reaching to get a box from the buggy.

Hannah frowned. "Martha? May I ask, have you made your dress, yet?"

Martha stopped and stared at her soon-to-be sister-in-law. "My dress?"

Hannah's eyes widened in surprise. "Your wedding dress."

Rebecca turned, almost spilling the contents of one of her baskets in the twirl. "Surely you have been working on it."

The awe in Rebecca's voice wasn't lost on Martha.

"I... It... Uh...With the baptism and other issues, I totally forgot." A tear welled in her eye. "There is so much to do and I forgot to even make my wedding dress."

Rebecca put her baskets on the ground and embraced Martha. "There, there, Martha. We will fix it all." She smiled, noting the car to the side of the barn. "Your mother and father are here. One of them..." She grinned. "I would guess your mother – could drive us into town to get the material and we can have your dress finished before the sun sets today." Rebecca picked up the baskets.

"And your attendants," Hannah added. "We can get the material for them, too. I could sew some of them tonight and tomorrow."

Emma appeared on the back steps.

"Is there a problem?" she asked.

Martha sniffed, wiping the tears away. "I need to make my dress for the wedding, and–"

"I'll get the keys from Dan." She hurried down the steps to help carry the items in. "Let's get this stuff inside and we'll go to town. My daughter will have the prettiest blue dress."

The four women carried the containers into the kitchen of the house.

Rebecca turned to Emma. "You go with your daughter. Pick out the fabric." Rebecca gazed at Hannah who helped Aunt Mary take the items from the containers, all the while sneaking peeks at them. "Take Hannah to help pick out the fabrics for the attendants."

Hannah placed her hands on the edge of the cardboard boxes of canned tomatoes, beans, and corn. She smiled, happy for the chance to help Martha pick her wedding colors. "*danke*, Mama."

"I have the keys," Emma said while jingling the ring of keys. "Ready to go?"

Martha, Hannah, and Emma headed to the car.

"This is very exciting," Hannah said as she crawled into the back seat. "I do not get to go to DeMotte that often, and if so, usually only to the fabric store."

"Do you want to drive, Martha?" Emma asked.

Martha stared at her mother. "I am Amish, Mother," she said. "Amish do not drive cars." She pushed the dangling keys Emma held out. "You drive. I will sit and enjoy the trip while talking with Hannah about what color for my attendants."

Hannah smiled. "I see a beautiful blue – one not too light, yet not too dark – for you. Plus, a pure white apron." Hannah's eyes sparkled with excitement. "For the attendants... how many do you have?"

Martha frowned. "I have asked Ruby Mueller and..." She paused. "I hoped you would be one."

"*danke*," Hannah replied. "I would be honored."

Martha sighed. "I always hoped my sister, Bethany, would be a part of my wedding, but she is not Amish, so that will not be. I think I will ask my cousins, Rachel and Fannie Herschberger."

Martha gazed at her mother. "Do you think Rachel and Fannie will be here?"

Emma nodded. "Yes, I spoke with Uncle Paul and he plans to be here with his family, so yes. A few others from Shipshewana plan to make the trip to Centertown for your wedding." She eased the car around the double curve before the small town of Hayton. "I will call and ask Jennifer to visit Uncle Paul and make sure Rachel and Fannie are here to be attendants. By the way, which store in DeMotte has the fabric?"

"That would be the Charles store on the square," Hannah said. "They have a beautiful selection of fabrics downstairs."

# # #

"What do you think of this color?" Hannah asked while holding up a bolt of royal azure blue. She grabbed a bolt of white and held it against the blue. "Do you like it?"

Martha had a bolt of navy blue in her hand. "That is perfect, Hannah. Beautiful!"

Emma nodded in agreement. "Just perfect."

"Now I need to find a color for the attendants," Martha said. "Purple. Right?"

Hannah nodded. "Unless you see another color you would like."

"How about this?" Emma held up a shade of orchid.

"Too bright and light, Mother," Martha said and scrunched up her nose. She grabbed a bolt of cotton. "I like this. Thoughts?" She read the label. "It is called Dark Violet."

Hannah and Emma stared at the fabric Martha held. It was a dark shade, but not too dark, yet it had a richness to it.

Martha held her chosen blue bolt against it.

"I think we have our wedding colors," Emma said. "Perfect colors, Martha."

"Yes, Martha," Hannah echoed. "Perfect."

Martha held the three bolts of fabric: white, royal azure blue, and dark violet. She slumped and made a face. "Now how much do we need?" She placed the bolts on the cutting table.

Hannah grabbed a pencil and scrap of paper and started calculating. She passed the final numbers to the saleslady. "We need this much white." Hannah wrote a "W" beside the number. "This much blue." The marked the number with a "B" and wrote a "P" beside the purple. "Plus, this much purple."

The saleslady picked up the purple bolt and scrutinized it. "I don't think there is that much fabric on here."

Martha's eyes widened. "There has to be," she gasped. "Do you have more?"

The woman cast Martha a look of disdain. "I can check." She pursed her lips, rolled a shoulder, and left, headed for the back storeroom. She returned about five minutes later. "No. We don't have any more of this particular color, but I found three bolts of this shade." She smiled. "It is almost the same shade. Will it work?"

Hannah reached out and pulled the fabric loose, stretching it out to give it a good look. Martha leaned in. She couldn't see any shade difference. She grabbed the bolt and read the fabric name: Shadow Violet. It was by a different company.

Hannah put the two fabrics – dark violet and shadow violet – beside each other. She sighed. "Only the most discerning eye would see a difference." She grabbed the dark violet, rolled the fabric back onto the bolt. "Make it all of this." Hannah glanced at Martha. "I mean, if you agree, Martha. It is your wedding."

Martha nodded approval.

"No need to mix fabrics." Hannah took the dark violet back to the shelf where it had been found.

The saleslady cut the fabric, folded it, and handed the stack with a piece of paper. "The clerk on the main floor will ring up your sale." She offered a smile. "Is there anything else I can help you ladies with today?"

"Oh, we need thread," Hannah said. "I have white at home, but will need a blue and purple to match the fabric."

The saleslady showed them a rainbow rack with all the

spools of thread. She grabbed a couple of the blue and started testing for a match on the color. "This one," she said. "How many?"

"One," said Hannah.

The saleslady already had spools of purple and checking. "And, this one." She placed the spool on the stack of fabric.

"We will need at least two spools of the purple," Hannah said.

The saleslady placed a matching spool beside the one already on the stack. "Anything else?"

"Thank you," Hannah said.

"Yes, thank you," Martha added.

"Okay, girls. Upstairs and I pay for all this."

#

The clerk pressed the numbers on the cash register and then the subtotal key, repeating for each item. "Will that be all?" she asked.

Emma nodded and pulled out her checkbook. The clerk did a double punch of the subtotal button for a grand total.

The clerk glanced at the checkbook, noting 'Shipshewana' on the check. "We don't take checks from out of town. I'm sorry. Plus, you're from out of state."

"I have proper I.D." Emma offered her driver's license.

"This is quite out of the ordinary," the clerk said. "I will need to get the manager's permission. Excuse me." She turned. "Mr. Newcombe?" she called up toward the balcony. "May I have your assistance?"

"Be right there," a man's voice replied, followed by a wiry, older gentleman hustling down the staircase toward them.

He looked at Hannah. "Miss Yoder?"

Hannah nodded. "Hannah Yoder."

"It is so good to see you," Mr. Newcombe said, offering a sincere smile. "What seems to be the problem?"

"I wish to pay for this with a check," Emma said. "I'm from Shipshewana." She shrugged. "Out of town. Out of state."

"Oh, my," he said. "Do you have any identification?"

"I have my driver's license," Emma replied and gave it to

him.

Mr. Newcombe scrutinized the license, glancing up to compare the picture. "Well, I am quite familiar with the Yoder family."

"This is Martha Noble," Hannah said. "She is marrying my older brother, Daniel, on Thursday."

The older man glanced at the fabric and thread on the counter. "Wedding dresses?" he asked.

Hannah nodded.

Mr. Newcombe turned to the clerk. "Nancy, write down Ms. Noble's driver's license and get her phone number on the check. I will approve it." He grinned at the three customers. "There is no need to delay a wedding on something as frivolous as a check." He turned to Martha. "Congratulations, young lady. The Yoders have been shopping here for years. I do hope you will consider us when you need fabric or other sundries."

Martha smiled at Mr. Newcombe. "I most certainly will."

"Have a good day." Mr. Newcombe turned and headed back to the stairs and the balcony.

Emma wrote the check and handed it to Nancy who wrote down the license number and asked for the phone number. Nancy then put it in a small tube and placed the tube in a clear pipe leading up to the balcony.

"It will be just a minute," Nancy said. There was a whoosh as the tube slid up the pipe to the balcony.

Mr. Newcombe waved from the balcony, nodding while waving the check. There was a swoosh sound with a loud click. The tube was back beside Nancy. She removed it and handed a sales slip to Emma.

"Thank you and come back again," Nancy said.

# # #

Rushing into the house, Martha discovered the kitchen a flurry of activity. Three more women had arrived and were helping to arrange and organize canned goods, start to bake bread and biscuits, and, of course, clean up after themselves.

"Come with me," Hannah said, grabbing Martha's hand. "May I use your sewing machine, Aunt Mary?"

261

"Yes," came the reply from near the kitchen sink.

"I will need to get a few measurements. I will measure you, then you will measure me. I can start on our dresses. We will go to the school near lunch time and get the measurements for Miss Mueller."

Emma walked into the room. "Is there anything I can do to help?"

"When you call, could you get the measurements of her cousins so I can make their dresses?"

Emma stared blankly at Hannah. "Measurements?"

"Watch," Hannah said.

She measured Martha, getting her sizes needed to make the dress.

"Just ask Jennifer to get the measurements." Martha grinned. "I am sure Aunt Mary will know how and what to do."

Emma sighed. "I have forgotten so much of my Amish heritage. I haven't made a dress in over twenty years." She rolled a shoulder. "Still, I should remember some of it as I help." She laughed. "Just give me a little time to figure it all out." She gazed at the fabric. "First," Emma said. "I believe I need to drive into Centertown and call Jennifer." She laughed. "We don't have a lot of time. I'd best call Jennifer." She turned to Hannah. "If I remember correctly, the local grocery has a payphone. Correct?"

Hannah nodded.

"I'll be back very soon." She headed for the kitchen.

"Mary, I'm going to the store to call my friend, Jennifer, to get some measurements. I'll be back shortly to help."

"Emma." Mary turned to face her sister. "Go to the neighbor..." She pointed out the kitchen window. "They have a phone. It will be quicker."

Emma frowned.

"They are *Englische*, Emma. If you need an answer, Jim or Eilene will come here with the message."

"Thank you," Emma replied and stepped out the door onto the back porch.

She glanced at the house about a quarter mile down the road. I could walk, she thought. But, that would take too much time. I'll drive.

Emma got in the car to drive to the neighbor's house.

It is amazing how much of my Amish heritage I have forgotten, she thought. A tear welled in her eye. *To forget my daughter must make her own dress for the wedding...* She shook her head then wiped the tear away.

CHAPTER THIRTY: The *Newehockers*

Tuesday, May 26, 1964, noon-ish.

Martha and Hannah jumped from the car.

"I'll wait here," Emma said from the driver's seat. She watched some of the children play baseball, while others played on the teeter-totter and swings. The older girls sat in the early mottled shade as they watched the older boys in the ball game. She remembered her childhood, her Amish heritage and grinned as the memory of Dan stating he would help Mark with the farm chores in the morning. She shook her head, placing a hand to cover her spreading smile.

Dan had no idea what he was getting into, she thought. Waking up before five in the morning was a surprise for him. *He will want to go to bed early tonight*, she thought. *He might even skip the evening meal.*

#

"Miss Mueller," Martha said. "We have come to get measurements for your dress as one of my *newehockers*."

Ruby's eyes widened in surprise. "I thought you were attempting to appease me." Her hand went to her chest. "I am honored."

Hannah offered Daniel a glance and then nodded to the door.

"Perhaps I should step outside," Daniel offered. "Will you join me on the steps, Martha?"

"Go," Hannah said. "I will get the information."

#

"Have you chosen your *newehockers*?" Martha asked. "I have Hannah, Miss Mueller, and my cousins, Rachel and Fannie."

Daniel scuffed his shoe on the step. "Well, I would ask Jason, but he is *Englische*, so that will not work. I will ask my cousins, James Troyer and Matthew Yoder. I can also ask John Heffel." He grinned. "I think he likes Hannah and perhaps she would like him and..." He heaved a sigh. "She is enamored with an *Englische* boy named Jonathan."

Martha cocked an eye in his direction. "An *Englische*? You have a problem with *Englische*?"

Daniel smiled. "Hm? *Englische*. Well..."

Martha pushed him, knocking him off-balance so he stumbled down the steps. Daniel laughed.

"So, I need one more," Daniel said.

"Promise not to get mad at me? I asked Elijah Hochstetler for you." She hung her head. "He is a friend of my Uncle Paul. I decided to play..." She glanced back into the school to locate Ruby and nodded approval. "I want Miss Mueller and him to meet. I think they have much in common." She shrugged. "One never knows." She grinned. "You are doing the same for Hannah and John... are you not?"

"Fine," Daniel said with some exasperation. "We have our *newehockers*. Who do we ask to be *Forgeher*?" He hesitated. "I can ask my brother, Luke, and his wife."

Martha grabbed his hand. "I only have *Englische* relatives, except for Uncle Paul. I could ask..." She shrugged and shook her head. "I have none to ask."

"We will have three *Forgeher*. My two older sisters and their husbands." He gazed into Martha's eyes. "If that is okay with you."

"I have no issue with that, Daniel." She gazed into Daniel's eyes.

"If the two of you wish to stand here and make goo-goo lovey-dovey eyes at each other, that is fine." Hannah stood behind them. "I have dresses to make and little time to do it." She nodded toward the car. "Your mother is waiting."

Martha blushed, having forgotten her mother sat in the car and obviously watched them. She squeezed Daniel's hands, let go, and followed Hannah to the car.

Tuesday, May 26, 1964, 3:30 p.m.

Daniel watched the student's leave. He waved goodbye to Ruby. His younger sister, Mary, had his siblings in the buggy and snapped the reins on Beauty to go home.

"I will be home shortly," Daniel said. "I need to visit Rachel, Ruth, and Luke."

He waved at them until they were well on the way. He closed the school and was glad he had ridden his bicycle this morning, allowing his siblings a few extra minutes at the house. Rachel and Jacob Metz's house was only a little over a mile away. He rode fast.

Slightly out of breath, he raced up to the house and knocked.

"Daniel," Rachel exclaimed. "How nice of you to visit. Will you be staying for a meal?"

Daniel shook his head. "Nay, Rachel. I need to ask if you and Jacob will be *Forgeher* on Thursday at my wedding."

Jacob appeared at the doorway. "Of course, Daniel."

"Does Mama need help?" Rachel asked.

Daniel shrugged. "She is at Uncle Mark's house and I know Martha's mother is helping. You can check." He stepped down from the porch. "I need to ask Ruth and Luke, yet." He waved goodbye, got on his bicycle once again, and rode to Luke's house.

Miriam answered the door.

"May I ask you and Luke to be *Forgeher* at my wedding on Thursday?" He bowed his head. "I know it is late," he mumbled.

"Luke is working in the field, but I am sure he will agree." She smiled at Daniel. "Our answer is yes."

"*danke*," Daniel said. He sighed. "Now I need to go to

266

Ruth's house and ask her."

Miriam waved goodbye and closed the door.

"*guder nammidaag*," Daniel said as Ruth opened the door.

"Daniel! What a pleasant surprise. Come in. Come in."

He followed his eldest sister into the house.

"I just noticed Joshua coming in from the field," Ruth said. "He should be here shortly."

Daniel sat at the table. "I have a question... a request of you and Joshua."

"What is that?" Ruth asked as she mashed the potatoes in the pot, adding a little cream and butter to the mix.

"I would like you to be *Forgeher* at my wedding on Thursday."

The kitchen door opened.

"Daniel," Joshua said. "So good to see you."

Ruth placed the pot on the counter and went to Joshua, grabbing his hands in hers.

"Daniel has just asked us to be *Forgeher* for his wedding."

"You honor us," Joshua said. "Of course."

"*danke*," Daniel said, standing. "I must now get home so Mama knows I will be there for a meal." He sniffed the air. "Although, it does smell quite tasty here." He grinned. "My sister has learned how to cook. Yes."

Ruth snapped a towel at her little brother. "You behave."

Daniel dodged the towel and raced for the door. "See you on Thursday."

"Tell Mama I will be over tomorrow to help," Ruth offered.

"I think she is spending her days at Uncle Mark's house, helping there to get things ready."

"Who is watching the little ones?"

Daniel grinned. "Me. I'm the teacher. I am pretty sure she takes Ester with her to Uncle Mark's place." He laughed.

"Go on," Ruth said, faking a motion to chase him.

"Goodbye," Daniel said as the kitchen screen door closed.

#

Tuesday, May 26, 6 p.m.

"Papa?" Daniel called into the main room from the kitchen where he had been helping his siblings with their homework. "May we speak?"

"Come, Daniel. What is on your mind?" Noah folded the newspaper.

Daniel sat in the chair next to his father's rocker.

"I wish to invite some *Englische* to the wedding." He paused, waiting. He finally continued. "They are my friends, like Ben Hopkins, Jason Muirs, Molly Pearce, and Bob Sullivan."

"I see no problem with *Englische* at the wedding." He turned to face Daniel. "Although, I am quite sure they do not wish to be in attendance for the whole service. Perhaps it would be better if they showed later, between ten and ten-thirty." He placed a strong hand on Daniel's shoulder. "I knew this question would arise." He nodded. "You have spent much time with the *Englische*, it was to be expected." Noah stood. "Are there others you wish to invite?"

"There are many," Daniel said. "I would invite Miss Julie Bronson, Maestro Cardinale, and some others..." He let his voice trail. "But, they are too far away," Daniel mumbled. "Plus, there is very little time for them to arrive."

"As you wish," Noah said, and smiled. "Miss Bronson?" He nodded and smiled. "I remember her; she was an interesting woman."

"I will go over to Mr. Williams' house and see if they will allow me to use their phone." Daniel stood and left the room to visit their *Englische* neighbor.

CHAPTER THIRTY-ONE: The Wedding Day

Thursday, May 28, 1964, 5 a.m.

Daniel strode with his father and younger brother, Jacob, to the barn. On a whim, Daniel gazed at Jacob with a devilish grin.

"Race you to the barn," Daniel said.

Jacob took off, sprinting ahead. Daniel ran a few feet and quit.

Noah shook his head. "You did not give him a true run, Daniel."

"It was my last time to give him a chance," Daniel replied. "Strange to realize today I will marry."

Noah slapped Daniel on the back. "You are becoming a man, son."

"Beat'cha," Jacob yelled from the barn door then disappeared inside.

"Jacob is already in the loft," Noah said. "I will go to the far end to start milking."

Daniel nodded, knowing the routine.

# # #

Daniel sat at the kitchen table, waiting for his father to sit. The others were already at the table. It was a quiet morning. There was no school and no rush to get about.

Noah sat. "Let us give thanks."

Everyone bowed their heads and a moment of silence ensued as they gave thanks to God for the day and the food.

"Let us eat," Noah said and reached for the eggs to pass.

Daniel munched his breakfast in silence. *This will be the last time I will enjoy a meal with my parents and siblings in the morning*, he thought. *Tomorrow I will awake and be...*

Daniel stopped chewing and stared at his plate of food. Custom dictated the wedding night to be at the home of the bride's parents.

But, Martha's parents are Englische and live in Shipshewana, Daniel thought. *She is staying with Uncle Mark, but do we stay there?*

"Uh, Papa?" Daniel softly said.

Noah scowled at him. "Later." Noah continued to eat in silence.

Daniel tried to eat but the nagging feelings inside bothered him. He pushed the food around on his plate, nibbling this and that, finally finishing most of the food he had on his plate.

"We should prepare for the wedding," Noah said and pushed away from the table.

"May we talk, Papa?"

Noah strolled into the main room. "What is on your mind, Daniel. Something bothers you."

Daniel inhaled deeply. "It is customary for the groom to stay with the bride's parents on their wedding night."

Noah cocked an eye, struggling to keep a straight face.

"Martha's parents live in Shipshewana and are *Englische*." Daniel hesitated, wringing his hands. "I cannot go to Shipshewana. I need to teach school on Friday."

"Yes," Noah said. "Do you see a better possibility?"

"Since Luke moved out to marry, and I moved into his old bedroom – I am alone in there." Daniel fidgeted. "Since I cannot go to Shipshewana, and I see no reason to live with Uncle Mark because that is where Martha is staying..." Daniel's voice faded.

"You wish to live here?" Noah asked. "Until you can find a place for you and Martha? Is that your question?"

Daniel nodded.

"Your mother and I expected no less," Noah said and slapped Daniel on the back. "Son, we are family. This is your home. You are always welcome here." Noah hesitated. "And, of course, your wife, too." He laughed. "Now, that the awkwardness has passed. You had best prepare yourself." He grinned and gazed at the kitchen. "If you are still hungry, you best be out there before Hannah has all the food cleared. Otherwise, there is a wedding. My first. I must get ready, too."

# # #

Daniel harnessed Bronk to the buckboard. The sun was just cresting the eastern horizon: a golden glow revealing a beautiful blue sky. He stroked Bronk's forehead.

"Tonight you will have the honor of bringing my wife and I back here," Daniel whispered. "You never imagined that, did you?"

Bronk raised his head and whinnied.

"Oh, you did?" Daniel mocked. "I forgot."

Daniel rushed back to the house and up the stairs to his bedroom. He opened the chest and pulled the item carefully out. It was hand-carved and polished to a sheen.

"I hope you like it, Martha," Daniel whispered. "I made this for you." He set the clock on the dresser and stood back to admire it. The dark mahogany glistened, barely revealing the detailed scrolling. Only when you looked closely did you realize the scrolling was musical notes. Daniel rushed down the stairs and jumped into the buckboard to go to Uncle Mark's house.

# # #

He arrived at Uncle Mark's house, handed the reins of Bronk to his cousin, Amos Yoder, and rushed into the house where others awaited his arrival.

Dan Noble greeted him and placed an arm around Daniel's shoulder. "Today," he said. "Today you will marry my daughter. I won't understand most of what is being said, but I welcome you into my family." He let go of Daniel and rolled a shoulder, wincing, grabbed and massaged the sore area. "This getting up early in the morning and doing farm work all day." He shook his head. "Now, I see why the Amish go to bed so early."

Mark Yoder placed a hand on Dan's good shoulder. "You

271

have done well, for an *Englische*." He laughed.

Daniel noticed movement outside the front window. People were arriving.

"We best be about our *Forgeher* work," Luke said and headed for the kitchen door. He had a pastry in hand.

"Leave some food for the meal," Miriam jibed as she followed.

Ruby Mueller arrived with her brother and his wife. Just then a van pulled into the driveway. Paul Hershberger and his family clamored from the vehicle. A stranger stepped out and covered his eyes from the sunlight. Older. No beard.

Elijah Hochstetler, Daniel thought and immediately looked to find Ruby. He smiled. Ruby had noticed the unbearded Amish man. Daniel moved forward to introduce himself.

"*guder mariye*," Daniel said, holding his hand out to shake. "My name is Daniel Yoder. Are you Elijah Hochstetler?"

The older man nodded, but had a frown. "I still do not understand how I came to be your *newehocker*."

Daniel smiled. "It was a request of my bride, Martha Noble. She wanted you here."

Elijah smiled. "Then so be it. The Lord works to His will. Who am I to question?"

"Come," Daniel said. "Let me introduce you to my family and others who are here."

# # #

Thursday, May 28, 1964, 8:30 a.m.

Daniel sat beside Martha as the service began. She appeared stunning and the most beautiful woman he'd ever seen in her blue dress, white apron, and black prayer covering. The *Englische* wedding dress had been beautiful, but now, in her Amish attire, she was even more beautiful. They sat in another room with Bishop Yoder – Daniel's father – and listened to the congregation sing. He conferred with them, reconfirming their beliefs and agreement to the rules of the

272

Ordnung. They finally joined the congregation and finished the song currently being sung.

Bishop Yoder stood and offered a prayer, followed by a scripture reading. He then began his sermon. Daniel listened to his father. Finally, almost two hours later, Daniel noticed movement. He watched his brother, Luke, stand and assist some late-comers. It was Mr. and Mrs. Ben Hopkins, Mr. and Mrs. Bob Sullivan, Jason Muirs, and Molly Pearce. Daniel smiled. His friends were here. A few minutes later, there was another interruption and Luke went to check on it. He brought in some more *Englische*.

Daniel's eyes widened. Maestro Antonio Cardinale and his wife, Mei Lien, plus Mr. and Mrs. Chang entered. Behind them, a tall, blond-haired gentleman guided a black woman holding a child into the room.

Miss Bronson? How? Daniel thought. *I did not invite them.*

Bishop Noah nodded his head at the group of *Englische*. He stopped his sermon.

"I wish to welcome Daniel's *Englische* friends to this wedding," he said then continued his sermon.

Daniel's lower lip trembled, overwhelmed. Martha squeezed his hand.

"Now," Bishop Yoder said, finishing his sermon. "Will the bride and groom step forward."

He questioned them about their marriage, asking similar questions from earlier in the privacy of the room. Nodding with approval, Bishop Yoder blessed them.

"As father of the groom," Bishop Yoder announced. "I will be first to bless this marriage and hope it is as strong, happy, and fruitful as the one my wife and I have. May my son have the strength of his namesake, Daniel, in faith." Noah turned to Martha. "May Martha be strong like Sarah, to raise a nation." He stepped back.

The other ministers offered up their blessings.

Dan Noble stood. "I am unsure if I may have a say, but as father of the bride, I want to say I am very proud of my daughter. She has a strong will and I am ashamed of my earlier actions regarding the Amish. She will make Daniel a good wife, and Daniel will be a good husband." He sat. Emma squeezed his hand.

Bishop Yoder offered a final prayer.

The congregation stood and moved about, setting up the room for dining.

Daniel grabbed Martha's hand and pulled her to the befuddled group of *Englische*.

"How are you here?" he asked, staring at the group. "How did you find out?"

"I called them on Monday," Noah said coming up behind him. "It was only right the people who helped to form the man you have become should be here. I call Mr. Cardinale and he contacted the rest."

Martha reached out to the young child in Julie's arms. "Name?"

"Daniella," Julie said.

"I wanted to call her Dannie," Gary said. "But, Julie is adamant her name is Daniella."

Daniel grinned.

"There is so much activity," Julie said, watching the men move the benches and tables.

"Let us go outside," Daniel suggested.

Jason punched Daniel on the arm. "You did it, buddy. You got hitched. The old ball and chain."

Molly slapped Jason on the arm. "Behave."

"Are you two a thing?" Daniel asked.

"Whoa," Jason yelped. "Are you bonkers? I'm a free bird. I'm not getting my feathers clipped. At least, not yet."

Molly's eyes widened. "You think I would date a creep like him?" She pursed her lips. "No way."

Mei Lien leaned in close. "This Amish? Yes?"

Daniel snickered. "Yes, Mrs. Cardinale. This is Amish."

"You all rook arike. How you tell who who?"

"Hey, you come my place. You use my door. Hokay?" Mrs. Chang smiled at Daniel. "Velly nice here. Purdy Ohio."

Daniel noticed Mr. Chang watching the women cooking. "You will not be seeing any Chinese food today," Daniel said. "You will get to eat what I like to eat." He grinned at Mr. Chang. "But, I did enjoy your food, Mr. Chang."

Mr. Chang nodded, all the while stretching to see what the women were cooking.

"You know, Daniel," Ben Hopkins said. "They say the third time's the charm. This is your second wedding." He laughed.

"No," Daniel replied. "I am Amish. This is my first. The other one was a dream. It was annulled. It never happened."

"Well, again, congratulations, Daniel," Bob Sullivan said.

Daniel introduced all the people to each other and then introduced them to his Amish family and friends.

Ruby and Hannah came hustling toward them. "It is time for you to sit at the *eck*," they chimed together.

"Please," Daniel said. "Come back into the house for the first seating with my family."

"First seating?" Julie questioned.

"There will be at least three, maybe four seatings to get everyone fed." Daniel led the group into the house, taking a moment to watch the group milling about the yard. "I would say there are close to three hundred or more here."

"This isn't catered?" Gary asked.

Martha laughed. "Well, if you call having the community supply and help as catering, then, yes, it is catered."

# # #

Daniel said goodbye to his friends, still unable to believe they had come to the wedding. Jason and Molly were the first to leave, followed by Ben Hopkins and Bob Sullivan. Finally, the New York group - the Cardinale and Chang families left.

"We had best be on our way," Gary said. "Little Daniella will need to get to bed at the hotel and then we head out bright and early in the morning." He turned to Mark Yoder. "You have a wonderful farm here. Maybe some day I can have a place like this." He then found Noah Yoder. "You, sir, have a remarkable son. Not only does he have a beautiful voice, but inside him, he has a faith that is unshakable. I hope, if I have a son, he grows like Daniel."

"Daniel," Julie said. "I still can't believe you're a teacher. And now, a married man. New York City held such hope for

275

you as a singer, but, I know deep inside me, you are Amish and would never succumb to the wiles of the big city. Broadway and Hollywood have lost a wonder, but..." She glanced at Martha. "Your wife has gotten the best prize in the world. If ever in New York, look us up."

"You know I will not be in New York City," Daniel said.

"You never know," Martha said. "I still have my relatives in Bird-In-Hand. New York isn't that far away."

"Relatives?"

"Jacob and Naomi Longenfelter. He is my uncle."

Daniel frowned. "But, your mother's maiden name is Hershberger."

Martha nodded. "Yes, but Uncle Jacob was raised by the Hershberger's. His family died in a horrible accident; only he survived. Grandpa and grandma Hershberger took him in at the age of five."

Daniel nodded.

"We must go," Gary said, shaking hands with Daniel. "Again, congratulations."

# # #

The night was clear. Stars glittered in the sky above even though the moon was almost full. One could see the fields, smelling the freshly planted soil.

Daniel allowed Bronk to set the speed – a slow gait. Martha snuggled close. Daniel had his arm wrapped around her.

"Well, Mrs. Yoder, are you happy to be going home?"

"Yes, and no," Martha replied. "Yes, because we are now a married couple. I love you, Daniel Yoder. But, also no, because it will not be to our house." She looked up at Daniel and smiled. "We will find a place."

"We are a couple," Daniel said. "I love you." He leaned his head on hers.

They listened to the clip-clop of Bronk, the creak of the buckboard wheels, and the buzz of the spring insects.

THE END

About the Author

My name is Robert S. Nailor but most people call me Bob.

I'm retired from the federal government. I was a computer geek and still do some programming yet today. One would think I should have plenty of time to write but I actually seem to have less now. So, to make sure that things work out correctly, I force myself to sit down and write. That doesn't always work. Today, writing is fun and I find it relaxing. I get to visit those fantastic and strange places within my mind and well, if I don't come back right away, there is no longer somebody behind me writing on a pink sheet of paper.

I live with my wife, Violet, in a ranch home snuggled into a small wooded acre in NW Ohio. I was born in Sioux City, Iowa but my parents moved to Ohio in 1953. I have four sons and currently have ten grandchildren - 7 granddaughters and 3 grandsons. Plus, I have great-grandchildren – 2 great-granddaughters and 4 great-grandsons.

My interests are camping (have RV, will travel), gardening, music, cooking and reading. So where do I travel? I've been in 46 of the 50 states and strangely, Hawaii is one of the states I've visited. I have also visited two of our territories - Puerto Rico and the Virgin Islands. Traveling allows me to add the ambiance to my stories and to some of the characters, also. Gardening is a bit gamey since we live in the country and have the wildlife visiting us constantly — deer, rabbits, raccoon, birds, squirrels plus many others. So vegetables don't always make it to harvest but what does is more than tasty. There are flowers, sometimes too many, to keep me busy. Music? I love New Age music and my favorite group is Mannheim Steamroller... and not just because of their fabulous Christmas albums; I was hooked on them before that. I also have created some of my own electronic music which I've been told is pretty good. Should I mention cooking? I love to cook and do gourmet cooking. Having worked with Boy Scouts for several years, I have taught many boys the basics of cooking beyond hot dogs and beans. I have won quite a few contests. As to what I read; well, obviously a lot of science fiction, fantasy and some Christian. Horror, romance, adventure and other genres are also great reads when they catch my attention with an intriguing tag line or cover.

Bibliography

Novels:

The Secret Voice ~ Book 1 in The Amish Singer series
The New York Voice ~ Book 2 in The Amish Singer series
Pangaea, Eden Lost ~ a Barclay Havens, relic hunter misadventure
Ancient Blood: The Amazon~ a vampire series
Three Steps: The Journeys of Ayrold ~ an Irish fantasy for today
2012 Timeline Apocalypse ~ the Mayan calendar comes to an end
At Death's Door ~ a collection of "light" horror stories about death
Eternal Blood ~ a Barry Hargrove detective mystery
The Emerald ~ Book 1 in The Shiyula Realm series

Coming Soon...

The Family Voice ~ book 4 in The Amish Singer series
The Topaz ~ book 2 in The Shiyula Realm series
The Babbling Sphinx ~ another Barry Hargrove detective mystery

Anthologies:

52 Weeks of Writing Tips ~ tips to improve one's writing ability
Telling Tales of Terror ~ essays on how to write horror and dark fiction
Mother Goose Is Dead ~ a collection of favorite fairy tales, fractured
Dead Set: A Zombie Anthology ~ a collection of unusual zombie tales
The Complete Guide to Writing Paranormal-Vol 1 ~ various essays
Nights of Blood 2 ~ different takes on the vampire story
Guide to Writing Science Fiction ~ essays on writing science fiction
Firestorm of Dragons ~ an eclectic collection of dragon stories
Fantasy Writer's Companion ~ essays on writing fantasy
13 Night of Blood ~ 13 amazing vampire tales
Spirits of Blue & Gray ~ a collection of Civil War ghost stories

PLUS more at www.bobnailor.com